THE PHOENIX FALLACY

OVERLORD'S ORPHAN

JONATHAN SOURBEER

Published by Vulpine Press in the United Kingdom in 2022

Originally self-published in 2018

Cover by Claire Wood

Cover image by Daniel Fernandez

ISBN: 978-1-83919-384-2

www.vulpine-press.com

For Janelle:
Once the little sister who never listened, now the woman who's always willing to lend an ear.

Overlord,

As you commanded, I assigned most of our Inferni to oversee construction of the new facility. To make up for the loss of manpower, we have begun using the local gangs to enforce our will. I believe that we have discovered a new model for policing the slums, and it appears that other Overlords are rapidly following suit. These "gang rats" as they are dubbed, will also serve as excellent tools for rounding up the population you desire. As the more capable rats prove their worth and loyalty, I will have them trained as STs and moved to our new location. I have left a platoon of my finest Inferni for your protection.

Transmission received from Commandant Novus Martel
Location Undisclosed
2316-07-28.2318

—Recovered from the files of *Overlord Victoria Middleton*, Cerberus Corporation

CHAPTER 1
GHOSTS, DANCING

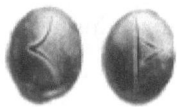

Janus awoke to the dark. His room was quiet, and the city of Valhalla was silent with it. Only a few days had passed since he, Celes, and Sergeant Wouris returned safely from the ruins of Phoenix Corporation.

As a wall panel slid open to reveal his armor, he reflected on the blur that had been the last week. The Titan outpost he and the ODIN Mercenary Legion had been contracted to strike had proved to be an elaborate trap. Now, with only a few snatches of a conversation to go on, Valhalla, the mobile home base of the ODIN Legion, was headed toward a distant mountain range known as Lightemann's ridge.

A new Loki pistol popped out in a drawer beside him. He had lost the last one in the battle that had cost him so many of his friends and fellow cadets. After giving the weapon a once over, Janus strapped it on and headed for the door. Val, the somewhat fickle Daedulus system that managed the city, opened it with nary a complaint.

The great windows of the hall were black, the pre-dawn light drowning out the stars, but leaving the horizon dark. The Legion had to navigate on its own now, hunting for answers.

His mind was a jumble as he jogged silently across the great hall in the middle of Valhalla. The hall was a massive, open atrium that surrounded a towering central column called The Trunk. So named because it looked like a huge stone tree sprouting in the middle of the city, the Trunk acted as the central way station for all the areas of Valhalla, its many branches connecting to every section. The stream surrounding it flowed silently in the dawn. Other than the night watch, most of Valhalla was still asleep, and Janus appreciated the early morning solitude. It reminded him of his original home, the slums of Cerberus, when the hot air grew still, and he and Clara could hear every noise for a mile.

When he reached the entrance to the mess, Janus turned to stare at the great seal of ODIN. The giant stained glass window, with the god Odin astride his warhorse, spear in hand, was a deep blood red in the dark. ODIN had more than a few scores to settle.

He found Lyn and Ramirez in the mess. Lyn yawned as he approached, unable to keep her eyes open.

"You're up early," Janus commented to her. He and Ramirez had often gotten up early in the past, but Lyn had never struck him as a morning person.

"I think it's late at this point?" Lyn replied, and then put her head down on the table.

Ramirez looked at him. Despite being sat down, he was essentially eye level with Janus. "She was helping Celes last night."

Janus's curiosity was piqued. "Oh?"

Lyn nodded sleepily. "Celes wanted ta look up Lightemann's Ridge. She felt like she had heard of it before but couldn't place it. We didn't find much. Just a note about how it was named after some Executor who fell during a war a long time ago."

"Spent hours in the database. No luck," Ramirez added. "Found her on the couches in the common room."

"And Celes?"

Ramirez shook his head. "Must have gone ta bed."

Lyn began to snore, and Janus chuckled. "Maybe she should head there as well?"

Ramirez shook his head. "Training with the Praetor t'day."

Janus nodded. "Right. Can't miss that."

The Praetor, the leader of the ODIN Legion, had summoned the surviving members of Wouris' cadets for special instruction that morning. Even though the man had somewhat mysteriously taken a shine to Janus, he had no intention of pressing his luck by missing out on what was certainly something important.

Janus went and got food, while Ramirez tended to the sleepy Lyn.

Sometime after breakfast, the day dawned bright and clear, seabirds wheeling lazily upon the warm updrafts rising along the outside of Valhalla as it glided over the ocean. Valhalla was already abuzz with activity. Anticipation inside the city was high, the Adepts eager to prove themselves.

Most of the new Adepts were already assembled in the Chariot of Voyages, the primary launch bay of Valhalla for all of their missions. Although Valhalla was a flying Avalon class fortress capable of reaching any continent or ocean, the Adepts of ODIN hardly wanted to put it directly in harm's way. It was slow and vulnerable in many ways, and incapable of surmounting especially high mountains. Most of the time, the Adepts flew to their targets in their Longboat transports.

As Janus, Ramirez, and a now slightly more awake Lyn joined the waiting Adepts, the sea breeze rushed between the open doors of the bay and swept along the line. The bright sun shone upon the hard metal floor at the edge of the bay, and Janus was glad to be standing in the shade. He felt more comfortable in the dark, and it was where Adepts did their best work. A single Zeus rifle had been mounted on a turret just a short distance from where they stood, pointing out over the open ocean, where large, gentle green swells rolled beneath them.

"Mind if I cut in?"

Janus smiled and stepped to the side without looking back. Celes jumped into the line next to him.

Janus stole a glance at his companion. "I didn't see you at breakfast this morning."

Her hair held a golden shine, like she was standing in the sun, and she flashed a beautiful smile. "Ate early."

"I heard it was late. Ramirez had to contend with Lyn's jokes this morning, too." Janus lowered his voice. "I heard a few of them… sleep-deprived Lyn… struggles with timing."

Celes held a hand to her mouth. "Sounds like it went well."

"Ya got that right." Janus turned to see Lyn with a devilish grin on her face. A few of the other nearby Adepts chuckled.

"Ramirez," Celes said politely.

The massive, brown-haired heavy gunner glanced down at her and nodded.

"Heard you had a fun morning."

Ramirez returned his gaze forward and nodded.

Marcus stepped up next to Celes, laughing. "Sounds like an understatement to me."

"And where were you, Marcus?" Janus prodded.

Marcus smiled confidently. "I learned in the Medusa Security Forces that when given an opportunity to grab a bit more shut-eye, you don't squander it. I'm not an idiot." He paused. "That reminds me, didn't you want a rematch in Brevis Bellum?"

Janus smirked. "Don't forget who won you that game."

Marcus grinned. "That's right, I did—"

"Praetor on deck!" Sergeant Wouris appeared like lightning, and the Adepts snapped to attention. Praetor Jennings approached, his

4

grey hair and handlebar mustache as trim as ever. He wore simple black armor with two golden ODIN horsemen upon the collar of his neck.

"Thank you, Sergeant." The Praetor took a moment to inspect them, tilting his head approvingly at Wouris, but he stopped at the sight of Janus. "Lieutenant Janus."

Janus stepped forward. "Sir."

"Please join the other officers."

Janus glanced down the line and saw Col. Keats and Col. Hawkes standing off to one side. The unpleasant expression on Col. Hawkes did not surprise Janus in the least, but Colonel Keats's disturbingly worried look gave him pause. Keats was holding parchment screen, a paper-thin Daedulus, while occasionally glancing at the turret which had several glowing red lights on the base. Occasionally, the turret would whir and click, moving back and forth, up and down. A cadre of combat medics stood ready behind them.

"Yes, sir." With a last look at his companions, Janus jogged quickly to stand next to Keats and Hawkes.

The Praetor smiled. "You all performed admirably during the battle, fighting well against overwhelming odds. More than a few of you still have raw feelings about the experience, and there has been little time to heal. However, you now stand as full-fledged Adepts, no longer cadets, and the future of our Legion is in your hands. We are about to embark on a mission that offers no payment other than the solace of bringing peace to our friends. But our time is short, and we have little choice—this travesty is something we cannot ignore. Our only clue is that Cerberus Corporation might be involved, including our old friend Overlord Middleton."

The name of the gaudily outfitted Overlord brought the taste of bile to Janus's mouth. Middleton had sold him to ODIN, forcing him to abandon his adoptive mother, Clara, and leave her to fend for herself. Praetor Jennings had secured her care from Middleton in exchange for his service, but Janus trusted Middleton about as far he could throw her. Which wasn't very far given her massive girth. As long as he was here, Janus would always be forced to wonder if Clara was still safe.

"Our only other clue is the name Delacroix and a mountain range called Lightemann's Ridge. Lightemann's Ridge is a well-known range to our east, and at this moment Valhalla is already on a course to put us within deployment range in the next few days. In the meantime, I expect you to train and prepare yourselves for the reality of another mission. Training is never over. We're getting back out there—we're going to make sure what happened at Titan doesn't happen again."

Out of the corner of his eye, Janus could see Keats shift uncomfortably, still staring at whatever filled the parchment.

The Praetor paused and stole a glance at the turret facing out over the open platform and ocean.

"As soldiers, you have trained for many months and had your physical limits pushed far beyond the average human. It is time to realize that, as Adepts, you can push your mental limits farther, as well. Are you ready, Colonel?"

"Yes, sir… However, I would like it noted that I am actively protesting this demonstration." One of the lights on the turret's base turned green as Keats looked up from her screen, voice quivering between irritation and worry. "There is an excellent reason why we decided to stop this form of testing, and now is not the time to resume."

Jennings looked back at Keats with a smile. "Noted, Colonel." He paced purposefully along the line of Adepts. "As all of you are aware, a Zeus rifle is an infinitely superior weapon to the electro-thermal rifles we use. It has immensely greater range and accuracy, and can hold much larger stores of ammo. Plus, with no moving parts, maintenance is kept to a minimum. It has a unique 'disadvantage,' however: as a semi-automatic weapon that is so incredibly accurate, it depends solely upon its user to hit a target. No spray and pray, as they say.

"Even the best Security Trooper, despite all the advantages of his suit, is still limited by two factors: how fast that Trooper can find his or her target and fire, and how fast the suit can react. Every suit of ST armor has this same limitation, despite all of its strengths. The armor does not react at the speed of the Trooper, but at the speed of its inputs. This moment between the man moving, and the suit reacting—that moment of slow acceleration—is inconsequential for most. But for an Adept, it provides the opportunity to change the very course of battle.

"The technique I'm about to show you is known as 'Ghost Dancing.' It is named in honor of the SHADE Legion, and was one of the principal reasons for its fame and success many years ago. This technique is very difficult, and very rare, even among Adepts. But it is one of the reasons that savvy Troopers fear us."

He motioned to the turret behind him. The final light flashed from red to green, the turret whirred one last time, then settled quietly facing the ocean. Keats sighed, as if disappointed.

"The turret that Colonel Keats has so kindly modified, along with our elusive tech-sergeant Chiles, is designed to mimic the limitations of an ST suit's flexibility and maneuverability. Its objective is to *try* to hit *me*."

Janus felt a jolt of excitement run along his spine. Beside him, Hawkes leaned over to Keats and whispered, "There's still time to kick it over."

"If you recall," the Praetor continued, "I told you that your abilities go far beyond what the Corporations have allowed you to think. You will learn that your faster reactions allow you to always stay a step ahead of an opponent. It is up to you to master this advantage."

The Praetor seemed to glide backwards, his footsteps seemingly making no sound across the hardened floor.

"Be warned, this technique is not for the faint-hearted, nor is it something for the foolishly bold. It is a technique of last resort. Which is why we do not even introduce it to cadets, and why we rarely allow even the best to practice it." The Praetor stopped rigidly in front of the turret, the Zeus rifle's long, rectangular nose pointing out behind him towards the green sea.

"Some of you may eventually perfect this technique so that a single ST will never pose a threat to you. Many of you will never even attempt it. And a rare few—a very rare few, indeed—will be able to face more than one opponent at a time. But only in the direst circumstances." He smiled. "Colonel." Keats hesitated, and the Praetor's eyes flashed.

Keats touched a button on the screen and a single green light appeared on the turret, and the air became deathly still. The Praetor closed his eyes and took a deep breath. Hawkes looked as if he had been forced to swallow slum garbage.

The light flipped to red, and the Zeus sprang to life. The Praetor leaped away in an elaborate dance: twisting, jumping, sprinting all around the platform as the hapless 'Trooper' turret tried to keep up. The Adepts gasped. The Praetor wasn't just fast, he was incredible. Despite his age, the Praetor's speed was far beyond anything they had seen before. But the turret's AI seemed to be learning, anticipating the Praetor's movements, snapping forward to hit the Praetor where he would land, but to no avail.

"He's a dancing blur," Jones commented in awe.

But Janus could see it was far more than that. One limb was always rooted to the ground, ready to spring the Praetor forward in any one of several directions.

"Look how he moves; he always has the ability to move in a new direction," Marcus exclaimed.

"Very good, Mercenary Auras," Keats said with forced calmness. "Ghost Dancing requires total body control, always maintaining contact with a surface so that an instantaneous change of direction can be achieved."

Walls sprang up from the floor. At first, Janus thought they would trap the Praetor, but they only seemed to give him more options, more ways to connect himself to a solid surface and escape the deadly hail. The walls moved closer, narrowing the field and giving the Praetor less room to maneuver. But all the while, he moved closer to the turret, staying just ahead of the barrel as it snapped into position to fire at him.

"Praetor, here!" Hawkes called out, unsheathing the Praetor's Ghostblade and flinging it towards him with a momentous effort. The Praetor leaped forward, catching the blade in midair and whipping it around in a tremendous downward cleave. The turret hardly seemed to move as the weapon passed through it, and the Praetor simply swept by. A moment later, the turret simply fell apart, leaving the base broken and unmoving. The Praetor stood slowly, smiling, leaving a smoking ruin behind him. Keats's jaw moved slightly as the sparking base popped and hissed, and she gave a sidelong glance at Hawkes. He, however, growled approvingly, and grunted at the gaping Adepts, "That's why he's the Praetor."

CHAPTER 2
THE MINT

The scouting ships left Valhalla early the next morning. Lightemann's Ridge was a large mountain range, and uncovering the Cerberus outpost would be no easy task. Praetor Jennings hoped that the flurry of activity Janus, Wouris, and Celes had discovered in the Phoenix ruins would translate into something that would give them a lead at Lightemann's. He called a council of war to give the preliminary plans for dealing with the outpost.

The Praetor's voice boomed out over the mess hall where all of ODIN had assembled. "This is a deeply personal mission for all of us, and I understand that many of you are eager to participate," he began. The anticipation buzzed around Janus.

"Adepts specialize in stealth, subterfuge, and silence. This time, we will fight *our* way." Cries of agreement sounded throughout the mess. "We will slip in and slip out without alerting the Cerberus forces to our presence." Dismayed whispers sounded here and there, but these were quickly silenced as the Praetor continued. "Many of you wish to take this opportunity to strike back, to make Cerberus pay for our brothers and sisters."

Cries of "'hear, hear" sounded.

"But this will be an intelligence gathering mission," the Praetor said pointedly fixing the room with a stare. He paused for a moment, struggling with his words. "The last time a Corporation made such a bold move, one of our fellow Legions was completely wiped out."

There were angry mutterings around Janus, but the Praetor held the room's attention. When he had first arrived at Valhalla, Janus had seen the ruins of Phoenix Corporation. Once the mightiest Corporation, Phoenix and another Legion called SHADE had obliterated each other in a mysterious battle. It had changed the balance of power in the world. And now Cerberus was up to something, but he had no idea what it could be.

"Cerberus is far and away the most powerful of the Corporations now, and if it has anything hidden up its sleeve, it is a cause for great concern. Therefore, our objective is simple: infiltrate the Cerberus base, discover what we can about their operations, and, most importantly, bring back evidence of that activity. If Cerberus is planning a move, we will need proof to convince the other Corporations and Legions into action." His voice became very quiet and solemn. "All of you understand what is potentially at stake—we will avenge our lost and dead in time." His voice rose. "Now, it's time to show Cerberus what we can really do." Cheers sounded throughout the gathering. A few of the officers cast guarded looks.

"The Praetor's walking a fine line," Marcus whispered, and Ramirez nodded behind him.

"A Corporation has not acted this boldly in decades," Celes breathed worriedly. "They've all been too afraid to violate The Phoenix Declaration."

"The Phoenix Declaration?" Marcus asked. Lyn and Ramirez looked just as nonplussed.

11

"It's a treaty between the Corporations following the destruction of Phoenix, describing how Corporations can engage in battle and what territories they control," Janus said.

Celes looked impressed at his knowledge. "Exactly. It covers everything from Corporate exchanges to banning the use of nuclear weaponry."

"Well, whether or not Cerberus is up ta something, ODIN is taking a major risk chasing them," Lyn interjected. She paused, looking thoughtful. "Ya don't survive the flood by beating back the river. Ya go ta higher ground."

Ramirez nodded appreciatively.

Lyn looked at the other three, noting the confusion on their faces. "Outskirter saying."

"Can't stop a Corporation, just get out of its way?" Celes interpreted. Lyn nodded.

Janus recalled that during his first meeting with her, Lyn had described Outskirters as people who lived outside of Corporate control, and survived by hiding. It didn't seem all that different from the slums in that respect.

"Well, I don't think the Praetor can stop the tide of this room, only direct it usefully." Marcus looked out over the gathered mass. "Whether or not we find anything, Cerberus is certainly planning something. And a lack of knowledge can be dangerous, too. Besides, none of us want our friends to die in vain."

"Too true," Celes said.

"No doubt Cerberus will be acting with only its best interests in mind." Janus grimaced.

"Tad bitter, are we?" Marcus asked. But Janus's reply was cut off by a signal from an Adept in front of them.

[Keats is] speaking.

"As the Praetor said before, this will be a small, covert operation. Therefore, we will have two teams infiltrating the base. After much discussion with the officers, it was decided that Sergeant Wouris will lead one group."

There were nods of approval from the crowd. Wouris was respected throughout Valhalla, and Janus couldn't think of anyone who he'd rather have at his back, other than his friends… or perhaps the Praetor.

"The sergeant also benefits from having been one of the three Adepts to infiltrate the Phoenix facility," Hawkes grunted.

Keats nodded. "Yes, and an important point, as the second leader was a harder choice. Although some disagreement resulted at first…" She paused. The Praetor cleared his throat, urging Keats to continue. "The officers eventually decided that Lieutenant Janus will lead the second group."

This time the murmurs were of disbelief. Marcus looked unsettled. Ramirez clapped Janus heartily on the back, and Janus nearly fell off his chair, both from the shock of the hit and the news. Ramirez quickly helped pull him back into his seat.

Keats raised a hand to quiet the crowd, who immediately settled. "Lieutenant Janus demonstrated excellent battlefield decision-making during our assault on the Titan complex, and Sergeant Wouris attested to both his willingness to listen to his teammates and his quick thinking during the mission. Furthermore, Janus is both from Cerberus and familiar with Overlord Middleton."

Janus was taken aback—he had only been promoted a few days prior, and already he had his first mission. Indeed, it had been the Titan assault where he had gained some measure of fame for his actions warning ODIN of the trap that had claimed so many of their friends, including many from his own team. *Isn't it standard to brief the officers before? Why didn't they tell me?* Janus wondered, but the voices around him interrupted his thoughts.

"He's too inexperienced, he's a mint," someone whispered to his left.

"But he obviously has the ability." Another voice to his right.

"Maybe they want to test his leadership skills. He has to start somewhere." From in front of him.

"Not for such an important mission," came from behind him.

Janus clenched his fists; how quickly they doubted his ability.

Celes turned and whispered irritably to the Adept behind them, "He and Wouris infiltrated the Phoenix complex just fine."

Janus felt a sudden rush of relief. He was going to turn and thank Celes, but he stopped. Marcus was staring at him with an inexplicable expression. Janus struggled to read his eyes.

Keats's voice, speaking to Janus directly, woke him from his thoughts. "…your own group, but you will defer to Wouris during this mission. The two of you will select your teams and be prepared to report to us the moment our scouts locate the Cerberus facility."

Hawkes stepped forward. "All right, that's enough for now. Dismissed."

Pushing Marcus's strange glare from his mind, Janus felt exhilarated. Many Adepts clapped him on the back as he left, wishing him luck. Others swept by, obviously not as pleased by the announcement. Everyone stopped to wish Wouris luck and offer congratulations. She shrugged this off and quickly left the mess.

Celes, Lyn, Ramirez, and Marcus all followed Janus out, and were soon joined by their fellow Sigma squadmates; they at least were pleased by the announcement.

"Excellent work, Janus."

"We knew you were officer material." Valers gave him a hearty shove to the back.

"You'll be amazing, I'm sure," Jones said.

"Remember, Janus, we're counting on you," Celes said.

"Yeah, don't let it go to your head," Marcus added rather coldly.

Janus gave Marcus a furtive look.

"He's right you know," a husky voice said. Janus glanced behind him; it was Colonel Hawkes.

Janus and the others came to attention. "Colonel."

"At ease. I'll talk to you for a moment, Lieutenant." He turned away from the group and walked towards a quiet corner of the great hall. Janus followed, somewhat cautiously.

"Yes, Colonel?" Janus asked expectantly, inwardly focused on his new promotion and mission. *Time to show them what—*

Hawkes's gravelly voice cut his thoughts off. "I'm sure you've realized not everyone is convinced about you leading on this mission." Janus shifted uncomfortably, now hanging on Hawkes's every word. Thoughts of his success suddenly seemed to dry up. "The Praetor, however, is confident in your abilities and believes you should be given an opportunity to prove your leadership skills. That's good enough for me." He paused. "But understand that we'll be watching you closely. Use your head. Sergeant Wouris expects you to act like you deserve to be here. She may be a sergeant, but I'd trust her over you any day. Listen to her every word and bring your people back alive"—Hawkes brought his face up close to Janus—"or you better be the one that doesn't make it back. Get me?"

Janus's gaze had not left Hawkes during the exchange, and he realized he hadn't been breathing either. He took a deep breath, and then replied, "Yes, sir."

Hawkes nodded in acknowledgement.

He felt compelled to ask, "Sir, what's a 'mint'?"

Hawkes's face was inscrutable. "It's a term for a new officer. One who lacks…experience."

Janus grimaced—he wasn't sure what sort of experience he had missed during the Titan battle, but he clearly hadn't impressed some of the other Adepts yet.

Hawkes shook his head. "Don't be too eager, boy. I'm afraid you'll understand it soon enough. Any other questions?"

Janus shook his head. "No, sir."

Hawkes gave him a lopsided grin. "Good. Now, your team will be critical. There's only four spots, and you'll naturally want your fellow Sigma Threes with you. I suggest you make your choices carefully. There's a fine line between you now. Ask Sergeant Wouris for recommendations. And train with them these next few days, just to get the kinks out. Dismissed."

Janus rejoined Celes, Lyn, and Ramirez in Sigma 3. Celes noticed Janus first. "So, what did Colonel Hawkes want to discuss?"

"Just some pointers," Janus said.

"And your squad?" Ramirez grunted.

"You three will be in it. I've seen how you work, and each of you has useful skills."

"Don't worry, Janus, we've got your back on this one," Lyn said.

"She doesn't want you hogging all the glory again." Ramirez grinned which looked good on his normally straight face.

Janus and Celes laughed at the surprising joke. But Lyn shot Ramirez a disapproving glare and he stopped smiling immediately, his face impassive once again.

"What about our fourth?" Celes asked.

"Marcus is the obvious choice," Janus said. "He's one of the most skilled in the squad. And both him and you, Lyn, led squads before. You'll have useful information about what worked and what didn't."

During the Titan assault, Lyn had led a separate cadet squad from Janus, and had ended up getting separated from both Janus's and Marcus's groups. In the end, she had gotten most of her squad out, but she had been forced to beat a hasty retreat from the Titan complex, and completely missed out on the action under the Phoenix ruins.

Celes nodded hesitantly. "I guess that makes sense."

"Come on, we've got a lot of work to do if we want to be ready the moment those scouts discover the Cerberus facility. Let's find Marcus," Janus said eagerly. He would show everyone the way to run a mission.

CHAPTER 3
THE FLASH OF LIGHTNING

They found Marcus in the Beacon of Need, Valhalla's highly advanced training arena. Janus had first experienced it when Sergeant Wouris had used it to completely demolish the entire Sigma Three cadet group single handedly.

Captain Rogers was instructing Marcus in Ghostblade techniques with a set of dummy Infernus units. The unpowered blade reflected the strange blue sheen of Immutium.

"Good," Rogers said. "The blade is used to counter the Infernus's superior strength and armor. Inferni, when attacking in crowded areas, will often land nearby so that they can make use of their flamethrowers. This provides an opportunity for a blade wielding Adept to decimate the Infernus ranks. However, the blade in and of itself is not an effective weapon. Only an Adept who understands how to maneuver, as well as the limitations of being confined to the heavy armor of an Infernus unit, can truly master a Ghostblade. Never forget that when powered, few things can stop the swing of the blade, and therefore you should have no problem slicing through brush, trees, or objects in order to connect with an Infernus unit."

Marcus finished his run through the Inferni by connecting his final swing to the head of an Infernus dummy. He smiled at Janus as he finished. "Janus! What did Hawkes say?"

"Just some particulars to keep in mind." Janus folded his arms over his chest.

Marcus held up the Ghostblade. "Like it? I wanted to learn how to use one after our experience at the colony, and the captain offered to show me some of the finer points after the meeting. I could have saved us some trouble if I'd had one of these at Titan." Marcus held it out to Janus, who took it and swung it around a few times. It no longer felt quite so heavy to him.

"Still interested in using one, son?" Captain Rogers asked Janus. "I was about to take Marcus to one of the platforms outside for some more in-depth practice."

Marcus smirked. "Come on, Janus. I can show you how a real Adept fights."

Janus took up the challenge. "I guess you won't be the one demonstrating, will you?"

More than a few of the new Adepts from Sigma Three were interested in learning how to fight with a blade, and by the time the little the group had moved to one of the unused launch platforms, quite a crowd had joined them. The sun was high in the sky, and a strong breeze pulled at the uniforms of the soldiers and the white clouds above them.

Within a few minutes, Captain Rogers had deployed several oddly shaped machines. These "dummies" were made of a strange, gel-like "healing" polymer on a Daedulus base. And they were like the turret Keats had deployed the other day—capable of moving without human input. Janus was always fascinated by Daeduluses. They, like satellites and many other technologies, were rare now, seemingly forgotten for reasons that were impossible for Janus to fathom.

Each dummy started as nothing more than what looked like a block of green goo on a solid pyramidal base. But as the gel reacted to a combination of heat and electricity from the base, primitive shapes began to take form. Basic armor, weapons, and either Adept or Trooper shapes appeared within seconds. Rogers tested the dummies, having each one unleash a wave of stinging red pellets from their bases at one another, quickly demonstrating not only that each could shoot, but that they could detect when they had been hit.

Captain Rogers brought out several training blades plus several real ones, all confined to their sheaths. They were all being kept in a solid looking cart, and Janus realized that even the dummy weapons were made of Immutium.

Rogers lined them up, a sheathed blade resting along his arm. Janus wondered how he could be so comfortable looking with such a heavy weapon. "Many of you are here because one of your fellow cadets used such a blade to great effect in our last battle"—he pointed at Janus— "but know that the Ghostblade is a difficult and dangerous weapon. Its origins lie with many of the martial techniques you have learned throughout your training. Created to fill a need for a close-range, silent weapon to deal with Trooper armor."

He walked along the line, watching the expression on every face. "When Trooper armor was first developed, it was almost impossible to eliminate an armored guard easily and silently, especially indoors. Standard combat knives were rendered useless." Rogers moved the blade from side to side as he spoke. "With the advent of Infernus armor, this inconvenience became an even heavier liability.

"The Immutium Ghostblade was created as a solution to this problem. As time has passed, it has become one of many invaluable tools in the Adept arsenal."

The gel-like Troopers moved around the room and into position. "Marcus, we've been practicing for a bit, why don't you start. If you let yourself get hit, those pellets will leave a nice red welt to demonstrate your failure." Rogers chuckled. "Everyone should step back now. We can use unpowered blades against the gel, but you should treat this as dangerous as any live fire exercise." The group took several steps back, while Marcus stepped forward. Rogers handed Marcus the sheathed blade, and said, "Are you ready?" as he set the dummies in motion.

Marcus unsheathed the dummy weapon, and Janus could almost visualize the change from deep red to a semi-transparent bright blue-white that a normal blade would undergo. The dummies melted back into their cube-like goo and slowly meandered around the platform. Marcus raised the blade in front of him and gave a slight nod.

In a flash, the two closest popped into shape in front of him. He quickly dispatched two 'Inferni' and then swept through to a third. The gooey adversaries whirled to bring their weapons to bear on Marcus, but he proved to be far too fast for them, quickly hacking his way through the group. For a final challenge, one ST dummy popped up far away from him. Marcus made several powerful leaps over to it and decapitated the dummy just before its weapon leveled on him."

Janus was impressed—Marcus's previous experience as an ST had undoubtedly given him some sense of how long the dummy would take to react. That, combined with his impressive physical strength, had let him close the distance. He doubted he could have done the same.

"Great work, Marcus! Quite good for a first try. Don't put so much flourish into your strokes though. The key is speed and effectiveness. It doesn't matter how good you look if you wind up dead. Most impressive; maybe this group will be able to move on to powered exercises sooner than expected."

The group cheered for Marcus, and he took a bow, using the blade's weight to smoothly lever himself over and back.

"Alright, Janus, since you're the one who got this group here, let's see what you can do," Rogers said. The dummies arranged themselves in a new pattern, as if pacing around before a battle. Marcus strode up and handed Janus the blade with great flourish.

"All too easy," Marcus said.

"Well, then, let me show you how it's done," Janus replied.

"Are you ready, Janus?" Captain Rogers asked.

Janus tested the blade. It felt good to have one in his hands again. "Yes, sir."

With a wave, Rogers set the dummies in motion, and Janus rapidly chopped the two Inferni that formed in front of him. It was a simple matter, and he moved through the dummies easily as they wheeled around, forming into passable imitations of STs and Inferni.

Only a few dummies remained when one popped up directly behind him. Janus whipped around the Ghostblade, leaving an imaginary blue trail as it arched.

He checked his swing just in time.

It was an Adept dummy. Janus flung the weapon high, giving the dummy a bad haircut and barely avoiding decapitating his 'ally.' The maneuver threw him off balance, the uncontrolled weight of the blade pulling his center of mass. There was a gasp of surprise from the group as he struggled to regain his momentum, and two new STs popped up near the edge of the platform, some distance apart. Janus grimaced as his eyes swept Marcus's concerned face. He couldn't reach both in time, but as his vision passed Celes, a thought occurred to him:

Why should I be limited to just the blade?

As the two 'Troopers' whipped around on him to fire, Janus let the weight of the blade carry him and pulled out his pistol. The Immutium blade firmly in his left hand, Janus shot the dummy farthest away while slicing through the other in one smooth motion. The clang of the round and of the heavy weapon digging into the base sounded together. Both stopped completely, the gel losing form and oozing down the sides of the dummies.

"Excellent! That is exactly how a Ghostblade is supposed to be used!" Rogers exclaimed. The far dummy fizzled and popped where a round had punched through its base. With some effort, Janus yanked the unpowered blade from the base of the other. It may not have been active, but it was still pretty much an Immutium club. The oozing gel pooled into the smashed top.

Rogers grimaced. "Though I probably should admonish you for destroying two perfectly good combat dummies." He rubbed his chin and glanced over his shoulder. "Sergeants Chiles and Graham aren't going to be happy about this, especially after the stunt the Praetor pulled on that turret earlier." He waved a hand. "We'll sort it out. Besides, knowing when to shoot is the key to making effective use of a Ghostblade."

He turned to the other Adepts. "That's exactly the type of lesson I want all of you to learn. It wasn't perfect, but it was a great start." Looking back at Janus, he smiled. "We'll have to make sure you learn how to check the momentum of the blade, but that will come in time."

Janus smirked at Marcus. "Told you I would show you how it's done."

Marcus looked slightly ruffled, but congratulated him nonetheless.

Janus glanced over at Celes with a smile, but she just shook her head, looking none too pleased.

He shifted uncomfortably, the congratulations of the others strangely hollow.

Chapter 4
Gathering Thunder

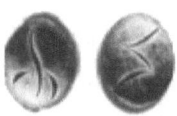

The next few days were a blur as the five prepped for the mission. It was constant training. Wouris had agreed to Janus's selections, but he had the impression that she was watching him like a hawk.

Now Celes, Marcus, Lyn, and Ramirez spent nearly every waking moment with him while they honed their skills. With the eyes of ODIN upon them, Janus pushed them relentlessly.

When Janus wasn't training, he was contemplating. During the nights, when he should have been resting, he tossed in his bunk. During meals, while the others talked, Janus sat quietly, alone in his thoughts. Most everyone in Valhalla let him be, watching him carefully from a distance. Even Celes left him alone, although it may have been because he had become such a brutal taskmaster.

Janus, however, wasn't thinking about the mission. Despite all his efforts to focus on everything else, he was thinking of Clara. Wondering what she was doing, and if she was all right. He knew it must be rough in the slums, suddenly all alone, not knowing whether he was still alive or not. How long had it been now? How many months? He just wasn't sure anymore.

Tired of another night staring at his ceiling, Janus slipped from his bed, and put on a light training suit. He wandered from the halls of Sigma 3, and into the great hall. The mess was mostly empty, though a few raucous voices emanated from it. He turned towards the Trunk, summoning a lift.

The lift flew upwards, stopping only once for a sleepy looking attendant who was leaving the medical branch. Otherwise, all was silent, and Janus stared up at the seal of ODIN, which had become a deep red-black in the darkness.

On a whim, Janus stopped the lift at the seal. Above him was Odin's Torch, the command center of Valhalla. Below, the Trunk stretched out its branches to all the various levels of the city. Waterfalls cascaded from cracks in the Trunk, and the sound of rushing water gently filled his ears. He looked around. To his right were residences, mostly reserved for the senior officers. To his left, Odin's one eye watched him fiercely. Janus chose neither, taking an oddly small path ahead. He crossed over the looming chasm of the hall and came to a small oval alcove. The sounds behind him became muted, and he discovered two windows with a wide view of the world outside. The ground below was dark with a new moon, and Janus couldn't tell if Valhalla was traveling over darkened hills or a rolling ocean. But it was peaceful, with a silence borne of its solitude. Benches built into the walls pressed up to the window, and Janus sat with his back against a column, staring into the sky.

A meteor streaked overhead, and the clear, dark skies lit up in brilliant bursts of blue and green, while bright stars glowed behind him. Janus pressed against the window in awe.

What would Clara say to this?

Soft footsteps sounded behind him. He turned and was surprised to see Wouris. She moved across the small alcove and sat back in the window across from him, staring at the meteor shower for several long moments before asking, "What's on your mind?"

Janus returned his gaze to the outside. "Nothing, really."

Wouris cocked her head at him. "I see. Then why are you staring into space in the middle of the night, not getting any sleep for the mission in two days?"

Janus sat bolt upright. "We found it?"

"Yes. It was luck, but I'm not going to complain. We caught a transmission between Cerberus and the facility. Looks like Lightemann's Ridge is going to have an important visitor in three days. We think we can use that to slip in. We're completing the scouting of the area surrounding the Cerberus facility right now. Two nights from now, our teams will have a go for the mission."

Janus felt the rush of expectations upon him once again. *What else do I need to do?*

Wouris seemed to read his mind. "Let your team rest a bit tomorrow, have some fun. Make sure *you* are fully recharged for the upcoming mission."

Janus paused, unsure whether he would heed her words. Then he shrugged. "There isn't much more they can do now anyway."

Wouris got up, taking a few steps away from the window. "Oh, and Janus, I think she would tell you off for worrying so much, putting both your team and yourself at risk by not getting enough rest."

Janus could not hide his surprise.

Wouris smiled. "I met her at Cerberus." He stared at Wouris for a moment, wide-eyed. Nodding, he slowly stood up and, giving one last look out the window, went to bed.

The next morning, Janus gathered Celes, Marcus, Lyn, and Ramirez in the common area and let them know about their upcoming departure. A strange sense of relief washed over the group.

"No more waiting. No more training. Just time to get the job done," Marcus said.

Celes agreed. "Maybe we can learn what on earth is going on. A Corporation, acting so aggressively…"

She became lost in thought, staring at the small table between them.

"Something about that really troubles ya?" Lyn asked her.

Celes shook her head as if caught off guard. "It's nothing." Lyn's eyes never left Celes.

Celes dismissively waved a hand. "It's just something I remember my father saying should be avoided at all costs."

"Well staying out of a Corporation's way is always a good idea, if that's what he was saying." Lyn said.

Ramirez crossed his arms. "Sounds wise."

Celes smiled faintly. "Yes." She looked down at her feet.

Janus cleared his throat. "Well, Sergeant Wouris dropped some wisdom on me, and I've decided to let all of you have the day off."

Lyn took the hint and focused her attention on Janus. "Finally realize that everything will be fine?" she teased.

Janus shook his head. "No, but Wouris raised the excellent point that if you all fell over from exhaustion, you wouldn't do *me* much good. Oh, and it would be bad for all of *you*, too." He gave them a smirk.

"Yeah, yeah." Marcus stretched and leaned back against his chair. "Your concern for your squad is deeply appreciated."

Ramirez stood up and Lyn motioned towards him without even looking. "We're going to grab some breakfast, if anyone cares to join us?" Lyn asked.

"I ate before meeting you all here." Janus shrugged apologetically.

Marcus and Celes nodded to show they had done the same. "I was trying to get some food in me so I wouldn't keel over in the morning training session. Sorry." Celes smiled reluctantly. Marcus motioned as if to say, *What she said.*

"So you can blame Janus," Marcus added.

Lyn pouted. "Well, fine. Ramirez and I didn't really want you guys, anyway. We'll have a nice leisurely breakfast with the other, more social Adepts," she huffed and leaped back over her chair, landing lightly on her feet and heading for the door. Ramirez nodded his head with a smile and followed, easily catching her with his long strides.

"Ever notice how Lyn always makes decisions for 'Ramirez and I'?" Janus asked with a grin.

Celes giggled. "Yeah, but he never seems to mind, does he?"

"Well, I'm not sure Ramirez is ever bothered by anything," Marcus commented dryly. "Anyway, I'm heading down to see if there are any Brigg's games to watch in the arena. I think Forrenza's squad was planning on playing. Anyone care to join me?"

Janus's interest was piqued. Brigg's Ball was the sport of choice for Adepts, and he had never actually had a chance to play as a cadet. In fact, it had been strictly forbidden.

"Not really, I think I'll pass for today." Celes shook her head.

Marcus seemed stymied for a moment. "What about you, Janus?"

Janus's mouth was half open as if to respond, but he glanced at Celes and back again. "Some other time."

A brief frown crossed Marcus's face. "Sure. Some other time." He turned and jogged out the door.

"Bye, Marcus." Celes called after him. He turned to smile at her as he left.

"Well, what should we do?" Celes asked wistfully.

"*We?* Why do *we* have to do anything?" Janus joked with a smile.

Celes gave him an exasperated look, and he quickly cleared his throat. "Err, sorry, habit. You just reminded me of Clara."

Celes frowned at him.

Janus suddenly looked towards the door. "I'm just taking it easy. Make sure I'm fully rested for tomorrow. Maybe I'll review what Valhalla's computers say about Cerberus, see if something valuable doesn't turn up."

"Good idea. I was thinking of heading up to the Garden," Celes said.

"The Garden?" Janus asked incredulously.

"Yes, the Garden," Celes said. "It is the perfect place to relax, and you can always bring a portable display to read from Valhalla's library."

Janus shrugged. "I guess so…"

"You've never been up there, have you?" Celes asked in amazement.

Janus mumbled something incoherent, then said, "I've been busy."

"But it is so beautiful up there!"

"Sure…" Janus shrugged.

She scowled. "You don't even know what it is, do you?"

"Uhh… of cour—" Janus was jerked forward as Celes grabbed his hand and pulled him towards the door.

"Well, we're going to change that right now. Come on!"

CHAPTER 5
THE GARDEN

The door to the Garden was heavy and solid, made from the same material as the glossy white exterior of Valhalla, designed to seal off the area completely in case of attack. Set into the stone were new runes Janus had never seen before: two small bent lines or Ls angled and wrapped around each other, and a rune shaped like a 'P.'

Janus studied the glowing red runes at the door. Celes smiled. "They translate to 'harvest of joy.'"

Without further ado, she stepped forward and the gateway slid open. "Come on." Celes pulled him in.

Janus gasped and stopped.

They were standing in a field of orange and blue wildflowers.

At his feet, a purplish-blue flower bloomed and he crouched down beside it. Carefully, he bent over to smell it, and a rush of memories came flooding back. A single flower in the slums. His wonder at it. And of Clara teaching him that not every good thing lasts.

He rubbed his eyes and looked up.

Adepts walked among the trees and grasses, their black-and-grey armor a stark contrast to the bright and vibrant landscape. But their faces reflected a simple joy as they walked, and suddenly, it seemed perfectly natural for them to be there.

Janus had assumed the Garden would have the same bright and rigid greenery of the Cerberus upper levels. This was much more wild. There were no paths, no organization. Things just grew. Simple gardening Daeduluses tended the plants as insects hummed lazily among flowers, grasses, and reeds. A brook bubbled cheerily nearby, flowing over natural stones. It was bright, and Janus looked up at the sky—the sun shone overhead through the clear, domed roof. The Garden wasn't even a quarter of the mess in size, but it felt open and free, and out beyond the walls, Janus could see the rolling clouds. It was like standing on an island in the sky.

It took Janus a moment to realize Celes had let go of his hand and was walking towards the brook. A breeze blew by him, and he looked to his right, where a small cluster of trees lined the wall, forming a tiny forest. Glistening fruit dragged down their boughs. Beyond them, special vents opened along the dome, letting fresh air in.

Right in the middle of the Garden, however, was the centerpiece. A giant tree—standing alone, and stretching nearly high enough to brush the top of the dome. Celes sat down on a rock protruding from the ground nearby, the brook babbling happily.

Janus followed her, carefully stepping to avoid the flowers, and feeling the temperature change as he moved into the shadows of the branches. The sun was warm and inviting, but Janus leaned against the tree. He wasn't sure what type it was, but he liked it. Although his

31

eyes had adjusted to the bright sunlight, he realized his years of skulking in the dark of Cerberus had left a mark on him. He was much more comfortable in the shade.

"I like to come up here sometimes and let my mind clear. I haven't been up here since the assault. Now seemed like a good time to do it," Celes said, her back turned to him.

Janus stared at her, but said nothing. The soft yellow sun filtered through the tree's leaves, cascading down all around her, giving her a heavenly glow.

Her hair shimmered like gold and she suddenly laughed. "Don't you just love it up here? It reminds me of home."

Janus averted his gaze, and glanced around, asking, "Really? How so?"

She blushed. "Never mind."

Janus looked at the ground, and then rubbed the back of his head. "It does seem nice."

Celes smiled sheepishly at him. "Neither of us like talking about home, do we?"

Janus swallowed, but didn't respond.

"Some people, like Valers, seem to only have good memories." She looked up at the sky. "But sometimes, it's a mixture. A place like this can remind you of the good."

Janus looked around once more at the flowers. "That's true." He cleared his throat hesitantly. "Was it bad?"

"Back home? Not always. But I had to leave."

"You had to leave?" Janus stood up from the tree. "Did an Overlord force you to go?"

Celes shook her head and pursed her lips. "No, nothing like that…"

Janus leaned back. "Sorry."

"Were you forced to come here?" Celes asked hesitantly.

Janus glanced into her eyes, and then looked away.

"Yes. That's why I had to leave Clara behind."

"I'm sorry."

A fresh breeze rolled across the meadow.

After a moment she added, "That's why I like it here. I can see the good times, and reflect on the bad. It reminds me why I'm here. You don't have a place that you go to sort things out?"

Janus shrugged. "Why would I need to? If my experience back home taught me anything, it's that I should spend as much time as I can learning and training."

"What about reflecting?"

"On what?" he asked cautiously.

She motioned back towards Valhalla. "On all of this. On what we do—we're mercenaries, Janus. We wage war for a living."

"We fight so that we can have some semblance of freedom. A chance for a real life," Janus replied.

"And what about those we fight?"

"STs? STs are scum—men and women who terrorize the innocent." He couldn't understand how anyone could think differently.

"Not all of them."

"Every one that I've met," Janus retorted.

"What about Marcus?" she asked.

Startled, Janus did not respond. A sudden rise in the chirping of insects pulled his attention back to the garden.

Celes searched for a new topic. "I love this tree. I've never seen such a large yew, and it's right here in the middle of the Garden." Her gaze traced a line up the trunk.

Janus looked up at the crooked branches. "A yew?"

"Yep. I heard the Praetor planted it himself long ago and had it brought here," Celes said. "Why do you think he favors you so much?" she asked absentmindedly.

Janus was taken aback at the question, and Celes quickly covered her mouth, as if the statement was unexpected.

"Not—not that there's anything wrong with that. What you did at the Titan outpost…" She struggled to find the right words. "But…"

Janus shifted uncomfortably. He felt the same, and even more so with the pressure of the upcoming mission. He couldn't quite explain it.

Celes locked eyes with him. "But from the moment you came here, it's clear that you've been treated differently."

Janus cleared his throat. "I don't know. Ever since that day in Cerberus when I was told I would be sold to ODIN, so many things happened so quickly. Norm was practically dancing with joy when he heard the news. And then when the Praetor shot me…"

"The Praetor shot you? Wait, what do you mean you were sold?" Shock emanated from her.

Janus grimaced.

Celes composed herself. "Why would he do that?"

"He thought he was doing me a favor."

"How could he possibly think…?"

Janus shifted uncomfortably and diverted his gaze.

Celes took the hint. "Still, I can't imagine he would show someone favoritism for something like that."

Janus shook his head. "He wouldn't. Maybe he came from the sl— the same area I did, and he feels that we're the same."

Patterns of light filtered through the branches of the yew tree, dancing across the ground.

Celes considered for a moment and then shook her head. "I don't think so. It seems so odd. There is so much we don't know about him, but I get the sense that he wouldn't intentionally show favoritism to anybody. It's got the others baffled too."

"Lyn and Ramirez?"

Celes nodded. "Yes, but it doesn't bother them. Marcus doesn't get it either."

"I didn't realize you talked about me so much." Janus coughed. He wasn't sure whether to be flattered or embarrassed.

Celes laughed. "You're our team leader now. We say all sorts of terrible things about you behind your back."

Janus chuckled. "Fair enough."

"May I ask who Norm is?"

Janus watched a dragonfly hover near the rock Celes was perched upon.

"He's a strange old man who apparently helped Clara with money and supplies when I was young. I don't really know him all that well, but he would often talk with Clara during their time on the lifts. The day I left…"

The dragonfly flitted away, along the brook.

"The day I left, he told me that going to ODIN was 'a great gift,' and that Cerberus would regret it."

"That seems strange."

"How so?" Janus asked curiously.

"I don't think many Corporate citizens anywhere know much about the Legions, let alone have a positive opinion about them."

Janus frowned. "I thought it might be just me. How do you know so much about Corporations, anyway?" It was Janus's turn to catch himself, and Celes quickly turned her head away.

Celes was quiet for a moment. "My father thought it was important to know."

"And why are you here?" He couldn't help himself.

After a moment, she returned his gaze. It was a hard look. "The same reason you are, to better my lot in life. To experience freedom away from the Corporations."

Janus felt a pit in his stomach.

"Hey, Janus!"

Marcus approached at a run, providing a welcome diversion. Janus gave one last hesitant glance at Celes, but she was now watching the brook.

"Glad I found you," Marcus said. He was covered in a sheen of sweat. "Captain Rogers is about to start a game of Brigg's Ball. Now that we're full Adepts, we can join in. If you play, we can have a three-team battle!"

Janus immediately popped up from the tree, eager to escape the awkwardness of the moment. "Count me in!" Brigg's Ball was a challenge he could understand.

"I thought you wanted to take it easy today," Celes said quietly, her back still turned.

"I wouldn't want to pass up my first opportunity to actually play Brigg's Ball, now would I?" Janus smiled, but Celes was unable to see it.

"You're welcome to come watch, Celes. I wish you could play, but Janus makes six," Marcus said.

Celes kept her back turned, staring up through the translucent roof at the sky. "Thanks, but no thanks. I think I'll stay. I came here to avoid a battle."

Janus wasn't sure she was talking about Brigg's Ball.

Marcus opened his mouth for a brief moment before deciding against it. He waved at Janus as he headed back towards the reinforced door. "Come on, the game's starting in just a couple of minutes."

Janus followed, but stopped after a few steps. He cleared his throat and spoke to Celes's back. "I bet this place would look beautiful at night."

He suddenly felt a chill, despite the warmth of his surroundings. Celes turned her head towards Janus and smiled, but only slightly.

"I'm sure it would." She returned her face to the sky, tilting her head back and closing her eyes as she let the sun play on her face.

Marcus called out, "Let's go," and Janus hurried after him.

CHAPTER 6
THE LEGEND OF BRIGG

The arena sat directly under the Trunk and great hall. Two simple runes swept over the entranceway:

which meant "Challenge and Victory."

Janus felt his body tense and tingle as he jogged swiftly down the ramp, Marcus just ahead of him, an electric buzz in the air. Janus had heard of Brigg's Ball as a cadet, but tradition stated only Adepts were allowed to play, and he had never found time to watch a match. Marcus, however, had quickly discovered a passion for it.

"It's said that Brigg's Ball was conceived by one of the first officers. A Major called Brigg," Marcus stated excitedly.

The space was like a rabbit-warren, and Janus spied large and stony root-like tendrils creeping down from the ceiling, forming the supports for the bubble-like wall of the playing field.

"First officers of what?" Janus asked.

Marcus waved a hand and shrugged. "I presume some early Legion. But it's not important."

"Brigg was strict, but principled. Someone who looked out for his men. But one soldier irked him to no end: a layabout called Boomer. Boomer was bright, but lazy and insubordinate, and he could always find a way to bend the rules in his favor."

A roar went up from the packed crowd. A game was already in progress, and the arena was filled with Adepts enjoying their downtime. Bleachers surrounded the round, slightly recessed field.

"Quite possibly the worst combination one can have in a soldier," Marcus ruminated.

"One afternoon, instead of normal training, Brigg asked them to play a game. He held up a red ball, and pointed to two sets of trees at opposite sides of a field. The goal was simple: shoot the ball between the other team's trees. The team with the highest score was the winner, and the game would end at sunset. The soldiers liked this plan. Playing a game was much, much better than their usual training."

"That's a mistake," Janus said bluntly, interrupting the tale.

Marcus laughed. "Of course. But we've had Wouris, and Hawkes, and everyone else. We know better. But that's not the point of the story."

He paused to motion them towards some bleachers up near the top. "I see some seats. We can wait up there until we're called up."

As they sat down, Janus watched as two teams shook hands and left the field. The playing field was slightly sunken into the ground, and as two teams climbed up the stairs back to the main floor waving, the crowd applauded. Apparently, the cheers had been for the end of the previous match, and so Marcus resumed his story.

"Boomer was wary, however, and asked if there were any other rules they should know.

"Brigg simply smiled. 'What? Do you think I'll spring some fancy twist on you after we start?'

"The soldiers nodded. Boomer was bright enough to know how the rules might bend, and if he had his guard up, they probably should as well. But Brigg shook his head and laughed. 'Nothing that clever, I'm afraid. Just a simple game with no other rules. Besides, I'm going to play with you. Do you think I'd cheat at my own game?'

"And so put at ease, the squad agreed to play, lining up on the field against Brigg and a few other officers he had recruited. Brigg was even kind enough to give Boomer the first try."

Two new teams jogged into the circular dome to raucous cheers, and Janus could almost envision the two teams being replaced by those in the legend.

"But when his men took the ball, and the game began, the unexpected happened. They had fun. No awful drills. No punishing exercises. Brigg and his team simply went for the ball and left it at that. It really was just a game.

"And as the day came to a close, the score was tied. The soldiers were surprised. They could win. They could defeat Major Brigg. At his own game, no less. And with the sun falling, Boomer confidently called for the ball and rushed forward, ready to lead his squad to victory.

"From out of nowhere, Brigg slugged Boomer, knocking him flat on his back, and taking the red ball for himself. And his team did the same to every other one of Boomer's squad on the field.

"Boomer watched helplessly as Brigg scored the final goal, winning the game as the sun touched the horizon.

"For a moment, some of the soldiers cried out, 'Cheater!', but Brigg silenced them with a wave of his hand.

"Boomer simply asked, 'Why?'

"'I told you there were no other rules, didn't I?'

40

"The men, including Boomer, sat in stunned silence.

"'You could have done the same from the very beginning. But you didn't. You arrogantly assumed that I couldn't outwit you. That I thought like you.

"'But we were enemies. Fighting on either side of a war. While you enjoyed yourself, you thought you were setting the rules. And when you were most comfortable, most relaxed, and most confident, I crushed you. Because I don't think like you do. Because there is no greater mistake a soldier can make than believing they understand an enemy they've never bothered to study themselves.'"

There was a huge thud and a resulting "oooo" from the crowd, and Janus suddenly realized he hadn't been watching the game. Several nearby onlookers visibly winced and a couple of white-clad Medical Branch Adepts pulled a limp figure from the playing field as the game continued on behind them.

Janus spied more than a few officers cheering as the game resumed. Brigg's Ball had apparently become even more brutal than its namesake, but he suspected the officers liked it that way. If the legend was true, this was a game designed to remind soldiers how to fight, without the risks. Or at least nothing more than a few weeks' docked rations couldn't fix.

An older Sergeant named Walters, wearing an odd, bright orange-and-yellow striped suit of armor signaled to Marcus and waved them down.

Marcus smiled. "Time to gear up."

Janus nodded confidently. "Let's show them what we can do."

"So how do you play?" Janus asked as they headed down.

"A Brigg's Battle is held between teams of five," Marcus began. "Our arena can accommodate two to four teams playing simultaneously."

"All at once?" Janus asked.

Marcus nodded. "Yes. Up to four teams playing in the same game. Makes for interesting tactics.

"We'll be playing with two teams today, Lieutenant Forrenza's Flames and Captain Rogers's Rangers."

"Does every team have a terrible rhyming name?" Janus interjected as they approached the prep area.

"Pretty much par for the course." Captain Rogers was warming up with his team and smiled at the pair as they passed. "Are you even playing Brigg's Ball if you don't? I hope you've got your name ready. We might just disqualify you otherwise."

"Uhhhh…" Marcus trailed off, looking at Janus. Janus was equally at a loss.

Rogers laughed. "I'm just kidding." He slapped Marcus on the back. "The whole stadium will boo you, but you won't be disqualified." The rest of his team nodded in agreement.

"So we've got to think of a name," Janus said as they walked further past them, towards where Sergeant Walters waited. "I thought you knew the game."

"I do," Marcus said defensively. "I just didn't think of a silly name for our squad because we haven't even had a chance to practice yet."

"Well, keep telling me the rules then," Janus said. "We've got three teams, so I'm assuming we've got three goals? And I think we'll have multiple balls in play?"

"Boomers, they're called boomers. Like in the story. The others will give you a funny look if you say otherwise," Marcus corrected.

Janus shot him an annoyed look. "Okay, boomers. What are the rules for those?"

Walters waved them to a prep area for their team. Jones, Valers, Kirsten, and Holloway were waiting for them, already tossing around a bright red ball. Valers' green eyes sparkled as they approached. "All right, the two aces join us! There's no way we can lose now!"

Janus smiled uncomfortably at the praise.

Marcus held up a hand and Jones tossed the boomer to him. With a flick of his wrist, he passed it to Janus, who caught it and rolled it around in his hands. It had a bit of give to it, constructed from a translucent, hard rubber. The red color came from a light inside the ball.

"There are two types of boomers: blue and red. Blue boomers represent defense. You can score them in your own goal for a point. Red boomers represent offense. Score them against another team and they'll lose two points."

"Interesting," Janus mused. "So why the light, not just solid colors?"

Valers pointed at the ball. "They can change colors during the match, so you have to pay attention, just like the ebb and flow of a battle."

"And there can be multiple in play at once." The short but stout Jones reached out, and Janus handed it to her. The ball flexed as she pressed it. "Basically, assume there is one in play for each team."

A slam against the nearby arena wall caused the group to look up, just in time to see one of the current players carrying a red boomer being forcibly checked into the glass, smashing against the wall with a loud thud.

Janus grimaced as the Adept stumbled to his feet to resume play—the circular playing field was confining, and it was clear that attacking a player with the boomer was highly encouraged. Sergeant Walters was going to be their ref for today, and she merely nodded approvingly at the hit. Janus presumed his bright orange-and-yellow armor was to make it clear he was not to be touched.

Marcus nodded. "That's pretty much it. Let's see, was there anything else?"

"Don't forget the goalie," Valers stated.

"Right." Marcus nodded. "Each team can have a goalie. They have to stay within a certain area, but they basically have carte blanche to annihilate anyone who comes into their zone. And you lose a point if you touch them."

"You get gut punched at the same time your team does," Kirsten summarized.

"Play never stops," Jones added. "It's one continuous battle without breaks."

Marcus snapped his fingers, "Of course! That reminds me of the most important rule!"

The team turned to look at him. Marcus smiled. "It's not a penalty if you don't get caught. That's an official rule, by the way."

To accentuate the point, a section of the crowd booed as one Adept tripped and slammed an Adept without the boomer into the ground while the ref was distracted. Another group cheered as their team scored on the cheap shot.

"So what's the ref for?" Janus asked in confusion.

"Rule on egregious stuff. And penalize teams that do get caught. You're not supposed to attack people who don't have a boomer."

With a loud horn, the previous match ended.

Holloway pumped a fist, his blond hair bouncing. "We finally get to play a Brigg's Ball battle. I've been waiting for this!"

Kirsten, her red hair running to her shoulders laughed and high-fived him.

"We still need a name," Marcus interjected.

"And we still need a team captain," Jones added, eyeing Marcus and Janus.

Janus wasn't sure how to react to that, but Holloway spoke up suddenly.

"Well, we aren't representing an officer's squad, but we could use the call sign from the last mission?"

Marcus's gaze shifted to Janus, but he rubbed his chin and said, "Wouris' Washouts? I think we need something a bit more intimidating. What about Wouris' Weapons?"

"I like that," Jones said. The others nodded again in agreement.

"And it seems to me like Marcus should be captain," Kirsten added. "He organized this for us."

Valers, Jones, and Holloway all nodded in agreement before Janus had a chance to say anything. He felt a buzzing in his brain that suggested he should do something about that, but he pushed it aside. They would be fine, and Marcus knew more about the game than he did.

Marcus smiled. "Gladly. Now that that's settled, let's get in there."

The team bristled with anticipation.

Chapter 7
Brigg's Ball

Walters, in her bright orange suit, waved for all three teams to meet her in the center. As Janus walked inside, Adepts roared against the glass, the arena seemingly vibrating with anticipation. It was clear that having new blood on the field was an exciting prospect for the fans. The Flames and Rangers sauntered in, confidence brimming. Five rectangular hexes lit up in front of each goal, showing the starting positions for each team, and another zone lit up around the goal.

"I want a good game, everyone. Remember, at the end of the day, you're all on the same team. Get everything out in here." Walters motioned into the middle. "Team captains, shake."

Lieutenant Forrenza and Captain Rogers stepped forward and shook first, giving each other proper respect. And then both turned to Janus and reached to shake. Janus was caught momentarily off guard; Marcus stepped in, extending a hand. "Actually. I'm the team captain."

The two officers pulled back, exchanging surprised looks with Sergeant Walters. "Marcus organized the team," Janus added quickly. Marcus's eyes flashed for a moment, but he was all smiles as he shook.

"Teams shake," Walters intoned, a brief frown upon her face. The three teams shook hands and quickly separated. Walters blew her whistle. "Alternates to sub-stations. Teams to the line."

"Kirsten, you're the alternate. We'll bring you in when one of us is gassed," Marcus said as they headed towards their goal.

Kirsten sagged a bit, but nodded and quickly ran towards a door beside their goal.

As Janus reached the glowing hexes, he became very aware of how little he knew about Brigg's Ball's overall strategy.

"Janus, take my left. Holloway right. Valers, are you comfortable taking up goal?"

Valers rubbed his hands together. "Born ready."

Jones laughed. "I'll take center defense once we start."

Marcus agreed as Janus toed the line of his box nervously. The other teams moved methodically into position and he exchanged anxious looks with Holloway. Marcus remained eyes forward, seemingly unshaken.

Across the arena, Lieutenant Forrenza moved to the back of her line, while Rogers took a wing position with his squad. A woman named Emmanuel with short black hair took up the lead striker of the Rangers. It was clear that both captains acted in supporting roles.

Walters blew her whistle and the arena went very still.

After a moment, a single boomer launched high into the air from the center of the arena, as if it had been waiting underground. Janus jumped off the line.

An alarm sounded, and Janus stopped. No one else had moved. A flashing FALSE START appeared in bold letters on the scoreboard. He heard some light laughter among the crowd and looked towards his team, and they motioned him back.

"You've got to wait until the ball's at the apex," Valers said.

"Wouris' Weapons, false start. Rotate your line," Walters said.

"I've got it, Marcus," Jones said. "Take my box Janus, we'll switch back our positions as soon as the game starts."

Janus walked to Jones's box, ignoring the subtle head shake from Marcus. Janus looked back just in time to see the boomer slide back into floor.

Walters blew her whistle once more, and Janus tensed. He wasn't sure what the penalty for a second false start was, but he didn't want to find out.

After a few interminably long moments, the launcher flew open and fired another boomer. This one flew even higher, and Janus realized it was flashing rapidly back and forth between blue and red. The flashing became almost hypnotic as the boomer slowed towards the top of the arena, the color changes taking longer and longer. Blue…red…blue…red…blue. As it nearly brushed the bottom of the scoreboard, the ball turned a bright red and began its rapid fall.

Marcus exploded off the line, heading for the ball.

As Janus watched his team launch towards the boomer, he suddenly had an epiphany, and realized how lucky it was the ball was red.

"Marcus! Hang back!" Janus called out as Jones fell in beside him, and Valers moved into the goal area.

Marcus did not stop, but Holloway slowed, and Janus was shocked by the speed on display by the other teams. Emmanuel was incredible and had snatched the ball well before Marcus was even close. Janus would have to figure out how she did that later.

Holloway came running up beside him. "What's wrong, Janus?" he asked worriedly.

Janus shook his head. "Nothing. But I don't think we should go for that ball."

The three of them backpedaled closer to Valers, forming a wall around the goal. Marcus, stuck in the middle with no support, decided to retreat back to the rest of the group.

"Why not?" Jones asked.

Emmanuel launched a flying kick and pummeled the boomer towards the Flames's goal, but Forrenza was there, and deflected it to her teammates. "Better luck next time, Rogers," she called out derisively.

Marcus came running up, an angry expression on his face. "What's wrong with you, Janus? You didn't even try."

Janus shook his head, looking at the scoreboard. "Sorry, Marcus. I just thought we shouldn't go for the ball, er, boomer."

"Why not?" Marcus asked, echoing Jones's question.

"Because there's no benefit. Red ones just hurt teams, right? They aren't worth any points for us?"

"Yeah."

"So there are three teams." He pointed to the intense melee between the Rangers and the Flames. "And those two probably don't think we pose any threat."

Marcus looked at him shrewdly. "Of course."

The others looked at him for an explanation, and Marcus watched as an Adept nicknamed 'Dozer' on the Rangers slammed one of Forrenza's teammates to the floor, sending the boomer flying free.

"They're going to attack each other. Whether we score on one of them, or they score on each other, it's effectively the same result. So we should just defend, and make sure we don't get scored on."

Jones, Holloway, and Valers all nodded in understanding.

"We've got another thirty seconds before boomer number two shows up." Jones looked up at the scoreboard.

Janus glanced out at the crowd, which seemed to be swelling by the minute; word of the match was going around. Janus suspected they were interested in seeing how the newly minted Adepts, and their newest lieutenant, performed.

An errant pass from one of the Flames brought him back to reality, sending the boomer hurtling to their goal. Marcus was ready, however, and cleared the ball back towards the other end of the arena with a swift kick.

A round of boos came from the crowd. Pure defense didn't appear to be a popular strategy, but Janus ignored them. "Good work, Marcus."

Marcus grimaced, but nodded appreciatively.

The high-flying boomer curved towards the Flames goal, giving the Rangers an easy attack, and as the Flames defenders struggled to run back, Rogers dashed by them. The Flames had overextended themselves, and Rogers used the opportunity to drive inside, passing to the lightning-quick Emmanuel. She leaped over a diving tackle by a Flames striker, clutching the boomer close.

Unexpectedly, it started to flash.

Blue…red…blue…red…blue…red…

"Time to move," Marcus said. The four dashed forward, leaving Valers behind to guard.

Marcus led the charge. "Jones, hang back near the launcher," he shouted behind him. "If that boomer goes blue before the Rangers can score, we'll need to intercept it."

Jones slowed, covering the middle of the field, watching the progress of the teams.

It seemed to Janus as if the arena suddenly stretched for miles. Rogers and Emmanuel were blazingly fast, and the rest of their team acted as a living wall of interference to the Flames strikers rushing back to defend. From the corner of his eye, Janus caught a Ranger defender rapidly peeling away from the group and heading center. Emmanuel quickly passed back to Rogers as the last remaining defender before goalie Forrenza moved to strike her.

"Faster, Janus!" Marcus called out, several lengths ahead of him.

Janus put on another burst of speed, trying to close the distance as the time the ball spent red became shorter and shorter. It would turn fully blue in just moments.

But now it was Rogers and Emmanuel vs. Forrenza. The Rangers had a two on one for the goal. Forrenza licked her lips in anticipation, and suddenly waved her arms unexpectedly. With a mental image of his training with Wouris, Janus barely jumped a sudden leg sweep from the Flames striker that Emmanuel had jumped over. He glanced behind him, watching as Jones and Holloway were unexpectedly blindsided by the Rangers and Flames respectively. The two teams were converging to the center, leaving Forrenza to her fate.

With Walters's attention focused on the goal, the Flames had taken the opportunity to knock out some of the extra competition.

They've already given up on this goal, while we're wasting our time going for a decided shot.

Janus made an about face. "Marcus, leave it!" He didn't look to see if Marcus stopped or not.

Rogers faked a shot on goal, and Forrenza was forced to dive. With a quick flick and a kick, he easily passed the ball to Emmanuel, who leaped into a flying roundhouse and smashed the boomer into the goal just before it finished flashing.

Janus glanced up at the scoreboard as a minus two appeared under the Flames's score. Immediately two Boomers shot out of the center launcher, and the Flames and Ranger squads both fought furiously for control. The crowd roared in appreciation.

"Looks like it really was 'next time,' Forrenza!" Rogers called out as he rushed back towards the middle to join his team. The Flames, with greater numbers at the center grabbed the first one easily. It was a blue. The second, a red, was more hotly contested.

Janus swore angrily under his breath, *Real good work team.*

The Rangers managed to grab the red as Emmanuel and Rogers rushed up to prevent the Flames from scoring the blue.

Janus glanced back to see Marcus jumping up from the ground. Rogers and Emmanuel had probably taken advantage of the new distraction to take him out as they passed.

Entering the chaos in the center, Janus realized trying to coordinate with Holloway and Jones was nigh impossible. They hadn't worked out any strategy, and were simply flailing, ineffectively rushing for whatever they could.

The Ranger Dozer broke off from the group and headed towards Valers as the red boomer erupted from the melee, flying in a long arc. Valers tensed.

With his team out of position, no one could support the inexperienced goalie. It was the perfect chance for the Rangers to solidify their lead.

A veteran vs. a mint—fantastic.

Janus abandoned the center and the battle for the blue, where a Flames striker was going at it with Rogers. If Valers somehow did stop the ball, he would need someone to whom he could pass easily or retrieve it on a deflection. Janus felt his breathing grow heavy as he ran.

In the corner of his vision a figure appeared, and Janus realized Marcus was sprinting neck and neck with him to help out Valers.

He's really fast, Janus marveled. He had covered a lot more ground than Janus had. Janus pushed himself faster and made a quick one-handed sign for separation to Marcus. With a nod, they split to give maximum coverage on a rebound.

Dozer shot.

As he watched the boomer sail towards the goal, Janus caught sight of Celes in the crowd, and he sprinted even harder. Marcus was already slightly ahead of him.

Valers reacted in slow motion, leaping lazily for the boomer; it curved in a gentle arc away from him and toward the corner of the goal.

The bile rose in the back of Janus's throat despite his labored breaths.

But suddenly, Valers's fingers brushed the boomer as it slid by, changing its course ever so slightly. As the red rebounded off the edge of the goal, the crowd let out a wild roar, approving of Valers's amazing save. Janus felt a pang of relief, and also pleasant surprise: *Valers is a good goalie.*

The cheers were short lived, however, as the bright ball bounced oddly, right back into Dozer's hands. Janus and Marcus hesitated; Valers was totally out of position. Dozer tossed the ball into the goal with a quick flick. Captain Rogers's squad cheered from the stands as a minus two appeared under the name Wouris' Weapons.

Rangers 0, Flames -2, Weapons -2.

Janus looked towards the center, expecting another boomer, but none arrived. Only the single blue boomer remained. He clearly didn't know the rules well enough.

Marcus shook his head in disappointment and took off, back into the melee. Janus looked to the group of Sigma Three Adepts who were watching the game; they looked slightly crestfallen. Celes simply shook her head. Janus turned away quickly and ran over to Valers to help him up.

"Good play, Valers. Sorry we blew it."

Valers looked a little dazed, but his broad smile remained and he said, "Hey, no problem. I'm as surprised as you are that I stopped it." Janus returned the grin.

Marcus called out, already near the center of the arena. "Come on, Janus, move it. Good try, Valers."

Leaving Valers to reorient himself, Janus rushed back towards center, the minus two looming overhead. The match was only twenty minutes long, and it seemed like every moment the clock was ticking faster and faster.

But few opportunities to change the score arose as the time slipped by. Neither the Rangers nor the Flames were able to score, and the inexperience of the new Adepts prevented them from making any meaningful plays.

Finally, after what seemed an interminable wait, another boomer entered play. It was red. The melee intensified, as there were once again two targets to distract and entice. And not much longer after that, with little progress made by any of the teams, a third ball entered the field of play. There were now two blues and one red.

Three teams, three boomers. If we're going to do anything, we need to do it soon.

A weak pass from the Flames gave them a chance, and Marcus leaped for the loose ball. Springing up from the floor with a red, and surrounded by Flames and Rangers, he whipped it over to Jones, who caught it and leaped over the Flames's right guard. The horde bearing down on her, she flung it over to Holloway. Unfortunately for him, possession was a relative term, and Emmanuel gave him a ferocious body check before the boomer had even arrived. As Holloway went flying, Emmanuel snagged the ball and headed for the Flames goal.

Holloway stumbled to his feet and gave a thumbs-up to the team, albeit somewhat less enthusiastically than before, his blue eyes looking a little dazed.

Janus glanced around, panting hard. His entire team was dragging. Even Marcus looked exhausted. While the more experienced teams were passing, and communicating, he and the other new players were running for every ball individually. His muscles felt as though they were turning slowly to lead. Even with their intense training, keeping up at full throttle with experienced teams was another level. As he watched one of the Flames strikers switch into the goal, leaving Forrenza to move forward, Janus knew they needed some new ideas.

It was Marcus, however, who signaled them to withdraw. They pulled back as a group to just in front of the goal box, leaving the Flames and Rangers to battle it out over the three balls. The crowd jeered at the tired group.

"This isn't working, we need a new strategy," Marcus breathed, keeping an eye on the battle raging at the other end.

Jones spoke up, pausing between breaths. "We need an edge...we don't have the coordination."

Holloway, his blond hair stuck to his forehead, was clutching his chest where he had been struck earlier. "Easier said...than done. They pass more than we do." Holloway looked at Marcus. "You're as fast as Rogers, if not faster. You and Janus can strike if you work together."

Marcus nodded, his breathing already slowing dramatically. "Agreed." A roar from the crowd momentarily distracted them as Forrenza finally shot a blue boomer into her own goal, adding a point to her team. The scoreboard flashed: Rangers 0, Flames -1, Weapons -2.

Marcus motioned with his hand. "Holloway, sub out with Kirsten."

"But—" Holloway protested, glancing at Janus, who nodded and shrugged.

Janus gestured at Marcus. "He's right. Good job, but that one shot really slowed you down. We need fresh legs if we want to pull this off."

Marcus's look was inscrutable as Holloway sighed and then hustled over to the sub-box where Kirsten waited.

Janus watched Forrenza try to take a shot with a red on the Rangers goal, only to collide painfully with the Rangers's new goalie, Dozer. Dozer mercilessly checked her and ripped the boomer from her grasp as she lay on the floor. Her supporters let out a disappointed cry as Walters signaled and the Flames's score dropped to minus two again.

Janus looked up at the time as Kirsten ran into the huddle. Five minutes remained. "We should pull Valers out of the goalbox."

Marcus shook his head. "Out of the question, we'll be too vulnerable. They've already taken advantage of a one-on-one before. How does that improve the situation?"

"What's the worst that can happen, lose by even more?" Janus shot back. "And there's only one red on the field right now." He flipped his head towards the other side of the arena. "Those two would much rather score against each other than us."

Marcus frowned.

Janus looked to the rest of the team. "If we strike together and focus on the blues, we have a chance to even up the game. Eventually they'll realize they have to deal with us, but it might give us the opportunity to change the pace of the game." Another roar from the crowd; they had lost interest in the huddle and now cheered as the Flames scored another blue boomer.

Rangers 0, Flames -1, Weapons -2.

"Sounds like a plan, Janus," Kirsten agreed. Jones and Valers nodded.

Marcus worked his jaw slowly, but studied the expectant faces of the group. After a moment, he said, "Just go for blues?"

Janus nodded his head. The crowd roared as a new boomer emerged from the center, with Rogers there to grab it. It was blue.

"Right." Marcus looked around the team. "We can still win this, let's get to it."

4:30 left...

Marcus signaled Valers out of the goal, and with fresh energy the young team reentered the fray to the roar of the crowd. Rogers bulled his way through a Flames defender, and was surprised by the sudden appearance of Janus and Marcus around him. He got off a weak pass as Marcus connected a heavy check to his gut. Kirsten, with her fresh legs, intercepted the blue boomer and broke for the outside. Leaping over a desperate tackle by a Rangers guard, she flung the ball toward the Weapons goal. It wasn't a great shot. Fortunately, Marcus was already racing to give it an extra boost. With a quick kick he sent it flying for the score.

The crowd cheered; the game had suddenly turned much more interesting.

Rangers 0, Flames -1, Weapons -1.

Marcus flashed a grin at Janus. And he noticed Celes in the crowd for the first time, too, sending her a wave. She cheered with the other Sigma members, encouraging the team on.

With only a single red boomer in play, the Weapons went on the defensive again, much to the chagrin of the other two teams. Valers temporarily rotated back into the goal, waiting for Marcus to signal him again.

Three minutes. We need some luck...

With the clock counting down, a deathly stillness suddenly settled over the crowd. Forrenza and Rogers surged towards the middle, and Janus followed suit, just as a boomer burst from the center. It was red, and Janus skidded to a halt along with Marcus beside him.

Patience, Janus struggled to calm himself. There were two boomers in play. He looked at Marcus.

"One still to go," Marcus replied to his unasked question.

As Janus backpedaled away from the center, he caught a glimpse of Celes watching from the edge of her seat. No team gave any quarter, and any red boomer that approached the Weapons goal was swiftly booted away to let the more senior teams battle it out.

Two minutes...

Janus could feel the stillness in the crowd again. Another boomer must be on the way. Launching forward, he raced towards the middle, Marcus already sprinting ahead of him. As Marcus reached the middle of the field, a boomer exploded upwards from the floor.

Blue!

With a high-flying leap, Rogers was there, snatching it from the air immediately, and delivering a heavy kick to Marcus all in one smooth motion. With a quick pass he sent the boomer hurtling towards his goal.

Janus pursued, ignoring the continued fighting over the two red boomers in play. He passed Marcus as he flipped himself back up. A Flames player intercepted, but almost immediately the ball had begun to slowly flash red. Janus felt a pit in his stomach, but he charged forward. Forrenza took control of the blue, and Janus rushed her, joined by Emmanuel.

Forrenza danced backward, looking for an open teammate. The boomer flashed faster, the red overtaking the blue. She dodged right, but Janus could see the same glint in her eye as when they'd played Brevis Bellum, the strategy game she, Marcus, and Janus frequently played together.

She's feinti— Janus collided painfully with Emmanuel, knocking them both flat. Forrenza smiled and launched the boomer to her open man with a powerful kick.

Marcus, however, was ready. Flying out of nowhere, he snagged the pass, and sent it flying back over the heads of the melee without taking a moment to look. And Valers was there.

With a high bounce the boomer landed right in front of him, almost entirely red. With one final surge, he leaped up and booted the bouncing ball as hard as he could.

It sailed true, but as it crossed through the goal, it flashed a solid red. Janus turned to the scoreboard: The score flashed, and a zero appeared. The Weapons were tied with the Rangers once more.

Rangers 0, Flames -1, Weapons 0.

The crowd erupted, and he breathed a sigh of relief. But there was no time to halt, as Rogers took advantage of the Flames's diverted attention to overwhelm their lone defender and drop another red into their goal. Janus glanced at the time.

50 seconds...

With only a red remaining and a score of -3, the Flames couldn't possibly win.

"Fifty seconds!" Marcus shouted. "Then it's just us and the Rangers!"

Sudden death. *We must keep playing but the Flames automatically lose...*

Hunched over and sucking in air, Janus glanced at the faces of Jones, Valers, and Marcus down the field. *Everyone is too exhausted...* The Rangers would destroy them. Faced with this proposition, Janus made a risky bet...

Straightening up, he bellowed to his teammates, "Attack! Give the ball to the Flames if necessary!"

Jones yelled. "What?"

"Just do it!" Janus yelled. Janus looked at Forrenza, who gave him a sly smile. The team pushed forward, and when the ball bounced in front of Marcus, he passed it directly to her after only a moment's hesitation. She was indeed surprisingly cooperative. Together the two teams pushed forward.

The clock seemed to slow –20...

19...

Even with both teams working together, the Rangers knew all they needed was defense for a few more seconds. Emmanuel booted an incoming ball away, launching it to the opposite edge.

We're not going to make it. Janus sprinted across the arena and smashed the boomer back towards Kirsten. He was racing back when Marcus's shout halted him.

"Stay there, Janus! We can't afford a late goal against us!"

"We don't have time for this!" Janus shouted back, glancing at the clock.

13...

"There are nine of us attacking, one more won't help!" Marcus commanded.

Janus clenched his fists. *We have to score!*

10...9...

A botched ball by Jones made up Janus's mind. He sprinted across the arena, desperate to clear the distance. The red that Jones had fumbled was still being kicked around in the scrum near the middle of the field. As Janus put in one final effort, it rolled free in front of him. It was a long shot, but his path to the goal was clear. He took aim as he bolted forward.

Emmanuel's sudden materialization in front of him caught him off guard, and her hard check in the gut sent him sprawling. She booted the boomer with a fearsome kick. But she wasn't kicking to the edge this time. Janus could only watch in horror as the ball curved gracefully towards his goal.

4...

The boomer landed with a high bounce, regaining the air and speeding towards the untended goal box.

3...

2...

The glowing ball seemed to inch towards the goal. Janus's gaze flitted rapidly between the ball and the time.

1…

The Boomer crossed the line as the buzzer sounded. Janus just stared at the score in disbelief: Rangers 0, Flames -3, Weapons -2.

The Rangers erupted into cheers, mobbing Emmanuel as she slid on her knees across the floor with a yell. Janus leaned on his knee, staring at the scoreboard. His fellow teammates were equally dejected. Disappointment etched their faces. Marcus ran over to him, livid.

"What were you doing?" he exploded.

Janus looked up at him. "Trying to win?"

"I ordered you to hold your position!"

Janus stood up, disgust and confusion on his face. "We couldn't win that way! Sudden death would have been a slaughter!"

"You don't know that! Maybe you couldn't do the job, but the rest of us could!"

Janus moved a step closer to Marcus. "Don't tell me you're so full of it you think you're that good!"

"I'm full of it?" Marcus turned away in exasperation. "*I'm…* full of it?" He turned back to Janus, sneering. "I'm not the one who threw away the game. I'm not the one who tried to be the hero by clearly going for a crazy long shot on goal. And I'm not the one who tried to take control after ignoring the *team captain's orders.*"

A large crowd was gathering, watching the pair. From the corner of his eye, Janus could see commotion at the edges, and he thought he recognized a familiar bob of red hair making its way through the crowd.

Janus sneered back, "*Captain's orders?* This isn't some Adept squad, it's a Brigg's Ball game! I'm the one who gave us a strategy that got us back into the match. You're too busy trying to be everywhere at once to notice your team is dead tired. And if you had just let me go instead

61

of ordering me around, I would have gotten to that ball in time and we would have won! Besides, in case you've forgotten, I outrank you now, so show some respect!"

Marcus bristled and Janus smirked at him. Wouris' face appeared in the crowd, and Janus was momentarily distracted. She shoved her way through, looking angrier than he had ever seen.

He turned back to see a fist moving towards his face, and with nothing left to do, he mentally braced for the upcoming pain.

The punch never landed.

Celes had stepped in between the two and blocked the blow. But it wasn't her sudden appearance that shocked them. It was the fire blazing in her eyes. Celes was smaller than both Janus and Marcus, but each of them took a step back from her penetrating stare.

Janus swallowed hard.

"What are you idiots doing?" she yelled.

Janus noticed Sergeant Wouris had stopped in her tracks, and she viewed the unfolding drama with great intensity.

Celes turned first to Marcus. "Are you trying to end up in the brig the day before a mission?"

Marcus clenched his fists and looked away, even angrier than before.

Janus was still stunned by the explosion of anger in Celes when she whirled on him. "And you? When did you become such an insufferable fool?"

Marcus whirled back to watch, mouth agape.

Janus immediately became defensive. "Now hold on—"

Celes cut him off. "Nobody gives a damn!"

Janus shut up. He had never heard Celes ever, ever lose her temper like this.

"The day before a mission you managed to get one of your own to punch your lights out. Not that I blame him—do you really think your new promotion makes you that much better than everyone else?" Celes's words were like acid.

"No, I—" Janus said meekly.

"So is it worthwhile to alienate everyone under your command to make a point?"

Janus opened his mouth, raising a defensive hand, but Celes cut him off again.

"It doesn't matter whether or not the strategy was correct!" Celes fumed. Janus closed his mouth.

"Marcus was your team captain. You were to follow his orders, whatever they may be. By ignoring him and disrespecting his authority, you undermine your own! Honestly, I thought you had some brains." She shook her head. "Marcus, come here." Marcus obeyed immediately.

Janus caught a glimpse of Colonel Hawkes joining Wouris. Both were looking at one another with eyebrows raised.

"Marcus, you're going to run laps around the trunk for nearly hitting a superior officer. But before you go, you'll give Janus an order for a task normally performed by the Valhalla maintenance Daeduluses. Janus, after you perform that duty, the two of you will meet, shake hands, and Marcus will promise to follow your orders exactly tomorrow when we deploy. Is that understood?" She gave both of them a hard stare.

"Uh, yes… uh, ma'am," Janus and Marcus chorused together.

Celes's pleasant expression returned. "Now what order will you give Janus, Marcus? I think it should be something unexpected, yet something that any Adept might be assigned as punishment."

Janus heard one adept ask Colonel Hawkes, "Can she do that?"

"Don't see anyone arguing," Hawkes grunted back.

Marcus thought for a moment and cleared his throat. "Uh, what about cleaning all the dishes in the mess. Is that fair?" he asked hesitantly, looking at Janus. Both had their heads cowed. Janus nodded.

Celes looked pleased. "Good." She smirked evilly at Janus. "Now, all that excitement has made me rather hungry." She addressed the crowd. "Would any of you like to join me?"

Chapter 8
Punishments

Janus scrubbed furiously at every new pot and pan, every stained tray and utensil, trying to relieve his boiling anger. But every new dish only seemed to increase his fury. He had never been so humiliated in his life.

"Well, maybe you deserved it."

Janus paused his scrubbing, staring at the tray before him. He could hear Clara's voice in his head. Admonishing him. But it failed to soothe him—it only added to the fire. He scrubbed once more.

He had been cowed at first. Embarrassed, but determined to do right. But the anger had slowly built up over the course of the evening. Quite a few of the diners had happily plopped down dish after dish upon him as they finished their meals. Occasionally, one would nod in thanks, or mumble "Sorry." But they were few and far between. Many had seemingly reveled in the fact that the upstart had been put in his place. And when Marcus had cautiously dropped off his single tray after finishing his lengthy run, his uncomfortable nod was too much. Even seeing Celes did not help. He could hardly even look at her, unsure if he was more embarrassed at himself or angry at what she had done. He had grabbed the tray from her as quickly as possible, and buried himself in the stack of dishes at the sink behind him. He could tell she lingered for a moment, but quickly left the mess. The mere thought of her brought the bile into his mouth, and after a few moments, he finally realized he had transformed the surface of the pot in his hands into a bright sheen.

His face was twisted in the warped metal. Clara's voice softened in the back of his head. *"Sometimes, you need to learn how to lose."* He quickly dropped the pot into the water.

He finally finished late into the night, but decided not to eat. He couldn't bear the thought of washing another dish. Besides, his stomach was still churning. Instead, he felt compelled to head up to the Garden.

Walking slowly through the trees, he tilted his head back to stare through the roof of the dome. It really was beautiful at night. Celes's rock, however, was deserted. He felt oddly relieved, and he sat down upon it, looking up at the night sky. The yew's branches formed dark streaks within the stars. The darkness was strangely comforting, like a little piece of home, and he could feel his anger start to slip away. The slums felt both close and far away, surround by the dark. The stars above were like the glowing lights of the upper levels, holding some great promise, yet always unreachable. The air was warm and still, and he took a deep breath.

Clara. What would she say?

Running his fingers through the coarse grass reminded him of his rough mattress in the slums. He could picture sitting on that mattress as a young boy, with Clara right beside him, when Janus had realized he was adopted. He had asked her many questions, and slowly he had begun to think only about all the negative things that had happened to them. But Clara had hugged him, bringing him back, and said, "Don't live in the past, Janus. You'll miss what you've got now."

Janus stood up from the rock. Everything seemed quieter now, even the brook. Walking slowly through the wildflowers, cast in shades of purple and red in the night, he wondered what tomorrow would bring. The sound of familiar footsteps stopped him at the open door of the Garden.

"Good evening, Praetor," Janus said, saluting.

"She told me I would find you here. At ease."

Janus relaxed, but only slightly. The Praetor watched him carefully. "But I wonder if you would rather have seen her?"

Janus did not respond and looked away. After a moment he motioned towards the Garden. "I was just doing some reflecting, sir."

The Praetor gave Janus a hard look. "You know, Wouris nearly had you demoted then and there."

Janus swallowed, but kept his head low.

"However, under the circumstances, I think the punishment concocted by Adept Celes is far more appropriate. What do you think?"

"I think the demotion may have been less humiliating, sir," Janus joked weakly.

The Praetor did not laugh. "Better to have a chance to learn from mistakes, is it not?"

Janus nodded, and met the Praetor's eyes. "Yes, sir."

The Praetor took a step towards Janus. "Pride can be a dangerous thing."

Janus swallowed hard.

"It can blind men. Lead them to believe they are incapable of evil. Make them overestimate their abilities."

The warm air of the Garden fought with the cool air wafting in through the open door, and it whirled around Janus.

"Great leaders must learn the difference between confidence and arrogance. A man cannot learn it without being humbled, yet humble him too much, and you will alienate him and destroy any chance you have to teach him." Jennings turned away. "Was Adept Celes's punishment too humbling? Would demotion have been more appropriate?"

"No, sir," Janus said simply.

The grey-haired man watched Janus carefully. "She might make an excellent Praetor someday, don't you think?"

Janus smiled softly. "She might indeed. But she might not want to deal with me."

The Praetor laughed, a deep laugh that surprised Janus. "You might be right. But you might also be surprised."

"Sir?"

"It's not important." The Praetor smiled. "Now, I believe Marcus is waiting for you. Perhaps you should go let him get to sleep, otherwise he might be tempted to drop his end of the bargain."

Janus nodded, stood at attention and saluted. "Sir."

The Praetor saluted back. "Lieutenant."

Janus found Wouris waiting for him at the entrance to the lift. She stared at him as he stopped in front of her. He gathered himself together under her wilting stare.

"I deeply apologize, Sergeant. My behavior was inexcusable."

Janus waited uncomfortably, and she gazed at him for several seconds before finally speaking. "We meet tomorrow at 0500 hours for final briefing."

They walked onto the lift together. "I expect the best out of all Adepts I train. Don't disappoint me again, Janus."

Janus saluted. "Yes, Sergeant."

Wouris gave him a hard stare. "You don't owe me a salute by default anymore—"

Janus cut her off. "I believe that since I now outrank you, I'm free to pay respects as I deem fit."

Wouris smiled and returned the salute. "Yes, sir."

As the lift arrived at the bottom, Wouris gave him one more hard look. "Oh, and Janus?"

He paused at the edge.

"I expect to see a proper victory next time you play Brigg's Ball. That or get a new name. No excuses."

Janus smiled and hurried off.

The common room was full. Everyone was waiting up for him, and the room immediately hushed as he entered. Janus felt a surge of apprehension.

Ramirez towered above the adepts with Lyn perched on a chair beside him. Both watched him with uncertain looks. Marcus sat in a chair, all alone in one corner of the room. Janus hesitated for a moment, the weight of his embarrassment pressing down upon him, but he quickly shoved it aside and strode forcefully over to Marcus. Lost in thought, he stared at a wall, his mind occupied. Janus waited behind his chair for a moment, then cleared his throat. "Marcus."

Marcus started and stood up swiftly, saluting. "Sir." It was awkward, and Marcus shifted uncomfortably. No one breathed.

Janus swallowed a gulp of air. "At ease." He stuck out his hand. "I prefer Janus." He caught Celes staring at them from her door in his periphery and coughed lightly. "Sometimes, a reminder of who we are is a good thing."

Marcus nodded. "Well, in that case, this was a good reminder for me too." He grabbed and shook Janus's outstretched arm. "Now, can we get some rest before we go into battle?"

There was a loud exhale from the room, and the pair turned to look at their audience.

"Yes. In fact…" Janus released Marcus's hand and motioned to the rooms. "I think we all should get some rest. It will be a very busy day tomorrow."

The crowd didn't react.

"NOW!"

"Sir, yes sir!" Adepts leaped from chairs, nearly colliding with each other as they sped towards their rooms. Janus felt a tug of delight at the sudden activity, and he struggled to contain it.

And then he saw Celes turn back into her room and the delight vanished.

"Celes, can I talk to you for a moment?" The Adepts hushed again and became still. Janus's eyes roamed the room. "Outside." Doors quickly slid shut.

Marcus gave Janus look from his door as if to say, *Be careful.*

Janus stepped back outside the common room, stopping by the large windows with their view of the bright night sky. He turned to watch Celes walk carefully from the common room, as if she were tip-toeing on glass.

She stopped in front of him, her eyes boring deep into his. He felt a slight surge of anger, and he couldn't contain the grimace spreading across his face. Celes recoiled and looked away.

For the first time since they had met, Janus thought he had seen a small glimmer of doubt deep in her eyes. He immediately felt himself lurch in discomfort.

He cleared his throat. "Celes…"

Her gaze dropped to the floor. "I don't know what I was thinking. I'm sorry for getting you stuck back in the mess."

Janus was shocked, unsure of how to respond.

"I could hear what some of the others said during dinner and I think I let things get carried away," she continued. "I don't understand why I was so angry. It really shouldn't be my problem—"

"Wait, Celes. I'm not angry at you." Janus finally found his voice and raised his open hands.

Celes looked up, her eyes searching his face. Janus pulled back and looked away. "Thanks, for what you did. You probably saved me a demotion." He rubbed the back of his head.

Celes's eyes opened wide.

"It wasn't pleasant. But it was necessary—Clara wouldn't have let me live it down. And some of those things said were probably spot on. What kind of idiot fractures his team right before a mission?"

He sighed and leaned into the window.

Celes looked down again with a smile. "You might be surprised."

Janus chuckled, and glanced back at her. After a moment, he looked back out the window once more. "The Praetor said that you were concerned with how I would react. I'm sorry that I even put you in that position."

She gently touched his hand, and Janus shifted uncomfortably.

Celes gave him a small smile. "Well, I was afraid I had gone too far." She paused. "Sometimes the most terrifying things are those that force us to question ourselves."

"Sounds like something Clara might say."

"Well, you can credit my father." She squeezed his hand. "But you won't have to worry about me."

"I'm glad for that," Janus said solemnly. He looked down at the hand Celes was grabbing. "Why were you so angry?"

Celes pulled her hand away and turned to look out the window. "I think it reminded me of something that happened in my family. An argument that hasn't ever been resolved."

"What was that?" Janus asked curiously.

Celes shook her head. "Not today." She turned back to Janus and smiled. "Not unless you want to tell me all about your home as well."

Janus tried to hide his mirth. He suddenly didn't feel quite as ashamed. But he wasn't quite ready to talk.

"Maybe next time then."

"Next time you act like a massive idiot?" Celes asked with a smirk. "I was hoping that wasn't going to be a regular occurrence."

Janus chuckled. "Me too."

"Well," Celes said with relief, "think we're ready for the mission tomorrow?"

Janus became more serious. "Yes, though I'm still worried about what the others think."

Celes nodded. "You shouldn't be concerned about Lyn, Ramirez, or anyone else for that matter. I'm sure they were disappointed, but they still trust you. And though Marcus will take time, I have no doubt he will stay true to his word."

Janus nodded solemnly.

"So what do you think Clara would say if you stood out here all night and headed out on a mission with no sleep?"

Janus chuckled. "She'd probably say I'm an idiot, and that there's nothing left to do but do better tomorrow."

They crossed back into the common area together and headed for their separate rooms. He paused at the sliding door.

"Celes…"

She stopped and looked at him from her open door.

"Thanks."

"Anytime."

CHAPTER 9
TO LIGHTEMANN'S

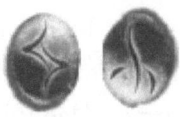

Janus stirred at the sound of a light tapping noise. He rubbed his face ruefully—he was a little sore from the beating he had taken during the game yesterday, and from the hours of scrubbing pots. He made a mental note that dishwashing apparently worked muscles he didn't know he had. Now he would need to go in for a Nanyte injection to meet spec for the mission.

That will be costly. He winced. Very costly.

It took him a moment to realize that it was still very early, and that it wasn't his alarm that had woken him. The tapping sounded on his door, and he hurried to open it. He was surprised to find Wouris there.

"Wouris…?"

She looked serious. "Come with me."

Janus quickly threw on a training suit and his boots and chased after her.

She led him to the Beacon of Need. Only the pre-dawn moon above shone through the high skylights, granting a measure of light. Janus paused at the door; the black Infernus armor with the skull face from his training sat silently in the middle of the room. It looked as intimidating as ever.

Wouris walked over to it, motioning for Janus to follow. "I want to show you something."

Janus stepped carefully into the room, remembering the last painful lesson he learned here from Wouris during their training. Getting trapped in here and attacked from all sides by the room itself is the last thing he wanted this morning.

"Do you remember when you first faced this monster?" Wouris asked.

Janus nodded. When he had been training as a cadet, they had faced 'Death' in a mock battle. Janus had been disarmed and knocked backward by the powerful armor. Had it been a real battle, he would have surely died.

"I am going to show you a technique for killing an Infernus if you are completely unarmed."

Janus was surprised—he hadn't realized such a thing was even possible.

"How?" he asked. "Why now?"

"It's an extremely dangerous technique and should only be used in the direst of circumstances. At best, you will break your foot, and at worst, the Infernus will kill you. Repeat that."

"At best I'll break my foot, and at worst I'll be killed. But why now?" Janus asked again in confusion.

Wouris looked him once over, as if debating how to answer. "When you weren't making a fool of yourself on the Brigg's Ball field, one thing became clear. Something I want you to remember. When you aren't bogged down by arrogance, you have good instincts, and good decision-making. It's the reason why we made you an officer."

Janus felt a swell of pride.

"Now, are you going to stand there like a pufferfish or do you want me to show you how this works?"

Janus coughed. "Please, Sergeant."

She pointed to the narrow slit of the visor on the massive hulk. As far as Janus knew, it was the only vulnerable spot on Infernus armor.

"It requires absolute precision and perfect technique to execute. You must connect the hardened toe of your boot with the exact center of the visor. If done correctly, the visor will shatter, sending it into the face of the Trooper inside. At the very least, they will be exposed, injured, and disabled—if not killed outright by the force of the blow. Very few people know it. I learned it directly from the Praetor. Fewer still can claim to have done it. We don't teach it because, frankly, there is almost no case where it applies in battle. And we don't want you to practice it instead of other, more valuable techniques. But we are about to engage in a highly dangerous mission in enemy territory with no idea of what we are getting into. Who knows what situations we will find ourselves in?"

Janus nodded in understanding.

She motioned as if she were about to jump.

"The goal is to torque your body so that you can apply maximum force to that tiny area. Stand over there." She pointed to a spot beside the Infernus. Janus had a side profile of the fearsome armor, its red visor just glinting in the dim light.

Wouris walked a short distance away. She took a running leap, and flipped herself over in mid-air. In the moonlight, she seemed to move in slow motion, far too slow to harm anything. In an instant, her body whipped around, and the toe of her boot streaked by overhead—just at the height of the visor, and for a brief moment, the two seemed to collide, and Janus could imagine the visor shattering under the force of the impact. And then Wouris tumbled by, using the momentum of her kick to roll by the Infernus and spring to her feet.

"Do you understand?"

Janus nodded.

"Good. Now you have a mission to prepare for."

Janus felt a rush of excitement as he returned to his room. A new shelf had appeared in his wall racks, and there, gleaming in the middle of a red felt cloth, was a Ghostblade.

A small note sat glowing on the screen of his desk.

"Janus, talked to the Praetor and thought you might be able to use this until we can make you one of your own. Godspeed, Captain Rogers."

Janus looked in delight at the weapon. Two power cores lay beside it, ready for use. Janus grasped the handle of the unpowered weapon, pulling it from its sheath. It was simple, but that only added to its beauty. The double-edged blade was thinner and longer than the Praetor's Ghostblade. Whirling it above his head, he tested the balance and the speed of the weapon. It was slightly heavier in the pommel to compensate for the added length, with a good balance. But it still didn't feel perfect to him—just like the Praetor's more ornate weapon. Perhaps it was impossible, but he felt there should be more...snap.

Janus pulled a power core out from the shelf, and with a twist, installed it into the weapon. Immediately, it began to hum with energy, pulsing with heat. Satisfied, he tested both cores, examining the brilliant colors of the blade as he did so. It was said that the Praetor himself had a hand in the making of every Ghostblade in Valhalla. That he was a master sword smith and that he marked each blade with his symbol. Janus flipped the weapon over, searching for a sign. Near the base of the handle, he found it. A small crescent moon stamped into the metal. Taking one last look as he removed the core and the blade turned a dull red, Janus grabbed the sheath and strapped the weapon to his back. He smiled at the familiar weight.

Being an officer does have its perks.

Janus ran to the medical ward where he was given an injection and a clean bill of health.

"You are being docked three weeks' pay for the booster injections. Your Immutium reserves will be reduced accordingly. The rest of the team has already passed through and the charges for Adept Marcus were added to your account," Major Yalla said, as Janus resealed the collar of his grey-black armor. "As his commanding officer, you're responsible for ensuring his health on the mission, especially since you decided to play games yesterday," Yalla admonished.

Janus winced at the old soldier's words, but there was little he could do at this point. At least this should help smooth things over, a little voice that sounded a lot like Celes's spoke in his head.

Janus chuckled and said, "I sure hope so."

"What?" Yalla asked in confusion.

"Uh, sorry, sir. Just uh… reflecting on some advice from a friend." He quickly headed for the door, waving as he left. "Thanks, sir!"

Yalla shook his head with a sad smile, watching Janus leave and whispered, "I still talk to my squad mates, too."

Janus arrived in the Beacon of the Tree right before 0500 hours. An intimate auditorium used for teaching and planning, the Beacon of the Tree was one of three places within Valhalla designed to focus and hone the Adepts of ODIN. So named because the runes representing it meant both wisdom and tree; it was bigger than the war chamber at the top of the city within Odin's Torch, but much smaller and more comfortable than the huge mess. It was the perfect spot for teams to discuss their upcoming missions. Celes, Ramirez, Lyn, and Marcus were already there, waiting beside Wouris' own squad of troops. Colonel Keats and Hawkes spoke quietly off to one side. He joined his team just as the Praetor walked into the room.

"Good timing, Janus," Lyn commented.

Janus nodded and took a seat next to her and Wouris.

Colonel Keats stood up as the Multidimensional Projector emerged from the floor, swirling with drops of light as it rose. "As you all know, we have located the Cerberus facility in an area south of a mountain range known as Lightemann's Ridge. Our surface intel reports that the facility is heavily guarded."

"Much more so than it should be," Hawkes grunted.

Keats glanced at him and tilted her head in a subtle but firm nod. "Correct." Her gaze returned to the glowing plates of the MuDi as it showed the mountains and nearby foothills. "We suspect that the presence of the SPARTAN Adept Legion, and the upcoming arrival of this Cerberus VIP has put the base on edge. We're not sure who hired SPARTAN, or how they found this base originally, but with the cat out of the bag, they have thrown stealth out the window. There is something very valuable inside that facility. Something Cerberus and Overlord Middleton are unwilling to share with just any passerby."

"But we are going to do a little more than just pass by," Hawkes interjected again with a chuckle.

Keats gave him a withering look, and continued, "We are going to insert your two teams into this marsh west of the facility"—the MuDi highlighted and zoomed in on a large marsh on the map—"at the base of the mountains. This is as close as we can get you without risking being spotted by the numerous patrols in the area. From there, you will have to hike through the marsh, and into these lowlands at the base of the mountain range to reach the facility. The structure is almost certainly entirely subterranean, running beneath the range, presumably through a series of tunnels. We've only been able to locate one entrance, wedged between the mountain and the surrounding marsh."

A series of images appeared and coalesced into a three-dimensional map. The MuDi swooped along the ground to highlight what appeared to be a concealed metal platform, hidden beneath dense foliage. "Our scouts have constructed this image for us. We believe this is actually a receiving platform for supply drops."

Lyn raised a hand, and Keats acknowledged her.

"So presumably, more materials are going into than out of the facility?"

Keats nodded. "If our assumptions are correct, yes. It also means that we can't fully estimate the size of the facility, though it seems unlikely to be very large."

Troopers and Inferni appeared, patrolling the perimeter in likely patterns. Dense trees and foliage concealed the pad and made it appear as nothing more than a tiny patch of dirt.

"We do believe, however, that the platform is configured to receive a small Cerberus transport, and based on the evident activity, we expect one to arrive any day now."

A Cerberus Styx transport appeared at the edge of the MuDi's map, swooping in to land. In a subtle shift, the dense brush and trees moved ever so slightly, granting just enough room for a skilled pilot to carefully lodge the craft between the trees. In moments, the Styx had disappeared underground, and the trees had done their subtle dance back into place, leaving the same patch of dirt, and numerous guards.

"These are all just projections. We won't know for sure until you investigate. It's possible there are other landing areas, but this is the only one we've managed to find. However, we did manage to stumble onto these..." The MuDi pushed through the foliage a short distance away, where four small ventilation shafts were barely visible through the brush. "Major Winters's team discovered these when a windstorm caused them to 'howl' during the night. They might just be your ticket inside. Ramirez, I suggest you bring something to grease yourself up with, as it is definitely going to be tight."

"Do we know what they are used for?" Marcus asked.

Keats shook her head. "We barely got close enough to see them, let alone investigate them. Major Winters gave her team strict orders to avoid any potential contact with Cerberus forces. We couldn't afford to let anyone know we were there."

One of Wouris' Adepts, a man named Riggans, spoke up. "So we'll be going in blind, and need to evaluate them as we arrive."

"That a problem?" Hawkes asked gruffly.

Riggans smiled at him. "No, sir. Just making sure that the sergeant knows how much in extra rations this is gonna cost her."

Hawkes chuckled, and Wouris waved a hand. "Just make sure you pull your weight this time." The rest of her team laughed. Janus smiled, though it was strange to see Wouris joking with her team. He wondered how long it took them to earn that.

"Ninety-six hours," Keats said. "That's your window to get in and back out to evac. Should the primary evac point be compromised in any way, just signal through an open channel with a single ping, and we will automatically respond by proceeding to the second evac point. Any questions?" Keats asked.

"What if we run into SPARTAN forces?" Celes asked.

Hawkes worked his jaw as if ready to speak, but he remained silent. Keats cleared her throat, glancing not at Hawkes, but at the Praetor. "We don't know their purpose there. Perhaps another Corporation has hired them to investigate. Perhaps it is chance. They undoubtedly know about the base like we do. The difference is, they don't know we're there. So whatever happens, do not engage. Simply go on your way, and they should go on theirs. They have not been contracted to engage us as far as we know, and it would not be profitable for them to do so," Keats concluded.

"But don't trust them any farther than you can throw them," Hawkes grunted. "They'll sacrifice their mothers for a coin."

Surprisingly, Keats nodded in agreement. "Any other questions?"

The room fell silent.

"Then I shall ask the question everyone has on their minds." The Praetor stepped forward. "What if the mission has already been compromised?"

Tension filled the room.

The Praetor continued, "Odin help us if it has, but no matter what, we are Adepts and we do not shy away from our mission or our principles because of danger, and certainly not for the shadow of doubt. Get the mission done and we'll be one step closer to understanding what happened back at the Titan colony. Dismissed."

A playful breeze swept across the Voyages bay as the giant doors opened. In the shade of the bay, the breeze was cool, but the air was warm—the summer months were approaching.

There was a slight acceleration as the massive engines keeping the citadel afloat powered up to push Valhalla over a group of rising hills. It was unusual for the floating fortress to pass over land; the open ocean had no obstacles and left no trail of destruction from the hot, hurricane force winds emanating from the engines. With the Cerberus facility so far away, however, the Praetor had decided to push inland. Valhalla would be in place to support them during extraction or, if necessary, launch a full-scale assault—assuming the two teams could hold out long enough. Valhalla would still be some distance away in order to avoid detection.

Janus waved his team onto the second of two Longboats already powering up their engines. A short distance away, Wouris gave him a nod before hopping into hers. Janus leaped aboard, and sat down beside Ramirez. Marcus and Celes waited calmly in the jump seats across from him, and Lyn sat on Ramirez's other side. Janus gave a thumbs-up to the pilot and felt the lurch of acceleration as the Longboat lifted off and flew from the launch bay, the rolling hills sliding by underneath.

Sitting in the Longboat, the weight of the mission felt magnified and the rising craft seemed to press him further and further into his seat. Each rivet on the floor reminded him of a different Adept depending on him. It was different from the first mission, when they had been riding high with confidence, and there was a whole Legion of Adepts ahead of them. Now, they were the tip of the spear. And ODIN was depending on them to get to the bottom of what Cerberus was up to.

He looked up, realizing the atmosphere was strangely stiff. Each of them sat in an uncomfortable silence, and Janus knew that all of them were thinking the same. He racked his brain, but as he glanced around, he couldn't figure out what to say. Marcus, usually so confident and composed, sat stiffly. Ramirez hardly ever said anything anyway. Celes opened her mouth, but as she met eyes with Janus, she stopped and looked away.

They're all waiting on me to say something. Because I'm in command. He silently berated himself for his outburst in Brigg's Ball once more.

"What did the Cerberus ST say ta the Infernus when the Adepts attacked?"

Janus looked at Lyn in surprise. No one spoke.

"AAAA!" she yelled, making everyone jump.

They stared at her in stunned silence. She shrank back into her seat. "Sorry..."

"Is everyone all right back there?" the pilot yelled at them through the speaker. "I heard someone screaming."

Janus punched the intercom to reply, "We're fine. Don't worry."

He had just finished speaking when he heard a deep, powerful laugh. Ramirez was laughing. It was odd, but it was infectious. And soon, they were all short of breath from it.

"Come on, Lyn!" Marcus heaved. "You can't do that to us!"

"You're supposed to attack the enemy, not us!" Celes was wiping tears from her eyes.

Janus looked around Ramirez, gave her a big smile, and quick nod of thanks.

And when the laughter subsided, they rechecked their weapons.

"What do ya think we'll find in there?" Lyn asked as the Longboat made a slight bank and hugged the bend in a river.

Celes leaned forward. "A lot of Corporations have secondary outposts they maintain. Sometimes for mining. Sometimes for food. Sometimes simply to act as a military base."

"Probably not any of those," Ramirez stated plainly.

The others looked at him, and he shrugged. "It needs more transport capabilities."

Celes nodded in agreement. "If it was food or mining it would need the ability to ship things out en masse. And a military outpost would probably be able to deploy troops, or be able to act as a communications or observation center. It certainly doesn't appear to be the case here." Celes looked at Ramirez questioningly. "Did you have experience with Corporate outposts before joining ODIN?"

Lyn smiled sheepishly. "We may have raided a food supply once."

The others looked at the pair in shock. "You raided a Corporate food supply?" Marcus asked incredulously.

"Raid's a strong word." Lyn shrugged. "As Outskirters, we would normally avoid Corporate controlled areas. But sometimes you need to be a little creative with food options, especially when trying to feed a village. Corporate farms usually aren't too heavily guarded, especially for the volume we were grabbing."

Celes rubbed her chin thoughtfully. "That makes sense actually. Many of the farm foods are reserved luxuries—they're not necessities."

"Yeah, all the Passers we ate were grown on the industrial level," Marcus added. "At least, that's how it was at Medusa anyway."

"What was it like there?" Celes asked curiously.

"I suppose it was better than some." Marcus looked pointedly at Janus. "But it wasn't easy. My parents worked in the battery plants."

"That's pretty important. But you said 'worked'..."

Marcus smiled grimly. "Yep. Entropic batteries are hardly ever used anymore. Fusion energy has replaced pretty much all of it. I joined as a Security Trooper soon after the Executors decided to shutter their plant."

He shifted uncomfortably, and then looked at Lyn. "Where did you raid?"

Lyn glanced at Ramirez and shook her head.

"You won't say?" Marcus asked. "I'm not going to be mad if it's Medusa!" He laughed. "I just know that you're not the biggest fan of Corporate Security."

Lyn chuckled. "Sorry, it's not that. You're our friends, and it's not that we don't trust ya. But we swore before we left never ta risk the village."

"It must be nice," Janus mused. "What's life like there?"

Lyn smiled. "It's beautiful. There's something about the air. About the very atmosphere. Whenever we went on a raid, we could tell something was different there. About those places under Corporate control. That's not to say everything's perfect. It can definitely be a bit rough. And we're always on the lookout for Corporations."

"Is that why you hate STs?" Marcus asked. "Because you're always on the lookout?"

Ramirez sat forward with a hard expression. "More than that."

"But you still say it's good?" Janus asked.

The pair nodded simultaneously. "We're free, and the things we do belong ta us," Lyn said.

Celes smiled sadly. "It sounds lovely."

The sudden static from the intercom cut the conversation off. "Arrival in five," the pilot said.

The conversation went quiet. After a moment Janus spoke up. "Let's get this done so we can all go back home."

Four heads nodded in agreement.

Chapter 10
Alastor

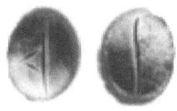

The Longboat hovered over a dry patch of marsh—or at least as dry as could be found. Janus hopped out of the craft and promptly sank into the mud. The fibers of his armor immediately locked together, a chain reaction starting within his boots triggering the armor to close its pores and become waterproof. He squashed swiftly into the deeper waters, sinking low to conceal himself in the murk, and held his weapon just inches from the surface. Tall reeds obstructed his view as much as they hid him. The cold water fought to suck the warmth from his insulated suit.

He saw Wouris' team drop silently into reeds several hundred meters away. "Check, check," Janus said. His mouth barely moved as the vibraphone picked up the minute whispers of his voice box.

"Loud and clear," Wouris responded into his ear.

"All clear," Marcus sounded.

"Check," said Celes, Ramirez, and Lyn.

"Full count, Lieutenant?" Wouris asked.

"Yes. And you, sergeant?"

"Aye."

He watched her turn and motion to the pilots, who rapidly pulled their Longboats around and away, disappearing over water-logged trees and stumps. Wouris signaled Janus, and he spoke clearly over the shared channel. "Nine-six hours, starting now. Lyn, find our path. Let's move out."

The going was slow at first as they swam and trudged their way through the marsh, but Lyn kept them moving. More than once, she would make seemingly random directional changes, but after a few moments, Janus would realize they had hit firmer ground, or shallower water. Her knack for pathfinding impressed even Riggans, Wouris' veteran scout. Between the two of them, they helped the team find its rhythm, keeping a good pace going with only infrequent pauses, as the occasional airborne patrols passed overhead. It was clear, however, that they did not expect to find anything so deep in the marsh and did not look particularly hard.

Eventually, however, as they ventured deeper into enemy territory, the teams naturally split. Separating for a lower profile and to cover more angles. Riggans disappeared into the high cattails with Wouris and the rest of her veterans close behind.

Six hours into their journey through the cold, muddy swamp, Wouris whispered into Janus's ear, "Contact."

Janus froze. He quickly flashed signs to his team, who were already disappearing into the dark waters. **Spread.** They silently fanned out, taking up better positions in the muck.

Janus searched the marsh for signs of life. Nothing moved. Wouris was nowhere to be seen.

"Coming your way, moving fast. Bearing west-southwest."

Janus sank lower, covering himself in weeds.

Suddenly, the sound of jump-jets echoed dully around the marsh and he watched a group of seven Inferni leap over his head. They deftly landed on a tiny dry patch of land slightly behind him. He noted the symbol on the leader's arm, and the customized armor. In moments, they were bounding off again. When the sounds faded, Janus whispered back into the com set, "Clear."

"Did anyone else notice something odd about those Inferni?" Lyn asked.

"Yes, they were good," Celes said.

"Good enough to make adjustments in mid-air to land on a patch of earth that small." Wouris' voice was clearly wary.

"It's a good thing that this marsh is relatively warm and teeming with life; we weren't picked up on their thermal sensors," Riggans said.

"Did you catch the leader's rank? It was a Novus," Marcus added.

"That's troubling," Wouris added calmly. "If a Novus is on patrol then there's definitely something valuable inside that facility, or our incoming visitor is very, very important."

"Maybe both," Riggans added cheerily.

"Guess it won't be a wasted trip," Lyn chimed in.

Two more hours of hard trudging and the ground started to firm up. Janus was glad to be free of the morass, though the biting insects remained. Lyn expertly guided them, helping the team avoid the occasional muddy patch as well as stinging nettles and cutting branches. The roots of large trees and heavy brush gave the ground structure and provided concealment from prying eyes. They moved fast, avoiding open areas where Inferni might deem to land; now that they lacked the protection of the marshes' waters, their suits could only do so much.

After another hour of tense marching, they eyed the landing site just over a small ridge. The patrols had evaporated, and Janus wondered what might have happened, but he soon had an opportunity to find out. Melding with the shadows and brush, Janus took his team left to skirt towards the pad and was unpleasantly surprised to see a number of Inferni and STs patrolling the area.

"They must have pulled back for the arrival of the VIP. How very odd, it's almost as if they expect the VIP to be trouble," Wouris commented over the radio.

Janus was about to ask for her position when Lyn interjected, "Incoming, five hundred meters north-northeast."

A small, sleek transport and two escorting Typhon class fighters were descending towards the area. A large, fearsome Cerberus sigil was emblazoned on the side, and it looked like a piece of black obsidian, reminding Janus of the lift system back in Cerberus.

Janus's training forced him to keep his guard up and look around, and he quickly noticed that the same could not be said about the STs around the perimeter. They were entirely focused on the landing craft.

He signaled to the team. **Advance.**

They crept forward, passing so close to a few STs that Janus could have tapped them on the shoulder. The thinning growth forced the team together, and Janus wasn't sure if his order to take the opportunity was wise, or reckless. He stopped near the edge of the pad, just as the craft began to slow for a landing. The nearby trees shifted ever so slightly to allow for just a tad more room, and a gigantic woman suddenly appeared on the pad to meet the incoming visitor.

Janus felt his face flush. "Middleton!" he whispered.

Overlord Middleton waited calmly, surrounded by an elite cadre of four Inferni. On her right waited the same Infernus he had seen earlier, his shoulder emblazoned with the starburst of the Novus rank. He scanned the forest as he waited, but the sudden strong downdraft of the transport diverted his attention.

Middleton's hair blew wildly in the wind, and Janus noticed it was now a soft autumn blond-brown, no longer so strongly silver. But her massive girth was unchanged, nor her preference for gaudy outfits. As the craft deftly landed, the two escorts darted away, quickly lost amongst the trees, and Middleton flattened the bright yellow-green dress that had been buffeted by the rushing wind.

Janus shifted from one leg to the other for a better view. As the obsidian cracked open, Middleton's face twitched involuntarily in irritation. Six Inferni walked slowly down the ramp, followed by a tall, thin man with black-and-grey-tinged hair and a beakish nose. He wore a poorly concealed smile, all eyes upon him.

"Ah, Middleton, so good to see you again," the man said.

Middleton scowled. "Alastor…the grey looks good on you."

Alastor sneered slightly at her. "Yes, even without the dye, I must say I am envious of your perpetual youth. It must be because I never seem to eat quite as well as you do." Middleton's eyes flashed. Alastor glanced around the landing pad. "Your operation is well hidden."

"Indeed, not even the SPARTAN dogs you sent could find it." Middleton had calmed herself immediately, and was taking jabs once more.

Alastor smirked. "Your ability to hide the truth is most admirable, although I'm afraid this base isn't much of a secret, now that the Executors have forced you to reveal its location. Pretty soon this will be on Corporate maps the world over. My only disappointment is that you had time to arrive early."

"Forced?" Middleton exclaimed in feigned surprise. "Why would I need to be forced? I serve Cerberus loyally and gladly reveal my secrets to the Executors. But they hardly wish to hear about every mundane operation I run. I certainly wouldn't want to trouble them while they direct the future of our great corporation."

"Well, for your sake, I hope everything is as *mundane* as you claim."

"You dare threaten me?" Middleton bristled.

"Threaten…? Of course not, I am merely stating a fact, my dear Middleton."

Middleton scoffed, returning to her calm demeanor immediately. "Well, I think you will find everything is in order. Although you did come at a bad time. With the recent SPARTAN patrols, my STs have been on edge. It would have been truly tragic had we accidentally mistaken your craft for one of those dog's scouts."

Deep within the marsh came the sound of a rushing engine, and Janus caught a glimpse of a Pegasus, a smaller Cerberus transport, lifting out of the swamp. It was just starting to push forward through the air when a missile streaked into it. The craft exploded into a fireball and careened towards the ground, causing a boom that echoed around the swamp. The STs around the edge rushed to protect Middleton, but those guarding Alastor didn't move. Nor did the Novus. In a roar, the two Typhons streaked over the landing zone.

Middleton's face displayed only a hint of annoyance, waving her guards off. "That was Cerberus property, you know. With your arrival, some of my regular transports needed to find another spot to land. It will take days to clear that wreckage."

Alastor looked surprised, and then smiled. "Terrible, terrible shame. My Typhons must have thought it was a merc scout. You should really let us know if you're planning on moving anything from this base." He chuckled. "Oh, well, we know how these unfortunate *accidents* can happen. I'm sure the Executors will understand. But I have complete trust in you, Middleton. Why do you think I came myself?"

Middleton turned her back to him and scowled. "You have nothing to fear, of course, Alastor."

"Good. The Executors are waiting for their report."

Janus blinked. *The Cerberus Executors have sent another Overlord to investigate Middleton?*

Middleton waved to the Novus and led Alastor to the lift from which she had emerged earlier. The Novus followed her and signaled to Alastor's guard as well. Four followed while two remained on the pad.

The obsidian transport and landing platform began descending slowly into the earth, while Middleton and her group had already disappeared elsewhere. The armored and camouflaged doors laboriously strained to close as the rest of Middleton's Inferni fanned out for their patrols and leaped away. Alastor's guard stayed at the edge as the pad descended, standing watch over the closing doors.

Janus made a snap decision, hastily flashing a pointed hand. **Engage.**

Looks of surprise appeared across the team's faces, but they obeyed instantly as Janus broke cover from the marsh, throwing his rifle on his back. If the first Infernus was surprised by the sudden appearance of an Adept, he did his best not to show it, quickly bringing his flamethrowers to bear, and crying out to alert his companion. Janus rushed straight ahead, hoping he had made the right decision. His faith was rewarded as the first guard's visor exploded from a well-placed shot from over his shoulder. He'd owe Celes a couple extra rations. The second Infernus immediately averted his visor and raised his flamethrowers as Janus took a flying leap towards him. Landing between the Infernus's outstretched arms, Janus could feel the heat of the flamethrowers behind him, and the Infernus turned his head just in time to see the Rogers's Ghostblade as it sliced him diagonally across his body. He toppled off the dirt pad and into the marsh.

"Janus, what are you doing?" Wouris yelled into his ear.

"Sorry, Wouris, you're on cleanup. Find another way in if you can, but we can't miss our opportunity to get inside. You heard Keats; she was doubtful about our chances to get into the facility. We have to go now."

"What about the guards?"

"They're part of our visitor's entourage, and I'm counting on them not being missed."

"But—"

"No time, Wouris. Good luck." Janus leaped between the closing doors, followed closely by Marcus, Celes, Ramirez, and Lyn. The doors slammed shut as they fell.

Was it rash, Clara? Janus thought as the daylight disappeared behind him. *There's no going back now.*

Chapter 11
Into the Depths

Janus executed a swift tuck and roll as he fell on top of the transport, sliding off the edge and landing catlike on the pad. The noise of the machinery, somewhat masked outside, was nearly deafening inside. A couple of mechanics stood waiting with tools and fuel for the transport as it settled to a halt at the bottom.

I think they need to focus more on oiling the landing pad, Janus thought as he slunk behind a charging station. Lyn, Ramirez, Celes, and Marcus joined him, and within a moment, they slid quietly from the bay, nothing more than five dark flashes at the edge of the mechanics' vision, as the echoing noise of the lift slowly subsided to be replaced by the clanking of tools.

Just around the corner, Janus found a disused parts storage room opposite what appeared to be the lift Middleton had used to reach the surface, and signaled the team inside. Old and disused fans and motors raised the hairs on the back of his neck.

Look, Lyn signaled, pointing out the old equipment. Janus appreciated her discretion, both for signing, and for recognizing the ill omen.

(I've) got a bad feel(ing), Marcus replied. None of them could forget their experience at the Titan outpost, or the fact that disused equipment had been their first clue something was off.

The five checked their weapons, and Janus looked around. Rocky cave walls surrounded them, and Janus could feel the pores of his armor slowly opening, allowing air to flow. With the mechanics clanking noisily behind them, Lyn flashed a series of complex signals. **(What) now, (oh) fearless leader?**

Janus smiled. *Well, not too much discretion.* He signaled back rapidly, using a mix of short and long signs. **Stick (to the) plan. Presume Wouris (will) remove Inferni up (top). We (operate) independently now, assume no contact (with) Wouris. Be aware—Wouris' team (may be) inside.**

Formation(?) Marcus asked.

Janus considered the room.

We'll need to move fast and tight. If the outside hall was any indication, we're trapped like rats in a maze. He began to rue his snap decision. *Our formation will presumably determine who, if anyone, can see anything ahead.*

Rotating point. Passages (presumably) narrow. Vanguard (and) rearguard (to assume) no mutual sight.

The hall immediately outside the room was devoid of life, the mechanics presumably too busy to come down the hall, and not important enough to warrant visitors. Janus listened carefully. Clomping boots and excited voices could be heard echoing distantly from further within the base. Despite his intentions, the team advanced slowly, leap frogging one another eager to avoid any unnecessary confrontations. The experience was nerve-wracking. The base so far seemed to be one long tunnel, cutting a jagged path through the earth that left them exposed as they skulked along. Blocks and edges of natural rock stuck out at odd angles from the wall, cutting their visibility and narrowing the passage even more. Water pipes and electrical lines hummed with the rush of water and power, running every which way along to the ceiling. Low supports made the experience even more claustrophobic, and the heavy metal floor slowed them down as they crept to avoid the thumping of their boots upon it. Only the occasional room, seemingly placed in a haphazard fashion, provided any sort of hiding place. Much to the team's relief, every single one was empty of Troopers. He could only assume Middleton and her guest had come this way, and that most of the base was turned out for patrols and the like, but even still, Janus found it oddly disconcerting.

Crouched behind Marcus as he peered around a corner, Janus heard Lyn whisper to herself, "Why don't they ever have one big sign saying 'SECRETS HERE'?"

Janus gave her a look. She smiled and then looked apologetic as she mouthed 'sorry,' tapping her rifle nervously.

Not even the narrow alleys of the slums were this claustrophobic and twisted, and Janus realized that if he was feeling the pressure, his team was likely feeling it worse.

(It's) fine. (Stay) calm (and) focused.

Janus took a deep breath. He heard the others do the same, and then looked back. The tapping had stopped. With no apparent influx of traffic, he took a moment to get his bearings, like he was in the slums once more. Tracking the passage in his mind, he realized they had to be moving straight under the mountain.

And yet, despite the singularness of the passage, they had yet to encounter a single ST or Infernus outside of the landing pad. It seemed impossible to think that with the number of STs that must be running around, they could do anything other than trip over themselves in the tiny facility—but where were they?

As if to answer, the long tunnel suddenly opened up and the noise level increased dramatically, splitting off into three separate directions. The sound of heavy boots and loud voices echoed all around. There was a veritable mass of Troopers somewhere ahead of them.

To the left, on the floor, was a symbol for a bed.

Dormitories.

To the right, a wrench, above what appeared to be a stencil of a Zeus rifle.

Weapons repair? Mechanics for something?

And straight ahead, a plate and fork.

Mess hall. What a strange design. What is Middleton doing here?

(Which) direction (?) Celes signed.

Janus was at an impasse as he examined all three branching tunnels. Splitting up to cover all three tunnels seemed like a bad idea, but the more time they took...*Where would Middleton hide her secrets?*

After a moment's consideration, Janus smiled, signaling the team: **Straight.**

The tunnel ahead resumed its jagged path, but now branches appeared here and there, along with the occasional room. To the right, the Zeus and wrench stencil appeared again. They passed through an open, empty room with several large tables. The footsteps were growing louder, seemingly coming from all directions. Peering around a corner, Celes signaled. **ST Patrol Incoming. Eight.**

Janus quickly signaled for retreat only to turn and find Marcus signaling frantically from down the hall behind him: **No (go!) Incoming Patrol(!)**

Janus glanced around, down the hall near Celes stood a closed door. They had not scouted it yet, but it could hardly be worse than being caught in a narrow hallway between two patrols.

Janus waved his hands rapidly, pointing to this objective: **Door(!) Go(!)**

Celes immediately flung it open, signaled **Clear**, and leaped inside. Ramirez and Lyn were hot on her heels. Janus stopped just inside, ready with his weapon, as Marcus sprinted towards the open hatch. He jumped back to let Marcus tumble into the room as Celes swiftly and silently shut the door.

Moments later, the sounds of the marching patrol could be heard passing them, followed shortly by the patrol from the other direction. The footsteps slowed as they passed the door, and Janus pressed to listen. There was nothing but the sound of marching. Something about it seemed off, but he relaxed as the sound faded away. Inside the room, the constant din of boots had lessened.

Janus took a moment to examine his surroundings. As appropriate for the plate and fork symbol, they had stumbled into a small kitchen and pantry, most likely servicing the area outside.

"The layout is difficult," Ramirez mused, gently tapping a hanging ladle over a large stove with a finger. "Makes it tough to move around."

"Those patrols are odd," Marcus interjected.

Janus looked at him. "How so?"

"Did you hear them talking to each other?"

Lyn shook her head in surprise. "Ya must have good hearing, because I couldn't hear a thing."

"Exactly," Marcus agreed. "They didn't talk to one another. That's not a standard patrol. You get to know your fellow Troopers. You talk to them. You at least acknowledge them. There was nothing like that here."

"So what does that mean?" Celes asked.

"So either they have been ordered to do something odd, or they don't know each other all that well."

"Maybe both," Lyn added. "This facility can't be a troop deployment center." She peered around the small pantry. "Unless there are about a hundred more rooms like this and the Troopers don't mind tripping over each other. This place has ta be for supporting or guarding something."

"Maybe both," Janus added. Lyn nodded.

"As an Overlord, Middleton would have the ability to bring fresh troops quickly in an emergency," Celes said thoughtfully. "And based on the Praetor's accounts, in secret as well. She could be using her own, loyal troops to support her in an emergency."

"That's good... I was looking for more skulls ta knock around," Ramirez said dryly.

Everyone stared at Ramirez for a moment, but no one laughed. His expression made it difficult to tell whether he was joking or not. Ramirez shrugged his shoulders and carefully selected an apple from an open bag, chewing it reflectively. In between bites, he added, "Probably built this place in a hurry. It follows the natural cave system."

"Of course," Celes exclaimed, placing an open hand on one of the walls of exposed rock. "That explains the strange layout. The tunnels simply follow it and rooms are placed wherever space is available. But why build a facility like that, why not build it normally, unless..."

Janus shared a look with her and finished the thought. "There wasn't enough time. Middleton had to construct this place in a hurry and in secret."

"But we still don't know why," Marcus said.

Janus signaled for Lyn, who carefully opened the door and peered outside. **Clear.**

He turned to Marcus with a smile. **Let('s) find (out).**

Patrols appeared more and more regularly as they followed the main tunnel, and their movement became a race between each successive room, the thrum of marching boots always just ahead and behind them. Some were personal quarters. There were a few more mess areas with attached kitchens. The occasional power relay or water pump maintenance room. And all of them were mercifully empty.

Every ST, every officer, simply everyone in the base *had* been turned out for Alastor's arrival. The patrols became so frequent they didn't even have time to signal clear or shut the doors fully. But it didn't matter. Janus wasn't sure they would have noticed their presence anyway.

(But) why(?) Lyn signaled.

They had finally been diverted from their main path when two patrols had nearly caught them in between two rooms. They had ducked down one of the halls marked with a wrench, and barely avoiding a third group, leaped into a small armory. Through the crack in the door, Janus watched a group of Troopers clomp by, carrying several large cases between them and seemingly headed for the landing pad. All of the Troopers were occupied with moving these large crates. Every patrol carried cases upon cases between them.

What (are) they carrying(?) Marcus asked rhetorically.

The footsteps grew momentarily quieter and Janus took the opportunity to close the heavy door and sized up his team. Ramirez was stooped into a crevice near a workbench, staring at some new mining equipment that had been opened and then clearly abandoned. Lyn crouched next to Celes, counting silently in rhythm with the receding steps, then shook her head and instinctively looked over to Ramirez.

Celes looked at him circumspectly. "It's getting almost impossible to move through the base. Sooner or later we are bound to get caught."

"Even the worst STs I ever met would notice an Adept running into them," Marcus agreed. He was pressed into the space behind the door, ready to leap into action should the unexpected happen. Beside him, a shelf full of newly maintained helmets sat in a line.

Janus looked around the packed room. *We've made it this far. But how can we navigate so many patrols?*

Lyn waved at the group excitedly and Janus looked at her with a raised eyebrow.

She pointed at Ramirez. "Ramirez has an idea."

They turned to look at Ramirez, who had somehow managed to make himself look almost comfortable in the tiny space. Janus realized he must have had to deal with spaces being too tiny for him for many years now.

Ramirez stopped staring at the mining equipment and grunted. "Do what you did before."

Janus was curious but slightly confused. "What did we do before?"

"Wouris dressed up in armor ta move through the Titan troops. We can do the same."

Janus looked around more closely, realizing that while there were no completed suits, all the pieces lay scattered around the room.

Ramirez looked down at Lyn, who was smiling.

She laughed. "Been a while since we raided a supply cache, but I'm always game."

Chapter 12
The Man in the Painting

It took some delicate 'fitting' to squash Ramirez into one of the suits, but eventually everyone was relatively comfortable in their new uniforms. But they soon ran into another problem.

"No weapons," Marcus pointed out. Not a single Zeus was to be found.

"They must be handled by another room," Lyn groaned. "Who designed this blasted base anyway? We can't go around carrying ODIN issued weapons."

"And I don't care for the prospect of us going unarmed," Janus agreed. He paused for a moment. "Most of the patrols are carrying supplies, anyway."

Celes kicked a couple of the large drilling crates and smiled. "Something like this?"

Janus nodded appreciatively. "Exactly." He clomped over to the mining equipment. "Here. Help me empty the rest of this junk." Together, they quickly moved the heavy gear, the suits making it surprisingly easy.

Janus looked at the empty boxes. "Put all of our weapons inside, except strap your pistols in an easily accessible place inside your suit, if possible. We might need them."

Ramirez handed his pistol to Lyn, who had considerably more room in her suit than he had. After a reluctant moment Janus dropped Rogers's Ghostblade into the crate and closed the lid.

As they grabbed the boxes, the door pushed open. The team turned in surprise. "You five, what are you doing?" An ST Battle Captain was standing there, and Janus cursed silently in his suit. Lacking a better option, he made a motion to the crates and the junk around them. The inside of his suit suddenly felt very hot.

The captain looked around the room for a moment. "Good, good." He raised his hand in appreciation, as the confining suit did not allow him to nod particularly well. "Most of the collection is already being handled, but Overlord Middleton wants anything we can grab headed for the transport bay. Just keep loadin' 'em up. I'll send some others to stop by this shop and pick up what they can. Good work." Without another word, the captain stepped out the door and hustled off.

Celes turned to the group, and though Janus couldn't read her face, he knew it was one of confusion. "Collection?"

Marcus raised his visor and shook his head with a smile. "Who knows? But at least it looks like things are finally going our way."

Lyn chuckled. "Well, we better get a move on then. That certainly can't last for long."

Janus agreed. "Let's go."

"If that captain was any indication, there are probably a lot of well-trained troops here. Middleton must have called in her best," Marcus whispered from the front of the little group.

"How do you know?" Celes asked.

"He used his hand and didn't automatically nod to acknowledge us. That's a sign he's well-acquainted to his armor."

Janus found himself nodding and then stopped himself, realizing that no one else could see him. "We'll need to be careful then. Marcus, you've got the most experience in this armor. Can you signal us in your suit?"

Marcus held a gloved hand a little to his side. **(A) little.** "I'll have to stay with basic stuff."

Janus raised a hand like the Battle Captain in acknowledgement. "Warn us if we're doing something wrong. Everyone share a crate. Except you Ramirez, you're the biggest, most menacing ST I've ever seen; you're on point. Clear a path for us and don't let anyone push you around."

Ramirez let out a small chuckle, clearly enjoying the prospect.

"It's too bad we don't have an Infernus suit for ya Ramirez then no one would get in our way," Lyn added with just a slight hint of adoration. Janus couldn't see their expressions through their visors, but he knew they were sharing a smile. When he realized everyone was looking at the pair of them, Ramirez shifted uncomfortably, and then straightened stiffly and opened the door.

Janus, Celes, and Marcus had a hard time suppressing their laughter.

Travel through the base suddenly became a breeze, and speed was their friend as they rejoined the main tunnel. The ST suits were awkward, and limited, but comfortable enough. Marcus had quickly taught them how to lock the arms of their suits into one position, so the armor carried all the weight of the crates.

They passed a few more groups of STs, but it was a group pushing a large wooden crate that gave them pause. Even Ramirez had to step aside for that one. It was right after that they finally understood.

They had stumbled upon a scene of total chaos. STs rushed by in all directions. They had entered one of the largest rooms yet, filled with art. Paintings. Sculptures. Books. Jewelry. All being stuffed into cases. Into crates. Being lifted from walls. The Troopers struggled to be as delicate as possible, while still rushing quickly in their bulky armor. Works of art were scuffed and scratched, and it was clear that no one knew exactly how they were supposed to handle it all.

In the middle, two of Alastor's Inferni spun around helplessly. One had parked himself right in the entrance, stopping patrols, while the other kicked open crates in frustration, revealing some new bust or jewel. When the second kicked open a wooden crate and smashed a painting of a massive bull, the stopped Troopers started to argue with the pair, and the team rushed by them, moving deeper into the base, and readily ignored by the rest.

More tunnels branched off, many strung with makeshift lights and looking as if they had only just been completed. More Troopers emerged from them, but they paid the group no mind, focused only on moving their current cargo. The team was truly invisible.

"Has Middleton really turned out this many Troopers for this?" Marcus whispered. "Why go through all the trouble for this?"

"Have you noticed the art? There are pieces from all the Corporations here," Celes said. "That bull painting has been missing from Minotaur for more than three decades."

"But why send the base inta such a furor?" Lyn asked. "Surely this Alastor fellow isn't just here for art?"

As one, the team stopped. Passing through an arch, they were greeted with a magnificently tiled foyer, as if they had passed into somewhere entirely new. Dim lighting gave the room a mysterious air. A large golden figurine of a Medusa with what appeared to be emerald snakes for hair sat upon a pedestal off to their right. A winged lion with topaz-colored eyes sat like a sphinx in a painting to their left. The sound of clomping boots had disappeared; they had wandered beyond the chaos, though for how long was unclear.

Celes stared at the statue of the snake-woman. "It's like the bunker we found. A haven. But most of this isn't from Cerberus…"

"Is that a problem?" Janus asked. "I wouldn't be surprised that Cerberus has taken a few things here and there from other Corporations over the years."

Celes shook her head. "You don't understand, the Phoenix Declaration had lots of little amendments and by-laws to the agreement. Things like this art were supposed to be returned."

"And are ya surprised they weren't?" Lyn asked skeptically.

Celes shook her head, which was more of a shoulder twist in the Trooper armor. "No, but a collection this vast is a huge breach. I very much doubt that the Executors at Cerberus would approve of Middleton having a large collection, especially only for herself. If this Alastor is to be believed, the Executors had no idea about this base."

Ahead of them were a pair of Oaken doors. They reminded Janus of Middleton's estate at Cerberus, and as he approached, he realized they had been left ajar.

Alert.

The team carefully moved through the portal, entering a richly carpeted hall interspersed with paintings throughout. Now more than ever, Janus felt the hairs on the back of his neck, and the feeling of déjà vu. The carpet was a deep wine color, and a great bird made of fire seemed to be the center of every piece. Janus paused, examining the title at the bottom of a particularly graphic painting depicting the fiery predator burning away a huge army. *"The Rise of the Phoenix."*

Doors lay along the hall, and a crashing from just ahead of them halted them in their tracks.

"Idiot!" a raspy voice sounded from a partially open door.

"What do you want me to do?" a gruff voice asked in a mocking tone.

Janus signaled the team to halt while he advanced. Carefully poking his head around the corner, Janus was surprised to see two Inferni standing in the center of a small library, their backs turned to him. The library had been turned upside down.

"Overlord Alastor gave us orders not to destroy anything!" the first replied.

"Yeah, but he also told us to find out what is going on here," the second responded. "Have you found anything?"

"Well…"

"So shut up! I'm more concerned about what Overlord Alastor will do to us if we don't find anything than what Middleton will do after we trash her stuff."

"Well, we still don't want to be discovered and stopped while we search!" He carefully picked up a book. "And making a mess won't help if what we're looking for is small."

"And do you know what we're looking for?" the second asked.

The first sighed. "No."

"Then I suggest you let me handle things my way."

Janus quickly signaled the rest of the team by the arguing pair, and through the doors at the end of the hall. They entered another foyer, and Marcus carefully shut the door behind them. For the first time, Janus could tell they were no longer simply following a natural cave. This had been completely dug out. A hall lay to their left and through a door at the end, he could see a massive bed and frame. Straight ahead, past a golden statue of a phoenix with rubies for eyes, lay another hall.

"It's a shell game," Janus said suddenly.

"A what?" Celes asked.

Janus turned to his team. "This." He waved around at the crates and the art. "A shell game. They're popular in the…" He paused. "In

Cerberus. One person hides a prize: food, money, whatever, under a shell. They then mix up that shell with several others. Another person bets that they can guess the shell the prize is under."

Marcus nodded, familiar with the game.

"Doesn't sound too tough," Lyn said.

Marcus raised a hand in a *'well...'*. "It is all about deception, and usually the person betting loses. A good Sheller will remove the prize before the bettor even takes a guess."

"So all the Troopers, the chaos is the game," Ramirez said.

"Middleton is the Overlord of Intelligence for Cerberus," Celes said suddenly. "She's known, even feared, among the other Corporations."

"Ya heard of her before joining ODIN?" Lyn asked in surprise.

Janus glanced at Celes. Her expression was unreadable through the visor, but he knew what she was thinking. "It's not important. The point is that even if Middleton's caught red-handed with this stuff, what will the Executors of Cerberus do to her?"

"Nothing," Marcus concluded. "If she's that valuable—that powerful—they'll give her a slap on the wrist. It's not like the other Corporations have any idea about her treasure trove. So Alastor must believe there's something else here."

"Exactly."

"And Middleton is using the chaos of the shell game ta distract him," Lyn added. She made a motion to the door behind them. "Do you think they'll find anything?"

Janus glanced around the room, taking in the spectacle of the red and gold art.

Celes stepped forward in her armor. "No. If we believe she needed this base functional in a hurry, whatever is here would have been here since the beginning." She waved a hand at the art. "This... this is a distraction."

108

"All these rooms have been dug out," Ramirez grunted.

"Yes. Middleton is using her stolen goods to hide something else."

Janus stared down the hall which seemed to run even deeper into the base and then suddenly bend. "Do we have any idea how deep these caves run?"

Lyn shook her head. "When they found the base, Major Winters had the scouting teams look for old records from the area. There are still some old maps and diagrams that we have access to from before Corporate control. Nothing that mentions this cave system survived."

Janus nodded and carefully moved towards the end of the hall, passing doors to other rooms. The team fell into line behind him. He passed a set of open double doors to an office strikingly similar to Middleton's Cerberus estate. Carefully peering around the bend, he found the hall forked just beyond, splitting into two directions, with two new wooden doors. But the fork didn't hold his attention—instead he was transfixed by the space between the two doors.

He walked forward slowly, staring at a large painting that occupied the entirety of the far wall. It was a picture of a battle, great Corporate armies clashing in the background. In the foreground stood two men, clad in massive red-and-gold Command armor, clearly leading the charge. It was not their forms, but their faces, however, that was so encompassing.

On the right, a serious-looking blond youth was surveying the battlefield. Even with so many years removed, Janus recognized Norm immediately. Norm—the old man from the Cerberus slums who had helped Clara raise him. The old man who struggled with large crowds and tight places.

His gaze departed Norm's face as Celes stepped up next to him, focused intently on the figure to Norm's left. "Janus…" she breathed. "It's you."

CHAPTER 13
BEYOND THE DOOR

Janus gaped at the picture from behind his visor. He looked down at the title: *Victory at Lightemann's*.

"Or at least, a very good likeness," Lyn interjected. "The face is a little thinner. The hair's darker, almost black."

Janus noted more of the differences, but they were slight. The resemblance was unmistakable.

Suddenly, a tall man with a pointed nose and wearing an apron popped out of the door to the left, carrying a large tray of delicacies.

"What are you doing here?"

Janus remembered him from Overlord Middleton's estate, and breathed a sigh of relief that they were wearing Trooper armor. His name was Albert, and he was Middleton's personal butler and servant, and Clara's supervisor. Ramirez stepped forward, pointing at the boxes, grunting.

"Out of here, fool!" Albert hissed. "Now is not the time for that! Miss Middleton is entertaining Overlord Alastor, is and not to be disturbed!"

"Albert!" a voice called loudly from inside the room to their right.

Albert looked alarmed. "Yes, Mistress? I am coming…" The butler swept away, muttering under his breath, "Thickheaded, moronic…"

He paused just before the door. "Go on. Leave." He waved them away as he ducked into the rightmost room and disappeared, the door swinging behind him.

Janus wanted to study the painting in more detail, but now was not the time. He moved towards the left door and peered through the circular window. Inside waited a large, neatly arranged kitchen, completely devoid of anyone else.

Janus turned to the group. "If you were Middleton, where would you hide something within your already secret base?"

Lyn laughed. "That's just cruel, Janus."

Janus raised his hands in defense. "We don't know how deep this place goes. And if you were forced to hide a secret within a secret, where would you hide it?"

"You might not have the luxury of deciding where to put it, only how to hide it," Marcus agreed. "You would want people to dismiss it any way you could. And even be willing to play on someone's biases to protect it."

"Worth checking," Ramirez agreed.

"Come on, Albert will be coming back shortly. We need to move," Janus said. "Lyn."

Lyn slid over to the far door, and deftly opened it a crack. She made a quick handwave, and the team rushed into the kitchen.

"Drop the crates in the corner. We'll have to hope Albert will be too busy to check them for now if they're out of the way."

The space seemed far too large for one man to manage, but the aroma of delicate spices and sweets filled Janus's nostrils, permeating even the Trooper armor.

Lyn came in behind them and gently shut the door. "Clear, temporarily. Albert's serving the main course, and it looks like he's busy carving whatever they're having while making drinks."

Janus nodded. "Good. Spread out. Marcus and I will take the outside edge. Celes and Ramirez, through the middle. Lyn, keep an eye out. We'll need to act fast if he comes back."

On an island in the middle, a stove simmered with a large steel pot of soup, while adjacent to it, a sugary confection sizzled and boiled, concentrating it and filling the air with a sugary aroma. Janus ignored it and began moving around the outside, clockwise from the door. There were several large sinks on his side, and a few ovens, but everything looked as though it was recently and frequently used.

"Don't forget to check the vents," Lyn noted from her vantage point.

Marcus gave a raised hand in acknowledgement, and then paused for a moment, opening his visor. He had been moving counterclockwise from the door, and with some flexibility fished a small, flat wedge from inside his Adept suit. Pausing by a large vent over a prep area, he used it to quickly and carefully unscrew the vent cover. After a brief moment of searching and patting the inside, he shook his head, and moved on, quickly replacing the vent.

Janus passed by another huge oven which was baking a set of small, round cakes. Celes glanced over at them as she searched a long island of cabinets with a huge cutting board and grill. "Mmmmmm, Cornucopia Cakes."

Janus looked at her curiously.

She smiled. "They're a semi-sweet cake filled with fruit or cream cheese, and then drizzled with the brown sugar and butter concoction boiling on the stove." Everyone paused briefly to glance at her, and Lyn grabbed her stomach. Celes smirked as she resumed patting the inside of cabinets. "They're delicious. My father used to sneak a few back to my room for me when I was little."

"Not to change the subject," Marcus said as his stomach growled, "but we still have no idea what we're looking for." He opened a huge walk-in pantry and glanced around, quickly inspecting a few sacks of potatoes before moving on.

Suddenly, a timer started to go off just behind Janus. Celes glanced at the oven. "It must be for dessert!"

"If I know anything about that guy, he'll be back any moment. Come on, everyone out!" Janus whispered urgently.

Lyn waved them back. "Inferni!"

"Alastor's men!" Marcus said.

"Albert just ran into them in the hall!" Lyn added, ducking down.

"Here," Ramirez grunted, pointing to a huge refrigerator, wide and long enough for several STs.

Janus was the last in, shutting the door to just a crack as the kitchen door opened and Albert strode in. As soon as the kitchen door closed, Albert muttered to himself, "The poorest manners I have ever seen. Dinner is dinner; it should not be disturbed by unpleasant conversation." He turned off the timer with a simple flick and opened the oven, examining his creation closely. After nodding appreciatively, he removed the pan of cakes carefully, and set them on the center island. As he turned to leave, however, he halted unexpectedly. He walked over to the crates the team had dropped in the corner, shaking his head in anger as he stood over them. "STs." But he did not examine the crates any further and instead walked straight back out the door.

The team breathed an audible sigh of relief.

"It will take about thirty minutes for them to cool. Hopefully that will buy us some time," Celes said.

"It'd be nice to know what Alastor and Middleton are saying," Marcus lamented.

Janus glanced back along the now crowded fridge. "Lyn, do you think you can get close enough to listen in? That would also give us a little bit more warning when Albert comes back. And we're close enough that the cave might not impede our radios too much."

Marcus jumped in, "You know, if you got out of that armor, Lyn, you might be able to slide into that vent I checked. I bet it's airflow for this section of the base and I'm pretty sure it leads straight into the next room."

Lyn took a quick glance around the door, sizing up the vent. "I think you're right." She nodded appreciatively to Marcus. "Ramirez, get me out of this thing!" She lifted up her arms, and Ramirez helped her quickly pull off the huge suit.

"Meanwhile, we still need to figure out where we haven't searched." Janus glanced out of the fridge door and roamed the kitchen with eyes.

"Janus," Celes said.

"One second." *Whatever Middleton is hiding has to be here. But where...?*

"Janus..."

"Give me a moment, Celes. I'm trying to—"

"Janus!" Celes, Marcus, Lyn, and Ramirez whispered.

"What?" Janus said irritably, turning around.

Celes was pointing at a hastily constructed shelf full of fruits and veggies. It appeared as if everything had been recently moved, the neat ordering of the shelves lost. Some of the fruit had large bruises, as if they had fallen to the floor. Behind it, just peeking over the top of the shelf, was the outline of a heavy door.

Janus gaped. "Oh." He recovered quickly. "Marcus, help me move this thing."

Moving the shelf was a breeze in the strength-enhanced ST suits, and revealed a large, rounded hatch recessed deep in the back of the fridge. No other security existed for the door. Janus could only presume that it was never supposed to be found.

They pulled. With the sound of a pressurized seal releasing, the door opened slowly, the cool air pouring out into the space behind it. Janus stepped into the darkness beyond, his breath catching. Celes cautiously followed. "Janus, I think we've seen this before."

"Yes, we have," Janus breathed, as soft blue lights on the floor illuminated the room. Before them lay a long hall, ending at a door with a familiar sigil: A fiery phoenix.

Janus quickly stepped back inside the refrigerator. His mind was a whirl. "Celes, how long has Middleton been an Overlord? I heard Alastor make a quip about her age on the pad."

Celes raised a gloved hand to her helmet. "Decades, I think."

Janus looked back at the rest of the team. Lyn was out of her armor. "Ramirez, help Lyn get a quick boost into that vent, and then move her armor into that hall. The three of us"—he pointed to Celes, Marcus, and himself—"are going to move forward. Adjust radio frequency to low band 23.84. Since we're splitting up, we want to be able to penetrate the walls as much as possible."

Ramirez poked his head out of the refrigerator. "Clear." He crossed to the door in a moment, and checked for Albert. "Clear." Silently pulling the vent cover from the wall, he turned and gave Lyn a quick boost all in one smooth motion. Lyn slid soundlessly into the vent, arms extended forward, barely clearing the edges. Ramirez silently replaced the cover and immediately returned to the fridge followed by Marcus, Celes, and Janus, carrying the two crates full of weapons.

Lyn's radio came across clear as they stepped into the fridge, the steady sound of her breathing as she worked her way silently along the vent. "Seems like it's sturdy enough for me, I'm moving forward," she said. The sound of Middleton's and Alastor's voices grew until finally, Lyn moved into position.

"—Alastor, Alastor. Did I not promise to show you everything? You certainly don't need to be in a rush."

"A rush? Never, my dear Middleton. I simply don't enjoy my meals as much as you do." There was a pause. "You think I won't be able to keep track of everything if you rush it around and mix it up?"

"Will you?" Middleton asked.

"Of course I can manage such a simple little test, but even if I couldn't, nothing is escaping this facility without my seeing it. My Typhons are patrolling the area and watching your landing pad. Try as you might, you won't sneak anything out from under me. Any transports within twenty kilometers will either be boarded or shot down. I will find what has been going on here and what you are up to."

"We'll see."

Janus waved for Marcus, Celes, and Ramirez to get moving while they listened. The four moved into the dimly lit hall, closing the heavy door behind them. Immediately static sprung into the feed.

Heavy door. Marcus signaled with a smile, and then closed his visor once more. **Middleton (must have) needed (all that) food (for) strength.**

Celes mimed covering her mouth and shook a finger reprovingly at him, while Janus struggled to flash a signal to Ramirez, who fortunately understood what he wanted. **Wait. Boost.**

Ramirez nodded, and slowly signed **49.27.**

Janus, Celes, and Marcus quickly shifted their radios, listening to the feed now sent via Ramirez from Lyn via relay.

(Bring) crate, Janus signaled to Celes and Marcus. The pair nodded.

"Twenty kilometers is a big area, Alastor. Are you sure that you can track everything?"

"I found this place, didn't I?"

The three marched smartly down the hall, leaving Ramirez to wait and help Lyn. Despite an intimidating-looking display, the giant door with the Phoenix emblem was not locked. "STAND-BY MODE" flashed across the screen to its right.

As the three crossed the threshold and into another hall, the static became worse, but still manageable with Ramirez' boost. This hall had many doors leading off, as frequently as they could be crammed in. All the doors were open, and Janus glanced into them as he passed by. The first looked like a large security room, with hundreds of cameras, but all of the screens were off. The next appeared to be a showering and changing facility, while the room connected to it was completely gutted and empty. The sound of Albert pushing his chair back could be faintly heard over the radio, and Janus paused briefly to listen, as their voices grew fainter.

"I must admit, Middleton," Alastor said slyly, "I am slightly disturbed by the volume of Phoenix Corporate lore that occupies this base."

Middleton sighed audibly. "Simply a remnant and a prize from the razing, nothing more, Alastor."

"I often forget you were there for the invasion," Alastor said with a somewhat troubled tone. "I didn't become an Overlord until years after."

Janus could almost hear the smugness in Middleton's reply. "Yes, well, you had to wait for your father to die, didn't you?"

Alastor chuckled, though Janus couldn't tell if he was sloughing off Middleton's remark, or laughing along with her.

Many of the rooms beyond the first few had been stripped bare, and Janus quickly reached the end of the second hall, another elaborate door with the Phoenix symbol. Inside was another armory—a complete one. Full suits of Security Trooper armor waited along the walls.

Strange, Celes flashed with some difficulty. On the left, Cerberus suits stood along the wall, but the right wall was empty.

Marcus carefully opened the door at the far end of the armory station. Janus followed him inside.

At first Janus thought he had stepped into a supply room—and then he realized he *had* stepped into a supply room. Mops, brooms, and crates of Passers, the ubiquitous Security Trooper meal alternative, were all were visible on shelves stacked like a maze in the room. Although he couldn't see their faces, it was clear that Marcus and Celes were just as confused as he was.

"Seems like a lot of work to hide a storage room," Marcus commented wryly, looking around.

The door closed behind him and Janus paused, cocking his head at the strange sight—their entry had disappeared. From this side the door had been cleverly concealed as part of the rocky back wall of the room. It had been much more carefully constructed than the one within the fridge. It took them a moment to realize how to open it again.

"There must be more here," Janus said, stepping over the littered boxes and supplies, which had clearly been moved in a hurry. Working his way around several strewn cases of 'beef' Passers, he found another closed door with a window. Peering through it, Janus could see a short hall hewn from the natural rock, with a sharp 90-degree turn at the end.

They carefully left the storage room, following the rock hallway, and peered around the corner. It failed to provide any great enlightenment either. The first few rooms off the hallway appeared to be nothing more than barracks, each labeled with a number and an armoring station. The rooms were almost completely devoid of any remaining equipment or furniture. Only the bed and armor symbols on the walls and floors gave them any clue. "Look, they must have added rooms over time, and added space, as well," Janus said, pointing to the numeric labels. "The numbers are all out of order, and you can see where the barracks were eventually expanded in some of the older rooms."

"The Phoenix seal is everywhere," Celes murmured, placing her armored hand over an engraving in the wall. The symbol dotted every room—the rising bird, wreathed in flames.

They moved past a cleared-out armory and onto another barracks. "The population must have exploded here," Marcus commented, gazing into an empty room. "Middleton must have constantly had men working to extend this area." He pointed to the rock. It changed colors, becoming lighter as newer rock was exposed to expand each room. Three times this particular room had been expanded, each time far larger than the last—it was like counting rings in a tree.

Alastor's voice crackled over the radio again, "Still, there seems to be a certain reverence that you hold for this... art."

Janus paused. Lyn must have moved somehow. He strained to listen, hoping to hear more about the strange painting of Norm and himself.

"You know full well of my collections. I simply could not let such fine displays of corporate prominence be destroyed, even if they were of an inferior corporation to the great Cerberus. Yes, I'm afraid the Executors simply wouldn't understand."

Janus's eyes traced the pipes that ran overhead. The solid rock was far from ideal for expanding outward, so it was clear that Middleton had stopped well short of the upgrades that had occupied her quarters. Simple showers and faucets were visible in some of the spaces, their pipes simply bolted to whatever was available. He stopped at another room which seemed to confirm his suspicions. Simple beds lined the walls. There weren't even dressers or places for personal effects. Just a trunk at the end of each bed. Apparently this room had been forgotten in the shuffle. Alastor's laughter diverted his attention.

"Are you trying to tell me that this whole base is simply a hiding place for your contraband art?" Alastor sounded incredulous. "Do you take me for a fool?"

"What do you think, Alastor?" Middleton's crackling voice responded.

"Do all Overlords hate each other this much?" Marcus interjected as they listened. "Or is it just them?" Janus shrugged his shoulders and together they stepped back into the hall, keeping an eye out for any signs of movement.

"Wait!" Celes exclaimed in revelation.

"What?" Janus asked, turning back around to stare at her still within the room he had just left.

Celes was staring at the beds and held a gloved hand to her face. "Look."

"I don't see anything," Janus said.

"Look again." She motioned to Marcus to put down the crate with her at the edge of the room, then walked past it to stand beside one of the beds.

Suddenly, Janus realized what was wrong—he couldn't fit. "They're for children." He felt a pit form in his stomach.

"Come over here," Marcus called worriedly from the hall. Janus and Celes walked across to where Marcus was standing. Janus swallowed hard, and Celes gasped.

Stretching out before them was a firing range, hundreds of meters long, extended deep into the rock many times over.

"Overlord Alastor! Leave me be, old man!" The rumble of an Infernus bursting in, compounded with Albert's protests sounded in Janus's ear.

"What is the meaning of this?" Middleton exclaimed angrily.

"Ah, Pyrus Reynolds. Do you have something to report?" Alastor seemed positively delighted at the intrusion.

Reynolds responded breathlessly, "We did exactly as you ordered, sir. We've been searching the place top to bottom. We hadn't gotten a report from Bretts or Cobb in a while, though, so I went up to check on them, with the radio static and all. I can't raise them, sir."

Janus dropped behind a wall and froze. He looked at Marcus and Celes, who had instinctively pressed themselves back into what shadows could be found in these empty spaces.

"What do you mean, you can't raise them?" Middleton interjected over Alastor. She actually sounded concerned.

After a moment's pause, the Inferni replied, "They aren't responding to comms."

"I'll have you know, Middleton, that the Executors are expecting my report, if—"

"Oh drop it, Alastor. We both know you won't be coming to any harm here," Middleton retorted. "Not today, at least," she muttered. Janus had to reflect in awe how close Lyn must be.

Her voice became louder, clearly directed at the Infernus. "Now what—"

It was clearly Alastor's turn to cut Middleton off. "I don't think the Pyrus has finished his report yet, Middleton."

"No, sir. As I came back, Inferni Shanks and Lire had just finished inspecting everything but the back area of the residence."

"You did what?" Middleton yelled.

"Please continue, Pyrus." Alastor ignored her.

"Yes, sir. The dining room and the kitchen area. Anyway, Lire reported that they were about to enter the kitchen now that Overlord Middleton's assistant—"

"Butler," Albert corrected.

"Assistant," the Infernus ignored the man. "Now that her assistant was not impeding us. When Lire was about to enter the kitchen, she witnessed a set of Troopers enter the refrigerator together with a set of crates. After several minutes, it became clear they weren't coming out again. She is now investigating to find out where they went."

Janus rushed headlong back into the hall along with Celes and Marcus. Reaching the storage room door, Janus felt his heart sink, cursing himself for his stupidity. *Mint mistake.* Peering inside through the window, Janus could barely see that slowly but surely, the hidden door was opening. Suddenly, a huge hand reached out from the darkness and pulled Janus back. He turned to see Ramirez put a huge armored finger to his helmet and point to one of the empty rooms. The storage room door opened and the sound of clomping feet could be heard coming down the hall. They quietly moved into the nearest room and pressed against the near wall, clutching their pistols at the ready. Janus felt his heart sink. The rest of their weapons all sat in a crate a few rooms away.

Alastor's voice was suddenly less crackly, and he sounded positively elated. "What do you have to say for yourself, Middleton?" He already seemed to have forgotten his missing men.

Down the hall, Janus could hear the metal toes of the Infernus clacking on the rock. Janus looked back at his team. All three were incredibly still, as if they weren't even breathing. They wouldn't be able to pass themselves off so easily to Alastor's men. And if they were brought back to Middleton, she would know them instantly. So if Lire found them, they would have no choice but to fight. With pistols. Against an Infernus.

Middleton's voice was pleasant as she replied. "I suppose I'll have to show you some more of this base." The utter lack of concern in her voice made Janus think that for once, Middleton was panicking inside.

"Come, Reynolds. Show me to the kitchen." The voices began to fade away, clearly leaving Lyn behind.

The clomping grew louder and paused at the room just down the hall. Janus's mind began to race.

Marcus signaled him. **Plan(?)**

Janus took a deep breath. **Fight.**

He fully expected some resistance at this, but Marcus raised a hand in agreement. **Pin (and) press.**

Janus signaled confusion, and Marcus elaborated, signing to Janus, Ramirez, and himself, then making the sign for Infernus. **(Use us to) pin (the Infernus).** He signed at Celes. **Press pistol (to visor).**

Janus nodded in understanding. **Good.**

The clomping continued towards them, the metal toes scraping the rock and creating an unpleasant *tap, tap.*

The four pressed themselves forward. They would have one chance to surprise the Infernus as it came into the room. They couldn't afford to let it ready its weapons.

Suddenly a raspy voice sounded from just beyond the threshold. "Yes, sir. I'll proceed ahead immediately. These first few rooms already appear to be emptied, so I wouldn't bother with them at all."

The heavy footsteps proceeded deeper into the facility quickly and Janus let out a deep breath that threatened to fog his visor.

Distantly, a voice could be heard calling over the radio. "Come along, Middleton. I'm in a bit of rush."

"Of course, Alastor," Middleton called out. She had clearly not moved. Her voice dropped dramatically. "Martel, do you read me? Alastor has two missing men on the surface. Find out what happened to them. And make sure Magnus knows. I'll be keeping our guest entertained as long as I can." Her voice suddenly became labored and started to fade away. "Sorry, Alastor. Just...taking a moment...to catch my breath."

CHAPTER 14
ABANDONED TREASURE

"Interesting," Alastor commented dryly, his voice drifting down the passage as he spoke to Middleton, their entourage clomping behind them. "Just what were you doing here, Middleton?"

Janus pressed himself against the wall of the empty barracks, listening intently, and the party walked by them without stopping.

"Empty barracks. Empty armories. It's almost like you were training troops here. But as Overlord of Intelligence, you know that any deployment center must be monitored and approved by the Overlord for War—by me." Alastor's voice was smug.

"Overlord Alastor, sir," Reynolds interjected. "Lire's found something."

Suddenly, Lire's voice crackled out from a radio, "I think you should come see this—wait, what are you doing?" There was scream and the radio cut out.

The footsteps stopped, and there was a notable pause. After a moment came the sound of claws extending and a Zeus powering up.

"My dear Middleton, we're not about to have a problem, are we?" Alastor's voice was grave. "Need I remind you of who sent me?"

Middleton's voice was calm once more. Janus felt like he was listening to a snake. "Don't be silly, Alastor. As you can see, I'm unarmed, and I have no intention of putting myself in an unfavorable position with the Executors. I suspect some of my soldiers got a tad overzealous about my warnings regarding intruders. But may I suggest we both arrive together to prevent any further misunderstandings."

"Of course." The Zeus powered down. "My own soldiers have been known to be temperamental, so let us ensure no further misunderstandings occur. Why don't you take the lead?"

"My pleasure."

Janus looked at Marcus, Ramirez, and Celes. *If something happens to either Alastor or Middleton, all hell will break loose.* As the two Overlords disappeared down the hall, and their voices faded away, Janus turned to Ramirez keeping his own voice calm. "Get Lyn. I'm sure she's tired of being crammed in that vent." Ramirez nodded and swiftly disappeared. Janus turned to Celes and Marcus. "Let's see what other secrets Middleton's hiding, before it's too late."

They gave the two Overlords some distance, and then rushed to grab their crate of weapons. Janus could only hope they wouldn't run into anyone else.

But as they moved past more and more empty rooms, it was clear he did not need to worry. Middleton had obviously made an effort to clear out the facility as quickly as possible. Non-essential items—beds, foot lockers, tables and chairs—had all been left behind. But judging from the size of these hidden rooms, Middleton must have had significant notice. *She must have known she would be discovered as soon as Alastor started looking.*

"She probably knew the moment Alastor sent the SPARTAN legion after her," Celes commented.

"But where is all of it going? Surely the Troopers haven't been moving back through the base?" Marcus asked.

"No. I don't think so," Janus responded simply. He looked at Celes. She had seen the same thing under the ruins of Phoenix that he had; the massive factories producing armor and weapons.

"But if Middleton is training up an army, without the knowledge of the Executors, where is it? This place feels big when it's empty, but it couldn't accommodate a fraction of what was below Phoenix."

It wasn't the beds, the sheer size, or the Phoenix emblem emblazoned upon every door and surface that truly added to the mystery, however—it was one unassuming room, smaller in size than many of the others.

It was beyond all of the barracks, the firing range, and the mess. Beyond the classrooms, the libraries, several huge rooms of weights, obstacles, and tests. It stood at the very end of the long, jagged hallways.

It had never been expanded and was of a solid metal construction throughout. Not one ounce of exposed rock peeked from any wall or surface, just heavy electrical connections.

And it was totally empty, with one exception.

Framed in the light of the door, tall, thin plates of a silvery metal were stacked in groups of three. They lay untouched and forgotten in the rush. Marcus lay a gloved hand across the metal. "It's definitely Immutium." A short-lived attempt to lift one of the plates confirmed his remark.

Janus hadn't known about Immutium for very long, but he knew enough to recognize that the amount left behind was worth a small fortune.

Janus tapped on his visor lights, highlighting a large door in the center of the wall, wide enough for the three of them to stand abreast, and read the lettering upon it. "Transport."

Celes pointed upward to a track along the ceiling that ran all the way to the door. "There are rails for moving something."

"Janus." Marcus pointed to the far side, where two smaller doors sat. One was marked "Transport Access." It was closed, and had a glowing green button beside it. The other was "Gel Processing," and it was simply open, the button red. Leaving Celes to guard the hall, Janus and Marcus slid inside the open room.

It was totally black inside. Only the light from their suits shone against the darkness. And it was empty but for a small, glowing puddle of blue goo in the middle of the room. Janus crouched and ran an armored finger through it. It tingled.

"Electrogel," Janus whispered.

"What's that?" Marcus said, pointing to a conspicuous hole in the floor. It was only a few centimeters wide, and he moved closer, listening intently. "I can hear running water. It's too deep to see, but I would guess it connects to a water supply."

He stood up. "Are you thinking what I'm thinking?"

Janus nodded, extremely troubled. "What could have been in these rooms that was more valuable than what was left behind?"

As they returned to the first room with the Immutium, Celes quickly signaled the alarm. **Someone(s) coming. Hall.**

The three quickly grabbed the crate and retreated to the second room, pressing themselves against the wall. A moment later, Ramirez and Lyn, back in her Trooper armor, swept into the first room.

Janus quickly signaled them

"Took me a while ta get out of there," Lyn said. "Middleton must have installed extensive ventilation for her own comfort. Gave me good access ta the talks she and Alastor had, however."

"Good work," Janus agreed. He quickly filled the pair in on everything they had found.

Lyn motioned to the door marked 'Transport Access.' "Guess nothing left but ta see what's there," she said casually. Janus opened his visor.

"We don't know what's on the other side. I'll open the door and then quickly signal to continue or retreat. If it's retreat, don't wait, just book it the way we came, and get out of the base any way you can."

The other four opened their visors. He could see grim determination on their faces, and each one nodded. Janus smiled and closed his visor, the others doing the same. He turned to back to the smaller 'Transport Access' door and took a deep breath. Then he pushed the 'open' button.

Chapter 15
The Collector

Janus braced for the worst. The area on the other side of the door was large. Very large. It was by far the largest they had found so far. And it was filled to the brim with Inferni and STs. But not one stopped what they were doing to pay any attention to him. They were all working—and not the controlled chaos of earlier. This was deliberate.

Advance.

The large room was circular in shape, and completely covered in equipment, wires, and pipes. Only a patch of rock here or there poked out from the ceiling.

Janus could hear the clomp of his companions' boots as they walked carefully into the room, carrying their crates between them.

Three levels of a heavily braced platform ran along the outside in a ring, with two large crane arms resting in the center. They stood on the middle level, and as they moved along the edge, Janus glanced up. High in the top of the cavern, a fusion generator glowed, providing the power for the base. Across the room, on the ground below the platforms, a long, flat railcar waited silently before a gaping black maw, traveling through what must have been the heart of Lightemann's Ridge.

Dozens of STs laboriously moved long, coffin-like metal boxes onto the railcar, placing them in perfectly shaped indentations. Electrical connections sat exposed at every indentation, and a recessed plug was visible on each of the coffin-boxes as the assisting cranes carefully pulled more from the topmost level and placed them on the waiting railcar. A small side track sat empty, as if waiting for another car.

Along the edge of the room on the bottom floor, a stack of broken crates, spilled electrical components and Immutium bars seemed out of place until Janus noticed a limp arm poking from the mess. Even Infernus armor couldn't withstand tons of Immutium

"I have a feeling I know what happened to Lire," Marcus interjected quietly, staring at the arm.

Janus nodded. "Keep acting naturally."

Stepping calmly but smartly along the raised middle walkway, the five approached a lift that ran along one of the support spines.

Alastor and Middleton were a level below them, and Alastor seemed to be studying the spectacle with reserve. One look at the pair made it clear they were both walking on eggshells. Alastor's forehead was glistening with a sheen of sweat, despite the calm on his face. He moved with careful consideration, shooting glances at Middleton repeatedly. Middleton, to her credit, seemed perfectly calm, though the deepness of each of her breaths seemed to demonstrate it was a forced exercise.

"This room seems familiar," Celes said softly.

"Really?" asked Lyn, surprised. "How so?"

"I don't know," Celes replied.

Janus tilted his head in agreement. He felt like something in his brain was trying to piece together where he had seen the same.

Janus motioned to the lift. "Let's head down."

As they moved forward, however, two Inferni stopped them, glancing at the group's armor. The pair towered over Janus, but he resisted the urge to step back.

"You aren't supposed to be here. Go back to the other side."

The vehemence in the Infernus's voice was alarming. Janus did a quick check of the two Inferni's armor for an officer's insignia and was surprised to see a fiery Phoenix emblazoned upon the shoulder and a gold flame below it. Janus studied the Infernus for another fraction of a second. "We follow orders. Miss Middleton wants this done. Or haven't you noticed that Overlord Alastor is posing a larger problem than expected."

Janus heard Marcus politely cough behind him, and added, "Pyrus."

The Infernus studied Janus for what seemed an eternity, and Ramirez stepped forward. It took the Infernus a moment to realize that Ramirez met him at eye level, and Ramirez chuckled. "Some of us are quite good at moving dead weight."

The Infernus didn't flinch and the pair stared each other down, until finally the Infernus made a motion with his head. "Fine. Take the lift to the railcar, and help the cranes load up those Cryochambers. They need to be on the final shipment out."

Janus raised a hand in acknowledgement as Marcus had showed him and together the team stepped onto the lift. His mind raced. If they thought they were in the thick of it before, they really were now.

The lift moved agonizingly slow, or at least it felt that way. Here and there, more STs, with the Phoenix emblem emblazoned on their shoulders would pause for a moment to look at them.

"Cryochambers?" Lyn breathed. But no one responded.

Janus stole a glance at the pair of Overlords as they descended past them. Alastor was staring intently at one of the metal box-coffins, and paused, seemingly counting on his hand. He stopped, looked at Middleton, and then shook his head, counting again. Middleton's large frame was very still, as if she was simply watching the spectacle unfold now.

As the lift jolted to a stop, they carefully disembarked with their crates, and deposited them upon the railcar. The cranes were stacking chambers near the car, and a set of specialized arms attached to the train sat ready for more to be included. Janus could only assume this is what the Infernus had meant, but honestly, he had no idea what they were supposed to do. Ramirez took command of a treaded pallet, moving it towards the chambers and pulling one from the wall. Some of the other STs around them paused and glanced at each other.

Lyn moved to pull another chamber from the wall and jerked to a stop. She pulled again and nearly slammed into the strange device. "Heavy," she said ruefully. Ramirez moved next to her and pulled two from the wall at once, sliding them smoothly onto the pallet.

"Show off…" she muttered. Ramirez just shrugged.

Marcus moved the pallet to the railcar and together, he and Janus moved one coffin into an empty slot.

(There's a) Display (on this) side, Marcus discreetly signed.

He bent swiftly over, feigning a quick adjustment, and popped back up. He raised a hand to sign once more but stopped, staring at the box. Janus moved to the next crate, and Marcus snapped back to reality. As the other three brought over another pallet, Marcus turned to them and spoke in the barest of whispers. "I think… I think they're people."

On the next crate, Janus did his own check: Subject: Gamma 3147-8, Sex: Male, Height: 185 cm, Weight: 75.4 kg. Status: Green.

After a brief pause, Janus simply lifted a hand in acknowledgement.

What(?) Celes asked.

Look, Ramirez discreetly signed as he deftly maneuvered the pallet towards the next set of chambers.

The group turned to watch an extremely grim Alastor descend to the ground floor on the lift. Behind him, the sweat on Middleton's large face made her appear even more piggish. The three remaining Inferni now surrounded him like a bubble.

Janus could almost taste the uncertainty in the air, and all around him STs were stealing surreptitious glances at the pair. Janus and the team quickly resumed their efforts to move the metal coffins. Despite their curiosity, the other STs had not stopped.

"Where does the railcar go, Middleton?" Alastor asked as the group stepped off the lift. "What are you doing with these...things?" Alastor motioned to the coffins.

"Simply some research, Alastor. Simply research."

"Last I checked, research such as this would not be your purview. Especially without the Executors' consent," Alastor retorted.

Middleton said nothing.

The arrival of an Infernus through the door above distracted Janus from the Overlords' verbal sparring. The armor was of Cerberus, and it had a large starburst on the shoulder. It was one of Middleton's guards from the landing pad, with a slightly shorter, stockier customized set of armor. The Inferni at the lift saluted him immediately as he approached, and he simply leaped to the bottom floor, the heavy mechanical legs thudding on the metal.

"Martel?" Middleton said in surprise. "Do you have something to report?" She fiddled with her radio as if surprised he had come directly.

"The comm lines were cut when they ripped out the rest of the equipment. And this part of the base is too well shielded for good radio communication." Martel's voice sounded like gravel, and Janus wasn't sure if that was the suit or the man himself. He moved forward to speak with Middleton directly, but Alastor interjected.

"Do you have news, Novus?"

Martel paused. The evil red visor of the Infernus armor stared silently at the impetuous Overlord. Middleton gave him a slight nod.

"We found the Overlord's missing men. They had been pulled away from the landing pad and covered in mud and debris to hide their heat signatures."

Middleton's nostrils flared. "Mercs."

"Likely another Legion, seeing as SPARTAN is contracted by the Overlord." Martel motioned a clawed hand towards Alastor.

The screech of another railcar coming down the track echoed down the tunnel.

"I sent word to the Executor via our overland radio stations. I expect that is him now."

Alastor turned to Middleton in surprise. "Executor? The Executor Council assured me they were unaware of any of your activities."

Down the tunnel, a light appeared along the single track, and there was a screeching of brakes as a second railcar slowed into the chamber. A Trooper rushed to a manual lever just ahead of where Janus was working, and switched the track so that the car could stop. Peering over the cryochambers on their own car, Janus could see it was brimming with Troopers, all carrying Zeus rifles.

"Ah, good, Martel. It appears you've alerted Middleton to the situation." The eerily familiar voice stopped Janus in his tracks.

As the Troopers parted, Janus could just make out a long mane of white hair passing through the crowd.

"And you are?" Alastor demanded.

The man had his back to the group, and Janus struggled to get a better look.

The man performed an elegant bow. "I am Executor Delacroix. And you must be Alastor. I've heard so much about you." The sarcasm dripped from his voice.

134

A quick signal from Celes caught Janus's eye. **Above.** Janus looked up and saw that the Troopers above had stopped, watching the scene expectantly. The room suddenly felt very quiet after the din of moving chambers. Middleton no longer looked as though she was in control of the situation at all, and she took a few steps back from Alastor and his remaining entourage.

Get ready. It was all Janus felt safe to signal in the bulky suit. He hoped his team knew what he meant.

Alastor paused, the sudden silence not escaping him, and glanced around the room. His three remaining Inferni stretched their claws and scanned the crowd. The Troopers around Delacroix tightened the grips around their rifles. Raising a hand for them to hold, Alastor took a moment to look back at Middleton, then gathered himself.

"Executor…Delacroix?" Alastor's voice took on a note of pleasant curiosity. "I'm afraid we haven't met. I don't seem to recall an Executor by that name on the Cerberus council."

Delacroix chuckled. "I suppose not. I don't sit on the Cerberus council."

Alastor nodded eyeing the Troopers around his little group. "It seems that you have some sort of deal with Middleton. I'd be interested to hear it. The Executors are expecting a full report, but I could see myself making some adjustments to it. No need to get them riled up with any unfortunate misunderstandings."

"You understand the situation quite well," Delacroix responded. "I must say that Middleton's reports about you are quite intriguing. You are a credit to your caste. Very few Overlords I've met could be considered the same."

Martel stepped forward. "Overlord Alastor is quite a credit to Cerberus. And his soldiers are top notch." He carefully moved between Alastor and Delacroix.

The Troopers took a step back, exposing Delacroix, who did not move. He wore a black-and-silver suit, with his white hair cascading onto his shoulders.

The Inferni around Alastor relaxed slightly.

Delacroix motioned towards the Novus. "Impressive. Martel vouching for your character is something indeed. Titan could use someone like you."

Down at his waist, Delacroix's hand flashed into an unmistakable symbol.

Kill.

Martel slammed a clawed hand into the first Infernus's visor. Before the dead soldier had started to fall, Martel had whipped both arms out and executed the two other guards in an instant with a Zeus round to each of their chests. The nearby Troopers ducked instinctively as the rounds slammed into the walls behind them, leaving sparks in two of the open coffin recesses. All three were on the floor within a heartbeat. No one moved.

Alastor looked at the dead men surrounding him and the dread began to flush his face. "If something happens to me, the Cerberus Executors will know something has gone wrong. Middleton can't cover this up! There will be hell to pay!"

Delacroix's voice took on a light tone. "I certainly hope so." In an instant, a pistol appeared in his hand and he shot Alastor dead between the eyes.

CHAPTER 16
MAGNUS

Middleton fell back in shock as Alastor's body hit the floor. Martel swiftly moved to her side and helped her up.

"Magnus, what have you done? The Cerberus Executors will pursue me to the ends of the earth for this!"

Delacroix's voice was smooth and calm. "They'll pursue someone. But not you. This will only fuel the fire. Our friend Alastor stepped out a little too far this time. He hired SPARTAN to find you, but I'm guessing that *little* expense was never going to be brought to the attention of the Cerberus Executors. At least, not until after he had some evidence of your duplicity. And that gives us an opening."

"How?" Middleton implored.

"SPARTAN did its job—they found this place for him. And since their contract ended, I've now paid them to eliminate all Cerberus Typhons in the area. Alastor's little air fleet is in for a surprise. I told SPARTAN to leave one Typhon alive to report back to Cerberus. They were more than happy to accept the second half of the Immutium shipment we never intended to deliver to ODIN."

"But what about Alastor? What about my troops? How will I face the Executors?" Middleton asked, her voice still a little shaky.

"Tell them the truth." Magnus laughed.

Middleton narrowed her eyes, and Martel interjected. "I've already reported on official channels that mercs are in the area, and we believe they've infiltrated the base." Martel motioned to Magnus with a claw.

"And I appreciate that, Novus," Magnus replied. "Tell them that Titan hired SPARTAN. You can omit the part where Alastor hired them first. The Executors will make the logical conclusion."

"And that is?" Middleton asked, but she seemed to have already guessed the answer.

"Titan hired a Legion to strike at Cerberus in response to the attack on their mining colony only a short while ago. Or in response to your repeated spying on them. Our dear Overlord Alastor, unfortunately, was caught in the crossfire."

"And what about this?" Middleton waved her arm across the room at the cryochambers.

"Give them the Immutium, the art, anything. Even throw in an unused chamber if you want. They'll drool all over it. Say you've been trying to pull relics from Phoenix for years—which is true. Tell them you've been following up on Titan—which is also true. Alastor's own Typhons are probably relaying they're under attack right now. You can claim anything you want in the interests of Cerberus. Research. Art preservation. You'll think of something. The SPARTAN attack will cover the rest. And perhaps we'll even have a body to give them."

"How so?" Middleton asked.

Magnus tilted his head in the direction of Martel, but Janus still couldn't quite see his face.

"ODIN is here." Martel stated plainly.

Janus forced himself not to react, but he couldn't risk turning around to check on his team.

"ODIN? Jennings? How do you know?"

"No one contracted SPARTAN for ground operations. And only one Legion would have the expertise or the interest in investigating this area," Martel added.

Middleton sidled up to Delacroix and grabbed his arm. "But surely you don't think that ODIN actually slipped into Phoenix, do you?"

Delacroix remained silent.

Middleton's eyes narrowed. "Well, they couldn't have slipped into the base without us knowing."

"Perhaps…" Delacroix said reflectively, as he glanced down at the pistol in his hand. "But experience has taught me to never underestimate an Adept."

Middleton sighed. "We both know that well."

Martel moved over to Delacroix's entourage. "Sweep the base." He turned to Delacroix, his voice rasping out, "Shall I leave a guard with you, sir?"

Delacroix waved a hand dismissively, pulling it away from Middleton's grasp. "That's not necessary, Novus. That will just make me stand out more." And then he motioned in Janus's direction. "Someone clean this mess up. Finish loading up those containers and get them moving." He looked at Middleton. "When you're done with the chambers, destroy anything left and leave; don't worry about the Immutium. We're abandoning this base."

Janus hesitantly motioned for help from the others.

"Why do you think I had so many troopers here? But why not take our time now that Alastor is dead?" Middleton asked.

Celes and Lyn picked up one of the Inferni between them, while Ramirez grabbed another and threw him over his shoulder. Even Delacroix took notice, watching as Ramirez walked over to help Marcus with another. Janus struggled to get a glimpse of the Executor's face while awkwardly grabbing Alastor.

Delacroix turned back to Middleton. "This base has little to offer us now—other than further possibilities for exposure. Let the Cerberus Executors have it. Everything will be concentrated at the Phoenix facility for the final phase. And I want the full results of the ODIN assault against the Titan outpost. I need to know how effective our troops were against them. Even if ODIN didn't find us in the ruins, they can still do far too much damage. Adepts stopped me before—it won't happen again."

The team moved away towards the railcar, piling the bodies on the back. Janus tried not to hurry too much, despite his eager desire to be rid of his loathsome burden.

He was just about to drop Alastor when Delacroix called to him, "Stop."

Janus froze. *He knows our hand signals. Did he see us earlier?* "Yes, sir?"

"Come here," he commanded.

Janus moved hesitantly, Alastor's body blocking his view, and he turned to see Delacroix's boots facing him.

Delacroix studied him as he approached. "You are a Cerberus ST, are you not?"

Janus felt his stomach turn, but he kept himself outwardly calm. "Yes, sir."

"Why are you here?" Delacroix asked. Janus hefted Alastor's body, trying to adjust its positioning. He caught a glimpse of Middleton staring suspiciously. He promptly lowered his head, shifting Alastor along his shoulder as he did so.

"I was ordered here, sir."

"By whom?" Middleton asked abruptly.

Janus knew he was going to be caught in a lie, and his mind raced, trying to stay a step ahead of the pair. "By you, miss." Janus kept his head bowed, but tried to peer along the top of his visor at the pair.

Middleton reacted immediately. "I did no such thing."

"Well…" Janus stuttered, buying time. "I assumed it was your order, miss, but it came from your servant…Alex…Alb…Andrew," Janus murmured.

"Albert, you moron," Middleton said, taking a step forward.

Janus took a step back, speaking quickly. "Sorry miss. He said that the—uh," he stuttered intentionally and hefted the body once more and sped up his tempo. "Uh, Alastor. Andrew said he was causing problems and…and something about helping our Mistress, and not worrying about the art in the back anymore. Then I saw those Inferni go into the kitchen."

Delacroix motioned towards Celes, Marcus, Lyn, and Ramirez. "And what about them?" Janus glanced back at the team. They were facing the railway, and their crates, ready to grab their weapons. They couldn't see Delacroix's face, either. Janus tried to shift Alastor again, but Delacroix began to circle him, moving to the edge of Janus's vision, his head bowed in thought. Janus forced himself not to turn to look.

"Well, I certainly wasn't going to face an Infernus alone, even if we're both from Cerberus," Janus responded in a whiny grumble, "uh, sir." He had nearly forgotten that part.

"And why didn't you try to help your Overlord while we killed him," Delacroix asked curiously.

"Well, sir, I work for Miss Middleton, and she didn't do anything about it. Besides, it seemed like a good way to get killed." Janus nodded in respect to Martel who was watching the scene impassively, "Even if he was an Overlord."

Middleton sighed. "Let the oaf be, Magnus. I was bound to get a few in the rush to get Troopers here."

Delacroix, however, sounded unconvinced. "Of course, of course. You're a smart man to feel that way…what was your name again?"

141

"Bynes, sir," Janus answered immediately.

"Let me see your face."

Martel's armor seemed to subtly lean forward, and Janus felt beads of sweat form across his forehead. Behind him, he could feel the others flinch at the question. Middleton would surely recognize him. Janus reached for his helmet, his mind reeling. Delacroix finished his circle and stopped in front of him, gazing him right in the eye.

Janus froze, his hand on the edge of his helmet. Delacroix was the youth in the painting. *He...looks like me...*Delacroix's hair was long and white now, and his face seemed harder, less joyful—but it was him, just as youthful and unlined as the day he had been painted.

"Is something wrong, Trooper?" Delacroix said.

Janus was thrust back into reality, his hand still at the edge of his helmet. "Um...I'm sorry sir, but I can't..."

Middleton perked up, staring intently at Janus. "And why not?"

"Because...because..." Janus tossed Alastor to the ground with a shudder, whining, "I'm sorry, Miss. I stole a bit of that sugary stuff on the stove, but—but when you asked me to pick,"—Janus motioned with his hand at Alastor and looked away—"him up, I threw up all over my visor. I didn't want anyone to know. But now, because of disease protocol, I can't open it without a trip to the armory..."

As if on cue, Marcus laughed, and the other Troopers followed suit. Soon the entire room was laughing. Except Middleton, who stepped away repulsed.

Delacroix glanced at her with an amused expression, and smiled at Janus. "You may go."

As Janus turned, from the corner of his eye he caught Delacroix's hand quickly flash a symbol.

Janus dove to the ground, sliding as a Zeus round screamed overhead. Martel was firing at him, reacting to Delacroix's command.

Celes and Marcus flung open the weapons crate, while Ramirez and Lyn quickly levered one of the cryochambers onto its side and across the back of the car. The Troopers were moving slowly, still not grasping the magnitude of what was happening, and Janus rolled to his feet, dodging sideways to make him a harder target.

Celes immediately returned fire while Marcus tossed a weapon to Ramirez, who caught it with one hand and tossed the closest Trooper away with the other. Martel's Zeus hit all round him, but Celes's fire kept him occupied, shielding his visor from the fire peppering him.

As Janus scrambled towards the railcar, Lyn and Marcus also began firing, urging him on. Ramirez hit the switch for the track and leaped into the driver's seat, setting the railcar rolling. An impact struck Janus in the middle of his chest as he flopped over the cryochamber, and he caught a glimpse of Delacroix's pistol flashing with an ornately wrought bird carved into it.

"Janus!"

Celes fired back at the Executor, but he had already stepped back behind Martel, using the large armor as his own cover. Martel, firmly planted with his arm over his visor, and up against the team's Skadis, might as well have been a solid wall.

And finally, the rest of the Troopers joined in, and a hail of Zeus fire rained upon them. The team hunkered down, waiting for the inevitable, for the weapons to tear them to shreds. But there was only the sound of bolts *plinking* unexpectedly off of the Cryochambers.

"They're bouncing off!" Marcus yelled, pressing himself even closer to the floor.

"They—they must be made of Immutium!" Celes crouched over Janus, staring at him.

But all further conversation was silenced as the railcar accelerated loudly into the tunnel, Delacroix screaming in anger after them.

CHAPTER 17
OUT OF THE DARK

The car raced through the mountain, craggy rock whizzing over the team's heads. The noise was deafening.

After a moment, Janus groaned intensely.

"You're alive!" Lyn yelled.

"Are you okay?" Celes bellowed loudly to be heard over the screeching of the railcar. Ramirez was sending them down the track at a breakneck pace.

Janus took a moment to look at his midsection. There was a huge hole in his Trooper armor. But underneath, his Adept armor held, though it looked a little worse for wear.

"It's a good thing that wasn't a Zeus round," Marcus shouted over the din.

Janus nodded.

"Where do you think we're going?" Lyn shouted.

"Through the mountain, to a hangar on the other side," Marcus cried back.

Janus agreed in his head, taking a moment to recuperate. *They must be transporting the chambers somehow.*

Dim lights rushed by overhead as the tunnel sloped upward, but the car continued to accelerate. Janus felt his breath recover and sat up. After a moment, he clamored up to the front of the car next to Ramirez.

"How long until they can follow us?"

Ramirez shook his head. "Not very. Couldn't disable the track switch. A minute?"

Janus grimaced. "We'll have to move fast. Do whatever you need to do."

Ramirez grunted, keeping his eyes on the track.

A bright light appeared at the end of the tunnel.

"Get ready for a hot welcome!" Janus shouted over the rushing wind. "There's probably more Troopers waiting!"

The others moved forward, joining him just behind Ramirez, just as the tunnel opened into a large, well-lit cavern with a raised landing pad and a massive Behemoth transport. Its six giant, rectangular engines were already humming, ready to lift the great belly of the beast. A full dozen Inferni waited at the end of the line, ready for the next shipment of Cryochambers.

Lyn grabbed Ramirez's shoulder and he nodded. She turned to the other three. "Brace yourselves!"

All five hunkered down, and Ramirez slammed the brakes, the loose cryochamber sliding dangerously forward. Janus was nearly thrown from the car.

Several things happened at once. Lyn shouted, "Jump!" The Inferni, suddenly aware that something was wrong, raised their weapons at the railcar. And Ramirez hit the accelerator again.

The team leaped from the hurtling train, firing at the Inferni as they went. Janus rolled roughly, tumbling and sliding towards the wall.

The shocked Troopers were unprepared for the resulting physical reality of the railcar as it slammed into the end of the track and flipped, sending tons of Immutium crashing down upon their heads. Some continued to fire at the car, others desperately fired rockets at the hail of cryochambers. None moved quickly enough. The resulting noise, explosions, and wanton destruction shook the dust from the walls, filling the cavern.

Pulling himself up by the crate of Zeus bolts he had rolled into, Janus made a quick check—only twitching, clawed hands and limp two-toed boots could be seen. He took stock of himself. His helmet visor had shattered. His rifle was gone. His left arm hung uselessly and his shoulder was in excruciating pain. *Why is it always my shoulder?*

He brushed it aside and whispered into his mic, "Everyone okay?" Static. Janus reached inside of his helmet with his good arm and ripped out the broken headset, a piece of his visor firmly embedded in it.

The screech of metal on metal rang out as a clawed hand reached around a cryochamber and began to slowly push the ominous shape of an Infernus from the wreckage. Janus ripped his helmet off and struggled to find Rogers's Ghostblade in the wreckage. As the Infernus's red visor emerged from the debris, Janus knew he only had moments to deal with the threat before—

"Janus, down!" Marcus cried.

Janus dropped like a stone and the Infernus whirled at the noise. A sudden burst from a Skadi rifle smashed through the demon's visor and dropped it back into the heap of Cryochambers. Janus carefully rolled onto his uninjured side to see Marcus upside down and clutching a Skadi rifle to his shoulder, his boot caught between two crates, leaving him stuck. Janus got to his feet and pulled Marcus upright with his good hand.

"Thanks. You okay?"

Marcus coughed. "Fine. You?"

"Shoulder."

"Everyone else?" Marcus asked.

Celes came limping out of the dusty fog. "Ramirez and Lyn are over here."

Lyn was tending to a gash in Ramirez's side, which if the number of faces he was making was any indication, was clearly causing him great pain. "Stupid Infernus. We nearly got away scot free, and he had ta go fire a rocket at us." Lyn grimaced.

Ramirez pulled out a jagged triangle of shrapnel from the side of his armor and quickly pinched close the vessel that had been bleeding profusely.

"Marcus, find us a way out of here," Janus said before turning to Ramirez. "Can you move?"

"Sure." Clenching his side, and with assistance from Lyn, he stood slowly. A sudden shift caused him to grunt loudly. Lyn gritted her teeth into an awkward smile. "Well, we didn't say anything about doing it quietly."

"Over here, the Behemoth's ready to fly," Marcus yelled. The sounds of another railcar approaching filtered down the tunnel. Making sure Ramirez was good to stand, Lyn leaped over a railing to a control panel by the wall. High above them, solid doors opened in the cavern, and further up, Janus could see daylight. The pad was deep in the mouth of the cavern.

"Time to go," Celes said. Marcus warmed up the ship as Ramirez, Lyn, Celes, and Janus made their way over.

"Too bad we lost Alastor's body, Janus," Marcus said from the pilot's chair. "Any Inferni survive we could capture?"

Janus looked back at the scattered wreckage and shook his head. "No time to search." Marcus turned back to the controls. "Wait." Janus held a hand up, struck by a sudden thought. He jumped off the transport and raced over to the scattered cryochambers, his arm swinging wildly back and forth, his adrenaline still pumping too hard to notice. He scanned the destruction, and spotted it. He clamored over to a cryochamber that had ended its careening journey against a wall. The chamber was undamaged—its control panel was not. Reaching in, he yanked out a cracked isotope drive. He gave the broken, translucent chip a doubtful glance, and then with the sound of the railcar ringing in his ears, clamored back to the Behemoth.

"Go!"

The Titan transport leaped into the air, its claw-like landing gear pulling in like tiny legs on a massive insect and hovered just over the surface of the bay as the second railcar arrived. Marcus pushed the throttle to maximum and the unladen transport shot off as Martel and several squads of STs arrived. In a moment, the team cleared the doors, squeezed through the cavern mouth, and emerged out over a giant mountain lake.

"Nice view," Marcus remarked, banking the craft as it quickly reached its slow and steady top speed.

Janus helped Celes secure the Behemoth's door, then turned to Ramirez. He leaned against the wall of the large transport. Lyn perched on a jump seat next to him and gently probed his side.

"Celes, do you mind taking over?" Janus asked. "Lyn, you're unhurt, so you should be up front, acting as co-pilot. If anything happens, Marcus might need you." Ramirez grunted in agreement and Lyn moved towards the cockpit, gazing back for a second as she did so.

"Thanks for the cover."

Ramirez simply nodded.

"Let's hope your help won't be necessary." Marcus looked over at her with wry expression. Lyn strapped into the chair and began checking the controls.

"With ya there."

"Keep an eye on the—" He glanced down at a glowing screen between the pair. "Incoming!"

"Alastor's Typhons!" Lyn exclaimed, glancing back through the side window.

"They're pinging us on radar and locking on!"

"Ramirez, get into the other jump seat, and both of you strap in," Janus ordered, and then moved to the front, leaning on the co-pilot's chair and letting his bad arm hang.

"Get low," he said to Marcus. "We might be slow, but without any cargo, I bet this transport can turn on a dime. Get us back into the mountains."

"Already on it. I wouldn't have thought they would come out this far," Marcus said through gritted teeth.

The Behemoth banked, heading for the edge of the craggy valley. Janus moved a step back and grabbed a handle that jutted out from the bulkhead between the pilot's chairs and the cargo area.

"The SPARTAN forces might have driven them this way," Lyn added grimly. "Engines at full power. They've got a lock!"

The Typhons fired as Marcus desperately dodged. Linked Zeus cannons peppered the transport, rounds flashing through the cabin. Janus instinctively ducked, although the thin armor of the transport might as well have been paper. "Everyone okay?" Janus yelled as Marcus banked again.

But there wasn't time for a response.

"Missile lock!" Lyn yelled.

Marcus rolled the craft into a steep dive, and Janus felt himself yanked from his handhold. He tumbled helplessly around the cabin, narrowly avoiding one of the heavy supports forming the skeleton of the ship. His injured shoulder collided with a wall, and he nearly blacked out from the pain. Sucking in his breath, Celes grabbed him, and yanked him into her lap, wrapping her arms and legs around him.

Another hail of fire hit the ship and the canopy shattered, engulfing Marcus in a wave of jagged glass.

"Marcus!" Lyn screamed, lunging forward to wrestle the controls. Alarms sounded throughout the cabin as Lyn struggled to pull the craft from its dive. She pulled them up as they entered the valleys of the mountains, just as the left engine exploded from the strain. The Typhons screamed past them and up, suddenly going far too fast for the narrow rocks and slow transport.

Marcus emerged from the glass, decidedly bloody. "I'm fine," he assured them. "The heavy stuff got stopped by my armor."

Through the canopy, the wind rushing in their faces, the team could see the Typhons make long, wide loops, coming around for the kill. Janus felt his heart sink. There was nowhere to go. Lyn tensed for a last-ditch dive.

A streak from above caught them all by surprise, and suddenly the left Typhon exploded into a fireball. The right immediately veered away.

"Look!" Marcus cried. "Three o'clock!" Two sleek, spear-like ships came screaming in, chasing the remaining Typhon through the mountains.

"Achilles fighters," Ramirez said.

"SPARTAN!" Celes exclaimed happily.

Lyn chuckled. "Thanks, Delacroix!"

Janus, suddenly reminded of the mysterious man, grimaced. "Take us home, Lyn. I think we've had about enough of this for one day."

CHAPTER 18
PLANS AND PLOTS

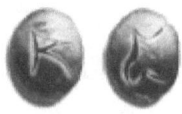

Valhalla had moved back over open ocean by the time the Behemoth transport managed to catch it. After intercepting the Longboat waiting at the rendezvous point, they had been unwilling to abandon the free transport, and so had limped back to Valhalla with Lyn and Celes constantly nursing the engines. Ramirez was moved over to the Longboat for medical treatment, and was eventually joined by Janus and Marcus, after Celes had volunteered to take over and assist Lyn. The three watched as the pair flew the heavy transport into the Dawn bay for storage and repairs. With the Behemoth safely tucked away, the Longboat raced around the glittering citadel into the Chariot of Voyages, where Hawkes waited to meet them.

"Lyn and Celes will meet us in the Praetor's briefing room. Assuming you can make it for another few minutes without medical attention, follow me," Hawkes growled as Janus hopped out. Janus looked grimly at his team, but Ramirez, Marcus, and Lyn nodded. Hawkes marched away, and the three fell into line behind him.

"Any word from Wouris?" Janus asked.

Hawkes shook his head and continued marching. They had returned early, so it wasn't necessarily a surprise.

A row of Longboats waited in the back of the Voyages bay, worked on by the most skilled mechanics in Valhalla. Valers, drenched in sweat and wearing one of the mech's uniforms—with a green stripe for engineering, and decked in tools—was wiping his hands free of grime and waiting for them.

"Valers," Marcus called, "what're you doing here?"

Valers hustled over, slowing to a walk beside the three. "Armory rotation. Just started, Wouris recommended me." He smiled. "I watched you guys fly in, figured you wouldn't mind a friendly face." He glanced at Hawkes, who scowled. "Was the mission successful?"

"Well—" Marcus said.

"You will get the debriefing when everyone else does—after the command staff," Hawkes interrupted, giving Valers a harrowing look. "Don't you have duties to perform?"

Valers did an about face and ran back to the waiting Longboats, calling out, "I'll be sure to go find some, sir."

The Praetor, Keats, Northcott, and another Adept waited for the team in the briefing room. Col. Keats wore a smile, but the Praetor and Major Northcott were more reserved. The unnamed Adept had long black hair, and her armor had a green stripe running along it. Light filtered through the thick dome skylights, and the bustle of Valhalla's command deck faded as the door shut.

"We are glad all of you made it back in one piece," Keats said. "You can head to the infirmary after the debriefing."

"We will try to make this as quick and painless as possible," the Praetor said. "Please have a seat."

Lyn and Celes jogged into the room at that moment, saluting in respect.

The Praetor saluted back. "Welcome back, Adepts."

The Praetor sat down at the round table, Keats on his left, North-cott on his right. Hawkes sat next to Keats. The unnamed Adept remained standing.

Major Northcott leaned forward. "Perhaps you would like to begin with Sergeant Wouris."

Janus shook his head. "I'm afraid I don't know where she is, sir." Janus gazed around the room. "But nothing would lead me to believe she is in direct danger. We arrived well before the deadline. Why?"

"Generally, our teams arrive together, and not bloodied from a fight," Northcott said pointedly.

Janus cleared his throat. "We separated due to one of my orders, sir, but at the time, there was nothing to indicate her team would be in any unexpected danger. In all honesty, I expect that when she returns she will have fared better than my team did."

"Then perhaps you should start from the beginning," Keats said calmly.

Janus focused his breathing and closed his eyes. The memory of the day flooded back into his mind, and he slowly recounted what had happened. Talking through the marsh and some of the close calls at the base, he stopped to explain the discovery of Norm in the painting.

"And who is this Norm?" Keats asked.

"An old man who lives in the Cerberus slums. He's known my mother for many years, although I only became more familiar with him just before I came here."

"And you're confident it was him in this painting?" Northcott asked.

"Yes, I recognized his face."

"He's that recognizable?" Hawkes said.

"Well, yes," Janus said, scrunching his face in thought. "It isn't that he looks strange—it's more like, his age has made him tired. The features were unmistakable, though he certainly looks older. In fact, I don't know anyone in the slums as old as him," Janus added, deep in thought.

"And this painting? Could you describe it?" Hawkes asked.

Janus glanced at the others nervously. Marcus was lost in thought; Lyn's face reflected a combination of fear and excitement; Ramirez simply nodded in support; Celes smiled at him.

"Well," Janus cleared his throat, "it was a battle scene. There were hundreds of Security Troopers celebrating a great victory over a fleeing enemy. All the cheering soldiers had the Phoenix emblem on their armor."

The Praetor sat forward.

"There were two figures featured in the middle and front of the scene—two Overlords, dressed in red and gold. They were both smiling, like they had been the victors. One was Norm, and the other..." Janus hesitated, thinking of Delacroix.

"—Someone who looked like Janus," Celes finished.

Janus gulped.

The Praetor narrowed his eyes. "How much like Janus?"

"Related features, just a few slight differences, hair and eye color, mostly," Marcus said.

The officers murmured to each other around the oak table.

"It couldn't be..." the Praetor mused, holding his chin. He stared at Janus and shook his head. "It couldn't be."

Janus looked around anxiously. The Praetor waved a hand in apology, as if regretting his outburst. "Please continue."

Janus took another moment to regain his composure. He swiftly recounted the events after they found the painting, the discovery of the secret base, and the team's harrowing escape.

"Did anyone get a look at Delacroix's face? After your encounter with the Titan Executor down in Phoenix, it would be nice if we had a better picture of who we are up against," Keats interrupted.

Janus paused, struggling not to shift in his seat. He was about to speak when he noticed the others shaking their heads. "He stood too close to Janus, and we couldn't move much without attracting attention," Marcus said. Janus nodded. "But he did somehow know our hand signals," Marcus added in concern.

Hawkes sat up. "He knew our signals?"

The group nodded.

"Seemed like only that Novus, Martel, knew to respond, however," Lyn added.

"What did he—" Hawkes went silent at the Praetor's raised hand.

"But as you described him prior, he has white hair?" the Praetor asked.

All five nodded.

A distant look came over Jennings's face, and he glanced at Janus again.

Janus cleared his throat and pulled out the translucent green drive he had pulled from the wreckage of the railcar. "This, sir, is the isotope drive I pulled from a cryochamber." He handed the drive to Keats. "Hopefully, it will contain something more."

"Well done," Northcott said. He studied the four around Janus. "And the way you worked together suggests any fears we might have had were misplaced."

Celes and Lyn beamed. Even Ramirez had a slight grin on his hard jaw. Marcus simply inclined his head.

"You've given us a quite a few clues, to start," the Praetor added. "Cryochambers—surely it couldn't mean effective cryogenics?"

"Cryogenics, sir?" Lyn asked, the confusion stamped upon her face.

The Praetor nodded. "The study and implementation of preserving life through carefully calibrated freezing." He stood up and kneaded his hand, as if he were confirming that he wasn't somehow dreaming.

"It is an ancient, rather unsuccessful science. I know Chiles and Graham have even attempted it. All we ended up with was a bunch of frozen rats."

"ODIN has tried to create cryogenic chambers?" Celes looked skeptical. "But why?"

"Every Corporation and Adept Legion has tried to make it work," the Praetor said knowingly. "Cryogenics is one of those technologies associated with the fountain of youth. It's a crude method, one that only buys time for something better, but I can't say I blame some for trying. ODIN's primary interest in cryogenics, however, was for battlefield medicine. If we can slow down or stop the biological processes enough on the battlefield, we could always get an injured Adept back in enough time for an effective Nanyte treatment. If we could succeed with Cryogenics, barring catastrophic head trauma, every Adept on the battlefield could be saved.

"But that requires us getting it to work." The Praetor sighed. "Anyway, every few years, someone else will attempt it, but inevitably fail. We usually learn about it through our contacts or by Corporations attempting to sell their research to us. The reason is always the same: expensive, impractical, ineffective."

"Especially if it requires so much Immutium," Marcus added. "But how do we know that Titan has made it work? Assuming Titan controls the Phoenix and Lightemann's bases."

"The Corporations aren't stupid. If Titan has put so many people into storage at such a high cost, you can bet it works," Northcott said.

"But why the secrecy? It is certainly noteworthy, and undoubtedly useful. But if Titan has developed it, why risk exposure by working with Cerberus?" Keats mused.

"I don't like having my enemies working together," Hawkes growled.

Keats looked at the Praetor. 'We should consider alerting the other Legions about this—"

"Only after we've looked at the isotope drive," the Praetor interrupted. "We may have a great deal of valuable information to offer, but it is only valuable if the other Legions see it that way. We Adepts are no more allied now than before the Phoenix Corporation attack on SHADE."

The Praetor's face reflected a fury Janus had never seen before, and Keats quickly motioned the unnamed Adept, who had been standing for the duration, holding up the translucent drive. "Sergeant Oleri, take this to the tech sergeants for analysis, if you would."

"Yes, sir." Oleri carefully took hold of the drive. "I'll let you know as soon as we know something." With a turn on her heel, she left.

"Now," the Praetor said, returning his gaze to Janus and the rest of the team, "report to the infirmary and get prepped to head back out. As soon as we can move into position, you're being deployed to Cerberus."

Keats looked at the Praetor skeptically. "Now?"

Janus sat bolt upright in his seat.

The Praetor's look was deadly serious. "We can't afford to be caught flat-footed."

"Are you sure about this?" Hawkes asked.

The Praetor glared at the Colonel for a moment.

Janus glanced around the table uncertainly, and then realized the Praetor was looking directly at him.

"Cerberus is the next logical step. Middleton will be forced to return to deal with the Executors. If we can get into Cerberus, we may be able to catch her off guard. And this man named Norm, you've already said he is there is well. It appears he may know far more than you realized, Janus. We have a brief window where we know exactly where several of our key players will be."

"What about Wouris?" Northcott asked irritably.

The Praetor gave a hard glance to Northcott, but finally relented. "Sergeant Wouris is no doubt perfectly well. However, we will leave behind a Longboat and a couple of Adepts in case she attempts to make contact." Northcott relaxed visibly. "I am sure we will have no shortage of volunteers," the Praetor added.

"And what about getting into Cerberus? That won't be an easy task. Sneaking into outposts and sneaking into a Corporation are different beasts entirely," Northcott added.

The Praetor stared at Janus. "I believe we have an expert on that."

Northcott nodded in agreement. "Hmmmm, yes, that does seem like it might work."

Celes, Marcus, Lyn, and Ramirez all stared at Janus in confusion. Janus felt at a loss.

"Now, Major, if you have no further questions, I want you to begin campaign preparations."

Northcott nodded. "I'll alert Tuorneg and begin right now." Major Tuorneg was the control deck commander, and responsible for all of Valhalla's movement around the world, among other things.

Northcott quickly saluted and left the briefing room, heading into Valhalla's command center.

Hawkes looked at the Praetor. "Do you really expect it to be that bad?"

"I suppose we'll soon see." He glanced at Keats and then back to Hawkes. "Any other questions?"

Hawkes sighed and shook his head.

"Then you know what to do."

Hawkes and Keats stood up simultaneously and saluted. "Sir!"

The Praetor stood and returned their salute. Then he looked at the five remaining Adepts. Janus knew it was time to leave and stood.

"Good work, Lieutenant." He nodded to the others. "All of you. Colonel Yalla is waiting for you. Dismissed."

Five smart salutes. As they left, Janus heard the Praetor say, "Valhalla, display Jennings's personal effect number one."

As the door closed behind them, Janus heard Val say, "Aye, Praetor," and glimpsed a picture of a beautiful brown-eyed woman. The last thing he saw was the Praetor staring at it, deep in thought.

CHAPTER 19
QUESTIONS UNANSWERED

"The Praetor's sending you out again?" Colonel Yalla asked skeptically. The setting sun filtered through a window in the medical wing, casting his white hair in an orange light. His back was turned to Janus, but he could hear the frustration in Yalla's voice.

"Yes, sir. We're supposed to get patched up and ready to head out again," Janus stated for the second time.

Yalla was hunched over one of the Nanyte dispensers, shaking his head. He turned to one of his medics. "Get Alexander on the line."

The medic paled a little bit, but immediately hopped into action. Janus looked at the others in confusion. Yalla turned and stared at the torn-up team, folding his arms across his chest. "You should have been sent to me immediately."

It didn't take long until the attendant poked his head around the corner. "Sir, the Praetor's on the line."

Yalla unfurled a parchment screen to his left, and Janus could see Praetor Jennings on the other side looking rather fierce.

"Alex."

"Colonel, how may I help you?" The Praetor paused and took notice of Janus and his team behind Yalla. "Good to see all of you getting fixed up."

Yalla threw his hands up. "That's the problem! You know as well as I do where they're at with doses. I send you a report as soon as individuals start hitting their limits. Nearly the entire team's going to be brushing up against their monthly maxes. Once I treat them, half this team can't get any more Nanyte injections for at least three weeks. You can't risk sending them out again."

Janus did a quick count and realized how often he had been getting injections. He looked at the team, they all had been getting beat up quite a bit over the past few weeks. More so than normal.

Jennings shook his head. "I'm sorry, Colonel, but we don't have many options here. The Lieutenant and his team have proved indispensable, and they are going to be needed once again."

"You're putting them at risk! I won't treat them, if that's what it takes. You won't send them out in their current condition, I know that much!"

Marcus coughed uncomfortably. He had been sown up, but there were some nasty gashes on his face that he probably didn't want to have to deal with for much longer. And Ramirez was certainly going to have a problem working at full capacity with his side as it was. Lyn was in the best shape, and even she could probably use a touch up from their past mission.

"I can, and I will. I know I can't force you to cooperate, and your medics will follow your lead, but I'll come down there myself and administer the doses if I have to. There is too much at stake, I'm afraid." Jennings rubbed his forehead. He suddenly seemed very tired. "I know your complaints and the risks, Colonel. If I didn't think this was the course that would be best for ODIN, I wouldn't be doing it."

Yalla looked back at the team and then up at the ceiling.

"They won't be going in alone," Jennings continued. "I've already spoken to Captain Rogers. He'll be joining them. But we absolutely need Janus. And in that case, his best chance is to have his team."

Janus instinctively reached for the Ghostblade strapped to his back and suddenly winced. Rogers would not be happy to hear about the mission. He returned his focus to the Praetor and Yalla and realized that Jennings had fallen silent staring at the old medic. After a few tense moments, Yalla sighed.

"I'll patch them up. But I'm giving them the absolute minimum. They'll be running on fumes for a few days, so I suggest you give them some time to rest."

"They'll have two days, but I'll make sure they aren't given any duties."

"Suppose that's the best I'll get."

The Praetor gave him a gracious nod. "Thank you, Colonel."

"You're welcome. And Alex?"

The Praetor paused as if he were about to disconnect. "Yes?"

"You should get some rest. You look terrible."

"Good night, Colonel."

The screen went black and Yalla turned to the team. "Well, let's get to work then."

Janus's arm still ached horribly, but he could feel it being mended by the Nanytes as it sat in the sling Yalla had provided. It was an odd sensation, as his arm seemed to waver back and forth between the extremes of pain and feeling better as the nerves in his arm were repaired.

Stopping along the branch from the hospital ward, Lyn turned to face the group. "Well, I guess we better get some res—" She stopped suddenly, staring at the team as they hobbled after her. Covering her mouth, she grabbed her sides and bit her lip.

"It's not funny," Ramirez said.

Lyn burst out laughing. "I've never seen ya like this, Ramirez. And the rest of ya…" She leaned against the rail.

Ramirez folded his arms against his chest, made an uncomfortable face, and lowered his arms again. Lyn laughed louder. "I'm sorry Ramirez. I really am. But ya'll will recover, and ya just look so pathetic."

Janus looked around. Celes was limping along, wearing a thick boot. Marcus still looked as though he had mistakenly cornered a rabid wolverine. And try as he might, Ramirez made a deep grunt with every breath, though he at least walked tall with some dignity. And suddenly more aware of the surroundings, Janus could see a few concerned Adepts watching them from afar, ready to rush over if one of them collapsed. Their little group looked anything but heroic.

For the first time in a long while, Janus laughed. They had survived, and mostly intact.

"We all made it!" Celes said with a great big smile.

"You know you didn't do half bad," Marcus said, throwing an arm around Janus. "Though pretty sure I could have done better."

Janus winced and danced away.

Marcus gritted his teeth. "Sorry."

After Janus had recovered, he waved a hand at him. "Come over here, Marcus, you've got something on your face."

Suddenly aware of his discomfort, Marcus raised a hand, and then lowered it in frustration and growled at him. Yalla had been adamant that his face would heal, but he had advised strongly against scratching.

The nearby Adepts all turned away, shaking heads, but with smiles on their faces.

Janus stared out at the Trunk and looked up at the great Red Eye. A sobering thought hit him, *But what about Wouris?* Janus looked at the group of four around him, still laughing at their absurdity, and realized that if he could get back with his team intact, he had no reason to be concerned. He chuckled to himself, *Wouris is probably already at Cerberus.*

They had all been too tired to eat and Janus awoke to a hunger he hadn't felt since he had lived in the slums. Even the pain of his shoulder hadn't been enough to keep him from falling asleep. Slipping from his bed, he found the common room empty, and returned to his room to better size himself up. He had pretty much collapsed into bed, not even bothering to change from his armor and, staring into the mirror, he realized how frightening the team must have looked last night and decided it might be best to grab a shower and clean up before heading to the mess. Plus, the fact that he couldn't smell himself suggested that he probably hadn't been this fresh since he was last in the slums.

"Val."

The Daedulus system awoke in his room. "Yes, Lieutenant?"

Now that he was awake, he realized there was something he wanted to do first.

"Have you heard of 'Victory at Lightemann's'?"

"I'm not familiar with that, Lieutenant. Would you like more information on Lightemann's Ridge?"

Janus pursed his lips in disappointment. "Sure."

"Lightemann's Ridge is the name now given to a portion of a larger mountain range called the Eastern Treaty Line and extends nearly five hundred km."

Janus looked at his terminal. "Why is it called that?"

"It was named after the conclusion of the period identified as 'The Fusion War.'"

"The Fusion War?"

"An ongoing conflict between the Corporations that involved Cerberus and Medusa against the remaining five Corporations."

Janus waited a moment and looked at the terminal incredulously. "And?"

"And what?" Val asked.

"What was the conflict about?"

"Presumably about fusion," Val answered in a voice that sounded awfully sarcastic.

"Don't you have any more information?"

"I have plenty of information. Just not necessarily about every random topic you decide to investigate on a whim. The Fusion War period happened many decades ago, and my records are dependent upon the Corporate histories we acquire."

Janus sighed. *It's never easy...*

"May I assist you in any other way, Lieutenant?" Val asked in a tone that suggested the Daedulus wanted to do anything but.

Janus smiled and stood directly in front of Val's camera. "Yes, actually..."

He spread his good arm wide, letting the computer get a full view of his ripped and torn armor, and severely unkempt look. The resulting noise from the somewhat ornery system made Janus think it had been unable to figure out whether to laugh or cry. A towel practically launched itself from a drawer, and a fresh uniform popped from the wall.

"Showers. NOW!"

He arrived at the mess to find the other four already digging into their breakfasts, looking much cleaner themselves. Grabbing a Passer called 'Bagel and Lox,' plus one called 'coffee cake,' he headed back out to their shared table. They were already deep in discussion about what they had found at Middleton's facility.

"Well, if it's that well protected, it's probably very interesting," Marcus said between bites of a Passer that had the consistency and flavor of oatmeal.

"Hopefully it gives some explanation as ta the nature of those chambers. It would be nice ta have some questions answered before new ones arise," Lyn said.

Janus looked at Celes as he sat down, carefully moving his arm to avoid bumping the table. "Cryochambers?"

She nodded. "Word came down that it's going to take a while to decipher the isotope drive. Apparently, Chiles and Graham haven't seen tech this old, or this encrypted, in some time. They're very excited."

"I wonder how much it will tell us about Middleton's and Delacroix's plans," Janus asked rhetorically.

"Magnus's plans," Marcus corrected with a wave of his fork. "They're on a first name basis."

"I'm not sure that tidbit will make a difference," Celes said looking at Marcus with a smile. She glanced at Janus. "But I suppose we shouldn't dismiss anything at this point. Perhaps that drive will tell us something about Phoenix and give us some clues about that painting."

Ramirez took a huge bite of his 'eggs' and grunted, "Too much ta hope for…"

Lyn nodded. "Yeah, unfortunately, we can't just expect all their plans ta be conveniently on one isotope drive. Especially since it was in just one of those chambers."

"No hope for 'SECRETS HERE'?" Marcus asked with a smirk. Lyn stuck her tongue out at him.

"Hope springs eternal," Celes said simply.

Marcus nodded with Celes and then sighed, poking his food. "Frankly, I'm not too keen about the idea of breaking into Cerberus."

"Ya telling me! An outpost is one thing, but a Corporation? Phah! And this time we won't have the advantage of the STs thinking no one even knows they're there," Lyn said.

"Nor the disorganization and chaos of unfamiliar Trooper squads all working together," Marcus added.

"Getting in is the real issue." Ramirez said succinctly.

Celes nodded in agreement. "If we can get the proper credentials and access, it won't matter how many Troopers there are, they'll let us pass. Which reminds me…" She looked over at Janus. "How does the Praetor think you're going to get us in?"

Janus rolled the remaining half of his 'bagel' around on his plate. The answer had come to him last night as they had listened to Colonel Yalla and the Praetor argue. It was actually fairly obvious.

"Janus?"

Janus looked up. Lyn, Ramirez, and Celes were staring at him. Marcus had a wry smile on his face but wasn't looking at him.

"Sorry. I heard you. I was just thinking about it…it's actually fairly simple. All of the Corporations have a major security weakness they all discount."

"The slums," Marcus interjected. He looked up at Janus. "No Corporation ever fully patrols or monitors the slums."

Janus met eyes with Marcus. But only for a moment, then he nodded in agreement towards the rest of the team. "With the right look, we can simply walk into the slums, and no one will even look twice."

"But what about the lifts?" Celes asked. "How are we supposed to gain access to the upper levels?"

Janus hesitated and Marcus rolled his eyes. After a moment, Janus sighed. "Clara has access to the upper levels. We can use her to get into Middleton's estate. And Norm lives in Persephone, so we should be able to reach him as well."

Lyn made a little 'ah' sound. Ramirez shrugged. "Seems like a decent plan to me."

But Celes tilted her head. "Clara? Your mother? Why would she be... oh." She paused for a moment, and the table went quiet. Janus looked back down at his plate.

Celes swallowed awkwardly and looked around at the others, avoiding Janus's eyes. "Well, I agree with Ramirez. I think it's a solid plan."

Janus nodded. "Yeah, well, seems like things just lined up perfectly for it."

Celes nodded uncomfortably. After a moment, she stood up, grabbing her tray. "You know, I'm feeling pretty full already. I might just go find a place to read up on Cerberus. Prepare myself for the mission."

Without waiting for a reply, she quickly deposited her tray on the dishwasher line and left the hall.

Lyn watched her go and then turned to Janus. "When we first met, I thought ya were from another village of Outskirters. I don't think our lives were all that different in many ways." Ramirez nodded in agreement. Lyn looked at him and then added, "If anything, being here shows how little the Corporations know about people anyway."

Janus smiled slightly.

Ramirez leaned forward. "One of our elders came from the slums. Chimera. Didn't like ta speak about it much."

Janus raised his head.

"Based on her, I would say that anyone who underestimates someone based on their social status is making a big mistake," Ramirez said.

"And that to get here says a lot about you," Lyn added.

The sound of Marcus standing up pulled her attention away.

"Something wrong?" Lyn asked in confusion.

Marcus lifted up his tray, and slowly shook his head. "Just... just needed to stretch my legs. I think I'm going to go for a walk."

Ramirez looked at Lyn. "I'll come along," he said.

Marcus hesitated and then nodded. Ramirez quickly got up and the pair left the mess, Janus and Lyn staring after them.

"Seems like everyone's got something on their mind..." She looked troubled. After a moment of watching her stare off into space, Janus shook his head. *Still a mint...*

"And how... are you doing with all of this?" he asked hesitantly.

"Me?" Lyn seemed surprised. "Oh, I'm fine. I mean, breaking into Cerberus won't be easy. But frankly, it's something we always wanted ta try."

"You and Ramirez?"

She laughed. "Of course! Whenever we raided some Corporate outpost, we always wondered if we could go bigger. Bring something better home for everyone. But it would have been too risky. Too big an undertaking. And Ramirez, well he's always been concerned with everyone around him. I guess it comes with the territory." She paused and looked around at all the other Adepts at their tables. "When you're the biggest and strongest, people either fear ya, or depend on ya. One way or the other, he has ta act carefully."

"So what about you?"

Lyn took a big gulp of water from her mug. "I guess I never really treated him differently. That's why he likes it here. He doesn't always have to be the leader." She shrugged and looked at the tray of food he left behind. "He can be himself." She grabbed it over and began shoveling the leftover eggs into her mouth. "And I... can be... myself."

Janus laughed. "I guess that's true. I've never really thought about that." He looked through the windows of the mess, out at the morning sun. "Well, I'm glad I've got you at my back."

Lyn looked up from her food for a moment and mumbled through a mouthful, "Well, we try."

"Not sure we would have made it out of there without the two of you working your magic."

Lyn flushed slightly and stopped eating. "Well, I'm just glad we all got out okay."

Janus stared at her in curiosity.

"What?" she asked.

"Sorry, I just wondered—are you ever worried about him?"

She looked in the direction Ramirez and Marcus had traveled, and her demeanor became much more serious. "We've been through a lot together. We watch each other's back, and we've always known there were risks." She eyed Janus's uneaten half-bagel. Janus pushed it over to her with a smile. "But I'm not worried about him." She picked up the bagel and pointed it at him. "As long as we're together, ya won't need ta worry about either of us."

She took a big bite of the doughy concoction. "It seems ta me…like ya've got nothing…ta be ashamed of… Done pretty well so far."

Janus looked sheepish, and then said, "Well, I try."

She gulped down the bite.

"Well, maybe ya should try and talk ta Celes then."

"Uhhh…" Janus wasn't sure how to respond.

She waved the bagel as if to shoo him away.

Janus stood up. "This is how you treat Ramirez all the time, isn't it?"

She gave him a dangerous look and said, "He knows when ta listen."

Janus wandered away from the mess, wondering where Celes could have gone.

The common room was empty. Jones sat alone, reading a tablet.

"Has Celes come this way?"

Jones looked up from the armchair she occupied, and then shook her head. "No one's been through here since I got off duty."

"Thanks."

Jones nodded and then went back to her reading.

He decided to check the Garden next. Taking a lift up the trunk, he watched several squads jogging around the central canal, and felt odd not to be doing the same. Even with his arm in a sling, he felt compelled to train. Already it was feeling much better, but Yalla had been adamant. Leave it in the sling as long as possible. Janus suspected that the Colonel would have given the same order whether they had been intended to ship out in two days or twenty. He wouldn't need that long.

Stepping through the heavy door, Janus caught the bright morning sunlight directly into his eyes. After a moment, his vision recovered, but was disappointed to find no trace of Celes. Her rock was empty, and the large willow sat silently in the morning air. A few Adepts wandered around, clearly enjoying the cool morning, but he doubted Celes had even come up here.

Janus scratched his head. Where could she have gone?

Do you even know her that well?

A little whisper of doubt came from the back of his mind. *What does she think about? What does she think about you?*

Janus swallowed. He walked back to the Trunk and stared out over the myriad branches. The many places within Valhalla.

"Lieutenant, you appear to be lost."

Janus started. He hadn't heard anyone around him, but as he looked around, he was alone. Only the smooth stone-like outside of the trunk sat behind him. A trickling stream of water cascading down the trunk splashed down just a bit further away.

"Can I help you, Lieutenant?" The voice came from a wall speaker.

"Val, is that you?"

"Yes, Lieutenant. May I help you?"

A screen lit up on the trunk, and Janus approached it.

"Uh… were you watching me?"

"I track all of the new Adepts and Cadets."

"All the time?"

"Yes. Many Adepts choose to turn off this feature, although I still track door entries as a matter of security."

"I... had no idea."

Val's voice sounded concerned. "Most Cadets from Corporations are aware of similar systems. Corporate Daedulus are usually more limited..." Janus could swear he could hear a hint of smugness in Val's voice, "but they are employed in certain areas. I had you marked as coming from Cerberus, is there a mistake in my database?"

Janus shook his head. "No." He paused. "I'm just not from one of the places that happens."

"I shall make a note then for the future."

"Is that all?"

"Yes?" Val sounded confused.

Janus looked around—he was still alone. "I thought you might to know why."

"Is that important?"

Janus stared at the glowing screen for a moment.

"Lieutenant? Is that important?"

He shook his head. "No, no. I guess it isn't. You just shouldn't assume someone from a Corporation knows these things. Or someone from anywhere, really."

"Noted. Thank you for your input, Lieutenant. Did you need anything else?"

Janus shook his head. "No. That's all."

"Okay, then—"

"Wait!" Janus raised a hand.

"Yes, Lieutenant?" Val's voice was flat.

"Could you locate Adept Celes for me?"

"Certainly, Adept Celes is in the Dawn Bay."

"Thanks, Val. I really appreciate it." Janus ran off, waving a hand behind him.

"Certainly, Lieutenant." Val's voice trailed off behind him. If he had waited longer, he might have heard the 'hmph' that followed.

The sound of rifle rounds echoed around the empty landing bay. The Dawn Bay, or 'Chariot of Dawn' as it was known by the two runes that marked it, was mostly used for storage.

"I thought you were going to read up on Cerberus."

Celes looked up from her prone position on the floor of the bay, but she didn't smile. Before her, the open door exposed yellow rays filtering through rolling clouds. A silver practice drone hovered out over a jagged coastline.

"Hey." She was holding a Vider long rifle, a much larger, more powerful variant than the Skadi rifles they normally deployed with. "I changed my mind. Thought I would practice with this."

Janus sat down next to her. "Oh?"

"If I had brought this, we might have been able to cut off our problems at the source. Close enough range and this can penetrate Infernus armor."

Janus thought about how the Novus named Martel had shielded Delacroix from their weapons and shook his head. "It's not guaranteed. And Martel's armor looked top of the line. Besides, that rifle doesn't make it easy to sneak around."

"Some of the more senior Adepts have done it."

Janus sighed and shrugged. "Well, if I had been able to reach Rogers's Ghostblade, that also might have solved our problem. Assuming that would have solved anything at all."

Janus felt like that was something Clara would say, and he stared out over the crashing waves. The clouds were rolling in quickly. He suspected that if he asked Lyn, they might be due for rain.

"You also probably would have died."

"At least I wouldn't owe him a Ghostblade then," Janus joked.

Celes's face did not change, and she suddenly looked away, focusing on the sight on her weapon.

He suddenly felt as though he was standing directly in one of those shining rays and felt very uncomfortable. He looked back at the rifle, trying to think of what to say. And Clara popped into his head once more. He looked down.

"Clara's really going to like you."

Celes turned back to look at him. "She'll like me?"

"Well, all of you. When you meet her," Janus stammered. "She'll be happy to know I've met so many people and that you keep me from doing anything too stupid."

Celes smiled weakly. "That's true." Her eyes still shone bright, but she looked as though she were about to cry. "I'm sorry that I didn't realize like everyone else where you were from. I'm sorry I made everything awkward."

Looking at her Janus couldn't understand why he felt compelled to laugh. She scowled.

Janus shook his head. "You? Don't give yourself too much credit. I'm the one who acted all secretive."

Her scowl was quickly replaced by a smirk. "There you go again. Trying to take all the credit."

Janus shrugged. "That's me. I'm the best, remember?"

She sat up. "Someone's got to keep you in order."

Janus nodded at the rifle again. He could almost hear Clara ask the question for him. "So why the rifle? Other than obscure chances to take out secret Executors cowering behind Inferni?"

She sighed and lifted the rifle. "It's my specialty. I realized today how little I know. Figured I might as well be good at something."

Janus looked at her quizzically and she looked up at the sky.

"Lyn's our scout, our survivalist. It's clear even Major Winters realizes how skilled she is. Ramirez is our heavy hitter. He can keep people calm and steady, and if something big comes up, he can knock it aside. Marcus, well, not only is he skilled, but he knows the Corporations. He understands Troopers and Inferni. He was one. More so than what we learned from Colonel Keats, he knows how they will act. He knows how they think."

She pointed at him. "And not to give you an even bigger head, but there's a reason you're a lieutenant. You see problems differently. You have good instincts."

She looked at the rifle. "And I'm…"

Janus raised a hand.

"Good at giving perspective. Helping teammates see their mistakes and how to learn from them. Knows a bunch of Corporate history and knowledge that catches even our most experienced officers off guard. And quickly becoming one of the best shots in Valhalla. So it seems to me like you need to dial it back, and let the rest of us catch up."

For the first time since they were on the Longboats to Lightemann's Ridge, Celes truly smiled. Her bright beautiful smile. And Janus felt like a weight lifted from his chest. They didn't say anything for a few moments, and Janus watched as dark clouds began to coalesce along the horizon.

"Thanks, Janus."

Janus got up and pointed at his chest with a smile. "Lieutenant, remember."

Celes made a stiff formal salute and said, "Thanks, Lieutenant Janus."

Janus laughed. "Come on, I think we're supposed to be resting, so let's go find the others."

CHAPTER 20
THE CHAMBERS

The announcement came suddenly a few days later.

"Come on," Marcus said. "Colonel Keats is waiting for us."

Janus sat up from his chair in the common room. "We're deploying?"

Marcus was already headed out the door. "Guess we'll find out."

Colonel Keats awaited the team at the top of Valhalla, at Odin's Torch.

"Good. I'm glad you came so quickly."

Passing through the main bridge, Major Tuorneg gave them a slight nod, then resumed her seemingly eternal watch. The little group headed into the main officer's room, and Janus looked around, surprised to find it empty.

"The Praetor has more to do than constantly brief your team, Janus," Keats said seriously.

Janus quickly sat down as the MuDi in the center of the large table created a holographic image of a fiery bird, wreathed in flames and surrounded by the words '*pax misericordis, bellus invictum.*'

"Chiles and Graham worked day and night to pull as much data as they could off the isotope drive." Keats pointed to the strange symbol.

"Latin—merciful peace, invincible war. It's an old Phoenix Corporation motto."

The MuDi changed and warped, revealing one of the cryochambers. "We pieced this together from the command codes on the chamber, and your description of the dimensions," Keats said.

It looked like a pretty close approximation, though Janus had the feeling one or two details were off. After a moment, part of the casket-like device was cut away to reveal the inside

The chamber was tightly packed, seemingly bereft of a place for a person inside. The chamber began to rotate, showing different angles, and Janus caught sight of a cramped space, just enough for a slightly larger than average man. Ramirez winced visibly at the sight of it.

"The tech-sergeants were only able to decipher some of the code so far, but it appears that some of the primary commands involve the dehydrator, and the charging plate."

"Charging plate?" Celes asked.

Keats moved closer and pointed to a set of thin plates within the cutout that would press against the occupant.

"Chiles and Graham believe that the chamber builds up a negative charge during the process to prep the occupant for the final stage."

"Freezing?" Marcus asked.

"Yes." Keats nodded. "It would seem there is quite a bit of prep to get the subjects ready for it."

"Why?" Janus asked, and then seeing the confused expressions, clarified, "Why the negative charge?"

Keats brought up a new projection. It was of a human body. "I'm borrowing these scans from Yalla, but hopefully they should suffice. According to Chiles, water's freezing point is lowered as a charge is applied to it." The model zoomed in on a cell. "Normally, when water freezes inside a cell, the cell bursts open and is destroyed."

"So if someone is frozen with water in their cells, they'll die?" Lyn asked.

"That's why cryogenics research has always failed in the past," Keats agreed. "You can preserve the bodies and tissues, but the cells themselves have already been destroyed. You can't bring someone back."

"But you can't just remove the water from someone. They'll die from that too," Marcus added.

Keats returned to the human body. "Exactly. We believe that Phoenix, however, figured out a way around that."

"Do both at the same time," Ramirez interjected.

Keats smiled. "Correct. Normally, dehydration will kill a person, but if you can cool them and slow their biological processes down, their cells can survive for longer. If you increase the charge, the freezing point drops, which means you can cool the body even more, slowing it further. By applying both together, you can dehydrate someone almost entirely while preserving their cells."

"It's brilliant," Celes said with a slightly worried tone.

"Two things that kill ya, combined ta keep ya alive. Sounds like a Corporation to me," Lyn said.

"If it works…" Marcus trailed off. "Though I wonder how many people it took to get right," he added.

Janus sat silently. Looking at the rotating image, he wondered the full extent of what it meant. *What could a Corporation do with the power to preserve people indefinitely?*

"How long does the process take?" Celes asked.

Keats shrugged uncharacteristically. "We don't know, but Graham suspects it could take days."

Celes stared at the tiny space for a person. "And how long is someone awake for it?"

Keats pursed her lips. "We can only hope a sedative is administered."

"How long can someone stay like this?" Janus asked.

"Decades… centuries maybe. We can't say for sure. And based on your experience at Lightemann's the chambers themselves require Immutium, probably for its temperature resilience. That's not something a Corporation could do overnight."

"So some of those people could have been frozen for hundreds of years now?" Lyn asked in surprise.

"Possibly."

Celes covered her mouth and looked over at Janus. "The beds."

Keats wore a grimace, as if she already knew the implications.

"The beds?" Janus asked in confusion.

"The rooms at Lightemann's Ridge," Celes clarified. "There were beds for children."

Janus's eyes went wide. "They could have been freezing people for ages…"

"Or at least trying to get it to work," Marcus added darkly.

"And of course it would be Cerberus," Celes added.

"What about it?" Janus asked.

"Cerberus has long specialized in Immutium production. They've produced the most of any Corporation for over a century."

"Which is precisely why you are being deployed immediately," the Praetor said, striding into the room. The five leaped from their seats to salute. "At ease. Colonel Keats, I want you to prep Captain Rogers for immediate deployment."

The colonel nodded and walked swiftly to the door, but stopped just as she reached it. "Any success, sir?"

"None whatsoever. Like talking to a wall. But it's still early."

"If anyone can convince them, sir, it will be you," Keats said supportively.

"One would think…" the Praetor said grimly. Janus had no idea what the pair were discussing, but it clearly wasn't going well.

"Are you ready?" the Praetor asked suddenly, looking at Keats.

"Yes, sir. The Longboat is prepped, though I would like a moment to speak with Adept Soltis before I go."

The Praetor nodded. Celes and Keats shared a meaningful look, and the pair politely excused themselves from the room.

Janus was about to ask what he was missing when the Praetor turned back him and the others. "I presume you have figured out a way to access Cerberus?"

"I believe so, sir. But the more people we bring along, the more attention we'll attract."

"Rogers's Wraiths are only coming along as a supporting role. They will wait in the slums for your return or communication."

Janus was hardly surprised anymore by the Praetor's seemingly prescient understanding of his thoughts. Janus motioned to his team.

"We'll head into the slums and use Clara as a contact point. She can help us reach the upper levels and contact Norm."

"Good," the Praetor said. "Find out what you can and get out. But be careful. I doubt Middleton will be caught by surprise again." He gave Janus a hard look. "And one more thing: a leader knows when to put his personal feelings aside for the good of his team. Do you understand?"

Janus felt the bile in his throat. "Yes, sir."

"You have a go for Cerberus. Major Northcott will provide you with whatever weapons you think you will need for the mission. I suggest you speak directly with Captain Rogers to coordinate his support. Any questions?"

Janus looked around at his team. Lyn, Marcus, and Ramirez all shook their heads. "No, sir," Janus said.

The Praetor saluted. Janus snapped his hand up smartly to his head.

"Get to it, Lieutenant."

CHAPTER 21
TO CERBERUS...

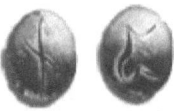

When Janus emerged from the Torch, he found Keats and Celes still in a conversation by the lift. Keats glanced at the oncoming group and nodded in thanks to Celes, then immediately jumped onto a waiting lift and headed down. Celes walked with them to a second platform, around the edge of the trunk.

"What did Keats need?" Janus asked.

Celes waved his question away. "We had an ongoing discussion about the Corporations we needed to finish."

Janus almost prodded further, but he was saved by Marcus who asked, "Where is the Colonel headed?"

"Diplomatic mission. Apparently, the Praetor decided we should be proactive about sharing the information we've gleaned so far with the other Corporations, in the hopes of convincing them that at least some part of Cerberus and Titan are up to something."

Lyn snapped her fingers. "I ran inta Valers yesterday, and he said he was helping getting one of the boats ready for an extended voyage."

"It'll take a while if she's planning ta visit them all," Ramirez added.

"That's why she's leaving now. There's no telling when we'll have more info or how quickly we'll have to move in the future."

The lift appeared in front of them, and the five stepped on board.

"It's a bit out of the ordinary, but based on the Praetor's orders, we should probably be ready to leave within the hour. I suggest we let Major Northcott know about weapons and then head back and grab whatever we need from our quarters," Janus said.

Celes nodded, looking out as the branches of the tree rapidly flew by them in their descent.

"The colonel already let Rogers know to get prepped. He's coming to meet us at the lift, and then will coordinate general supplies for the Longboats," she added.

Janus felt his heart sink. He had been avoiding Rogers for the better part of a week, keeping an eye out for him when he was in the mess or halls. Rogers certainly already knew why.

"What's wrong, Janus?" Lyn asked.

Janus coughed uncomfortably. "You may not remember, but I left behind the Captain's Ghostblade."

Marcus grimaced. "You still haven't talked to him?"

Janus shifted uncomfortably as the lift arrived at the bottom of the trunk.

"Ah, if it isn't the Lieutenant I've been most eager to see."

The team turned to find Captain Rogers already in armor and staring at Janus frightfully.

Janus saluted smartly. "Captain. Come to see us about the mission?"

Rogers smiled evilly. "You know, you're pretty clever for a Lieutenant." He leaned in close to Janus. "I believe you owe me something."

Janus swallowed. "Sorry, sir. But I'm afraid your Ghostblade was dropped during a skirmish in the last mission."

Rogers reflected thoughtfully with a hand on his chin. "What a unique way of saying... I lost your custom weapon, Captain. I'm so, so very sorry."

Janus looked anywhere but at Rogers. "I lost your custom weapon, Captain. I'm so, so very sorry."

Rogers motioned with his hand for more. "And I'm going to be paying you in lots of rations for a very long time to make up for it."

Janus sighed. "And I'm going to be paying for it for a very long time."

Rogers laughed, and his serious demeanor changed instantly. "Good enough for now." He looked at Janus with a questioning look. "Did you at least use it?"

Janus grimaced. "I was able to eliminate an Infernus that threatened the mission with it."

Rogers looked intrigued, and Lyn interjected, "Before he threw it in a crate and lost it."

Rogers bit his lip in disappointment.

He put an arm around Janus's shoulder. "Tell you what. When we're out there, before we reach Cerberus, we'll play a round of 'Ghost.' If your team can beat mine, I'll let you off the hook. But if I win, you owe me an extra week's worth of rations."

Janus looked back at his team in surprise. He had never played Ghost before, but he knew it was a somewhat frowned upon game Adept squads would play on missions. They shrugged. He turned back around. "Deal." No matter what, this mission was going to get interesting.

Two Longboats, their engines whirring, sat prepped in the Voyages Bay. Celes had opted to take the controls this time, and she signaled her fellow pilot, Glory. Glory was a veteran who had piloted for them during their first mission to Titan. She was also, as Janus was surprised to learn, a member of Rogers's Wraiths, which is why she was accompanying them today. Janus, who was sitting in the co-pilot seat, spoke into his link, "Yes, sir. Once we land, we'll rendezvous within eight hours at the designated coordinates." Cerberus was some distance away from Valhalla's current position, so their Longboats had been loaded with extra fuel. They would fly to Cerberus and hide the craft outside the city, each team landing in a different area, reducing the chance of detection and giving them two evacuation points, if needed.

Captain Rogers responded over the group channel, "Find a nice spot to sit tight, confirm you haven't been detected, and then head out."

A farewell from Valhalla came in the form of Major Tuorneg speaking to them directly. "Operation Hell Flea is a go. Good hunting."

"Hah! Thanks, Valhalla. We'll give 'em something to remember us by and take plenty of blood while we're at it," Captain Rogers's voice came over the com.

With one last look, Janus gave a thumbs-up to Glory, who led the way out of the Chariot of Voyages.

The two Longboats soared from the launch bay, dropping over the edge towards the sea below, skimming the surf as they sped on to Cerberus.

Janus looked back over his shoulder. "Might as well rest up back there. We'll shift every four hours. I'll take the first and last."

The flight would be long and tedious.

"Does it say something that I'd rather be sleeping on a rock than trying ta in a 'boat?" Lyn asked holding her stomach.

Marcus lay across several seats resting his head in his hands. "I've slept in worse. Some of the old Behemoth transports make you wonder if you'll wake up at all."

"Thanks, Marcus. That makes it so much better," Lyn replied.

"Lyn, do you get...sick?" Janus asked in surprise.

Lyn shrugged. "Me and vehicles don't always agree. But usually during a mission there's too much going on to think about it."

"Settling in," Ramirez grunted, leaning against a bulkhead and closing his eyes.

Lyn nodded.

"Reminds me of the treks back home. I only got sick after we had a few under our belt."

"Are you going to be okay?" Janus asked. They had hardly gone anywhere and she was already looking a little green.

Lyn waved him off. "I'll be fine. Just force myself ta sleep for a bit, and then I'll be right as rain. Always worked before."

Janus was skeptical.

"If it comes to it, I'll just hop into the pilot seat a little sooner. Being the driver always helps," Lyn stated.

"Don't worry, Lyn," Marcus added, nodding to Ramirez. "Me and Ramirez will make up for your lost sleep."

Ramirez had already apparently conked out in the space of mere moments, but he frowned, his eyes still closed. "Usually sleeping people are quiet."

Marcus laughed.

"Well, could ya at least offer me an arm or something?" Lyn asked. "Taking up all the prime real estate, ya big galoot."

Ramirez sighed and proffered a huge arm. Lyn leaned back comfortably, looking considerably less ill. "Thank you."

Celes giggled. "The taming of the beast." She lowered her voice so only Janus could hear. "Though it seems suspicious that she's already looking better."

Ramirez opened his eyes long enough to give her the evil eye, and Janus struggled not to laugh as the back compartment fell silent but for the sound of gentle snores.

The ocean always seemed endless, even though Janus knew better. He stared out the cockpit, peering at the blue expanse below him. It seemed strangely quiet. And lonely.

Involuntarily, he watched as Celes worked the controls, gently guiding the Longboat in a slow bank. Ahead of them, the second Longboat reflected dully in the sun.

"So how exactly are we going to get into Cerberus again?" Celes asked.

Janus realized he was staring and turned to look out at the sky. "You just like watching me squirm," he said irritably.

Celes didn't reply, but her smile was enough.

Janus looked at the speed gauge, as if he wished they could go faster. He grimaced. "It's been a while. I hope Clara is okay. I know the Praetor stated that he had made an agreement with Middleton to protect her, but down there..."

They were silent for a while, the whine of the engines filling the space.

"How bad is it really? The slums?" Celes asked.

Janus frowned. "You'll see, soon enough. We shouldn't take them lightly. There are rats, trash hazards, the occasional security sweep."

"Rats? Like the animal?"

Janus shook his head. "No, like gangs of criminals. They're all called rats. They roam around and take from folks who can't hide or defend themselves. Some of them even work for the Troopers." Janus looked troubled. "And I left her there..."

"She wanted you out here, remember?" Celes interjected. "I'm sure she can take care of herself."

"Well, she's had to do it alone," Janus said coldly.

Celes changed tact. "And who exactly is Norm?"

The engines' thrum echoed dully in the cockpit, and Janus stared distantly at the horizon. "That's a good question, isn't it? I thought he was just an old man who's lived in the slums for a long time. But if we can't find Clara, he may be able to help us."

"Help us to do what—locate Clara, or figure out what Middleton is up to?" Celes asked cautiously.

"Both," Janus said.

CHAPTER 22
HOME

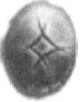

Celes eased the Longboat deep into a tiny clearing north of the city. The engines buffeted the trees back, but even still, only inches remained. After the trees had settled, the craft was nearly invisible, even from above. A few adjustments later, and the Longboat turned a mottled shade of green as the active camouflage adjusted and made it truly invisible to the naked eye.

Janus heard a yawn from behind him.

"Wait, are we there?" Lyn asked.

Janus looked over his shoulder. "You were sleeping pretty well, so we decided to leave you. Ramirez and Marcus took a shift earlier."

Lyn looked accusingly at Ramirez. "Did ya tell them to do that?"

Janus came to Ramirez's aid. "It was my call. I figured it didn't make sense for my scout to be exhausted."

Lyn gave him a glare. "I pull my weight."

Marcus gave the tiny merc a once over, which did not escape Lyn's notice. "What? Do ya have something to add?"

Marcus coughed politely and shook his head.

Janus raised his hands in defense. "Okay! Okay! Here, take these." He tossed everyone a set of brown rags.

"What are these for?" Celes asked, holding up the shredded and woeful articles.

"Put them over your armor. We're using them to blend in. I had Rogers ask Chiles and Graham to make them on short notice, so they're not perfect, but they'll get the job done."

Janus put on his own set, and he had a momentary flashback to his many years in the slums. But only for a moment, as the 'rags' were actually rather high quality, torn from any extra flak mesh Chiles and Graham could find. Apparently, they had complained excessively to Rogers upon pickup. One day they were asked to make armor. The next day, to destroy it.

Janus had yet to meet the pair, but they seemed to do two things very well: come up with ingenious solutions to problems, and complain.

Confident the Longboat was secure, the little group made its way carefully to the edge of the forest over the next hour. Peering from the shadows, Janus looked upon the dark mass that rose up above them. They were still some distance away from Cerberus, but the massive towers gave the same sort of illusion as mountains. They always seemed closer than they actually were.

"It's easy to forget how large the Corporations are..." Celes said from behind him.

Janus nodded, and his stomach roiled. Part of him was eager to return home. But he never quite imagined Cerberus looking exactly like this.

Great black spires dotted with sparse lights erupting from the earth. Twisting black lines of roads and rails circling it like razor wires and disappearing into it, like they were embedded in a monster. And the towers of steel and plasment rising higher and higher, like a mountain range piercing the clouds. But perhaps worst of all—just how dead it all seemed. It was like a corpse of a creature, laying there.

"Looks like a piece of hell pushed up through the earth," Lyn said simply.

Janus realized this was the first time he had seen a Corporation from this side, barring the ruins of Phoenix. He turned to Celes. "Do all the Corporations look like that?"

Celes shrugged. "Yes, and no. They are all massive. They block out the sky. But not all are quite so…dark."

Lyn pointed at the ground. "In a few hours, this whole area will be in shadow. Night comes early here."

Brown, stunted grass and trees became more and more sparse further ahead, eventually turning into dirty, dusty hills. The area around Cerberus was eventually nothing but rock and grime. But it made the rags they wore all the more perfect camouflage for their approach, blending with the greys and browns.

"Come on. We need to rendezvous with Rogers's Wraiths and move into the city before dark," Janus said. He motioned to Lyn, who took the lead.

Nothing moved. There were no insects. No birds. No animals. Janus had no idea if it was always like this, or just that they were interlopers in this land. And there were no patrols either.

It seems so different than when I left. Cerberus has always been bad, but it hadn't seemed dead. Dying.

Leaving and coming back had given him a totally different perspective.

Lyn kept them moving through the rocky foothills, staying low and between the rises, but eventually the emptiness got to her.

"It's odd, though, isn't it?" Lyn asked. "It takes up so much space and then it suddenly…"

"Stops," Ramirez finished.

Janus looked at the edges of the city, which abruptly went from the gigantic buildings to empty space. No outlying buildings—the edges had been built up, and seemingly abandoned.

"All of the Corporations are like that. None have expanded for years," Celes said simply.

"But why?" Janus asked

"You need a growing population. The Corporations are shrinking."

"Yeah, the Corporations keep adding Troopers so they can shrink," Marcus interjected sarcastically.

Celes shook her head. "It's not quite so simple."

Marcus cocked his head at her. "For who—" He stopped at Janus's raised hand.

"Do you hear something?" Janus asked.

The sound of voices. Laughing voices.

Lyn crept up to the top of nearby hill, just to the left of a boulder. After a tense few moments, she signaled.

It's (the) Wraiths!

Janus looked around at his team. After a moment, he smirked.

Game on!

The rest smiled. Looks like their round of Ghost was starting. Janus looked up at Lyn, who signed down to him. **Two.** And she motioned him up.

Janus crept up beside her, the boulder to his right, and stared out over an abandoned quarry. It had partially collapsed and filled from ages of disuse, long stripped of whatever was once of value here. Tough brown grass filled the bottom, subsisting on whatever had been left behind. Camouflaged within the mass was a spot of discoloration just next to a large divot in the ground.

Glory. The Adept pilot was lounging in the middle, seemingly unconcerned and unaware. After a moment, she turned and began to clearly talk to the rock at her left. It took Janus a moment to process what he was seeing.

Raleigh. He shook his head. The pair of them were nearly invisible, but for slight differences between their armor and the surroundings. They never would have seen them had it not been for their voices. Both were facing to his left, so he and Lyn were outside of their normal sight lines, at least for now.

He looked at Lyn, and she looked troubled. He pushed himself back down below the lip and signaled her.

(Something) wrong?

Lyn shook her head. **Where (are the) rest?**

Janus looked down at his team who were watching him expectantly. **Stay here.**

He slid quietly down the hill to Celes, Marcus, and Ramirez.

Raleigh. Glory. He mimed their positions. **Hit (from) back.**

(Rest of) Wraiths? Celes asked.

(Get) them. (Then we) ask.

(We'll) need two. Marcus signed. Janus nodded.

Ghost was a fairly simple game to play. The objective was to sneak up on another unsuspecting Adept squad and touch them before they realized. Seeing as it was slightly dangerous to sneak up on an armed Adept, it was officially frowned upon by Praetors and senior officers, but not actively discouraged. Unofficially, it was considered good practice. The only rule was that you couldn't touch more than one person at a time, akin to the difficultly of one Adept taking out more than one foe at once silently, and it was only a victory if the entire squad was touched, though it didn't have to happen at the same time. Since Glory and Raleigh were so close to each other, they would need two of their squad to sneak up together on them. Adepts were honor-bound not to jump in surprise or cry-out when caught. And they would never hear the end of it.

He pointed at Celes. **Take (the) hill (behind us). (Look for) others.** She nodded.

He looked at Ramirez. **Circle (clockwise).**

(You and me)? Marcus pointed between the two of them.

Janus nodded and motioned to Lyn. **Keep watch.** She nodded and resumed staring at the pair of Wraiths as if she couldn't quite believe what she was seeing.

The pair moved counterclockwise, staying below the quarry lip so that they could come up behind Glory and Raleigh. When they had gone far enough, Marcus turned and began creeping up the side of the hill. At the top, peering through a tuft of the tough grass, Janus looked down into the quarry. He could still make our Glory, though Raleigh appeared like a rock once more. He glanced over for Lyn, but any view of her had disappeared behind the boulder.

(Let's) do (this), Marcus signaled.

Janus nodded. **Go.**

The pair slipped over the rim of the quarry, moving quickly. At any moment, Glory and Raleigh could turn around. There was nowhere to hide, so their only option was speed and silence.

Janus crouched as he moved down the side, keeping his center of mass low, nearly walking on his toes. With each step, he tried to focus his weight as much as possible to avoid slipping on the scree. Looking at the loose rocks, he was glad their disguises did not sweep along the ground.

As they reached the bottom, Glory let out a loud yawn, stretching her arms up. Janus froze and dropped prone, hoping that if Glory checked anywhere, it would be the lip of the quarry. After a moment, she put her arms behind her head and settled back down.

Marcus gave him a pair of wide eyes, as if to say, *We need to keep moving.*

Carefully picking himself off the ground Janus was forced to move even slower, gently placing every foot to avoid the crunch of the tough grass. It was torturous. Finally, they reached the divot, and carefully sliding into it, Janus held his breath. He could hear Glory gently snoozing. Next to him, Marcus reached towards Raleigh's 'rock'.

Janus nodded to him and stretched a hand for Glory's head.

A hand fell across his back. "Dead."

Janus sighed. Invisible against the wall of the divot, waited two more Wraiths.

A few minutes later, Rogers slid into the crater with Celes, Ramirez, and Lyn in tow.

"Got you too, eh?" Celes asked as they walked dejectedly across the empty quarry.

Janus nodded.

"Don't feel so bad," a Wraith named Bravos said, "we never would've heard the end of it if a mint had snuck up on us."

Janus shook his head in frustration. *Still a mint.*

Glory looked in disappointment at the group. "Did you really think we'd do such a poor job hiding?"

Townes, the short and lithe Adept that had tagged Janus laughed. "Captain had you pegged for a while. Figured we could get you split up if we offered some bait."

Rogers threw an arm around Glory's shoulder. "And for your excellent acting, the Lieutenant will be providing us with some extra rations."

Glory smiled. "Well, it's hard to beat our troupe at the acting game."

Rogers gave Glory a tiny glare, but proceeded to do a deep bow. "Better luck next time, Lieutenant."

The edge of Cerberus gave off an aura of decay. The ground was tough, and infertile. Shoots of some sort of resilient weed stood in isolated islands in the cracked and dry earth.

Dressed in their brown rags, their little group didn't even warrant a second look from the wasted forms who foraged this desert. Heads down, the inhabitants ignored all but their search for meager sustenance, wandering like ghosts, insubstantial in both mind and body. And the few that did acknowledge the Adepts showed no fear—they had nothing worth taking.

But there were so many of them, driven to the edge of the city. Perhaps out of fear of what awaited them deeper inside. Here and there, one of the lowered heads would perk up, still connected to the world enough to be struck by the oddity of the new group. The traveler's determination. Their speed. Their strength. The fullness of their faces.

What a problem to have... Janus thought ruefully.

No one appeared surprised, except maybe Celes. She wore a look of disgust and sorrow that was impossible to miss. The others were harder to read. Lyn's grimace and shared look with Ramirez. Perhaps from an awareness now confirmed by reality. Marcus, a look of contempt, perhaps for the souls, or perhaps for Cerberus. The Wraiths remained impassive, too jaded not to have experienced such sights before, or too veteran to reveal they hadn't.

Slowly, the Wraiths adopted the characteristic stoops and coughs of the ones around them, yet never slowed their pace.

I've been away too long, Janus realized. His natural confidence amplified by the characteristics of an Adept made him stand out like a sore thumb. Rogers seemed right at home, and Janus realized that within the space a few moments, the man had become indistinguishable from the wretched mass around him. Janus adopted a limp-like hitch in his step, and soon his whole team had followed suit with afflictions of their own. Supporting one another, the group crossed the threshold of the city, passing into the broken and decaying buildings. Janus tilted his head back as they passed, his eyes watering as the city disappeared into the clouds. In the shade of the giant superscrapers, the air became still and the familiar smell of rotting garbage filled his nostrils. He took a deep breath. At first, he wanted to gag, but then he could feel himself reacclimatizing to the smell, to the dark, to the slums. A rush of emotions washed over him—each smell, sight, and sound brought back a memory. The sun disappeared completely and quickly, and the surroundings took on the quality of twilight. The city lights twinkled high above, like the heavens of stars. Small fires burned everywhere, occasionally surrounded by a small group of slummers seeking warmth. They scurried away at the group's approach.

"If we can locate a lift station, I can orient us properly. Then we'll be headed for the East-2 lift and from there…" Janus hesitated, momentarily ashamed, "I can take us…home."

Celes watched him with a guarded expression, and he quickly looked away, towards the dimly lit alleys of Cerberus. Without another word, he moved deeper into the shadows, the two teams just behind him.

Janus led them carefully into the deep of the city, where the garbage began to form small mountains, and the alleyways filled with the hot winds of the factories above. The angry whirr of Carrion Eaters and their gang rat pilots whizzing through the darkness told him that what he searched for was nearby. Long forgotten lampposts and wires, crackling with the electrical power and occasionally lighting the dark appeared along the thoroughfares, and Janus directed them onwards, avoiding the light, towards the beating heart of the city just beyond.

Finally, after hours of trekking across the uneven and treacherous terrain, they came upon their goal, its black obsidian exterior reflecting just as darkly and strangely as Janus remembered it.

"One of the Cerberus lifts," Janus whispered.

Lyn and Ramirez looked on in awe, while Marcus and Celes studied the architecture impassively. STs guarded it from a raised platform, strung out like a wire along the edge of a neighboring building.

Janus shrank back, melding with the dark, no more than the garbage around him. He could feel his old instincts taking over as he stared at the expressionless monsters that watched the lift from above. His voice was strangely muted, absorbed by the muck around them.

"How far have we traveled?" Lyn asked. "It's hard to tell with no sky…"

"Thirty to forty kilometers since we lost track of the sun." Janus eyed the lift station. "This is Northeast-1. Southeast from here will be the East-2 lift. At a steady pace it should take about five hours to reach it. From there it is another hour at least, to reach our destination."

The others nodded in understanding and slunk after him, only the rush of a factory wind through the narrow passages making any noise at all.

As they progressed, Janus quickly found the others could not match his speed or agility through the wet and slippery morass. Each squelching boot, every accidental slide seemed to echo through the buildings, and Janus slowed their pace.

Stealth (over) speed, Janus signaled while briefly crossing through a patch of light that emanated from a miraculously intact streetlamp before he disappeared back into the deeper darkness. He paused to listen from the top of a mound of broken and cracked plasment, long since dried and discarded from some abandoned construction project, while the others crept forward. Ahead of them, two crumbling brick buildings butted against one of the giant superscrapers.

"Are those…?" Celes asked in surprise as she came up beside him.

Janus nodded. "Remnants of the old city. From before Cerberus took over and rebuilt everything."

They were old apartment buildings, the first leaning perilously against the second. Twisted metal of former fire escapes knitted between the two, like they were holding hands. A pair of gaping holes in the second between the third and fourth floors made the building seem as if it had eyes, giving it an almost childlike quality.

"I recognize this area. Those are the sisters," Janus stated.

Lyn perched on a steel girder sticking out of the plasment and pointed to a set of murals, numbers, and letters along the side of the building. "And those?"

Janus shrugged. "A few different things. The letters and numbers are for the Cerberus sections above, so the pair serve as a kind of guidepost. The murals are from people who have lived there and decided to add something before they left."

"But those buildings look like they could collapse at any moment!" Celes whispered in shock.

"Shelter is shelter," Rogers interjected, looking up at the hazy murk of the factories. "I imagine mostly what people need here is a wall at their back."

Janus looked at Celes and explained, "You don't shelter from the weather so much as from the gangs. And gangs like easier targets than people prepared to fight them. People living in the sisters are usually transients, making the journey from one side of the city to the other, but every so often there have been communities that have sprung up."

He peered more closely at the buildings. "Doesn't look like anyone is living there now, though." He pointed ahead and smiled grimly. "We're close now. The lift is to our ten." He looked down at the little group. "We're entering rat territory again, be alert."

"Isn't everything rat territory?" Marcus asked skeptically.

Janus nodded. "Yes, but they tend to concentrate closer to the lifts. More targets that way." He waved the group to follow him. "Keep your heads low."

The trash piles had shifted again in his long absence, but the alleyways and corridors remained the same, and familiar sights and sounds greeted him as he journeyed through the wastes.

His heart soared as the final sight came into view: an old run-down hotel that took a tiny parcel of land for itself amongst looming giants. He was home.

CHAPTER 23
THE LOCKET

Snaking through the crumbling wood and concrete, Janus led the little group into the main lobby. In the gloom, he could see the familiar worn plaque just behind an ancient wooden desk. But as his eyes adjusted in the gloom, something felt off. The air was mustier. The dust thicker.

Leaping up the old stairway littered with remnants of the ceiling above, he cleared the gaping chasm in the floor with a leap, landing in front of room number 8. The old broken door swayed on shattered hinges. He pushed it open. Only the whistle of the wind outside echoed through the room.

"Clara?"

The books were gone, the makeshift shelf smashed and broken on the ground. Springs from his shredded mattress scattered across the floor as he stepped inside. The old armchair lay toppled in a corner, one of its legs shattered. The broken end table lay across it helplessly. He fumbled with the light switch—the bulb was broken.

"CLARA!"

The rotting wood quickly stifled his echo, leaving the hovel as silent as a tomb. A surge of anger came over him. "No!" He shook his head in denial. He grabbed the fallen end table shouting, "NO!" and smashed it into the wall. Holding its broken legs in his hands and ready to beat them against the wall, he glanced up.

Celes watched him mournfully from the door. Behind her, the others peered into the room.

He sank to his knees, taking in the room. A fine layer of dirt and dust covered everything. It had been this way for some time. "Clara…" he whispered, his heart sinking deep into his chest.

Celes's hand came to rest on his shoulder. "I'm so sorry, Janus."

"I shouldn't have left her. I knew that she couldn't survive forever on her own. I shouldn't—" He turned away.

Celes crouched down next to him, her hand squeezing his shoulder gently. "But she wanted you with us. She wanted the best for you. Would she have really let you stay?"

Janus looked at Celes, his eyes red with tears. "No. And there would have been no use arguing with her, either."

"The place is destroyed, but there aren't any signs of her. Which may be a good thing," Marcus said, picking up a piece of the broken shelf from the floor. Janus looked up at him.

"Would rats have taken her with them?" Marcus asked pointedly. "I'm assuming the ones here are similar to the ones in Medusa."

Rogers stepped into the room, glancing around. "How likely was someone to find this place?"

Janus shook his head. "You saw how we got in here. Only someone desperate would think to look here."

"Could Clara have left? Would she still be here if this place were discovered?" Celes asked kindly.

"Actually…" Janus stood up. "If she were here now, she would probably berate me for letting my guard down, not stopping to listen to make sure everything was…" He paused, suddenly aware of what he wasn't hearing.

Through the cracks in the walls, he could hear the gusts of hot winds, and the *whirr* of distant hovercycles. He stared at the broken bulb. It's reassuring buzz was gone. But something else was missing. Something even more important in the desert of the slums.

"The faucet," Janus said, "is it…fixed?"

"Would that… be a surprise?" Glory asked uncertainly.

Janus shook his head. "When I was young, I spent nearly a week carefully figuring out how to take the faucet apart while Clara was away and then another two months searching for the right washer. I thought I would surprise her by fixing it, and one day, I finally did. I waited at home, proud of my accomplishment. But when she came home, she nearly panicked."

"Why is that, Lieutenant?" Rogers asked.

"She thought the water had somehow stopped. That our supply was gone."

A look of understanding passed between Lyn and Ramirez, and comprehension dawned upon Rogers's face. Marcus crossed his arms and leaned against the wall, while Celes grimaced, staring up at him.

Janus smiled, a look of nostalgia crossing his features. "Clara loved the sound of it. No matter how rough things got, she could come home and know that she still had running water—a rare and precious thing.

"When I finally calmed her down to explain what I had done, she smiled and told me how proud she was… and then she made me put it back. I threw out the washer the next day. She never would have fixed the faucet. And if anyone else had bothered, they would be living here right now."

"So either the water is gone…" Lyn trailed off, and Janus stepped into the old bathroom.

He stared down at the old faucet, the sink covered in a layer of grime. He reached for the handle, but hesitated, pulling his hand back.

Thinking better of it, he stooped down to look at the water valve. It had been turned off.

He stood up once more and grabbed the faucet with one hand. It took him a moment to fish a flatheaded tool from his armor, and then he carefully unscrewed and pried open the base. Slipping his hand into a small hole, he felt around in the dark. A moment later, he pulled out his hand excitedly. Opening his palm, he found himself holding a jeweled locket.

"That's not something you find in a faucet every day," Lyn said with a wink.

"It's Clara's! There's a note attached!" Janus said excitedly. "It's from Norm?"

Janus paused and read the note aloud:

Janus,

Hope this letter finds you well. I assumed that someday you would make it back here, and something tells me sooner, rather than later.

To answer your first question—Clara is alive and safe, for the time being. Miss Middleton has recently moved her to quarters in E level. Unfortunately, since Clara's move, I have had to limit my contact with her, but she passed this locket along to me so that you might know she is safe.

Middleton has been increasingly agitated recently, and I suspect that if you have returned here, you may have something to do with it. No doubt you have many questions to ask, so come visit me. Either meet me at East-2 at 0500 hours (before my shift begins) or visit me directly in Persephone. I live at West End—just ask around and they will know me.

By the way, Clara wanted you to keep her locket. She says it belongs to you anyway, and she thinks it is time for you to have it.

I expect you will have many interesting stories to tell me when we next meet.

Regards,
Norm

Janus held the locket up. It was gold, in the shape of a bird with tiny ruby eyes and wingtips. It looked as if it had been through quite a bit, the edges worn. Carved into the front, where the metal was smooth, was a tiny inscription.

"Belongs to me…?"

He pulled the locket closer to read:

To Natalie, From Magnus
Eternal Love

The feel of a rough edge along his fingers made him turn the piece over. Scrawled writing was inelegantly carved into the back, as if done quickly with a knife:

may Janus remind you

He stared at the writing and then opened up the locket: a beautiful young woman stared back at him from the left. On the right, a smudged picture looked as though it had been waterlogged or wet. Whatever had ruined the picture had mixed the colors, making the blob under a streak of white impossible to identify.

"What's our next move, Lieutenant?" Rogers asked, pulling Janus out of his reverie.

Janus looked up at the captain, still ruminating on the locket as he considered the question.

Flipping the locket closed, he said, "We'll head for Persephone. We'll be safer there than here. Since this place has been raided, it's possible that the rats have been watching the area, and our group might have attracted unwanted attention. Persephone will at least give us protection from them, and we won't have to worry about the odd Trooper patrol."

He paused, looking up through a hole in the ceiling. "Let's get moving, we need to be there before dark."

Janus led the team through the alleyways once more, keeping the group moving faster than he normally would have liked. But dark was fast approaching, and they couldn't afford to be caught in the open. The gang rats would be out in full force. There were no complaints from the Adepts, but Janus knew that they were all out of their element, and he wanted to avoid any unnecessary encounters.

"Make sure you hide your weapons well," Janus said. "Persephone frowns upon weapons."

"What is Persephone, exactly?" Rogers asked.

"One of many 'towns' found throughout the slums—one of the largest in East Cerberus, actually. There are hundreds living there." He paused for a moment, peering at a particularly fetid trash pile that rose several stories above him. He shook his head and kept moving, not noticing the skeptical glance Marcus and Rogers exchanged.

"It sprang up around a still-functioning water supply station and protects the slummers in that area. It's a place where slummers can raise families without immediate fear of Security Patrols."

"So why didn't you and Clara live there?" Celes asked.

"The Dons," Janus spit.

"The Dons?" Glory asked.

"The people in charge. The Dons control the slum communities, and Don Vulle is in charge of Persephone. If you want to live in a place like Persephone, you better be willing to do whatever the Dons say. Clara had a problem with that. I think she made the right choice," Janus said. "Anyway, the Dons often form covenants with the local Trooper Sergeants to keep their communities safe from patrols and rats. It's just a pyramid of extortion really, with slummers at the very bottom of the pile."

Janus checked the sky above; the hazy mist of the factory levels was getting darker by the second. "We need to hurry, the gates will be closing soon."

"How can you tell down here?" Lyn asked skeptically.

"Slummers who do work on the upper levels need to know the time to make their shifts. You live down here, you learn to look for the signs. Cerberus factories work on rotations." He trudged onto another mountain of trash and briefly glanced up at the sky. "The haze is a dull blue-grey right now, which means that the food recycling plant is in its clearing phase, and the weapons plant is heating up a new batch of aluminum and cobalt. It's just after twenty-one thirty hours."

He began rooting through the pile he stood upon.

"You can tell all that by the color of the smoke?" Celes asked.

Janus wiped his brow with his forearm and looked down at the group. "Not just that. There's less light filtering from the mid-levels. The sun sets early for everyone below H-level. But when the factories are off-peak, and the workers are prepping for bed, the lights dwindle. You learn to notice all those things together, and soon, you just know the time."

"What time does Persephone close its gates?" Ramirez asked.

"Twenty-two hundred hours."

"So shouldn't we be hurrying then?" Lyn asked curiously.

"Soon enough," he replied, scrambling a little further up the pile. "There's still one thing we need."

Janus paused on top of the trash heap, letting out an "ah-ha!" and pulling a couple of old loafs of bread from the pile. They were in surprisingly good condition. He turned to look at the group triumphantly, who collectively looked at him like he was mad.

He smiled at them, tossing a loaf down to Rogers. "Stuff that somewhere it can be easily found." Rogers caught the loaf and stuffed it into his raggedy clothes without question. Janus pulled his rifle and pistol from under his rags and threw them to Celes. "Hang in the middle of our group, and hand over your weapons and anything that'll stick out too."

Marcus gave Janus a skeptical glance. "Are you sure you didn't breathe the fumes from that trash pile too deeply?"

Janus shook his head. "Just trust me."

"But what about Persephone?" Celes asked, slinging Janus's weapons under her own set of rags.

Janus took several strides up the mountain and pointed from the top. The two teams hastily made their way up. Below, nestled between four gargantuan Cerberus buildings, was a ramshackle gathering. "There it is," Janus said simply. Two enormous gates made of an amalgamation of wood, sheet metal, and other assorted materials, stood between them and the community. "Let's go," Janus said, "they're closing the gates, and I would rather not stay the night out here if I can help it."

A few straggling slummers were hurrying to get through the southern gate when Janus reached it.

The two guards protecting the gate were brutish looking and heavily muscled, hefting old and patched together Zeus rifles with sharp bayonets over their shoulders. Tattoos like sleeves ran up the left guard's arms. The right was missing an eye, a nasty scar evident around the edges of the hard metal patch he wore. Intimidation was just as effective a weapon down here as any gun.

"Hey! Stop there," the tattooed man said.

Janus stopped immediately, looking furtively at the two men. "Yes?" he asked timidly.

"Not from around here. Can't just walk into the Persephone," the second man added.

Janus took a few uncertain steps back, his eyes darting back and forth between the two guards.

"What'cha hidin'? Com'ere, 'fish," The tattooed man brought his weapon off his shoulder.

Janus glanced furtively at a bulge just in the folds of his clothes. "Nothin'."

The guard grabbed Janus roughly by the front, and yanked the bulge out, throwing Janus to the ground.

"Ho ho! Look at what we got, Pots!" the tattooed man exclaimed, holding his prize up. "Bread! Looks fresh!"

Pots smiled, his good eye glinting. "Nice, Fin. Wha'bout the rest? Don' make me use this 'ere gun." He glanced at the group menacingly, patting his patchwork weapon.

On cue, the two groups split, revealing a shaking Rogers, who glanced around looking like he had been betrayed. Janus had to bite his hand to prevent himself from laughing. Fortunately, Pots and Fin had moved swiftly past him.

The pair swiftly snatched the second loaf from Rogers, who handed it over with a dejected look upon his face. Pots laughed. "See, didn' cost much—go on." He motioned his head through the gate.

Janus marched the group swiftly through, as Fin and Pots joked behind them and closed the gate.

"You picked that up quickly, Captain," Janus said to Rogers as they moved out of earshot of the two burly guards.

"Quite the actor, sir," Celes said with a smile.

"He was part of a theater troupe that toured Hydra when he was younger," Raleigh whispered.

Rogers whirled around on him. "I thought I told you never to mention that." Rogers's eyes narrowed at Raleigh.

"Oh, yes, that's right. Sorry, sir," Raleigh apologized. "I'm sure it won't happen again."

"And now?" Lyn asked. Struggling not to laugh at the mischievous grin on Raleigh's face.

Janus looked around at the bustling night market of Persephone. "Now, we go find Norm."

CHAPTER 24
PERSEPHONE

Persephone was bustling with peddlers and tradesmen hocking their wares, even as late as it was. Ramshackle buildings haphazardly climbed up the sides of the Cerberus superscrapers, like vines up a tree. Multi-colored bulbs scrounged from wherever they could be found gave the market a dull yellow and red hue. Rising above the Adepts, merchants perched on platforms just a few feet from a terrifying drop to the street below calling out to the shoppers who climbed rickety ladders and balanced on the wooden catwalks than ran along the outside of the buildings. Here and there, shut curtains and shutters struggled valiantly to keep the noise out for the few who tried to sleep. A group of children protested as their mothers interrupted their game using an old, molding ball. And still a few unlucky souls shivered in the streets, covered in dirt and grime, and demonstrating that wealth was always a relative term.

Janus turned to the little group and said, "Spread out, don't stick too close together. And watch yourselves. The rule is that if you don't miss something when you first lose it, you probably didn't need it— and you'd be surprised at how good these people are at taking things off of you. Most aren't as thick as our two guards."

"Why would they think we have anything?" Celes asked, looking at her rags.

"And do you really think they could sneak something off of us?" Townes asked in surprise.

Janus jumped forward and grabbed a young boy by his shirt as he sidled away from Raleigh. The boy was guiltily fiddling with a variable grenade, clearly unsure of its purpose. Janus snatched it from the boy's hand just before he could activate the grenade at its maximum setting. Rogers gave Townes a bemused expression.

"Around here—" Janus said.

"You're still a mint," Rogers finished.

Janus stopped at several merchants as they moved along the market, inspecting their wares, and the others meandered some distance along behind him. Tiny stalls, illuminated with candles and sometimes filled with surprisingly valuable trinkets and tools, lined the avenue. "You'd be surprised exactly how much good stuff gets thrown away," Janus explained picking up what appeared to be an old wooden clock in remarkable condition. "It's just a matter of finding it and fixing a few pieces here and there."

Rogers wandered by, as if interested in the clock. After a moment, he leaned forward so only Janus could hear. "So is there a reason we're shopping right now?"

Janus leaned back and whispered, "Moving too fast will attract attention. Makes us seem like we have a purpose here."

Rogers nodded as if he already expected the answer, and went back to perusing the other wares, keeping a lookout for others who might try to grab something off of them. Underneath the clock was an old book, its cover pulled back together with twine. The faded cover showed a little girl looking up at a cat in a tree. Janus looked at the vendor. "How much?"

The man perched on a stool in front of him squinted through a single eyeglass, sizing Janus up. "Want the book? Can read, can you?"

Janus shook his head. "Just think they're neat. Maybe someday."

The man smiled, revealing a mouth with many missing teeth. "Noble goal! That's a rare book, there. Very valuable." He took the book from Janus, flipping the pages to show Janus all the writing inside, as if it were a mystical tome.

Marcus came up beside Janus. "So rare you have it buried underneath other junk?"

Janus gave Marcus a sidelong glance. He had the right tactic, if not the approach Janus was looking for.

The man scowled. "It's there because meatheads don't appreciate its value."

"So it's not selling," Janus chimed in.

"Depends on what you're offering." With a frown, the man folded thin arms across his chest, pressing his baggy green shirt against his frame.

Janus considered the man for a moment, and then pulled out two ration bars from underneath his rags, just holding them up so only the man could see. He lowered his voice to a conspiratorial whisper. "Got a couple of Passers from a discarded Trooper crate the other day. Found these in there too."

The man peered at the food, his eyes growing wide. He reached for the rations, but Janus pulled them away.

"I'm just seeing if it's real," the man huffed.

"It's real," Janus assured him. "Do you want them or not?"

The man gazed over at Marcus. "And what about you? You got any of those?"

Marcus shared a look with Janus, who signed discreetly, **One**. With a sigh, Marcus reluctantly handed Janus a single bar. **(Good) Touch.**

The old man reached out again, but Janus shook his head. "We don't want anyone trying to shake us down for our find, especially since we're busy trading it away. Is that a problem?"

The man nodded his head and reached out again.

Janus took a step back. "And we've got a friend in the East End." He pointed down an alley to the west. "Will that get us there?"

Old man shook his head. "You daft? That's the West End that way." He looked up. "Up ahead is a crossing on the third level. Wide area between four of the 'scrapers. Will take you to either the West or East End. Go right for east. If you head down that alley, you'll end up right in the middle of one of the Vulle's barracks. You two look strong, but best to stay away from there."

Marcus nodded. "Thanks."

The man scoffed. "I just prefer you not to say anything about me either."

Janus held out his hand for the book and the man carefully placed its battered pages in his hand, then quickly snatched the proffered bars and stuffed them inside his green shirt. Without waiting any longer he closed up his shop. Several others nearby were doing the same. He looked at Janus. "I suggest you get moving. Vulle's men will start patrolling the streets soon."

Janus raised a hand in thanks and quickly moved away, making sure the others followed at a distance.

Further along, he ducked into a relatively deserted alley, a few of the more destitute hunched within a wall constructed of old metal crates along the back.

As the group joined him, he explained what he had learned. He pointed out of the alley and ahead of them. Layer upon layer of reclaimed wood and sheet metal climbed six stories high, and right in the middle, a glowing thoroughfare showed a dwindling stream of slummers.

"It looks like the markets are finally dying down. We should stick together at this point, we'll look like any group just eager to get home before it gets too late."

Bravos nodded towards the structure rising above them as they walked through the hastily emptying streets. "I can't imagine it could get any taller without collapsing."

Ramirez and Lyn had taken the lead, and she looked back at the Adept. "Reminds me of some of the things thrown together in the Outskirts. Keep it simple, don't overengineer it, and ya can manage a lot with a little."

Ramirez grunted in agreement. "Easier to trust things ya make yourself." He swung onto a pole with alternating pegs that led to the third level and began climbing. Lyn followed him, with Celes and then Marcus close behind.

"It is amazing what people can do, even in the most desperate situations," Celes said quietly, quickly springing up the steps.

Janus smiled. "Cerberus has no idea how many slummers really exist down here."

Marcus looked back at Janus with agreement. "Someday, they may be in for a nasty shock."

As the group turned and gathered on the third level, Rogers looked at Janus. "How are we supposed to find Norm at this hour? It sounds like we don't want to get stuck out here either."

Janus looked uncertain. "We may have to ask. I've never stayed here overnight, so I had no idea we would have such a time crunch."

"Do you think Norm would be so well known?" Glory asked.

A young woman with dirty brown hair rushed by them, bundling some dirty rags together while hoisting a small toddler in her arms. Her face reflected her hurry, and worry.

"Excuse me," Rogers asked politely. The woman startled and jumped, eyeing him suspiciously. Janus pulled him back, then turned to her, his palms open. The young mother clutched her child closer and took a step back.

Janus felt a hand on his shoulder and Celes stepped beside him. **Back**, she signed.

Janus and the group took another few steps back. "Hello. I'm Celes." Celes held a hand to her chest, and then opened her palms the same way Janus had. The brown-haired woman eased slightly. "I'm looking for a friend who lives in the West End, and I'm afraid I don't know exactly where he is."

The woman looked around as the nearby lights from windows began to wink out, leaving only the main lamps along the throughfare, and stared at Celes uncertainly.

Celes smiled. "It's getting late, I just want to find my friend and get off the street."

The woman hefted the child, who stared at Celes in interest, for a better position. "Who are ya looking for?"

Celes looked around. "A man named Norm. My friend here"—she pointed to Janus—"knows him."

The woman's demeanor instantly warmed. "Are you Janus? Norm's been hopin' ya'd show up soon." She made a motion with her head towards a group of men wielding makeshift weapons now walking along the path to the gate down below. "It would be best for all of us to get inside. Can take ya to him."

"Apparently he *is* that well known," Marcus muttered.

She led them away quickly, shifting the toddler to her other arm. "My name is Sara and this," she smiled at the child, "is Julius."

Janus smiled at the little boy, who promptly hid his face.

"Since you're not from around here, you'll probably attract attention from the Don's men if you can't get inside."

Rogers moved closer to Janus and whispered in his ear, "I know that we're committed to this, but it seems like we're pretty vulnerable here. Lots o' potential hostiles. You sure Norm won't sell us out, either to this Don Vulle or to Cerberus? Seems like a good way to get ahead around here."

Janus shook his head, watching as Sara led them down another ladder, still carrying her load. "Not likely. Expressing a love of Cerberus here has a tendency to make life even more difficult. The upper levels may get the propaganda, but we get the scraps. The Dons support Cerberus out of necessity, and they'd prefer no one else have close ties to compete with them. And if you haven't noticed, most people don't care for the Dons either, they just don't have much choice. Norm has helped Clara many times. I doubt he decided to change now." He glanced back at Rogers and shrugged. "Besides, what choice do we have?"

Rogers nodded. "I'm with you, but I just wanted to hear you say it one last time, now that we're in it deep."

Janus smiled grimly. "I have a bad feeling we haven't really gotten into it yet."

Rogers chuckled softly. "Ah, I see you've already developed that old ODIN optimism. Try to look on the brighter side of things. Even if Norm betrays us, we're probably valuable enough to Middleton at this point that maybe we can use it to our advantage. See, the brighter side."

Janus grinned and said, "And if he is a Cerberus loyalist, I'm sure Middleton will keep us alive because she wants to torture us first."

Rogers scowled. "You, my boy, are a lost cause."

Janus chuckled to himself and quickly followed the others down the ladder as Sara rounded a corner into a side street between two massive supports for the superscraper above. To their left, the shantytown crawled up the side.

Sara motioned for the group to keep up with her free hand. "Norm's been around for a time. Got to know everyone righ' away.

Clever man, never forgets a name. Done enough around here that even the Don's men won't touch him. Must be the oldest livin' man in the slums. Few people here get to be as old and greyin' as he is."

Janus could see the sudden realization on several of the Adepts' faces, but Ramirez chimed in, "Ya, it doesn't seem like many live past forty or fifty."

Sara grimaced. "Had hoped that some of the other communities were doing better than we were, but I guess everywhere has the same problems. Suppose it's better than bein' an Outskirter, though."

Lyn and Ramirez shared a look at that.

"But wouldn't know anythin' about that, would ya? Where you from?"

Janus quickly jumped in. "We're from Aphrodite."

Sara raised her eyebrows. "Aphrodite! That's all the way on the other side of Cerberus! No wonder Norm's been waitin' so long. Travel the outside?"

Janus shrugged. "Well, we took a few cuts through the city to save supplies, but we skirted the outside to avoid the patrols. Took us about two months, once we had received word that Norm was looking for us and had gathered everything we needed."

She nodded. "Must be tired, then. No one has come from there in…" She looked at Julius. "Two years now."

She led them up another ladder, and surprisingly, into the side of an old brick building through a hole in the wall. Electric lamps, buzzing with electricity lined the walls.

"We've entered the luxury quarter," Marcus breathed.

Sara motioned around her. "Only the most successful merchants and the Don's favorites live here. Even got a connection to the water line, no need to travel to the well." She stopped before a thinning, wooden door, its dark red paint nearly gone.

"This is Norm's place."

Janus raised his hand cautiously and knocked.

Chapter 25
The Burden of Wisdom

A strong voice answered, "Yes? Well, whoever it is, stop standing there and come on in. Thugs and thieves do not knock."

Janus pushed the barrier open. A silver-haired man in a sharply pressed servant's uniform sat in a well-preserved armchair, with a wooden table to his right that looked as if it had been gnawed by termites. A multi-colored shade of reds, yellows, and oranges covered a stubby lamp that cast shadows from its perch, while a small pile of worn books sat beside it. The rest of the room was bare except for a hammock strung across a corner, a pile of rags neatly folded along one wall and an old sink that had several clear pouches of water hanging from its edge.

Norm's blue eyes gazed up from the raggedy book he was reading. His silver brows arched in surprise and he grinned. "Janus!" He stood up, waving Janus inside. "Come in, come in!"

Janus strode in, followed by Sara and the rest of the group, crowding the tiny apartment, despite the lack of furniture.

"And I see you have brought plenty of"—Norm looked over the group, his sharp eyes noting the fierce jawlines, and the strong muscles just beneath the rags—"friends."

He chuckled, smiling at Sara. "Thank you so much, Sara." He waved at the toddler in her arms. "And how is Julius doing?"

"Quite well, thanks to you. Will find a way to pay back the food, and the books." She looked fiercely determined.

"No need. I already have more than I should." Norm shook his head, his eyes distant and his voice quiet. He stared at Janus for a moment, and the strength in his voice returned. "I will see if I can bring more tomorrow. Now if you will excuse us, I would like to catch up with Janus here." He paused. "It's rather late. You shouldn't be caught outside. Please talk to Marietta, and let her know I sent you."

Sara smiled and did an awkward curtsy. "Let me know if you need anythin'." She quietly closed the door.

Norm grunted, "Good girl. She used to work on the upper levels, live in the factories. The boy is the son of her employer, an Overlord in charge of behemoth and styx production. When his wife found out, Sara had to flee into the slums. Ended up in Aphrodite, actually. But that wasn't enough, and she ended up traveling here. Did it alone and very pregnant, too." He shook his head, considering a thought. "Arrogance blinds us. We are all fools."

He paused, a hand to his lips. Janus exchanged a look with Rogers. Finally, after several moments, he looked at Janus as if he had just remembered he was there and said, "Well, you made it back. And I see you have a whole slew of Adepts with you."

The group raised their eyebrows at that, but Janus said, "You always knew more than you let on, Norm—and you still do."

Norm nodded. "Perhaps, although it took me coming here to realize how little I actually understood. And I think I have some more to learn right now…" He looked around the room. "Care to tell me what two Adept squads are doing in the bowels of Cerberus?"

"We were hoping you would give us some answers first," Janus stated firmly.

He met Janus's eyes. "In good time, lad. But first, I need to know what has been happening outside of my little bubble. It will tell me where to start." He studied the others. "And perhaps all of you should find a place to sit. We are stuck here until morning anyway, and I suspect there is quite a bit to discuss."

After introductions were made, Janus and Norm talked for a long while, discussing what had happened to him during his training at ODIN, and how his first mission, the attack on the Titan outpost, had started. But when Janus finally reached the disastrous end of the mission that had left many of his fellow Adepts behind, he hesitated. Now that Rogers had raised the issue, and Janus really thought about it, could he really trust Norm? Even now, he still had yet to tell them anything.

Norm watched the conflict in his eyes. He smiled sadly. "Trust is a difficult thing, isn't it? Misplace it and you may never get it back. Whatever you may think, Janus—whatever I may have held back in the past—it was to protect you." He turned to Rogers as if he could read the man's doubts. "I assure you, Captain, I am no Cerberus loyalist. Completely the opposite in fact, but I do not blame you if you thought otherwise."

Even the accomplished actor in Rogers struggled not to reveal his surprise.

He looked over at his collection of books, staring distantly, and then shook his head. "An outpost assault. Of course that was the logical route." He looked at Janus. "You found it, did you not?"

Janus stared at the old man in disbelief. Celes gave him a little reassuring tap on his shoulder, and after a pause, he nodded.

"Was it running?" Norm asked.

"Yes. Producing thousands of weapons every day."

Norm looked deeply unsettled. "I knew it would be, I just did not want to believe it. Please continue."

After that, Janus told him everything that had happened, from the Titan disaster onward, including the discovery of the painting.

"Hmmm, I had no idea Middleton was so...sentimental," Norm said, and then shook his head. "It really is a pity about Alastor. He was not kind, and often pompous. But he took his duties seriously. He truly did wish to improve Cerberus and the lives of its citizens. That is far too often a rare quality in Overlords these days, in my experience."

He looked around the small room. "But there is no time to mourn him, unfortunately. Time is short. If Middleton has connected the dots, we could be in for serious trouble."

Rogers jumped in. "Agreed. Norm, grab whatever you need. We'll be heading back to Valhalla as soon as the gates open."

"But what about—" Janus caught himself and bit his tongue. *Clara.* He looked at Celes, who was watching him with a mix of dismay and sadness.

Rogers's eyes narrowed. "Not your call, Lieutenant. Now that we've secured Norm, we head back."

"No."

Both Janus and Rogers turned to look at Norm in surprise. Janus didn't know how to react, torn as he was.

"What?" Rogers was flabbergasted.

"I'm afraid that we will not be leaving without Clara," Norm said.

"Why?" Janus was shocked he even asked the question, while the Adepts looked at Norm in surprise and alarm.

Norm wore the same troubled look the Praetor had worn—that look of awful loss and of terrible lessons—and it disturbed Janus greatly.

"Let's just say that I have obligations that must be fulfilled," Norm stated simply.

"What makes you think that we won't simply pull you out of here?" Rogers asked.

Norm sighed in disappointment. "Because you would find it extremely difficult, especially once the others around here caught wind of it." He looked at Rogers, and his eyes cut the captain right to the bone. "Because even if you could, nothing you could do to me could make me talk, because I assure you, I have seen and experienced worse." Norm's eyes softened. "And because you would be making a terrible mistake, creating a far worse vulnerability than you know. But we both know it would never come to that, Captain."

Rogers spoke softly with a mix of curiosity and dread. "Why?"

"Because you have a conscience."

Janus felt odd, listening to those words. It was why he was so torn—to save Clara and risk his friends.

"However." Norm's pause brought Janus back to reality. "That does not change our immediate problem. How to get you to her...?" He paused. "Middleton certainly won't be granting you special access this time, and without any identification, you won't even be able to get near the lift."

"I have the impression you might know a way though," Celes said to him.

"Indeed I do... Adept Celes, was it?" Norm studied her for a moment more, as if confirming some detail in his mind. "But it won't be easy with so many of you."

Janus quickly interjected, "Captain Rogers and his squad will remain as backup."

Rogers gave Janus a sharp look, but after a moment, he relented. "Our goal is to get in and out as quickly as possible. My team will stay behind if that will make it easier."

Norm grunted. "Well…that will help." He looked at the others. "I believe Janus and I have much catching up to do, so I suggest all of you try to grab some sleep. We have an early day tomorrow."

The Adepts bedded down for the night crammed into Norm's small space. While the others slept, Norm, Janus, and Rogers spoke late into the night, the darkness slowly creeping closer around them.

"So why can't you simply retrieve Clara for us, Norm?" Janus asked.

Norm shook his head. "My ID is very specific and specialized. I can only travel to H-level. To do otherwise would trigger many alarms. Moving outside my prescribed route will cause problems as it is. Heading to E-level is something I would only try in desperation."

"So, you have a plan for getting Janus up top?" Rogers asked succinctly.

Norm smiled. "You do not strike me as a man who enjoys being this brusque, Captain. But yes, I do have a plan."

"I don't enjoy the situation ODIN is in, that's all."

"Understandable. Well, let us see if we can resolve at least one of your concerns then."

"So how do we get onto the lifts, Norm?" Janus asked curiously. "As you said, I can't exactly expect a special invitation from Middleton this time."

"But in a way, you can," Norm said slyly.

Janus and Rogers looked at him curiously.

"The Overlords have always been at each other's throats, but it has been more pronounced recently. Many stepped up the recruitment of Troopers. Janus will remember this from when he left."

Janus nodded. "But I didn't expect it to continue this long."

"Normally, you would be right," Norm agreed. "But Overlord Alastor was quickly splitting the other Overlords into two factions.

225

Those who supported him, and those who supported Middleton. The Executors, probably considering it a necessary and entertaining power struggle, were keen to sit back and see how the dust settled between the two."

"You're a servant on the upper levels, correct?" Rogers asked.

Norm nodded. "Yes. I work… well, worked, for Alastor. I would often be privy to many details that were not common knowledge. And Alastor's death is not commonly known yet. I expect I am the first servant to have any idea in his household. That gives us an opportunity."

"How so?" Janus interjected.

"Security has stepped up recently, but my position is well known among the Troopers. Many recognize me as one of Alastor's. I may be able to convince them that I'm bringing you to bolster Alastor's ranks."

"But won't we be sent to the military blocks because of that? We can't get up to the top that way."

Norm smiled. "That's true. But it will get us closer. As for the rest of the way, I have an idea for that too, but first we'll need to see if we can get you onto the lifts at all." He glanced at Rogers. "This is why I hesitate to say I can bring all of you, Captain. There more I bring, the more suspicious it will seem, especially with your age."

Rogers looked offended. "I'm not that old!"

Glory and Raleigh rolled over independently and said together, "You're pretty old, Cap."

Rogers hung his head. "I'm only thirty!"

Norm patted him reassuringly. "You are a spring chicken as far as I am concerned. But that doesn't change the fact that there would be questions about why I am only bringing you now. The others I can pass off as younger and could have missed previous drives."

Rogers sniffed. "Won't they recognize Janus?"

"Possibly." Norm rubbed his chin. "But I doubt it." He looked at Janus. "Whether you realize it or not, you have changed quite a bit, since the time you lived here. Your face is fuller; your body is more muscled, less lean."

"But you recognized me right away, Norm!" Janus said.

Norm smiled. "Well, that cannot be helped…" And he left it there, trailing off.

After a brief moment of silence, Rogers interjected, "So I suppose we at least have the beginnings of a plan."

Norm nodded. "I hope you are satisfied."

"At least for now."

"Good. Now, Captain. I suggest you get some sleep. I suspect Janus and I will be up for some time still yet."

Rogers looked at Janus. "Don't exhaust yourself looking for answers that don't exist. You have a team to lead tomorrow."

Janus smiled weakly.

Rogers smirked. "Just remember, I expect you to perform better than you did at Ghost." With that, he tiptoed to a corner of the room and then suddenly plopped right in the middle of Glory and Raleigh, who startled awake in surprise.

There were muffled and irritated murmurings of "Captain!" and "What was that for?" before the room went quiet once more.

Norm chuckled, and Janus turned back to him, pulling out the small golden locket he now wore around his neck. "Norm, can you tell me anything about this?"

Norm's eyes widened slightly and he said, "Ah…" but the look quickly passed and he said, "…the locket. What do you know about it?"

Janus shrugged. "Nothing really. Clara wore it for many years, but she never let me even look at it. When I was younger, I apparently took it off her neck once while she was sleeping and started playing with it. When she woke, she apparently gave me such a scolding that I wouldn't even look at the thing. I never really asked about it again. I always assumed it was something extremely precious and sentimental to her, and she couldn't afford to lose it... but in the note she said it belonged to me. And there is this writing on the back, with my name." Janus pulled the locket over his head, and held up the inscription on the back so Norm could see.

"May I?" Norm asked.

Janus nodded and Norm took it carefully into his hands and peered intently at the scrawling.

May Janus remind you

Janus watched as tears began to well up in the man's eyes, but Norm instead handed the locket back and asked, "What else?" His voice wavered for only a moment.

"There are two pictures inside"—Janus opened the locket—"but I can only make out the woman over here."

"A very beautiful woman," Norm said with a sad smile, raising his eyebrows.

Janus could feel himself talking faster, but wasn't sure how to stop. "I knew from early age that I wasn't Clara's biological son, but I had no memory of my parents, so I didn't mind. And Clara has been as good as a real mother to me, better than most probably. But if this locket is mine, I've been thinking about it and I was wondering if maybe...maybe this woman in the locket *is* my real mother. And if she is, what happened to her? Clara told me that she found me, but she never really seemed to want to give me the specifics. She always just told me..." Janus put his head down to hide his embarrassment, his eyes shifting to the sleeping group. "That I was the best find she ever made."

"Clara cares for you deeply, but I can only speculate why she chose not to give you it earlier," Norm said honestly. "She wants you to have it now, though." His eyes once again returned to the locket. "I am afraid there is nothing for me to add at this moment that will help you. You should focus on Clara. Once she is safe, we can have a frank discussion with her. But for now, you should get some rest, as there is much to be done tomorrow."

Janus agreed, and found a small open patch on the floor to stretch out on. It seemed comfortable and familiar to him, and the temperature was just right. In moments, he was fast asleep.

Celes lay awake, her back to Janus and Norm. As the group's soft snores filled the room, she closed her eyes, pondering the conversation she heard.

"You know, Lady Celes, you should get some rest. Tomorrow will be a difficult day," Norm whispered softly. Celes rolled over to look at him in surprise. She was just able to make out his small frame in the dark, resting in the aging chair. "You have nothing to fear from me." With a turn of his head he added, "Captain, you should rest as well. Nothing ill will befall you during the night."

A surprised, but amused grunt emanated from the direction of Captain Rogers, and Celes felt strangely reassured. She studied him for a moment, and she whispered back to Norm, "You know Norm, the way you speak reminds me of my great-grandfather from when I was little."

Norm chuckled softly, "Your great-grandfather must have been very old-fashioned then."

But she had already closed her eyes again, and slumber soon overtook her.

Norm woke the party after only a few hours' rest.

"You are going to need to strip your Adept armor off. The risk of discovery is too high once Troopers get involved." Norm shook his head. "I suspect the delay in news of Alastor's death is only because Middleton has been laying the groundwork for Titan and you Adepts to be blamed, and word will be out soon," Norm said. "I imagine there will soon be talk of war."

The Adepts exchanged uncomfortable looks with one another.

Lyn gave Norm a puzzled look. "But why? I realize I might not be the expert on Corporate politics, but isn't she working with Delacroix? Why would they try ta start a war with one another?"

The troubled look on Norm's face did not ease Janus's mind.

Norm shook his head and looked at the group. "I cannot be sure. But right now, your priority is Clara."

Celes signaled Janus. **(He's) hiding (something).**

Janus looked back at Norm, who was pointing to the far side of the room.

"The piles of clothes in the corner are for your team. I have been collecting those for months now. I figured you would come back with others, although Ramirez might have trouble finding anything that will fit him particularly well. I suppose that will make it more convincing, though," Norm added as an afterthought. He tapped his chin. "No offense to the clothes you brought, but they are in far too good condition, and they might attract attention. Slummers might not notice, but there is an ST or two sharp enough to spot flak armor when they see it, even if it is ripped to shreds. Captain, you and your team can remain in your armor. Oh, and Janus, if you don't mind, I should hold onto your locket for now."

Janus hesitantly removed the jeweled bird from around his neck and then carefully handed it to Norm, who tucked it away.

Lyn and Celes both looked at the pile of 'clothes' dubiously.

"These are clothes?" Celes asked with a hint of concern.

Lyn held up a particularly gungy rag at arm's length and gave it a hesitant and distant sniff. Her surprised expression made it clear that was more than enough. The pair took a moment to find some of the slightly more complete and less rancid smelling pieces. After a few moments, Lyn held up her selection with a grimace. "Can't back off now."

Celes nodded and pulled off her flak rags, reaching to undo the collar of her armor. Janus and Marcus grew wide-eyed and Celes blushed, turning away from the pair. Lyn gave Ramirez a harsh look, and he quickly herded the two outside the room. Norm, Rogers, and the others followed, leaving the two girls to change, while Ramirez and Glory stood guard. When Celes and Lyn exited the room, Janus, Marcus, and Ramirez all quickly went in and exchanged their armor for the rags. The smell was even sharper than Janus would have thought, and he realized, in a strangely sad way, that he was one step further away from his life in slums than he had realized. He had been away for far too long.

"Bring your weapons, for now," Norm said when they emerged. "You can leave them with the Captain when we separate, but there is no point in not being prepared while we travel to the lifts. Take the water pouches on the wall as well, we will need them."

With that, Norm beckoned them into the eternal twilight of the slums.

CHAPTER 26
THE FORGES OF CERBERUS

Dim lights shone along the squalid streets, casting strange shadows with the flickering fires. A crowd waited at the gates of Persephone, ready to travel to the lifts. There was safety in numbers. At the appointed hour, the gates creaked and cranked open under the guidance of the guards and people streamed out in multiple directions, heading for the lifts to which they had been given access. Janus knew some would be gone for days—the journey to some of the lifts would take many hours, and factory shifts were long and hard. The men and women wore grim, tired looks. Norm moved slowly, letting the main group slip ahead.

Norm spoke quietly, "We need to let the others go ahead. The factory workers all have their own IDs, and we do not. So we will have to look for the right opportunity."

With a small gap between them and the main group, Norm increased his pace, and the others followed. Feeling more comfortable with the terrain than they had the day before, and with the safety of a nearby crowd, the group moved swiftly. And soon, the black obsidian mass that was the lift system shone before them.

Norm peeked over a small garbage pile and then turned to Rogers. "This is where we leave you, Captain. We are approaching the station and the last thing we need is for even more suspicion. Take the weapons and head back to Persephone, you will be safest there."

Captain Rogers nodded, signaling his squad into the shadows. "Very well, we'll take a bow then." He saluted Janus and the others. "Good luck, to all of you. Honor and Victory."

They saluted back, and within moments, Rogers had disappeared into the dark.

"Honor and Victory," Janus murmured, wishing somewhat that he could have joined them.

A line of slummers stretched from the large open doors of the pulsing obsidian rock. Black-and-purple armored STs outside paid little attention to the struggling people, seeming almost bored in their duties, mostly concerned with keeping them in line while a few officials at the front scanned IDs.

Norm studied the Troopers, and suddenly waved Janus and his team along. They hurried along the line, ignoring the curious and irritated looks from those they passed, and Norm quickly brought them alongside the front of the line. One Trooper took notice of them and tromped over, holding his Zeus menacingly.

"Back of the line, mudfish."

Norm lowered his head. "Sorry, sir. I work on the upper levels. For Overlord Alastor. He wants more Troopers, and my friends wanted to join up."

"And you thought we'd take trash like you?" the ST mocked. "We don't need an old man or his friends." He raised his Zeus. "Now get back before I splatter ya."

Janus reached to pull the old man back, afraid of what the overzealous Trooper might do to him.

Hold.

The signal behind Norm's back caught him off guard, and he stopped. First Delacroix. Now Norm. Their secret signals were apparently anything but.

Norm held his hand up. "Oh no! Oh sorry! Oh... oh, Lieutenant Simms!" Norm's voice suddenly became louder and he stared directly at another Trooper who was monitoring the entire line.

The officer perked up and swiveled his head around, finally settling his gaze on Norm, who was now waving his hand in the air, while the menacing ST watched the exchange in surprise.

"Norm! Good to see you!" the ST said warmly, striding over in several powerful steps. Janus had a hard time masking his surprise.

Lieutenant Simms turned to glare at the threatening ST. "Is there a problem here?"

Their erstwhile bully's imperious manner instantly dissipated. "Uh, well, sir... this... *gentleman* and his friends are trying to get access to the factory level for ST recruitment." He lowered his weapon. "Says he is one of Overlord Alastor's."

"And indeed he is. And a fine scout of talent, if I do say so myself."

Norm interjected, "I heard there were a few positions in demand, and although I *certainly* couldn't fill the role, I know my friends would make fine additions."

Simms lifted his visor, smiling warmly. "Well, I don't know where you get your information, but you certainly know far too much." He looked over the group, pausing as he noticed the strong muscles underneath their rags. "But I don't suppose there is a problem with letting you try," he concluded.

"But sir!"

"Oh shut it, Gibbs. The man has been a servant for years."

Gibbs motioned to the ID scanners, lowering his voice to a conspiratorial whisper, "Sir, the regs say that we can't let anyone through without an ID. You know that they've been stepping up reviews recently."

Simms raised a hand. "They state that we need a registration for recruitment, not an ID. But still…" He looked at Norm. "You understand, right Norm?" He leaned forward. "I'm sorry, but honestly, your friends might want to stay in the slums for now."

"I've got a registration," Janus interjected.

Simms looked at him in surprise. "Really?" Grabbing Gibbs, he took the Zeus from him and said, "Scan him."

After a moment, Gibbs had grabbed a small handheld device and brought it back over. He reached for Janus's hand, then thought better of it.

"Hand out."

Janus complied, and Gibbs put his hand into the small device. Janus felt a tiny prick, and a few moments later, the device turned green. Gibbs held it up. "He's in the system. Says he's greenlit for transfer, whatever that means."

Simms clapped Gibbs on the back heartily. "Good enough for me."

"But sir, what about…"

Simms gave him a glare and lowered his voice. "We both know the fact that we got one registration is a lucky break for this crowd. We've heard the rumors. We might need strong backs soon, or would you rather have someone decide we're needed for the forward squads?"

Gibbs remained silent.

"Thought not. Check them for weapons, then send them up on a factory lift."

Gibbs nodded.

Simms winked at Norm. "You know how to work magic, Norm. I'll give you that. Stay sharp, you wily old man!"

Norm smiled back. "I plan to. Stay out of trouble, Lieutenant."

Simms waved as he left, and soon enough Gibbs had sent them through.

Inside the station, Celes curled her lips in disgust, and Lyn cursed.

Janus stared at the pair, and Celes glared at him. "Gibbs didn't have a problem with me being a slummer when he was patting me down."

Janus gulped and turned towards the packed station. The crush of bodies was immense. A constant flow of slummers moved onto the lifts that formed the outer ring of the station. More lifts were active, moving many slummers to the factories. But across the way, over the heads of the crowd, Janus could see many of the gates for the highest levels of the city were closed and locked, guarded by more STs than Janus could ever remember seeing within the confine of the station. There was even an Infernus prowling amongst them.

Norm's breathing became ragged as they pressed deeper into the station. "What's wrong with Norm?" Marcus asked quietly.

"He doesn't like being enclosed by crowds like this," Janus said in a low voice.

"That would be a problem," Marcus whispered. Lyn and Ramirez agreed.

"I don't think we're going to move through this anytime soon," Lyn spoke softly.

Janus was at a loss. Norm's condition was getting worse. His breathing was becoming louder and others in the crowd were starting to look at him. Celes, however, wormed her way forward, and grabbed Norm's hand tightly. He stared at her in surprise and she smiled at him, patting him gently on the arm in the limited space, and took slow deep breaths. She kept his vision focused on her, helping him navigate the crowd, and gradually, his breathing slowed as well.

As another lift descended, the crowd roiled. Janus felt the mass push forward, trying to get onto the lift. A moment later, a counter push sent the mass backward, as the slummers at the front struggled to prevent themselves from being pushed under the lift and crushed.

The STs shoved the crowd together as the lift locked into place, and Janus found himself in a stream of people jetting aboard. Grabbing Celes's hand, he pulled her into the stream too, and the little group was swept onto the lift, and moved to the edge.

Janus whispered to Norm, "That was quite a bit easier than I remember."

"Well, we aren't done yet." He breathed heavily as the lift slowly accelerated. Relief was evident on his face—the lift was still crowded, but the STs had limited the numbers, quickly shoving back the crowd as the lift had filled. "But I have a few tricks up my sleeve yet."

"I certainly hope so," Marcus spoke in a hushed tone. "Walking into Cerberus unarmed like this is worse than that time Hawkes suited up in Trooper armor and fought us one on one." He paused. "What did we call it again?"

"The night of a thousand bruises," Celes chimed in softly.

"But... what about the time he would find a weak spot in our defenses and kept pounding that repeatedly?" Marcus asked in puzzlement.

"The bruise for a thousand nights," Lyn added.

"Ah, yes," Marcus reminisced. "Good times."

The lift slowed and stopped at the factory level and the rest of the slummers departed. Norm waved for the team to keep up. They had hardly exited the lift before it silently dropped away, heading back for the slums.

The workers were quickly directed through the station by the Trooper guards, and they soon found themselves outside in the smoggy air of the factory levels.

Norm coughed in the stale air. "Been a while since I was here. Come on, we should keep up with the others."

They followed the factory workers, who slowly began to diverge off in different directions. Norm, however, did not slow.

Hot air blasted out of nearby vents, while they passed doors giving off the orange glow of a forge, or the sounds of pounding machinery.

"I'm surprised we were able to make it through the station," Celes said once they were out of earshot.

"And how do ya know the ODIN hand signals?" Lyn asked. "No one else should even know they exist."

"And yet many seem ta," Ramirez added.

Norm looked surprised. "I have known those hand signals for a while. I did not realize they were specific to ODIN, but I thought you might know them too..." He paused, collecting his thoughts. "As for the station, Simms is a bright and capable man, enough so that I was able to get him into an ST position, long before Cerberus started grabbing slummers for their army. I have kept track of him since then through various connections over the years. I discovered recently that he had been promoted to a lieutenant and heard rumors he would be assigned to the station."

Norm took a few more steps before he realized that Janus was no longer walking beside him.

"You helped someone get out of the slums?" Janus asked. Norm shifted uncomfortably. Janus looked at him coldly and took a step forward. "Don't you think Clara or I would have liked to leave as well?"

Norm looked down, and he stammered, "I was... was trying to help... as much as I could."

He grabbed Norm by the front of his raggedy shirt, dragging him forward. "I always heard you were so helpful. But so far? I keep thinking that you're more committed to what's best for you. Why are you helping us get Clara, anyway?" Janus asked angrily.

"Would you have wanted to be an ST instead of meeting us and becoming an Adept?" Celes asked quietly.

Janus looked at her sharply. "Marcus didn't seem to have a problem!"

Norm gazed sadly into Janus's eyes. "If I could have helped you any more than I did, I would have… I'm sorry." He slumped, totally drained and dejected.

Janus stared angrily at Norm, his lips curled in disgust. Norm did nothing, awaiting his fate.

A gentle hand grabbed his arm. Celes was gazing at the pair of them. "Let him go, Janus," she said softly. "I think he is telling you the truth. Let him go."

Janus remembered his team. Marcus was staring at him shrewdly. Lyn's eyes were open wide, and Ramirez was watching at him with a troubled gaze.

Janus released his hand from the front of Norm's shirt. "We're wasting time. Let's get moving."

Norm nodded solemnly, and then started moving away once again, his steps seemingly devoid of their energy and life.

Norm led them deeper into the factory level. Hot winds gushed from firing furnaces and shouting voices sounded around them. Heavy cranes clattered overhead, while churning vats bubbled and protested against their contents. Occasionally huddling in dark corners, or passing through tiny alleys filled with pipes, they skirted the ST patrols and checkpoints that were scattered throughout the factory level. Those workers they passed that noticed them kept their heads down and their noses clean. They had more important things to worry about.

The smoky haze surrounding them became lighter with the rising sun and slowly faded as the sun set again. Janus felt no hunger as the day went on. He merely stewed, unable to shake his feeling of betrayal, or the fact that he felt like Norm was lying to him.

There was a tap on his shoulder. Janus looked back, and Ramirez nodded to the sky. "Gettin' late. We should rest."

Janus looked around. Celes, Lyn, and Marcus looked fine. "The others are fi—" He stopped. Norm looked ragged. Janus doubted the old man ever traveled nearly so far anymore. Not that he should. Janus could feel a surge of irritation and contempt at the man.

Clara.

Janus stopped. Took a breath, and looked at Ramirez, his face no longer filled with quite so much anger, and nodded.

"Norm," Janus called out. Norm did not stop or turn around.

"Norm! We should take a brea—"

Norm glanced at him. He looked extraordinarily sad, but he did not stop moving. In fact, he sped up. "We're close," he huffed. "Almost there."

Janus glanced at the others, and they hurried after him.

It took another twenty minutes or so, but finally Norm disappeared between a set of thick tanks, large enough to each fit a longboat entirely within them.

Squeezing through, past a set of pressure gauges long busted, Janus found Norm stopped and gazing upward. A maze of pipes soared overhead, connected to the tanks by valves and pumps, and together, they formed a small enclosure. The hulking mass made Janus think of some giant creature with hundreds upon hundreds of thick appendages protruding from its body. The others joined him, gazing up in wonder at the structure.

"Here. It's here," Norm breathed.

Lyn looked confused. "And where exactly is here, Norm?"

Norm pointed at the mass of metal and plastics, still breathing heavily. "This is part of the main water treatment facility for the entire city. Many years ago, I climbed these pipes. It took me two days, and I nearly died doing it, but you should be able to do the same."

Marcus barely contained his skepticism. "You want us to climb these to reach the habitation level?"

"E-Level? Yes," Norm said.

Lyn looked at the man as if he were crazy. "We climbed all sorts of dangerous things in the Outskirts." She pointed up the pipes. "But that's what? A kilometer? Using rusty nuts and screws for handholds and feet?"

Norm shrugged. "I did it. And there is no other way. Once up top, if you have not attracted too much attention, Clara's ID should get all of you down to the slums. The Troopers will probably be more than happy to send you down."

Janus looked shrewdly at Norm. "But how will we find Clara?"

"Are you actually going to do this, Janus?" Celes asked skeptically.

"How else are we supposed to get there?" he asked. He looked to the others for an answer, but they remained silent.

Celes shook her head helplessly. "Is there no other way, Norm?"

"To climb, or to have me answer your questions about Middleton and Cerberus?" Norm asked.

"Does your answer change?" Marcus asked.

Norm shook his head and turned to Janus. "Clara was moved to somewhere in Sector 3. You will have to find a directory to look her up. Be swift, but be careful. Oh, and take these as well." He pulled out a small package of supplies.

"It contains some of the energy rations I found in your suits. I figured that if we were stopped I would be the least likely to be searched, and if I was, it wouldn't seem as strange that I had them. I've also thrown in two credit swipes with about five Heads each."

Janus nodded—there wasn't much point in asking how he managed to slip the energy bars off their suits unnoticed. There were still too many other unanswered questions about Norm anyway. As for the money, ten Hound Heads, it wasn't much, but it was more than most slummers would see in months. He returned his gaze to the pipes climbing skyward.

Clara.

Without another moment's hesitation, he stepped forward and grabbed a pipe, hauling himself up and grabbing for another.

"Now we will see *who* defines you," Norm whispered.

CHAPTER 27
THE WORLD ABOVE

The going was easy, if precarious. At least at first.

Keeping his weight over his feet and stepping up for new hand holds, Janus found climbing the pipes was like climbing a ladder or steep stairs. The others formed a line behind him, following his path, without complaint. He moved steadily, but carefully, ducking pipes and signaling to those below to watch their heads for jagged corners.

Sometimes, the group was forced to backtrack, awkwardly climbing down just to head up again. When this happened, someone new would take the lead while the others waited patiently, watching from their perches on valves, thick nuts, or wide pumps. The tangle was a never-ending vertical jungle. Freezing liquid coursed through some pipes and covered them in condensation, making them slippery and numbingly cold to the touch. Others were boiling hot to the touch, creating billowing clouds of steam and mist, and making the travel even more treacherous. They stopped to rest frequently, whenever they found a suitable perch.

It quickly became apparent that Lyn was the best choice for leading their little expedition, while Ramirez was far from it. His excessive height and reach gave him a big advantage, and other than the occasional tight squeeze, he often could take paths that were far more difficult for everyone else to follow. After an episode where Marcus clung to a rusting and precarious pipe while pulling Lyn up so she could avoid a terrifying leap over empty space, Janus ordered the team to perform an awkward switch several hundred meters up to place Ramirez firmly in the middle of the group, and Lyn at the front.

Lyn made more than a few pointed remarks as she climbed by Janus and Ramirez, just to make her feelings clear.

The going after that, however, became considerably easier for everyone. Lyn's pathfinding seemed to have a knack for even metal jungles, and as the shortest among them, no handhold she chose was out of reach. And despite her dark words, she seemed keenly aware of routes that allowed Ramirez to move without trapping his great bulk between the narrow pipes.

Peering between the openings of the pipes, Janus could spy factory roads, and the occasional windows of the nearby superscrapers as they climbed higher. He had never quite realized that the city was really just new buildings built upon old buildings. Each layer of structures formed a base for the next one above, as the tops of one section gave way to roads, or offices, or even completely different factories all around him. Occasionally, they passed within meters of lit windows, and Janus wondered what the occupants might think if they looked outside right now.

As they climbed further and further upwards, the pipes began to disappear into different sections of the city. Movement became considerably more difficult. And when Celes tore off an old bolt and Ramirez snatched her hand, stopping a terrifying plummet into the misty abyss below, Janus called a halt.

He looked around at the space. It was perhaps one of the few spots with a bit more real estate, an opening where the buildings had seemingly veered away from the metal vines.

"We'll stop here for a few hours to rest," Janus said.

Lyn agreed. "This is probably the best we'll get."

Marcus eyed the decrepit and precarious pipes that formed not-quite-horizontal platforms around them as he clung to an old valve above a massive drop to another crisscross of pipes below. "You have an intriguing definition of rest."

Slowly, the group made themselves as comfortable as possible in their perilous surroundings. Celes and Lyn wedged themselves into a small crevice between a pump and a valve, resting on six small pipes that shot off into the darkness. Marcus settled into a recess between two large, angled pipes, his legs sticking out into space from where the pair suddenly dropped vertically. Janus wove himself between another set of small pipes, far from comfortable, but secure. Ramirez had the most difficult time, as his size made it almost impossible for him to find a comfortable position, let alone one that was secure. He eventually settled into a spot where his knees were pulled up to his chest, pressed between a filtering station and another valve, sighing as he resigned himself to it.

"Marcus, first watch," Janus said.

"I suppose it's more of a listen, though," Marcus said, sitting up and peering around a pipe to look at Janus. "Not sure how much I expect to see."

"Second," Ramirez added.

Janus nodded. "Wake him up in an hour, Marcus." I'll take third."

Ramirez shared a glance with Marcus.

"I don't think that'll be necessary. But I'll make sure Ramirez is awake."

With his hands behind his head, and a last glance at Celes and Lyn, exhaustion overcame him, and he drifted to sleep.

Ramirez touched Janus lightly, and Janus's eyes snapped open. It felt like only minutes had passed. "Time to go," Ramirez said softly.

Janus gave him a quizzical look, and Ramirez shrugged. "Marcus convinced me that we should each take an hour and half watch. Neither of us were sleeping anyway, and you looked much more comfortable than I ever was."

Janus tossed a look at Marcus, who was perched on a pipe, watching him. He felt the bile rising in his throat. Staring at Celes and Lyn, who remained asleep, Janus turned back to Ramirez, speaking so that his voice just carried to Marcus as well. "I'm in command, so you're my responsibility. We're a team, and I need everyone functioning at full capacity." Janus looked at the spots Marcus and Ramirez had been resting. "Or as much as you can, anyway."

Ramirez watched Janus thoughtfully for a moment and then put a hand on Janus's shoulder in assent. Janus looked to Marcus, who shrugged and moved towards the girls to wake them.

Janus peered over the edge, trying to fathom the distance that they had covered in the perpetual gloom. The mist and smog made it impossible to see the bottom, even if he could have seen through the maze running below him. Tilting his head back, he could see fewer and fewer pipes running upwards. As they left the factory level, the air was becoming more and more clear. It seemed like they were making good time.

Pulling the package of concentrated energy and protein bars from the small pocket in his clothes, he motioned for Ramirez to distribute a bar for everyone. The group ate in silence, the conversation muted by the gloom and the seriousness of their position. Janus chewed slowly, taking a swig of water from one of the water pouches, and reflecting on the fact that in the scheme of things, at this moment, he could hardly claim that he was better off as an Adept than a slummer.

"Take a moment to stretch out a bit," Janus instructed as they finished their meal. He could feel his muscles stiffening from their climb and break, and he couldn't afford to cramp up now.

They were soon moving again, at least somewhat refreshed by their short respite and meal. The climbing was slower, but smoother than it had been before their break. Bright light began to filter from above, and Janus realized that for the first time, he was experiencing a sunrise of sorts at Cerberus. The pipes began to break apart, angling upward to the left and right, and Lyn directed them along a larger pipe that rose up and to the right.

Smaller pipes forked off, and suddenly the climbing became much easier, as the pipes provided excellent footholds. Stepping into a shadow, Janus looked up and realized they were now underneath some sort of platform or building. The sound of machines and people filled their ears, and Janus looked back at the others in surprise.

Left, Lyn signaled along a narrow path of pipes that broke away and then climbed upward suddenly through the platform above them.

The path was narrow and treacherous, and the little group stepped carefully, avoiding the rivets and connectors that threatened to snarl and send them toppling over. There was nothing around them to grab onto anymore. Reaching the vertical pipes, Janus watched Lyn ascend, pushing her head through a hole just a few feet wide.

Hurry, she signaled.

Janus climbed after her, and as he pushed through the narrow gap, the volume intensified immediately. He was just beside a bustling bridgeway filled with the eager populace of Cerberus. He quickly pulled himself through the hole and behind the barrier that separated them from the citizens. Peering over the barrier, he studied the crowd while Celes climbed up behind him. Some wore fairly impressive tailored outfits, some had clothes nearly as poor as those living in the slums. But as they rushed about, they all seemed different—they lacked the air of oppression of the slums, and the haughtiness of the elites.

There was only one place they could be: they had reached the habitation levels of Cerberus. They had reached E-level.

When Ramirez had carefully extricated himself from the narrow space, the five casually hopped the wall during a lull in traffic. A few passersby gave them odd glances, but soon enough they moved on, seemingly more concerned about their own business than Janus's.

Lyn, Ramirez, and Janus marveled at the sight.

"So this is a habitation block?" Lyn asked quietly. It was completely different than what Janus had expected. It seemed... alive. Sunlight—real sunlight—filtered from above, muting the shade of the massive buildings. It was like they had stepped into a thick grove.

"Yep. Though this doesn't seem as crowded as Medusa." Marcus motioned with his head. "Follow me."

They were on the edge of a square, ringed by shops—real shops—not just shanties. And they were filled with goods Janus had never imagined, let alone seen in anything other than a book. He took in the variety with interest as he followed Marcus. Lyn and Ramirez were equally in awe. Luxury stores filled with exotic foods—apples, pears, and oranges. Stores with odd curios: 3-stringed musical instruments, strange games and playing cards.

"There's so much stuff!" Lyn said.

"And so many people," Ramirez added.

All around, bright signs and yelling vendors announced their wares. And of course, there were a good number of bars. There was a depth and energy to the place that Janus did not expect.

Their rags did not warrant much more than the occasional glance, and the team quickly joined a throng of people heading along another bridge.

"Do you know where you're going?" Janus asked Marcus.

Marcus rubbed his chin. "We're headed towards the edge of a sector to orient ourselves. But mostly I'm looking for a public Daedulus we can use to look Clara up with."

"How do you know where the nearest edge is?" Celes asked.

Lyn pointed up to the side of a nearby building. "The sectors are marked on the sides of buildings. See? Looks like we're in Sector 16-G. H is the one back there, so presumably we're moving towards an edge."

"Ah. We probably need to look for a way to the center of the city then," Celes said.

"Why?" Janus asked.

"If it's anything like Medusa, the lower the sector number, the more central the sector," Marcus interjected.

Celes nodded in agreement. "Most Corporations expanded outward in a sort of spiral shape over time. The lower numbered sectors are almost always at the center and often the oldest parts of the city."

"Ah, here we go," Marcus said, pulling them from the crowd. He stepped inside a small alcove marked CHT, next to a set of stairs where people were rapidly descending to a lower level. "It's the local transit system, and they have a directory for travel purposes."

The others crowded around while Janus peered over a nearby bridge rail to see a hovering train, loaded with people, depart into the darkness of a tunnel. Deeper down, through the mists below, a cargo train sat idle. One of its lights was missing.

"Does Clara have a last name?" Marcus asked.

Janus looked up in surprise. "I—I don't know."

"This might take a while then. Let me look for Clara and try to sort by last name." Marcus tapped the screen of the Daedulus several times, a picture popping up with each name.

"That's her!" Janus exclaimed.

Marcus looked surprised. "That was easy. No last name, so she just sorted to the top of the list."

"Looks like she's in E03-F47894?" Celes said.

"E-level, Sector 3, Subsection F, I'm guessing," Janus stated. He studied the rest of the numbers. "47894…"

"Block 47. Sublevel 8. Unit 94," Marcus corrected. "If we don't want to be walking for hours, we'll need to take the transport, but it's too expensive from here with a transfer. We'll need to head a bit further along and pick up a direct route. Come on, if Cerberus is anything like Medusa, it will be best for us not to be caught outside too late tonight."

They rejoined the throng, making their way towards the center of the city. Ground cars occasionally passed them, but most of the movement was foot traffic. And though the people moved without the weight of the slums or the highest levels, Janus's eyes slowly began to take in the decay of the city—the dull sheen of dirt and age on the walls. The city was in a state of disrepair that could not last forever. Flickering old lamps filled the tunnels and the gaps where the sunlight could not reach. And more than once Janus pulled his hand away from a railing or wall to find it covered in the dingy red of rust and grime from years of neglect.

"Here's our station," Marcus said, leading the group down some stairs to a train waiting below, paying for their tickets from an automated machine with the ten Hound Heads Norm had provided them. They just barely had enough.

Night fell once more while they rode the train, or at least an early twilight. Other than the dull hum of electricity from the magnetic rails below, the ride was surprisingly quiet, with very few people heading towards the center.

They stepped out from the CHT station in Sector 3 into utter darkness. The few who rode the train with them peered into the blackness in concern and then hurried off. In the distance a few lights flickered, unable to muster the energy to light the area continuously.

As the train pulled away from the station, its pool of illumination quickly disappeared down the tracks.

"Pretty dark," Lyn said.

"Older sectors sometimes lose power," Marcus said. He lightly tapped the floor. "It's steel. Not plasment. This section has been around for a while."

"A lot of Corporations invest the most in the top levels of the sectors, as that's where the Executors moved to. The centers are the first to be abandoned as people move up and out. Sometimes, the only maintenance is to make sure the foundations remain solid," Celes added.

"Stay on guard," Janus said. "This reminds me a bit too much of the slums." With his eyes adjusting to the dark, he could just barely make out Marcus's nod.

"You're not too far off there."

"Everything is taller here," Ramirez remarked.

Janus looked up. The superscrapers reached even higher. It explained why everything was so much darker, the sky was blotted out once more. It really was the slums all over again.

"Good to know Middleton is looking out for Clara..." Janus murmured under his breath.

"This way," Lyn said, pointing up at a sign that was almost illegible in the dark, and trotting carefully off the platform.

The group followed her, slowly spreading out more and more as their eyes adjusted. They traveled along a road that ran perpendicular to the station, walled in by what appeared to be narrow and uniform apartments stretching along the street. Occasionally, the streetlamps would flicker on for a moment, only to shut off again, leaving them to blink their eyes while they adjusted once more.

"Subsection F. Block 47," Lyn whispered. "We're here."

As she said it, the lights flipped on once more, but this time they stayed. They had entered an area that reminded Janus more of the factory levels than anything else. The road narrowed to a single bridge, surrounded by steel catwalks that led off to the apartments beside them. To their right, a small set of open-air lifts provided access to the levels below.

"We want sublevel eight," Janus said. A stenciled identifier on the side of the nearby building read E03-F479. "We're on nine now."

As they approached the lifts, it was clear only one was functional, with a single light on above it. Next to it, another sparked and flashed, greedily sucking the power from a nearby line. Below them, a third lift lay smashed several levels down, split in two and illuminated by a flickering lamp nearby.

"I don't see a set of stairs or anything nearby," Lyn said. "Unless we want ta climb it."

Janus peered over the red, peeling railing. If anything, the rust covered supports looked more treacherous than the pipes.

"Climbing down is harder than up, and if anything, that looks worse than how we got here," Janus said. "Besides, if anyone is watching, that will certainly draw their attention, so…"

"Down we go then," Marcus said with resignation, stepping onto the lift.

Janus nodded, and the team crowded aboard, closing the simple gate behind them.

He instantly regretted it as soon as the Lyn jammed the button. The lift screeched, filling the air with the most awful racket imaginable. Lyn tensed, as if ready to jump off. Marcus and Celes grasped the rail. Everyone winced, Janus particularly so.

The lift descended with fits and starts, and as it ground to a halt one level down, the power cut out again, plunging the whole block back into darkness.

"That went well," Marcus said sardonically.

They exited posthaste.

"Spread out. We're looking for apartment ninety-four," Janus whispered.

As his eyes readjusted, Janus could see the nearby catwalks, and he carefully moved to one. As he got closer, he could begin to make out numbers along the walls. The identifiers for each apartment.

63, 65, 67…

"Over here," Ramirez said from a distance behind him. Carefully, Janus made his way over in the direction of Ramirez's voice. After a few moments, the figure of the large Adept emerged from the gloom.

"Number ninety-four," Ramirez said as Janus approached.

The others joined them.

"Keep hidden," Janus whispered, carefully approaching the dark door. He knocked on the door with three taps. There was no response.

He knocked harder, trying to whisper through the door, "Clara, it's me!"

The door swung open as the lights came back on, and propped up within the simple room was one thing. A ghostblade. Rogers's ghostblade. Janus felt a deep well of fear within him, but he turned back to his team.

"RUN!"

And then he felt an intense pressure on the back of his skull, and the world went black.

CHAPTER 28
MIDDLETON'S TRIUMPH

"Welcome home."

Janus's head swam, and he felt a great disconnect between his mind and body. He knew he still had arms and legs, he just couldn't make them move.

"I can hardly believe it—are you really the same boy?" the voice asked.

Janus groaned and tried to roll onto his side.

"Answer!" a different voice growled and pain shot through Janus's gut, knocking the air from his lungs. He gasped.

"Now, now, Martel. That is hardly productive, or becoming of a Commandant, enjoyable as it is," the voice said.

"Of course," the Commandant responded.

Janus opened his eyes, coughing, and a blurry figure hovered over him. It was red, and as he rolled his head down, he could see two large toes upon the foot.

"Hmmm, it is you. Unbelievable. Well, we have much to discuss…" the feminine voice purred. It came from a second figure, behind the first, and Janus struggled to focus his eyes on it.

"I know why you're here, but we need to discuss specifics," she continued. Janus felt a wave of vertigo as the blurry figure slowly came into focus. The features were round. Overly ornate clothes, and jewelry abounding.

Middleton!

Martel hovered over him, the massive boots just in front of his face. Janus surreptitiously eyed his surroundings. He was in a small, metal cell. Thick, unadorned walls surrounded him and the floor was rough and uneven. The Commandant Novus stood between him, Middleton, and a very solid door. Two more Inferni stood at the exit, watching impassively.

"Oh, there will be no escape for you," Middleton said with a smile as she caught his gaze. "I am wise to all of your tricks—I've been at this a long time."

She sighed, looking regretful. "I'm very disappointed, though. Capturing you was much easier than when I killed your mother."

Janus's mind went blank with shock and he leaped up with blinding speed, lunging for Middleton, and screaming angrily, "You killed Cl—"

The Commandant's huge two-toed boot connected with his midsection with devastating force, and Janus skidded into the far wall, doubled over in pain. "Down mudfish." He chuckled.

"The slum girl?" Middleton chuckled. "Don't make me laugh. Why would I waste a good servant like that?"

Janus's mind raced. *Clara's alive? But what does she—*

Middleton's eyes went wide. "You don't know, do you?" She looked away thoughtfully, "But… why else would you have spent so much effort…?"

Janus struggled to keep his face impassive and she turned away from him, a strange expression on her face, as if considering some unforeseen possibility.

Janus tensed, but Middleton's body began to shake, the fat jiggling her dress, and the most horrid noise emanated from deep with the folds.

Middleton was laughing…laughing at him. Her girth heaved as the laugh rumbled from her gut.

"Dumb luck! A coincidence?" she howled. "That's all it was?" She held her hands out and looked at Martel. "And here I was thinking that I had beaten one of my enemies! An enemy I had created, no less. But now, now I realize"—she wiped away a tear as she returned her gaze to her prisoner, unable to contain her mirth—"that you are just as foolhardy as your traitor mother." A flash of contempt crossed Middleton's face. "That beggar." She regained her composure, smiling broadly at Martel. "Oh, I am going to savor this moment."

Martel, hidden behind his visor, did not stop looking at Janus for a moment as he lay pressed against the wall.

Middleton snapped her fingers. "Bring me a chair, a comfortable one." One of the two Inferni at the door bowed and knocked on it. The door became translucent, and a moment later the ST on the other side had opened it. The Infernus leaned forward and whispered to the ST, who promptly ran off. Middleton paced the room slowly as she waited for the chair, but her eyes never left Janus.

A large, cushioned throne appeared, carried by two Troopers. The STs set the chair in the middle of the room and hastily exited. The second Infernus closed the door and it reverted to its solid state.

Middleton sat down, carefully settling herself in the large seat. "Where to begin…?" She grinned, tapping her chin. "Well, perhaps we should start with some introductions. I feel like we never got the chance to know each other properly before, and there's so little I know about you."

She placed a hand on her chest. "I am Overlord Victoria Middleton. But I'm fairly certain you knew that." She motioned to Janus from her throne. "And you are?"

Janus remained silent. He braced for a kick, but Martel did not move.

"Let me help you. Your name is Janus. You are currently employed with the ODIN mercenary legion. But after such a long time away, the mutt came home, eh?"

She sat forward in her chair. "You were the ST who grabbed Alastor, weren't you?"

Once again, Janus remained silent. Martel titled his head nearly imperceptibly, but Middleton continued.

"I know the answer. You can see it in his eyes." Middleton rested her chin on her hand. "Did you know that? You can always tell how a dog is feeling by looking at its eyes. Your mother was the same. Lowly trash that bit the hand that fed her. I guess we shouldn't be surprised that he betrayed Cerberus, should we?" Middleton asked Martel. A lighting fast kick sprung out, slamming into Janus. He was slammed back against the wall, and then rolled in agony, trying to suck in air and refocus his mind. The only reason his ribs weren't broken was because he had exhaled as soon as his mind had registered the kick. And the fact that Martel had clearly held back. The Commandant Novus moved much faster than any normal ST. He took a step back, giving Janus some space.

Middleton sneered, "But you're not here because of her, are you? Little mercs wanted revenge for their failed mission? Discovered something under Phoenix, did you?"

She sighed. "Alastor's meddling probably led you to Lightemann's, didn't it? Even in death he's an inconvenience." But a smile came unbidden to her lips. "But now his death is working for me, so I guess I can't complain too much."

She looked up at Martel. "Can you imagine what went through Jennings's head the moment he found out?" She laughed. "What I would have paid to have seen that!"

She eyed Janus carefully. "So the question is, what did you think you would accomplish by coming here? What do you think is going on?"

He struggled not to react in any way.

"Did you think there was something I have as evidence?" Middleton stared up at the ceiling. "No, no. That's only part of it. There's something more..."

She glanced at Janus, as if suddenly struck by a thought. "Your vaunted *Legion* did teach you about Phoenix Corporation, did it not?"

Martel stepped forward and Janus cautiously nodded his head.

"Good." Middleton chuckled approvingly. "So you know Phoenix was once the most powerful Corporation in the world. Why don't I tell you a story, then? Yes, I think that would be nice. A story for the babe." She looked back at the pair of Pyrus Inferni at the door, and as if on cue, they chuckled.

"Years ago, Phoenix sought dominance over all the other Corporations, including dear, dear Cerberus. They made a gamble, attacking a mercenary Legion in an effort to seize their Avalon citadel."

Janus's eyes widened, but he remained silent. He had heard the story long ago from the Praetor, but for some reason, he wouldn't have expected Middleton to tell it as well.

"But the Executors of Phoenix made a critical error. The SHADE mercenaries fought back, and killed them." Middleton's face lit up with joy, and Janus shuddered involuntarily.

Janus scowled. "Why are you telling me this?"

"Because I'm just getting to the good part," Middleton replied sweetly. "Your mother was there. She caused me a great deal of trouble actually, when the Corporations banded together to finish Phoenix off," Middleton said reluctantly. Janus could sense Middleton was fishing for something, but he wasn't sure what. "Her meddling caused nothing but headaches, and she was supposedly my ally! Frankly, it would have been better if she had died there, but through a stroke of luck, she made her way here." Middleton paused, turning her head to look at Janus from a different angle. "A traitor and a fool, who dared try to make Cerberus her home." Middleton looked beyond Janus, her eyes filled with rage. "She dared to try to take what was mine."

Janus struggled to focus. To resist Middleton's barbed hooks. She was telling him this to get him to slip up in some way.

Sometimes, you need to learn how to lose…

Clara's voice echoed through his mind.

"I would have none of that, however. But by the time I was able to bring her to justice, she had a brand new little baby. You. A boy she had the gall to call Janus. A veritable slap in the face."

Middleton paused, casually allowing her eyes to fall on Janus's form. "She ran, you know. Like all cowards do. Struggled to stay ahead of my men and dropped you into the slums with hardly a word."

Middleton stopped as if waiting for a reaction. Janus clenched his fists.

Learn how to lose…

"Honestly, I took you for dead. Didn't even think to look." She leaned forward. "Frankly, that was a mistake I made when we first met. I simply couldn't believe that you were…" She motioned to Janus. "But few things brought me greater joy that day than watching the life slip from your mother's eyes."

Janus's heart pounded. Middleton's expression was too joyful for her to be telling anything other than the truth.

"I can only assume you landed in a trash heap, somehow survived the fall, and that slum girl found you. I'm surprised she was able to work up the pity to pull you out. It seems you are just as lucky as your mother. But your luck has run out."

She soaked up the moment in her chair.

"Why should I believe anything you say?" Janus spat.

Middleton gave him a broad smile. "Oh, I assure you, I have spoken nothing but the truth. But that brings me back to the question of *Why?* Why are you here? Your superiors wouldn't have simply given you the objective of saving the slum girl. Perhaps you thought she could give you access to my estate?"

Janus forced his eyes shut. He had no idea what Middleton was looking for, so he couldn't give her anything. Middleton chuckled.

"No. That's not all of it," Middleton added. "Something else. What am I missing?" She snapped her fingers. "How *did* you get to the upper levels? Martel was pinged as soon as your ID was verified, so I knew you were coming. But I can't just start making a scene with the Troopers at the station. Not yet, at least."

Janus tried to prepare himself mentally for what was likely to come next. He doubted Martel would hold back anymore.

"Well, if you can't tell me, I can always ask your... friends?"

Janus's eyes snapped open. She put her fat fingers together across her stomach. "Yes, I think that's what I'll do."

Janus took a deep breath, and sat up against the wall, meeting Middleton eye to eye. "Best of luck," he said with a smile.

Middleton put a hand to her mouth in mock surprise. "Never heard that one before!" She lowered her hand. "When I'm through with you, I'll make you beg. Just like your mother did that day." She paused, and Janus felt that this was something she had not meant to say. She looked at Janus shrewdly, then gave a quick jerk of her head to Martel.

The Commandant leaped forward, but Janus was ready this time, rolling to the side and springing to his feet, his back to the wall. The

Novus pressed his weight and strength advantage over Janus, clawing at his head. But it was clear the Infernus was holding back, and Janus took the opportunity to dodge right, attempting to use the Commandant's forward momentum against him and to find an opening around.

The armored Infernus, however, was too clever for that, and maintained his balance all while driving Janus along the wall. Middleton remained seated, watching impassively.

I have to reach Middleton.

Janus struggled to dodge and deflect the flurry of blows from the armored Commandant, the huge suit blocking every attempt to escape. As the Infernus pressed him into a corner, Janus felt his arms becoming leaden, barely escaping the attacks. Sensing the weakness, the cruel soldier pressed his advantage. Finally, after a series of devastating strikes, Janus suddenly dropped his guard and the Commandant was forced stop a clawed fist from embedding itself in Janus's head.

Janus smiled as he dropped to the ground, allowing the Infernus's momentum to carry him forward into the wall. Crouching underneath the massive arm as it passed overhead, Janus leaped for Middleton in her chair. Middleton remained impassive, and the two Inferni guarding the door suddenly appeared in front of her.

With a quick pivot, Janus twisted himself on his leg and launched himself into the flipping kick Wouris had taught him. Janus knew his aim was dead on as he felt his twisting body accelerate his foot to crushing speed.

In his mind, he plotted his attack. He would incapacitate the left soldier, and then be forced to land on his right and leap immediately for Middleton. He would have one shot, to grab her and hold her hostage. And hopefully, his leg wouldn't be completely broken.

And then the Infernus's hand appeared. Janus's eyes went wide with surprise as the soldier he had aimed for caught his leg inches before it connected with its visor, twisted him around, and flung him into the wall.

Janus felt his head smash against the steel, and he slammed into the ground. A blood smear marked where his head and the wall had met, and he did not rise.

Janus once again awoke in a cell, except this one was far darker, and he was now alone. The walls were of the same hard steel as before, but now there appeared to be no exit, no door in any of the four walls.

He felt the back of his head; crusted blood matted his hair, and purple splotches covered most visible parts of his body. He stood slowly, his body aching. A wave of nausea passed over him and he collapsed to the ground.

When the nausea passed sometime later, he propped himself up and walked slowly around his cell. The only opening was a small vent near the roof.

He steadied himself for a time against the hard steel, and then made a flying leap, slapping the vent with his hand. As he landed he listened for the sound. The noise was quickly muffled inside the dark vent. Janus sighed, somewhere along the walls was a door even better concealed than the one in the room where he had met Middleton.

He leaned against the wall and closed his eyes, thinking about what his next move would be.

CHAPTER 29
THE MISSING

Janus awoke suddenly. He felt the back of his neck prickle. The left wall was translucent and an Infernus stood there, watching him. It was a Pyrus, and Janus felt some relief that it wasn't Martel. Janus held his gaze with the intimidating figure. Finally, after several moments, the Infernus shook its head and touched something on the wall. The translucent door retracted into the floor, leaving the cell wide open. Janus looked around, no other Inferni guards stood anywhere. He got up slowly but the Infernus didn't move.

I won't go to Middleton again that easily...

The Infernus tapped the floor with its foot. "Transpicuoum. Huh, don't see that much anymore."

Janus kept himself relaxed, limping forward for added effect. *Just a little bit closer...*

"I wouldn't try it, if I were you." The Infernus looked up. "The last time didn't go so well for you. Although, it was a beautiful kick. Very well executed. It's just too bad you had to show it off in front of that fat hog."

Janus stopped in amazement. *Fat hog?*

"I do have to take pride in how well I trained you. I barely blocked that kick in time, and I knew it was coming," the Infernus continued.

Janus's mouth opened in shock. "Wouris?"

"She may be a pig, but she doesn't miss a beat. I suspect the only reason she didn't question me is only because I beat on you as hard as the others. Sorry about that, by the way, but I couldn't compromise myself by going easy on you," Wouris replied, lifting her faceplate.

"Wouris, it is you! How did you get here?" Janus said.

"By not diving in, but we can talk about that later. We need to get the others if we're going to make a clean getaway. They're further down this cell block. Middleton's been keeping you all isolated, but I think at this point the only reason any of you are still alive is because she wants to torture *you*, Janus. She plans on making you watch everyone else die before she finishes you off. I knew I had to get all of you out before that happened, so here I am. That woman is a monster, and she absolutely hates you, though I got the distinct impression from your *interview* that she didn't provide the whole story."

Janus smiled. "I got that too, although I had to take a few punches to drag the information out of her."

Wouris grinned. "Nothing keeps a good Adept down."

Celes was in the next cell block. She was crumpled on the floor in the middle of the cell. Wouris quickly opened the door, and Janus dashed inside.

"Celes!" Janus whispered. "Celes, are you alright?"

Her clothes were covered in blood. She stirred slowly. "Janus? Janus, is that you?" She turned her head to look at him and smiled, then grimaced, obviously in pain. "I thought I wouldn't see you again."

Janus smiled back, cradling her head. "Don't worry, everything's going to be fine."

Wouris watched the exchange silently.

"Can you move?" Janus asked.

Celes shook her head. "I am feeling a little weak right now..." She smiled again. "Why is it that we can never make it back without getting beat up?"

Janus chuckled. "But we always make it back, don't we?"

"We do..." Celes said, lapsing back into unconsciousness.

"She's in bad shape," Janus said, looking at the gashes on her face and neck.

Wouris nodded. "I wasn't there, but I understand she was very *uncooperative.*"

Janus looked at Celes with concern. "Good for her."

He picked her up, his face hard as he held her close. "Let's get out of here."

Wouris looked at him doubtfully. "Are you sure?"

"I'm fine. Besides, you're in better condition for fighting, so if it comes down to it, I want you to be ready. I'll keep up, don't worry."

Wouris nodded. "Let's go."

It didn't take long to have everyone out. Middleton hadn't posted any guards along the block.

"Will she be okay?" Lyn shot worrisome looks towards Celes as she stumbled out of the cell. Her face was puffed and purple and she held her wrist as her hand flopped limply around. The six of them were standing in the middle of the long metal cell block. A few bulbs burned dimly the dark surroundings.

Wouris shook her head. "I don't know. Only if we get out of here quickly."

"Where to now, Wouris? And where are the other guards?" Marcus asked, watching Celes. Both he and Ramirez clutched their sides, and Marcus's right arm was broken. Ramirez bore a very deep gash over his left eye, and crusted blood covered part of his face. His gait was uneven, and he gritted his teeth as he moved.

"Middleton didn't want to attract too much attention, so she kept the guards light," Wouris said through the heavy visor, which added a disturbing rasp to her voice. "She doesn't really expect you to be able to escape in your condition, but she also doesn't expect the guard she posted to be working with you, either. We don't have much time. They'll be coming again soon." She paused, pointing to the door out of the block. "We're going to be making a full-out run for the lift. Things are probably going to get a little nasty from here on out. Our only advantage is that Middleton doesn't want word of your capture getting out, so only her Troopers know you are here. They won't expect one of their own to turn on them, so we might be able to surprise them and escape, if we're lucky.

"This cell block is located in Sector 10, north of Sector 3. It's one of the least critical areas of Cerberus, which means that if we can get out of the main towers, we should have nearly a free run to the lifts. The closest is due north, about fifteen minutes at a run to make it."

Janus gritted his teeth, but said nothing and held Celes closer.

"Can you keep up that pace carrying Celes, Janus?"

"Just get moving, Wouris. I have no intention of dying in Cerberus."

Wouris nodded and took off running, the others struggling to keep up with her.

At the end of the long hall, Janus could see a solid door that blocked their way. Wouris signaled to them to keep running and put on a burst of speed, lowering her shoulder. She bulled straight through the door, bursting into the guard's room. The two Inferni present, resting on a solid bench designed to support their weight, were caught completely off guard. They had barely sat up before Wouris dispatched them both with a savage point-blank burst from her Zeus into one and a claw through the visor of the other. She was surveying her handiwork when the others came running in behind her.

"Still with me?" Wouris asked.

Panting, the others nodded. She immediately sprinted off, the team on her heels.

Sector 4 was in what could best be described as a state of disrepair. Absolute disregard would be more appropriate. Even the great superscrapers had begun to crumble around the edges, plasment supports chipped away in places to reveal metal beams beneath. A thick layer of dirt and soot covered the walls, making them a dark brown-black. The streets were devoid of light, and only faint moonlight and lamps from the level above gave any illumination. Only a few timid faces peered out at the group as they dashed by, realizing that whatever was at hand was none of their concern.

Janus's head throbbed as he ran, but he pushed through the pain. It helped keep his mind off of his legs and arms as he ran to keep up with Wouris, clutching Celes tightly. Several times he stumbled in the dark, but he kept doggedly going. Wouris turned on her flamethrowers, and they burned like little beacon fires in the darkness. He focused his mind on Wouris as he ran, like she was a finish line just a little further ahead. The others running beside him faded from his vision. All he could do was repeat a little mantra in his head. *Just a little further now...*

After what seemed an eternity, the lift came into view and Wouris slowed the group down. Far too many STs waited here for her to make a surprise attack. Wouris let the group fall in behind her and stepped forward confidently.

The STs surrounding the lift station watched the little group, but were hesitant to stop an Infernus. Wouris signaled the team to move into the station.

"Just taking these troublemakers down to the slums," Wouris said confidently.

"Not likely," said a gruff voice. Five Inferni appeared from inside the station, and more from Sector 4 behind them surrounded the group. Commandant Martel emerged from the darkness, Middleton just behind him.

"I was wrong—you're just as much trouble as your mother," Middleton said, flanked by another two Inferni. "And you"—she addressed Wouris—"are clearly not one of my Helltroopers. I've seen that kick before, but I wouldn't expect my Inferni to know it. An Adept officer, perhaps? Probably one who infiltrated our forces while young Janus here was causing such ruckus at Lightemann's?" The sarcasm dripped from her voice like venom.

The STs now raised their weapons at the pronouncement.

"These ghosts are the ones who killed Overlord Alastor?" an ST asked in surprise. "Well, we'll take care of them, don't you worry, Overlord Middleton."

Middleton smirked. "That won't be necessary, Trooper. Everything is well in hand right now."

"It has never been as *well in hand* as you believe, Middleton," a strong voice came from the shadows near the edge of the station.

"Who said that?" Middleton turned around. "Who dares question my authority?" Her two guards shifted towards the voice, putting themselves between it and their Overlord. Martel did not move from his position, but titled his head slightly, as if listening closely.

"I would not move if I were you. Unless you want Middleton dead," the voice said.

The Inferni stopped moving, trying to block multiple angles with their bulk, staring intently at one point in the darkness. Some of the STs watched the shadows nervously, unsure where the threat lay.

"Lower your weapons," the voice commanded.

The STs looked hesitantly at Middleton. She cocked her head at the darkness. "No. I don't think so."

A silver-plated pistol emerged from the shadows, pointing at Middleton. The voice laughed. "There are too many Troopers here, Middleton. Too many to deal with properly at least. So either you tell your troops to lower their weapons, NOW, or die. The options are simple. If I wait any longer, one of yours might get twitchy. But I have no fear of death, so the only way you are going to live is if your Troopers lower their weapons before I hit three. One...Two..."

"Lower your weapons," Middleton snapped nervously. The Troopers complied, and the Inferni kept their arms at their sides.

"Good," said the voice.

Middleton looked at the weapon curiously. "Do I know you? Your voice...sounds familiar. And that weapon..."

Janus took a closer look at the silver pistol, suddenly realizing that he had seen two nearly identical copies before. Both had shot him. One was the weapon the Praetor carried, and the other was the pistol Delacroix had held. The Praetor's had a crescent moon engraved upon it, while Delacroix's had had a fiery bird on it. This pistol had an open eye and shield carved into the side, but it was unmistakably of the same origins.

It can't be... now that they had stopped for a moment, his head was pounding, and it was hard for him to focus at all. He steadied himself, he had to be ready to act.

"It has been far too long, Middleton. I am ashamed that I have done nothing but hide for so many years. But I have bided my time, hoping for a chance to redeem myself. At last, that day may have finally come. Let them go."

"No." Middleton smirked.

"Still confident to the last, eh? You always were so sure of yourself, except when it came to her. She always had something you could never have." The pistol fired, hitting Middleton in the knee, and she collapsed to the ground in a wail of pain. The STs raised their weapons.

"HOLD!" Middleton screamed.

"I assure you, I am a much better shot and far less afraid than I was long ago. Natalie made sure of that."

Middleton's eyes went wide as she grimaced, lying on her side. "It—it can't be," she stammered. "You're dead. DEAD! I searched for you. You died on the streets of Cerberus, despondent and alone. I searched for you."

"You forget—without regular treatments, I have aged greatly. That and the fact that the slums age a man like nothing you could ever know."

The figure stepped out of the shadows.

"Norm!" Janus exclaimed.

"Impossible!" Middleton snarled.

"So now you realize our predicament," Norm said.

Middleton's face took on a look of panic. Norm smiled. "Yes, you understand how close to death you are in this moment. And you will let them go."

Beads of sweat formed on Middleton's brow, but she regained her composure, having one of her Inferni pull her up and support her, and Janus was surprised by her resilience.

"I will let them go. But only if you stay."

"Hmmmm. I will consider it. But first, we have someone else who needs to leave here as well. Come on." Norm motioned behind him with his free hand.

Clara stepped out of the shadows, looking nervous, as if not believing what was happening. Janus's eyes went wide. "Clara!"

Norm glanced at Janus. "No time for pleasantries, lad, get on that lift. Now Middleton—"

A streak of light slammed into the superscrapers towering high above them.

The concussive force was massive, knocking even the Inferni to their knees. The towers shook and leaned precariously. Janus scrambled upright, hauling Celes away. The closest building pitched over, slamming into another and crashing down through the elevated roads and walkways as it fell, destroyed everything beneath it. More streaks raced in, flashing throughout Cerberus.

"We're under attack!" one of the STs screamed.

"We are being hit by atomics!" an Infernus shouted over the din.

"NO! NOT YET!" Middleton screamed.

CHAPTER 30
...AND BACK

Janus, still carrying Celes, rushed forward and grabbed Clara's arm, pulling her from the ground. "Let's go!"

"Absolutely right, lad." Norm had somehow stayed up on his feet, and ran forward, grabbing Clara's other arm.

Janus yelled to the team, "Go! Go! Go!" and the group took off into the station. Missiles streaked into buildings all around them, launching fiery projectiles from the broken structures. A few STs made to stop them, but Wouris barreled them aside.

Martel had stayed on his feet and took aim at the fleeing Adepts.

"No, you fool!" Middleton shouted. "Forget them, GET ME OUT OF HERE!"

Despite his helmet, the Commandant looked almost perturbed for a moment, but then quickly signaled his troops, leaping away from the chaos.

"Take me to my estate!" Middleton shouted.

"But Miss," one of her guards protested, "that's in the middle of the city, won't that—"

"Do it now!" she screamed, and they picked her up and boosted away, while the other Inferni followed, abandoning the STs who cowered and lay scattered amid the chaos.

Janus caught a glimpse of them disappearing as he ran through the doors of the station, his pumping adrenaline making him entirely forget the pain and the exhaustion that was within him.

The station was empty, likely due to Middleton. Low rumbles reverberated through the ground, but the station itself felt fairly solid, and the explosions outside were muted somewhat by the structure. Lyn rushed into the guard station.

"The lifts are locked down!" Lyn exclaimed through a speaker, waving a hand at the red warnings flashing upon the screens, and the sealed doors preventing the lifts from moving up or down.

"It must be the attack!" Marcus exclaimed.

"Can you override it?" Janus asked.

"Not anytime soon," Lyn yelled.

"There should be an override that will send the lifts to the bottom!" Marcus said, rushing in behind her. "But it will disable the system." He searched around the station for a moment, and then pointed to a large yellow-and-orange button behind a glass screen. "There!"

"Get on!" Wouris shouted at them, pointing to a nearby vehicle lift.

The group clamored aboard. "Hang on!" Marcus said, grabbing a railing. Norm quickly did the same, while Janus helped Clara and carefully put Celes on the ground.

Wouris stepped over to the console with the button and smashed a huge fist through it. The warning sign turned to green.

"System Overridden," Wouris said.

In a flash, the doors below the lifts sprang open and their lift dropped like a rock. Janus grabbed a railing and held on as he began to lift off the floor, reaching out to secure Celes as well.

"Janus!" Clara screamed.

"The emergency brakes will kick in!" Marcus shouted.

The lift raced downward, faster and faster, as explosions peppered the city above them. Janus looked up and had the odd sensation of time being stopped as debris from above fell in parallel with them, looking like they were all stopped in time.

"Marcus!" Janus yelled.

"Once we get closer to the bottom!" Marcus replied.

They plummeted downwards through the factory level passing screaming people and shocked Troopers who stared dumbly at the chaos around them, or at the lifts that shot by them. Deeper and deeper they fell, the smoke and dust from above blocking out the light. Only the lights on their lift illuminating the rushing haze, and the feeling in their stomachs gave them any indication they were still falling.

Suddenly, the squealing of metal could be heard as the emergency brakes kicked in, and Janus felt a sudden and unpleasant deacceleration. Within moments, they were within the confines of the bottom station. Confusion and chaos reigned here as well as Troopers struggled to contend with what was happening above.

"LOOK OUT BELOW!" came the bellow from above, and Janus looked up just in time to see Wouris come flying out of the darkness, firing her jump jets at max power, slamming into the far side of the platform. The joints on the suit strained and popped as she fell backward, deflecting some of the energy from her fall.

Wouris struggled to regain her footing, the massive suit clearly damaged by the attempt to stop.

Immediately, STs swarmed her.

"Pyrus! What's going on?"

"Are we under attack?"

"What's happening?"

"What should we do?"

Wouris stood up and examined the situation. A moment later, another lift from above screeched into the station, carrying a bunch of terrified H-level citizens, who had clearly been caught off guard when the override was thrown.

Wouris held up a hand. "Cerberus is under attack. Get all of these people away from the station. If we're under attack, Cerberus is going to need every citizen soon, so leave no one behind. The edge of the city should be safer, so head that way. I've been tasked with protecting this group, so I'll be counting on you to take care of things here."

The Troopers instantly seemed more calm. "Yes, sir!"

Janus knew that would rankle Wouris, but she said nothing, and quickly rushed over to the group. "Let's move."

They quickly fled the station, moving out into the darkness that now seemed even more black. Lights from the factories above them flickered and went out.

"Where to now?" Wouris asked Janus.

Janus hefted Celes closer and looked at Clara.

"We're close to the North end of the city. This is actually about as good as we could have hoped for getting to evac, but we've still got quite a run."

The whirring sound of Carrion Eaters sounded around them, and both Janus and Clara tensed. Wouris noticed their reaction and raised her weapons. "What is it?"

"*Rats.*"

Norm stepped forward, and put a hand on Wouris' raised arm. "I suspect you might be in for a surprise."

The whirring became louder and then finally a group of several cobbled together bikes, if that's what they could be called, rounded a corner, with Rogers on the front, slamming to a stop in front of the group.

"Looks like you could use a lift, Lieutenant."

"Captain!" Janus exclaimed.

"Norm told us we might need a quick exit from here, and once the chaos started up, we figured we should watch the lift. We saw your lift come flying in," Rogers said.

"Seemed like a solid signal you might need help," Raleigh added.

Wouris raised her visor. "Well, we're glad you're here."

"Sergeant! I knew we shouldn't be worried about you. What's your status, and where's the rest of your team?" Rogers jumped off his bike.

"Hopefully back at Valhalla by now. But we can talk about that later. This team is hurt, some of them badly. We need to get back to Valhalla and away from this..." she motioned back in the direction of the station, where Troopers were hurriedly directing people out, "mess, as quickly as possible." A distant boom sounded from above them.

"Agreed." Rogers looked at Norm. "You got them out? I'm more and more impressed."

"Looks like you managed to procure a ride like I asked," Norm replied.

Raleigh smiled from over his handlebars. "Sure. We just asked some of the locals real nicely, and they were happy to help us out."

Clara cautiously stepped up behind Janus. "Are these your friends as well? Based on what Norm told me, I'm guessing they did a bit more than ask."

Rogers did a double take, as if noticing Clara for the first time. He smiled charmingly. "I assure you, we are always absolutely polite. But I'm afraid I haven't introduced myself." He performed a small bow. "I'm Captain Rogers of the ODIN Legion. And you are?"

"Clara." She smiled.

Janus stepped in with a stony look. "My mother."

Rogers looked surprised and said, "Charmed. I never would have guessed. You're far too young."

Clara blushed.

Janus cleared his throat and said, "I don't think this is the time."

Rogers shook his head at the young lieutenant. "Still so much to learn. Bravos, take Adept Celes out of the Lieutenant's hands. He looks about ready to collapse." He looked Wouris' suit over. "Will your armor hold up for a bit?"

"I think well enough for this."

"Good." Rogers nodded, motioning for the groups to divide themselves on the bikes. "Let's ride."

They had just enough room. Rogers had clearly searched out bikes large enough to support the extra people, and riding in twos and threes, they raced through the city as quickly as possible. The Carrion Eaters were essentially off-road bikes designed to handle the garbage filled terrain of the slums, and despite their patchwork nature, they handled it beautifully. Janus rode with Bravos, helping to hold Celes upright while Bravos steered them through the city.

Wouris kept up behind them, bounding along, the joints in her suit straining as she kept up the pace.

And it was a good thing too. Despite the fact that deep in the slums, the huge explosions above them sounded far away and muted by the stillness, it did not make them less dangerous. Parts of the massive Cerberus superscrapers fell near them as they sped on, bringing roads, pipes, and everything else with them. But they raced onward, sticking to back alleys, as Norm directed Rogers through the mess.

As they careened between buildings, Janus realized that many of the slummers they passed did not react at all, simply standing exposed and staring up at the sky as lights above them winked out, one by one.

To them, the massive attack seemed more a puzzlement to them than a threat. There was nothing of value to be taken from here. And the slums were well protected by the levels above. Even those who understood the meaning of the noise paid it little heed. Either a building would come crashing down on them or it wouldn't. They would have no warning either way. They simply hoped what little food, water, and money flowed their direction would not be affected.

Janus smiled at the sight of the curious men and women. For once, the slummers may have gotten the better end of the bargain. No doubt that people up above were dying and panicking, but down below, in the slums, an entirely separate world existed—one that would find a way to survive no matter what happened above. For the first time, Janus realized he may have been done a far greater service growing up in the slums than he ever could have imagined. It was a disconcerting thought.

Near the edge of the city, the distant booms suddenly stopped, and as the open sky appeared overhead, Janus looked back over his shoulder. Cerberus was burning. Fires raged across the black cityscape, and there was a constant low wail of sirens and people. He grimaced and looked over at Clara, who was riding with Raleigh and Lyn. She was looking back as well, shock and awe upon her face. No matter what happened now, he doubted Cerberus would ever quite be the same. He couldn't imagine what he would have felt had he known she was still stuck there.

"Glory, head to the Longboat and get us warmed up," Rogers shouted.

Glory nodded and peeled away. Marcus, riding on the back of the bike, gave a surprised look towards Celes, who drifted in and out of consciousness as they headed on a slightly different tact. Now beyond the city and with mostly flat ground, Rogers opened up the throttle, lurching ahead.

The others followed, and Janus looked at Celes.

"Just a little longer, Celes."

She did not respond.

Racing into the woods, Janus was relieved to find the Longboat undisturbed. While Rogers quickly helped Wouris out of her armor, Ramirez powered up the engines. Bravos helped Janus move Celes onto a medical stretcher, while Clara scrambled aboard, Lyn helping her strap into a seat, and then buckled in herself.

"I'll take over." Wouris grabbed the second seat next to Ramirez.

"Norm, you're with us," Rogers said firmly, mounting his Carrion Eater again. He looked at Wouris, yelling over the engines, "Valhalla should have moved closer for our rendezvous. We don't want to be caught by any overzealous Cerberus fighters that might have scrambled from the attack. Move fast. We'll be right behind you."

Wouris nodded, and Rogers raced off with Townes, Raleigh, and Norm.

Once Celes was secure, Bravos yelled to Wouris, "Hit it!" and Wouris pushed the craft to full power, punching out of the forest and zooming away from the chaos behind them. Janus and Bravos held on for dear life, not daring to leave Celes's side.

"How is she doing?" Wouris asked Bravos as they accelerated away from the city.

Bravos shook her head. "Not well. We are doing the best we can with what is available in the Longboat, but she needs treatment at Valhalla. It's internal bleeding, but I don't know how bad."

Janus hovered over Celes, wiping a thin trickle of blood from her mouth. She looked pale, and her skin felt clammy.

"Hold on, Celes. We're almost home," Janus whispered.

Strapped into her seat, Clara watched with worried eyes.

Janus lost all track of time, and every moment seemed interminable. He vaguely remembered hearing Ramirez give Wouris a heading as they left, and looking out the window at one point to realize they had left land far behind them. But the swelling waves seemed to have no end. They just stretched endlessly, and he had no idea how long they had been flying. He just stared at Celes, doing everything his limited medical training and Bravos instructed him to do. And he felt useless.

Suddenly, a voice crackled over the comm. "Longboat 879-Charlie, you're coming in fast, what's your situation?"

Wouris glanced at Ramirez. "What's the call?"

"Hell Flea-2," Ramirez responded.

Wouris nodded, all the while moving in a blur of speed, but keeping her voice detached, and calm. "Valhalla, this is Hell Flea-2, requesting emergency medical support."

"Confirmed, Hell Flea-2. Welcome home, Sergeant. Medical support will be standing by in Chariot of Protection. Platform is clear, so take it in as hot as you like."

"Roger," Wouris replied.

Janus looked to Wouris, as Ramirez asked, "How fast can you take us in?"

She grimaced. "Just watch me."

As they approached, Wouris yelled back, "Strap in! Janus, Bravos, I know Celes is secure, so jump into a seat."

The landing bay opened up like a maw in front of them, and Wouris took the Longboat in at full speed. As she did, she cut the left engines and spun the craft 180 degrees. The Longboat hurtled towards the rear wall of the bay, and Wouris punched the engines back to full power. The heat of the engines licked the wall, causing it to shimmer and dance, but the Longboat slowed and stopped with expert precision. Wouris quickly lowered the craft and cut the engines as medical personnel wearing red crosses swarmed them. The medics leaped aboard, and Celes disappeared in the flurry of activity. More medics stepped aboard to help the rest. Janus felt a sudden exhaustion wash over him. He staggered up from his seat, and a familiar hand steadied him. But the next moment it was gently pulled away, and the medics carefully guided him onto another stretcher. Before another thought crossed his mind, he had fallen asleep.

Chapter 31
Old Acquaintances

Janus awoke to a familiar feeling of warmth. The medical ward of Valhalla had not changed much, and the green glow of the sensors was oddly relaxing. He felt an odd sense of déjà vu with his first day in Valhalla.

But there was one change. Looking a combination of exhausted and relieved, Clara sat beside him, wide eyed.

"Clara."

"Well, I can see that your habit for getting into trouble has not improved since you left me." Clara smiled.

Janus laughed and then grimaced. Pain shot up his body. He remembered Yalla's words. He guessed that he hadn't been in bad enough shape to warrant a Nanyte injection. "I sometimes think that it has gotten worse, actually," he joked, and grimaced again.

Clara shook her head knowingly and looked him up and down.

Janus smiled. "It's good to see you again."

"I'm glad to see some things haven't changed," she said. "Barely surviving the day and all you can say is 'good to see you.'"

"Hey! I just—"

"You're safe, and that's all that matters to me," Clara said with evident relief. In a flash, she hugged him.

"Ahhhh, ahh—" Janus squirmed uncomfortably, trying to pull away from her firm grasp.

"Oooo, sorry," she said through gritted teeth. "Well, serves you right, making me worry," Clara scolded. "And getting yourself captured? They told me all about it. I can't believe how stupid you were."

"How was I supposed to know?" Janus asked skeptically.

Clara rolled her eyes. "You grew up in the slums. Surrounded by danger. You're supposed to know."

Janus looked at her blankly, and she sighed, exasperated, and said, "I thought you were supposed to be the smart one." Janus scowled, but Clara merely brushed his look off. "Middleton threatened me the very first time you met her, just to get you to cooperate. She commented on how we were late and punished the Trooper responsible! Just that one meeting should have convinced you that she's not to be underestimated. She tracks everything. She's Overlord of Intelligence, for crying out loud!"

Clara shook her head, and then looked out the window of the medical ward. She motioned through the window. "It's so beautiful here. It reminds me of her estate."

Janus looked at her curiously and she sighed.

"She came back from her travels agitated. More so than I've ever seen before. She was angry. Nothing was making her happy. I started fiddling with..." Clara hesitated, and pulled the jeweled bird locket from a small box next to Janus's bed. "I started fiddling with this."

Janus looked at it. "The locket... my locket."

Clara nodded.

"Middleton noticed it immediately. She seemed shocked. I guess she had never really studied it before, but she looked as if she had seen a ghost. She asked me where I got it, and I told her the truth—that I had found it a while back in a trash heap, abandoned."

Janus smiled. "All true."

Clara smiled back. "Anyway, she almost immediately dismissed me. It was if she had suddenly realized something and had no idea what to do. It was… frightening. But just before I left she told me to report to E-Level for better housing, and she expected me to be there that night. I knew something was up. I didn't have time to head back home, so I waited in the maid's house until Norm's shift normally ended and met him at the station. I gave him the locket and told him where to put it. He asked me why and I told him that I was being moved to E-Level. It was about that time that Troopers in the station forced us to go separate ways. After that, Middleton kept me confined there, until one day a Trooper instructed me to report to work as normal, as if nothing had happened. That's when Norm showed up and told me you were in danger." She shook her head in disappointment. "You were supposed to know that I would never have given this to you willingly!" she exclaimed.

Janus cocked his head at her. "But, if this is mine, why wouldn't you ever let me have it?"

Clara shook her head. "I'm sorry, Janus. I should've given it to you long ago…" She paused, her breath catching.

Janus looked confused. "But…"

"But—" Clara hiccupped. "I was afraid. I know I'm not your real mother. But you're my son. Ever since the day I found you. Ever since I realized you're my good luck charm." Tears streamed down her face. "Something…real and precious in a life filled with garbage."

Janus's eyes widened in surprise, and he hesitated, struggling to find the right words. "Do—do you remember the books that you found for me when I was young? So that I could learn to read?"

Clara nodded, wiping her face with her sleeve.

"Well, they were filled with stories. Stories about families. About how the people you love are the ones you share your life with, not necessarily the ones related by blood." He faltered, embarrassed. "And even if I want to know the truth, I owe my life, everything I've become, to you."

Clara smiled happily, but her face reflected confusion. "But you've never called me mother, or mom, or anything other than Clara, unless you were annoyed, of course. Why?"

Janus lowered his eyes. "I guess I didn't realize it was so important. I guess I thought it might be a—" He stopped, looking out the window. "I figured it was safer in the slums, to appear as though I had as little connection to you as possible."

Clara hugged him tightly. "Well, I guess I'm just as big a fool as you are, then." She pulled back, her face beaming beautifully, although her eyes were puffy and ringed with tears.

"Thank you, Janus, you really have been my lucky charm all these years. I'm so sorry for holding back on you all this time."

Janus smiled. "Well, it's not how you start, it's how you finish."

"That's true."

Janus looked pensive. "I think I have some serious questions for Norm, though."

Clara nodded. "I think we all do. But first, I thought you might want to check on your friend—"

Janus leaped out of his bed. "Celes! How is she? Is she okay?"

Clara looked shrewdly at him. "Why don't we go find out? She's just a few doors down." Janus rushed out, his pain and discomfort already forgotten. Clara called out after him, "Oh, and I forgot to tell you, the Praetor is willing to let me stay…"

She heard Janus yell "Great!" as he disappeared around the corner.

"Well," Clara half-grumbled, fighting hard to keep the smile from her face, "at least I got twenty years."

Janus bumped into one of the medics in the hall, the words coming out in a stream, "Adept-Celes-what-room-is-she-in?"

The medic pointed to a ward on his left. Janus ran to the room and realized that the medics might not appreciate him bursting in. He checked himself and carefully knocked. After a moment the door slid open, and he realized he need not have worried.

Celes was upright in bed talking to Ramirez, Lyn, and Marcus. Norm sat off to one side, listening. They stopped at the sound of the door.

Celes beamed at him. "You're awake! We weren't sure if you would ever wake up, you were so tired."

"Yeah, we thought maybe you were taking a good opportunity to catch up on all the sleep we missed as cadets while you had a chance," Marcus said with a smile.

Janus screwed up his face in confusion. "What are you talking about?"

Lyn's eyes lit up with surprise. "Didn't you know? It's been two full days since we made it back to Valhalla."

"What?" Janus exclaimed.

Wouris walked into the room with Clara behind her. "Ah, good. I just ran into Clara in the hall. We were about to give you a Nanyte injection, Janus, for fear that we had misjudged your condition. I am glad to see that all you needed was some rest."

"Well, he earned it. I can hardly believe you made it that far carrying me like that." Celes's smile became even larger. "Thank you, Janus."

Janus shifted uncomfortably. Marcus made a wry face.

Wouris eyed the pair and said, "I'm sure any of your teammates would have done the same."

Marcus nodded.

"Still, I can hardly believe that you made it as well as you did, Janus. That was quite the feat," Lyn proclaimed. She took a moment to note the marks everyone still bore.

Janus looked at his team as well. From the bruised and battered face of Ramirez to the heavily wrapped arm of Marcus, and even the black and blue splotches across Lyn's arms and legs. All in all, Celes actually seemed to be in the best condition, at least externally.

Wouris turned to Celes. "How long?"

She shrugged. "Another day. Major Yalla doesn't think I need another injection to heal fully. We're all over our recommended maximum doses, anyway. So now he's forcing me to rest instead. Another day and they will release me."

"Good." Wouris turned to Norm. "Will you talk now?"

Norm nodded. "Tell the Praetor that now that Janus is awake, I will tell him everything I know. But I want everyone in this room to be there. They all deserve to learn the truth, after what they have been through." He looked around the room. "And if you would be willing to share the information you obtained on your own…" Wouris cocked an eyebrow in suspicion at him and Norm shrugged. "The choice is yours, but I can better frame my story for you."

Wouris shrugged noncommittally. "I'll talk to the Praetor. Either way, he's determined to have you tell us everything as soon as possible."

Norm nodded. "That is all I ask."

Wouris looked at Celes. "I'll see if I can speed up getting you out of here."

After much protesting by the medical staff and Yalla, Celes was allowed to leave, albeit under orders to go easy and not to train for a week. The others were given similar warnings. Janus felt like his team was going to develop a reputation.

Wouris led the ragtag band to the officer's briefing room in the Beacon. High atop Valhalla, Janus quickly showed Clara the view from the bridge under Tuorneg's watchful eye, and then joined the others, only to find the Praetor, Hawkes, Northcott, and Rogers already waiting for them. Rogers wore a boyish grin like a lad waiting for a toy he had been promised long ago. Northcott was grimly stroking his jaw, while Hawkes scowled beside him. The Praetor was inscrutable. Soft light around the edge of the room gave everything a warm glow.

"Sergeant, good to see you again," Northcott said gruffly as the officers acknowledged the group.

"Major." Wouris lowered her salute with a smile. "It's good to be back."

"Have you reconnected with your squad yet?"

Wouris nodded. "Yesterday, thank you."

Janus sat next to Celes, and Clara sat beside him. She became as still as a maid serving an Overlord. Something he had seen her practice many times before. She was very aware of the gravity of the situation, and Janus smiled.

"Will Colonel Keats be joining us?" Celes asked cautiously.

The Praetor shook his head and glanced at Hawkes. "The Colonel is still on her diplomatic mission."

Celes looked concerned. "Has there been any word from—"

"No," Hawkes answered. His scowl deepened.

"Colonel Keats is more than capable of handling herself," Wouris interjected. "But talking to the Corporations is bound to be slow."

Hawkes gave a surly nod.

"Perhaps"—Northcott waved a hand towards Norm—"we should allow our guest to speak."

The Praetor agreed, "Excellent suggestion, Major." He looked at Norm. "Would you be so kind…Norm?"

Norm stood off by himself, deep in thought. At his name, he looked up. There was an element of relief on his face.

"Of course, Praetor... Jennings. Although my full title is Overlord Norman Garret Walden, Intelligence Branch of the former Phoenix Corporation."

Janus felt his jaw drop at the pronouncement. Everyone else at the table looked just as shocked. Everyone but the Praetor.

Norman cleared his throat, speaking carefully, "And you would be the former Colonel Alexander Jennings...of the SHADE Legion. Am I correct?"

The Praetor nodded once, slowly.

"It has been a long time," Norm said simply.

CHAPTER 32
THE BEGINNING OF THE END

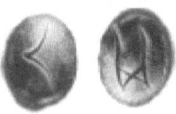

Janus leaped to his feet. "You're…" He wasn't sure what he wanted to say.

"Now is the time to listen, Janus," Norm said calmly.

Janus sat slowly, but he leaned in with the others as Norm took a deep breath.

"As some of you may know, several hundred years ago, the Corporations were all that survived the collapse." Norm's eyes flitted over Celes.

Janus listened intently.

"Adrift, and uncertain, these survivors each had a unique origin—identity, if you will—that allowed them to survive. Titan manufactured weapons. Medusa was an energy conglomerate. Cerberus specialized in mining and alloy production. Each had their unique background."

Norm walked towards the table, standing behind the open chair reserved for him. "Phoenix was a powerhouse of medical technology. Using these strengths, the Corporations were able to trade and thrive after years of hardship and famine. For centuries, the Corporations held a necessary, and oftentimes amicable, truce. However, as the world recovered, the Corporations started to provide for themselves. The great mixing of survivors from all over the world stopped, and the Corporations began to divide culturally and diplomatically. Eventually, a mix of cold war and active skirmishes broke out, with no one power able to emerge victorious. This period eventually became known as the 'Great Divide.'"

Norm shook his head. "At least the Corporate historians still occasionally talked to each other back then, I suppose."

He looked towards Janus and Clara. "Each Corporation searched for a way to gain an edge in their constant battles with one another, exploring fields in which they had excelled to produce an advantage. Titan created the Zeus rifles and Trooper armor. For years, they held an advantage, but eventually, those technologies were reproduced, and their gains were slowly whittled away. Medusa's entropic batteries gave it a powerful mobile energy source well before fusion power, albeit an expensive and short-lived one. Cerberus eventually created Immutium—something that would prove to be a world-altering discovery, but we will come to that."

Norm pointed to Celes, Marcus, and Major Northcott in turn. "Minotaur, Medusa, Hydra."

Janus hid his surprise. As did the others. Norm had seemingly guessed Celes's and Marcus's origins without any input. He glanced at Northcott, wondering just how much Norm knew.

"A cycle emerged," Norm continued. "One Corporation would develop something new, and have a brief advantage, only to eventually lose it. It became clear that for a Corporation to truly turn the tide, it needed a decisive advantage.

"So, Phoenix took a different approach, setting itself on a quest that would last centuries. It would not invest in material advantages, but in human capital." He glanced at Clara.

"Sounds rather compassionate," Marcus chimed in, folding his arms skeptically.

Norm clasped his hands behind his back and smiled grimly as he lowered his head. "The research conducted was the most highly guarded secret in Phoenix. Only the intelligence branch and the Executors knew of it. Many of my predecessors, and occasionally, my forebears..." Norm paused for a moment, "were consumed entirely by it.

"More than once, our research was nearly discovered, our progress lost. Phoenix gladly sacrificed years of research, or even the scientists themselves, to maintain the shroud that surrounded its attempts at"— Norm's gaze pierced Janus—"the fountain of youth. Hundreds of years passed, and though we always seemed on the cusp of success, death maintained its terrifying grip. But then something happened—"

"The advent of Immutium," the Praetor remarked coldly.

"Very good, Praetor." Norm nodded. "That remarkable metal." He paused, looking at the five young Adepts. "You found a painting in Middleton's possession, one that depicted me and another young man?"

"Yes," Celes answered, "he could have been Janus's twin—or relative."

"So it was you?" Northcott asked.

"And who was this person who looked like the lieutenant?" Hawkes asked.

Norm pursed his lips. "I will come to that in a moment. But to answer your question, Major, it was indeed me. I remember very clearly the day I sat for that painting actually. There was a huge celebration that morning throughout the streets of Phoenix. Any ideas as to when that painting was made?"

There was silence around the room. Finally, Janus spoke up, giving his best guess. "Well, it was before Phoenix fell, and you appear to be a young man—anywhere from thirty to fifty years ago?"

Norm smiled. "Not a bad guess… did you happen to see the name of the painting?"

Janus racked his brain. "I searched for it in our database after our return, but I couldn't find it. What was it…?"

"You probably had no idea where to look," Norm added. "And, with no offense to the Legion, I am not surprised that Valhalla's database might be lacking in historical data."

The Praetor and Northcott nodded in reluctant agreement.

"That being said, however, I would guess no one thought to ask you the title. Otherwise, I am sure someone here would have said something about it. It was a rather singular *victory…*"

Janus snapped his fingers. "That's it! Victory at Lightemann's."

"Impossible!" Northcott jumped up.

"Are you sure that is correct, Janus?" the Praetor asked urgently, glancing at Norm.

Norm smiled.

"Yes, I'm sure. Why?" Janus responded in surprise.

"And I say again that it's impossible," Northcott interjected, staring at Norm.

"Why, what's impossible about it?" Clara asked in confusion.

"Because"—the Praetor leaned forward—"Lightemann's Ridge was the final decisive victory by Phoenix and the other Corporations over the alliance of Cerberus and Medusa during the conclusion of the Fusion War. It was the battle that allowed all Corporations access to fusion power."

Celes raised a hand in shock and she looked around, waiting for recognition from the others. After a moment of silence and a nod from the Praetor she piped up, "It happened over one hundred and fifty years ago."

CHAPTER 33
THE PHOENIX'S TEARS

Janus gaped. "You're over a hundred and fifty years old?"

Norm chuckled. "You'd think I would be a little wiser by now, wouldn't you?"

"But that can't be right, Norm!" Clara exclaimed.

Norm held his hands up in defense. "Allow me to finish. Immutium changed everything. During the conclusion of the Fusion War, Phoenix was finally able to learn the secret of its production for itself. Since Immutium is not just produced by fusion power but is necessary for sustaining it, Cerberus and Medusa had jealously guarded it until their defeat.

"With Immutium, the Corporations entered a new era of growth and development. Titan developed its Advanced Trooper armor, a suit capable of withstanding the extreme heat of its internal systems through precision engineering of Immutium components. Its distinctive shape and massive heat generation that could be funneled as a weapon soon gave it a more fearsome name; Infernus armor. Minotaur created new construction techniques using Immutium hardened steel beams, creating the first superscraper just a few years after the conclusion of the war. And Phoenix finally had its breakthrough—and not just one, but two."

"I had no idea so much was developed together," Celes said in wonder.

The Praetor nodded. "Much of that history has been lost, or is only known to a few."

"Corporations aren't known for their honest retellings," Hawkes grunted.

"Not anymore," Norm said sadly. "It was not always the case."

"They all try to make themselves look great," Marcus said.

"Or cover up their failings," Wouris added with a shake of her head.

"And their sacrifices," Norm said quietly.

The room went silent.

After a moment, Norm took a deep breath and sat down at the table. He leaned forward, almost conspiratorially.

"The first of Phoenix's landmark achievements was cryogenics."

"Cryo-genics?" Clara asked.

Janus looked at her. "Freezing something to keep it preserved. Sort of the like the refridge units that you told me about at Middleton's estate."

Norm looked at Clara. "But for people."

"Freezing people? How is that useful?" Clara asked in genuine confusion.

Janus smiled at her in understanding. "It's good for keeping people alive who might otherwise die."

"But what about it?" Hawkes interjected, looking at Norm.

Norm nodded politely. "With Immutium alloy, Phoenix finally had a material that could withstand the rigorous process it had theorized could work nearly a century before."

"But other than for preservation, that doesn't really let a person *live* forever," Wouris stressed, tapping the table.

Norm shook his head. "No. But it does become of the utmost importance when I discuss Phoenix's second breakthrough…"

The Praetor sat forward. "Phoenix Serum? Is it true?"

Norm's expression changed, his eyes becoming more distant. Despite his seat at the table he suddenly looked very alone. "It was called many names in our efforts to hide it. Phoenix Serum…Phoenix Tears…Phoenix Blood. I was so very proud of it."

"Are you not anymore?" Wouris asked curiously.

Norm opened his hands on the table, examining the wrinkles. "The Phoenix… Tears were miraculous, and made us the most powerful Corporation on the planet. Our population exploded. We were more productive than any corporation could match. Our soldiers could outnumber and outperform anyone else on the battlefield. And fortunately for the Executors, our expanding workforce was just able to keep ahead of their own personal demands for it."

"But didn't you just say that this serum—that the whole population saw changes?" Marcus interjected. "You make it sound like the Executors needed it for something else…"

Norm met Marcus's eyes. And then he looked around the room, as if debating whether to stop there.

"What is it, Norm?" Clara asked, reaching for his hand.

Norm grabbed the proffered hand and rubbed his eye with his free one. "I'm glad you're here Clara."

"I have always called them Phoenix Tears. Not just because of their distinctive color, but from the way they act. Because the tears are actually two parts. Two agents. One that heals and restores. And one that ages and consumes."

"That's quite a trade-off," Wouris said with narrowed eyes.

Norm nodded solemnly. "Decades upon decades of research, finally realized through the application of fusion power and Immutium. We wanted to use it to help everyone. But it quickly became clear that it was far too expensive to produce. Our first year, it took the better part of a week to create one dose, and we quickly realized that the Phoenix Tears two halves acted against each other. Trying to cut the formula to levels we could produce for the general population simply resulted in a product that had no benefit whatsoever. The healing and destructive agents would cancel each other out."

"So how did the whole of Phoenix benefit, then?" the Praetor asked.

"A discovery by a recently promoted Overlord. The officer who had recently helped deliver the decisive victory at Lightemann's Ridge."

Janus shot up from his chair and exclaimed, "Delacroix? The Executor working with Middleton?"

The others looked back and forth between Janus and Norm. "Wait, Janus, why do ya think it's him?" Lyn asked in confusion.

"Because," the Praetor interjected, "Janus has seen Delacroix's face."

"But how?" Lyn asked. She looked at the Praetor. "Are you saying Delacroix is the man in the painting?"

Janus swallowed hard but said nothing.

"You saw him? At Lightemann's Ridge?" Celes asked.

Janus nodded cautiously.

"Why didn't you tell us?" Celes asked, unable to hide the doubt in her voice.

"Do you blame him?" Marcus asked, crossing his arms but giving Janus a shake of his head.

Ramirez leaned forward. "But how do you know this, Praetor?"

The Praetor locked eyes with Norm, "Because I have seen Delacroix's face as well."

Norm's gaze met the Praetor's and he sighed, carefully pulling out a jeweled bird with rubies for eyes. Clara's eyes went wide.

"That looks like my... I mean... Janus's pendent."

"It was a gift from my friend. Magnus Delacroix." Norm put it down on the table in front of him. "At the time, I was primary Intendant to the Overlord of Intelligence, my father. Magnus was one of my finest officers. It was he who orchestrated our final victory at Lightemann's. And as a result, he became the first person in nearly a century to be promoted to Overlord through a means other than inheritance.

"Newly privy to our most top-secret research, he eagerly dove into a new challenge: how to take advantage of our priceless discovery. But if anything, the war had taught him that no secret was safe forever. And that, eventually, the other Corporations would come knocking for anything that broke the balance."

"Was it really that difficult?" Marcus asked.

"Corporate secrets are like water in a leaky bucket. It had taken the utmost effort, and supreme sacrifice, to preserve years of research before it amounted to anything at all," Norm said simply. "Once we had it working, our advantage was too blatant. Rumors began to spread of Executors, elderly and on their deathbed, suddenly showing renewed vigor."

"So what did Delacroix do?" Northcott asked.

Norm smiled. "Magnus was Magnus. He figured it out."

"Figured out what?" Wouris asked.

"How to keep us rising yet preserve our secret." Norm put his head in his hands and rubbed his silver hair. "He never would have even thought of it before the war."

Clara put a supporting hand on his shoulder.

"What was the cost, Norm?" the Praetor asked.

Norm patted Clara's hand, and looked the Praetor dead in the eyes. "People. The population of Phoenix. We had perfected the idea of the Tears long before the Fusion War had given us all the tools we needed. Years of research had shown the secondary agent of the Phoenix Tears was terrible for people in the long term. But Magnus realized it was controllable. In small doses, it acts like a catalyst for the human body. Making it like a candle that burns at both ends."

"So you gave it to everyone who wasn't an Executor," Wouris said.

"Yes. As I said, it made our population more productive. And fertile. And at the mere cost of a dwindling lifespan. But we had plenty of replacements, that became clear soon enough."

Celes held a hand to her mouth. "Children. Middleton was using the drug on children!"

"She did what?" Hawkes asked angrily.

"In Lightemann's Ridge. We assumed Middleton was simply testing the cryochambers. But she wasn't, was she Norm?" Celes asked.

Norm shifted uncomfortably. "I cannot speak to all that Middleton has done, but at Phoenix, it happened slowly. Over time. And the people were happy. Our productivity made their shorter lives that much better. And the children didn't know that they grew faster than everyone else. But they knew they were taller, and stronger."

"Didn't anyone notice? Didn't anyone care?" Celes asked.

"Our citizens liked being the greatest Corporation in the world. The costs were mere rumors. The victories real," Norm stated simply.

"But... how could ya do that... ta kids..." Lyn spluttered.

"And that still doesn't explain how Delacroix kept these Tears a secret or how Middleton is involved," Northcott interjected.

"Yes, I am getting a bit ahead of myself," Norm stated. "After the war, everyone retreated to their little corner of the world, eager to lick their wounds and recover. Alliances fell apart, and communication between the Corporations became sporadic. It took years for the other Corporations to take the rumors of our youthful Executors seriously. For our population to truly show the signs of careful dosing. By then Magnus was already being hailed as a future Executor, '*The true successor*' to Lightemann herself."

Marcus interjected with a raised hand. "Who was this Lightemann?"

Norm nodded slowly. "She was the Executor Ascendant of Phoenix...and beloved by many, including Magnus. She fell during the battle. It is the reason why the area is named as such."

"And Magnus was hailed as her successor?" Wouris asked curiously.

Norm leaned back and stared at the table. "Very much so. Lightemann had left no heir, and the people of Phoenix, even without a vote in the matter, knew a spot on the council remained unfilled. Magnus provided everything the Executors desired. A popular hero. A man who had risen through the ranks of the Trooper corps, decidedly loyal to them and Phoenix. A vehicle to their own goals. And a fool to blame should anything go wrong."

"Something tells me he wasn't as pliable as they might have hoped," Hawkes grunted.

Norm laid his palm on the table. "No. But in the beginning, he was only focused on his goal. I remember... I remember the first time I saw his plan in action. I would sometimes head to the lower levels, discreetly, to talk with the citizens. There was a bar called Killjoy I would frequent, listening to unfiltered opinions about Phoenix drift by me." He tapped his finger on the polished surface. "One day, as I walked the streets, there was a woman who was wailing about her child. How he had been taken because of the plague. People kept walking by, avoiding her, but I stopped. I asked 'what plague?'"

Norm looked around knowingly. "Troopers had come to her home. Taken her son. Said that all the children had been exposed. I rushed back, and there I found Magnus and my father counting. Counting people. Criminals. Orphans. Undesirables. The ones that had disappeared, and the ones that were going to disappear. Just enough to cause alarm, but not enough to seriously harm Phoenix. To spread a rumor. Of a mysterious illness that was suddenly afflicting our people."

"Just enough to give the other Corporations pause," Northcott spat.

"What did he do with them?" Wouris asked, bitterness in her voice. "The people he made disappear?"

"He didn't kill them if that's what you mean. Magnus knew that we could only play this game for so long. Eventually, the other Corporations would catch on. Phoenix would need soldiers after the losses of The Fusion War. The armies of old would not suffice. He needed people whose sole purpose would be to fight. Indoctrinated. Trained and battle-hardened."

"That's why he wanted children," Ramirez said.

"Yes," Norm said. "And with a smattering of others to make it less obvious."

"That's monstrous," Lyn said.

"Yes," Norm said sadly. "But you might have felt different had you fought in the war."

"That's no excuse." Wouris' eyes bored into Norm.

Norm shook his head. "I will not claim that it is. But I would say it's not so different from what you do here."

"We don't steal children," Hawkes replied.

"No. But you do take in criminals, children, and undesirables from Corporations who have no other options for survival and train them to be warriors indoctrinated in your culture, do you not?"

"There's a difference," Hawkes said angrily, his face flushing. "I dare yo—"

"Colonel." The Praetor sat forward, and Hawkes immediately clammed up. After a moment of silence, the Praetor nodded in appreciation to him. Hawkes balled his fists in frustration but said nothing.

Praetor Jennings looked back at Norm. "Maintaining an army takes resources. A big one would be bound to get noticed. And this army would only last so long."

"Yes. People take space. And food. And energy. And so many other things it's amazing sometimes we function at all. We built underground labs and dormitories. We created firing ranges and schools. And as we grew richer, we expanded deeper and deeper. We would raise a group, accelerated in their growth in the space of a few years. They would be trained. They would be monitored. They would breed. And then they would be—"

Janus sat bolt upright. "Frozen."

Norm nodded. "Cryogenically preserved until Phoenix was ready to make its final push for domination."

CHAPTER 34
SACRIFICES MADE

Silence greeted his pronouncement.

Finally, Clara spoke up, so softly Janus almost missed it. "But why, Norm?"

Norm did not meet her eyes. "The Fusion War was a terrible time across the world. Phoenix had often been driven to the brink. Years of war taught us that nothing was more important than the prosperity of Phoenix and peace. And yet, we knew it could not last."

Norm looked around the room, his eyes tracing across their faces. "But Magnus proposed a way that the years of strife could come to an end. A way where, maybe someday, all people could benefit from Phoenix Tears. And in the meantime, under Phoenix, the populations of the world could be stronger and more productive than ever before. Prosperity could be brought to everyone."

"That seems like a stretch," Celes said.

"Sometimes, those sacrifices are worthwhile," Marcus replied, looking at her. "Especially to those who have grown up in the worst of conditions."

Celes shifted uncomfortably in her seat.

Norm's eyes roamed over Marcus. "Magnus had worked his way up the ranks. Some parts of his struggle are unknown, even to me. But after the war, he never once struggled with the decision to use the serum." Norm's gaze stopped on the Praetor. "Our compound soldiers were never treated poorly. Their lives were simple, but they did not lack compassion. Magnus saw to that. And the generations raised in our facilities did not know of what freedoms they lacked, so how could they feel denied? They would not even exist without our efforts— would they have preferred oblivion? Was our quest not noble?"

Norm paused and slowly soaked up the mixture of disgust and awe that surrounded him.

He took a deep breath. "We struggled to keep our secret under wraps. We were forced to periodically reintroduce our 'plague,' and the Corporations grew more suspicious every time. And while every year undiscovered made us more powerful, we lacked the capability to produce enough Immutium to meet our ever-expanding needs. Even after decades, Cerberus still remained far ahead of everyone else in terms of raw output. They fought to maintain their own secrets, I am sure," Norm added as an afterthought.

"So how did Phoenix overcome it?" Wouris asked cautiously, as if she suspected but didn't want to know.

Norm shook his head. "For nearly a century, we worked tirelessly. But time began to take its toll. The Corporations had recovered dramatically. Trade resumed, and secrets and subterfuge once again became the name of the game. But our secrets were more and more poorly hidden. The Corporations no longer failed to notice how very old our Executors were. Executors who had increasingly become obsessed with preserving themselves at any cost. And our advantage was becoming insurmountable. Instead of working to hide our secrets over years, it became months, and then weeks. My father was pushed to the limit. Magnus and I struggled to the point of exhaustion. There were too many potential leaks. And then one day, it happened."

"Someone stole the secret of the Phoenix Tears?" Northcott asked. "But no one has ever heard of this before."

"We captured the young woman before she could report back to her superiors."

"Young woman?" Wouris asked.

"Victoria."

"Lady Middleton?" Clara exclaimed.

Norm smiled. "Yes, Overlord Middleton. Though she did not have that title at the time."

"How did you capture her?" Janus asked.

Tears filled his eyes. "Naivete and betrayal."

"What?" Hawkes asked gruffly.

"My father was Overlord of Intelligence before me. He worked day and night for Phoenix. But only Executors were given full doses of the Tears. Our lesser treatments extended our lives, but did not roll back the effects of old age. Magnus and I were still quite young when our treatments started. We were heroes of the war, after all, and were given priority. But my father, he was very, very old. And very, very tired. Even with the Tears, at the dosage he was given, he would not last much longer. He had seen what the Executors had become and warned us that they were slowly spiraling. And that Phoenix would soon follow. So he made a deal. He promised the secrets of Phoenix's miracle in exchange for Immutium, and he promised it to the one place that could deliver. Cerberus."

"What happened?" Clara asked cautiously.

"My father... my father told me what he was planning." Norm paused. "And I... had no idea what to do. I could not simply give up on all the work we had put in. I could not understand how my father had done this. So I told Magnus. And Magnus told the Executors. I believed they would go easy on him. They would understand his desperation. He had served for over a century. I was a war hero pleading on behalf of my father…" Norm stopped suddenly, lowering his head. The room became deathly quiet but for the sounds of the old man's ragged breaths. After a few moments of silence, Norm raised his head once again, his eyes red with tears. He wiped his face. "But they did find out where Middleton was hiding."

He looked around. "My father's betrayal had shown the Executors that they could not afford to lose our support, or they would risk themselves. It also made them paranoid. But who could they trust better than the two war heroes who had turned on their father and mentor? I was 'rewarded' with my father's title. Magnus finally became the Executor the people wanted. Our promotion was broadcast across the Corporation to great fanfare. It was wonderful propaganda, especially since only the Executors and ourselves knew the reason for our sudden rise. Behind closed doors, we were given an offer: find a solution to our Immutium problem, and never worry about our dosages again."

"What about Middleton?" Janus asked. Norm raised a hand as if he were getting to that.

"Middleton was hiding in Phoenix, waiting for my father to provide her passage out, so she had nowhere to go. I for one was surprised to discover the beautiful Intendant my father had introduced me to as a possible match was actually a spy.

"But Magnus knew a good opportunity when he saw it. He knew my father was right, we needed more Immutium, and our best bet was Cerberus. So he made a deal with her, and this time I knew better than to tell anyone else." Norm shook his head. "As much Immutium as she could provide, and Magnus would provide her with her own personal supply of the Phoenix Tears. For her part, Middleton was more than intelligent enough to realize the implications. If she brought the Tears back to Cerberus, she would never be afforded enough for her own dose. And she was tough enough to propose her own terms, as well, even in her half-dead state. She would only be able to do so much as an Intendant. A shipment here. A shipment there. Irregular and infrequent. But if she could climb the ladder, she could do more. So she proposed a scheme of her own. One of intelligence sharing, not just of the occasional Phoenix information, but of anything Phoenix learned on the other Corporations as well. New advancements in Infernus armor? Relayed to Middleton for Cerberus to use. Medusa making improvements to reactor technology? Shared to Phoenix. Middleton became a true double agent, but the best kind: invaluable to her Corporation. After her return, a few weeks after we cleaned her up and sent her along with enough rumors and decades old research to delight her superiors, she quickly gained a reputation for being the best intelligence officer Cerberus had ever seen. With the combined power of Phoenix and Cerberus working for her, she seemed almost superhuman."

"This explains so much!" Celes exclaimed. "Even my father spoke with whispered tones about Middleton!"

The Praetor sat forward. "This does help explain her surprising knack for finding secrets."

"Don't underestimate her intellect, however," Norm cautioned.

"I think we have already learned that lesson," Marcus interjected.

Norm gave him an apologetic look. "She has perhaps one weak spot, however."

"Oh?" the Praetor asked curiously.

"She is desperately in love with Magnus."

"What?" Clara exclaimed.

"But how? You captured her!" Lyn asked, flabbergasted.

Norm stood up and walked away from the table. "I'm not proud of what I did. After what happened to my father, I blamed Middleton for his fall. In my mind, she had clearly corrupted him. I starved her. Had her beaten for information."

"Oh!" Clara made a little gasp.

"And Magnus was the one who saved her from all that?" Wouris asked.

Norm nodded. "While I was still unwilling to even hear the words from her mouth, he recognized her brilliance. Her value. After we turned her, she was firmly in Magnus's pocket. She and I, however, never quite saw eye-to-eye."

"But she supplied you with Immutium," Hawkes said.

Norm turned around, looking very tired. "Yes. More and more over time. And the Phoenix Executors never questioned where it came from. They were too occupied with their personal projects and works that stroked their egos."

"Was a golden, winged lift system part of that?" Janus asked, remembering the broken and destroyed ruins at Phoenix.

Norm shook his head in disgust. "One of many."

"So what went wrong?" the Praetor asked.

Norm studied him for a moment. "Yes, I suppose that is what you really want to know, is it not? Do you have a map of the territory surrounding Phoenix?"

Hawkes nodded, and made a few swift motions to the panel before him. A MuDi emerged from the table. "How far?"

"A thousand kilometers should cover it." Norm made a circle with his hand, and soon after, the MuDi projected a simple map. Norm pointed at several spots around the edge. "Minor skirmishes broke out along our borders as the other Corporations began to test our strength. Middleton began secretly sharing our information not just with Cerberus, but with other Corporations using our information and resources as leverage."

"And you let her?" Marcus asked.

"We encouraged it," Norm replied matter-of-factly. "Let the Corporations have small victories. Let us appear weak. As long as the Tears and our Cryogenic army remained secret, Phoenix would eventually win. But one day, we received word from Middleton. The Corporations had agreed to meet. Or should I say, the other Corporations had agreed to meet about how to deal with Phoenix. The power gap was too large. There was talk of war. And other than those of us at Phoenix who were receiving life extension treatments, there was no one left to remember the horrors of the last one. Magnus and I knew it was something we had to avoid at all costs."

"You had been prepping for decades, had you not? Was that still not enough soldiers?" Northcott asked.

Norm rubbed his chin. "It was far more than just soldiers. Our best case for preparation was still more than five decades away. And waking all of the already preserved soldiers would take time. Fighting a defensive war was the absolute worst case. For our plan to work we needed to strike first, with absolute precision. But that wasn't even the worst part."

"What was that?" Celes asked.

"Your vulnerability," the Praetor said.

Norm closed his eyes and nodded in respect to the Praetor. "Precisely."

"What vulnerability?" Hawkes asked.

Janus looked at Norm and felt his mind race ahead to all the possibilities he could imagine, and he realized that the answer was the same reason Valhalla always stayed on the move and did not engage in battle directly.

"Because everything was stuck at Phoenix."

The Praetor looked at Janus and smiled faintly.

"Yes." Norm looked around the room. "Imagine what would happen if the Corporations caught even a whiff of what Phoenix had planned. Of what was buried beneath it. What do you think they would do?"

"This was before the Phoenix Declaration. Before the banning of the complete destruction of a Corporation," Celes interjected in sudden realization. "They would have simply annihilated the entire complex and been done with it. Your army couldn't even defend itself."

Norm nodded.

"So is that what happened? You were discovered? Is that why Phoenix was destroyed?" Lyn asked in flurry.

"Phoenix was destroyed by its own hubris, but we haven't gotten there yet," Norm said simply.

"The attacks against us increased by the week. Mercenary Legions, which had begun to emerge at the end of the Fusion War and had been gaining prominence over the past several decades, began to strike us unexpectedly. Our standing army was being spread far too thin. It did not appear as though we would have time to implement our plan."

"So what did you do?" Clara asked. She had become fully enraptured by the tale. Janus realized that if he had not seen the clues with his own eyes, had he not believed Norm was telling them the truth, that it would be the most fantastical story he had ever heard.

"Magnus was an Executor now. He could act in ways that would have been impossible before. And he realized there was only one solution that could possibly save us: give up the Phoenix Tears."

"But I've never heard of them before!" Celes exclaimed. "No Corporate history I've ever read mentions them at all!"

"There are good reasons for that. The first of which was that we were very selective in who learned our secret," Norm explained.

"And who was that?" Hawkes asked.

"Titan," the Praetor interjected.

"Very good, Praetor." Norm nodded.

Chapter 35
A Call to Arms

The sound of the sliding door to the briefing room surprised Janus. So engrossed in Norm's story, the sudden appearance of an aide at the Praetor's side caught him off guard.

The Adept whispered in the Praetor's ear and he nodded in response before the aide disappeared in a flurry.

"We have a visitor," the Praetor announced.

A few minutes later, a man in a matte black uniform with gold trim stepped into the briefing room. The howling three-headed dog of Cerberus was embroidered onto his right breast in purple-and-gold thread.

The man bowed to the Praetor, who stood but did not make any move to greet him. The man seemed momentarily flustered, as if expecting some sort of greeting, but as none was forthcoming, he hastily began his speech.

"Noble Praetor of ODIN. My name is Jordain, an Intendant of Cerberus. I come with a message of great importance from the Executors of our mighty Corporation."

Northcott coughed loudly at that, and Hawkes rolled his eyes in disgust. The Praetor responded stiffly, "Well, out with it."

"Yes, sir," Jordain responded awkwardly, caught even more off guard by the hostile response. "The Executors wish to inform you of a terrible travesty: Titan Corporation has used nuclear weaponry against Cerberus in an underhanded assault against our noble people. According to the rules set down in the Phoenix Declaration, we must join together to crush this traitorous enemy."

The Praetor shook his head, his voice hard and cold. "I'm afraid you're mistaken, Jordain of Cerberus. We are an Adept Legion. We are not bound by your treaty. The Phoenix Declaration has no hold over us."

"Yes sir, but such a travesty—" Jordain stammered.

"Has not gone unnoticed. Tell your masters that ODIN will consider its request. You may inform the other Corporations of our potential support, as well."

The messenger bowed deeply, looking somewhat relieved. "Thank you, noble Praetor. I will relay your message immediately." He promptly turned on his heel and left the room, escorted by two armed Adepts.

The Praetor sat down, sighing. "I have been expecting that for some time now."

Wouris looked at Janus, explaining, "While you've been recovering, Cerberus has been blasting out messages in any way they can looking for an audience with whomever they can get."

"What kind of messages?" Celes asked.

"Urgent requests to parley. Just over twelve hours ago the Praetor gave us permission to make contact with Cerberus scouts." She looked at the Praetor. "They must be very serious if they sent us a representative so fast."

"Titan crossed a line that no Corporation has been willing to touch in over two decades," Celes added. "The Phoenix Declaration states that any Corporation that presents itself as a global threat will be destroyed by the unified power of the other Corporations. The others will almost certainly respond to Cerberus's request."

"Do ya think the Corporations will act, sir?" Lyn asked.

"I suspect they will. There is too much at stake. But they must know Titan would not act without reason."

"You might be surprised," Norm disagreed. "I may have been stuck in the slums of Cerberus for the last couple of decades, but I have seen more than enough to know that the Corporations are becoming desperate. And with Middleton and Magnus in the mix, the other Corporations have no idea what is coming for them."

"But why attack Cerberus?" Marcus asked. "Why not another target? Surely Middleton could have aided Delacroix?"

"Perhaps not," Wouris said. "If Alastor's suspicions were representative of the Executors, Middleton may have fallen out of favor."

"But the panic of an attack might drive them right back to her. It was clear that Alastor had no idea that Titan might be her partner," Northcott added.

"She could have been 'warning' them for weeks," Hawkes huffed. "All the while knowing she was setting herself up for redemption."

"That would certainly explain why she was so eager to return to her estate," Clara interjected.

Janus looked at her knowingly. "She knew that she would be safe there. And that would imply this strike has been a long time coming. The Corporations have no idea everything that has been set up against them."

Lyn looked troubled. "I can't believe I'm rooting that at least some of them have the brains ta figure this out."

"Does that mean we will aid the Corporations, sir?" Ramirez asked the Praetor.

The Praetor looked over at Norm. "I suspect we will be forced to. But how we do it depends somewhat on what else you have tell us. Why Titan?"

"Titan was the weakest corporation at the time. We wanted to shift the balance of power just enough to discourage war. And since they had no idea about the existence of our Cryochambers, they could not build an army to rival our own," Norm said.

"Ingenious," Marcus said. "With a leg up, they would be unwilling to help the other Corporations level the field."

Norm nodded. "Unfortunately, our biggest obstacle was our own Executors."

"They did not agree," Celes said with a tinge of annoyance in her voice, as if she were unsurprised.

"Exactly. Magnus argued the case beautifully, but the Executors' paranoia and protectionism of their precious secrets had only grown since my father's betrayal. They nearly accused Magnus of treason to suggest such a thing, but they simply could not see the inevitable."

"The Corporations are immense. Their armies and defenses, gigantic. To completely overwhelm them and then hold that territory would have taken decades more, and that is assuming we could have continued to accelerate. But when I ran the numbers, no matter what I did, I kept coming up short. If we went to war before we were ready, even with a first strike, it would be the end. We would lose the war of attrition."

"But Phoenix had such an advantage," Celes stated. "Why would you lose?"

"Too many mouths to feed. Too many dependencies on others. War would cut us off from the many secret deals we made. It would make us the biggest target. The Executors had driven us to the brink for years in an effort to expand their power. And everything we had built was dependent on being able to maintain our dosages and our productivity. If that slipped, even slightly, everything would spiral out of control, and very, very quickly."

"So what did you do?" Ramirez asked.

"Me? Nothing. I was committed to remaining the loyal Overlord, to make up where I had failed as a son. But Magnus? Magnus had no such compulsion. He had become increasingly convinced the Executors would doom us all. And worse, they had insulted his pride. So, unbeknownst to me, he went ahead with his plan anyway."

"You didn't know? What was his plan?" Lyn asked in a flurry.

Norm's face twisted into a sad smile. "I think when I betrayed my father, whether I realized it at the time or not, I changed the relationship with Magnus. I had shown that my loyalty was to the Corporation above my family. That I couldn't be trusted. And I suspect Magnus had been feeling the same way as my father for years."

"What was the plan?" Hawkes grunted.

"Phoenix would have to lose the war."

"What?" the group exclaimed in unison.

"Please explain, Norm," the Praetor said calmly.

"When war started, no matter what happened, Phoenix would inevitably be destroyed. The other Corporations would not, could not, allow it to escape unharmed. Even in the best case, it was nigh impossible for us to stop retaliation upon Phoenix. The Corporations, after the Fusion war, did not possess much in the way of the weapons of mass destruction they once had, but they had enough. Even with everything we lost in the War—the knowledge, the people—they had enough. We had no doubt that in their death throes, the Corporations would launch what they had at us. Phoenix would burn if we won. And it would burn if we lost."

"Go on," Northcott said, clearly beginning to see the strategy unfolding before him. Janus tried to think several moves ahead, as his games with the Major at *Brevis Bellum* had forced him to do so many times.

"The Corporation would burn, but not necessarily the people," Janus said with sudden realization, looking at Norm.

Norm nodded. "Magnus realized that Phoenix was the people, not just the giant structures we had built. We simply needed a place to put them."

"Another Corporation!" Lyn said. "But no Corporation is going to let you simply walk in and take over. How could you manage it?"

"If we could launch an attack that would make the others believe we would destroy our opponent, but in actuality conquer it with minimal incident, we could pull it off. But as you said, no Corporation would simply let us walk in, and anyone we attacked would be heavily damaged if not destroyed. Without careful planning, the whole Corporate structure would be at risk of collapse."

"You needed a way to surprise and weaken a Corporation without the others knowing," Northcott concluded.

"What exactly did Magnus give Titan?" Wouris asked skeptically.

"The accelerator. The portion of the Tears that burned the candle at both ends. And he leaked careful instructions for dosing..." Norm stopped. "It's even more monstrous when I say it aloud."

He shook his head.

"He gave them just enough information to maximize its power, without realizing its full effects. And carefully calculated that the average person, after a set period of time..."

"Would drop dead," Janus realized.

Norm's eyes met Janus, and then he nodded once.

"What are you talking about, Janus?" Clara's eyes, however, reflected that she understood the disturbing truth.

Janus looked at her. "What better way to eliminate a competitor than to have them poison themselves? By the time they realized what was happening, it would be too late for them to do anything about it. And from what you've described, Norm, they probably felt invincible right up until the end."

"Subjects often felt euphoria from the drug. Coming down was often a bad experience, especially depending on the length of time one had been exposed."

"The water!" Celes said.

Norm and the rest gave her a quizzical look, and she turned to Janus. "Remember when we were stranded under Phoenix, and we found a water supply that we used to refill our canteens with? How it tasted wonderful and felt great, but we all got sick when we were on the trip home?"

Wouris nodded. "That's right. I've hardly ever felt so nauseous in my life. I figured it had to be something else, because our canteens have purifiers in them. How long did the side effects last?"

Norm rubbed his chin thoughtfully. "For someone just on the accelerator, with none of the healing properties? Someone who had been injecting it for years? Probably weeks of illness. Possibly bad enough to be incapacitating."

Janus shook his head. "Delacroix. He knew Titan would be unable to wean themselves off of it. Even if they discovered the truth, stopping would leave them helpless. But if they didn't…"

"They would all die from the aging effects. Because Delacroix knew how long it would take," Ramirez added.

Norm looked around the room speaking quickly, "That was the basics of our plan. We would launch our attack simultaneously across all the Corporations, launching what few weapons we had, assaulting others outright. And we would take Titan, making it our new home…"

"But that clearly isn't the whole story," Marcus said.

318

Norm's eyes seemed to deepen into his skull, and he looked almost sickly as he recalled it. "We needed to move quickly. Taking Titan with minimal destruction and losses was critical. But it would be impossible to move our forces without anyone knowing. And if Titan had any time to prepare, even in its weakened state, it could be devastating. Not every soldier would be weak. Not every person would be dying. We needed a way to strike without warning. Not even Magnus had figured out that piece of the puzzle."

Norm smiled sadly and glanced at the Praetor. "I was so proud when I realized the solution. A way to have Titan invite us in with open arms, and welcome us into their midst, not even knowing what they were doing. It was my greatest contribution to the plan yet. And all we needed was—"

"A Legion." The Praetor had stood up from his seat. Janus realized his face was a mask of rage and sorrow like he had never seen before. "You. You were the one responsible," the Praetor said in a hoarse whisper.

Norm looked at him, the sorrow deepening in his eyes.

Janus realized the officers had stood up as well, but they were all watching the Praetor carefully, looking as if they were about to tackle him.

The Praetor pulled out an ornate pistol. As Janus looked closely at it, he could see the inlaid sigils of a half-moon and a crossed Immutium blade and Legion-style rifle. He glanced at his officers as if to warn them not to interfere and then pointed it directly at Norm's chest.

"You—you are the responsible for the death of SHADE. My Legion. My home. And for the death of my daughter."

CHAPTER 36
LOST LOVES

Norm stared directly into the Praetor's eyes. "May I have a chance to finish my tale first? And then you may shoot me if you wish."

The Praetor narrowed his eyes.

Norm reached behind him and slowly, carefully, pulled out a pistol of his own. The one with which he had rescued Janus and the others. And Janus realized they must have had the same maker. But this one had a different design, that of an eye and a shield. Norm eyed the weapon lovingly. And then he presented it to the Praetor, carefully putting the beautiful weapon upon the table.

"She was quite the weaponsmith."

"You—you knew Natalie, my Natalie?" The Praetor's gun lowered slightly.

Norm smiled warmly for the first time since he had begun telling his story. "Yes. For a number of years."

"She... lived?"

"Yes. But I think you already knew that, didn't you? Your grandson is sitting right there." Norm nodded at Janus.

The Praetor collapsed into his chair, looking suddenly exhausted as he stared at Janus. "I suspected, but it seemed impossible to be true."

"Well, he does look more like his father. But his eyes, and his name, should have been more than enough."

Janus's head went into a whirl. And Clara asked the questions he suddenly could not.

"Wait, you knew Janus's parents, Norm? You've known who his family was the whole time?"

For once, Norm ignored her question and looked at the Praetor. "Do you still have a picture of her?"

The Praetor nodded. "It was the one thing I was able to save. The one thing that I could keep." He pressed a few buttons on the table. "Valhalla."

"Yes, Praetor?" Val's voice rang out through the room.

"Display Jennings's personal effect number one."

"Aye, Praetor. Personal effect number one. Portrait of Natalie Janus Jennings."

A beautiful young woman appeared on the screen and Clara gasped. She was smiling and at her neck was the insignia of Lieutenant. An Adept Lieutenant. Janus recognized her right away. Trembling, he pulled the locket from around his neck and opened it up. Inside, the young woman smiled at him. He looked at Norm, and pointed to the locket.

Norm gently held the locket in his hands as he held Janus's gaze. "Natalie Jennings, Lieutenant of the SHADE Legion and daughter of Colonel Alexander Jennings, is your mother."

"And the other side?"

"Magnus Delacroix. The Security Trooper who became an Executor of Phoenix. The man in the painting, and who leads Titan at this very moment, is your father."

The Praetor still seemed to be in a state of shock as he muttered, "So what really happened that day?"

Norm stood up straighter than he had in a long time. "I think it is time you finally found out what happened to your family, Alexander. But I need your help. There is one part I do not know. One part I need you to tell."

"What's that?" the Praetor asked in a daze.

"The beginning," Norm said quietly.

— END OF BOOK II —

APPENDICES

APPENDIX I
CORPORATE and MERCENARY
HIERARCHIES

CORPORATE RANKINGS IN ORDER OF GREATEST TO LEAST

Executor Ascendant—Leader of the executor council. There is but one
Executor—Supreme leaders of the corporation. They elect the Executor Ascendant. There are often six
Overlord—Delegates that control the everyday workings. There are
dozens. Lesser "High and Mighty" (As dubbed by STs):
Intendant—Highest ranking assistants to Executors and Overlords
Nobles. These Include: families of Ranking Executors and Overlords,
Ranking Assistants, and High Ranking Military

A Special Note on Overlord Rankings:
Most Overlords are subservient to a specific executor, but a core group
of five overlords is considered critical and supposedly impartial. These
overlords control the most important aspects of each corporation and

are second only to the executors—they have the power to enact whatever they wish, as long as those wishes do not conflict with the executors. They are:

The Overlord for Intelligence

The Overlord of Sustenance

The Overlord of Diplomacy

The Overlord of Production

The Overlord for War

Newly Promoted Intendants are strongly advised to learn the identity of these individuals immediately!

ST MILITARY RANKS

Commandant Bellus—Commander of all st units

Assault Commander—Up to three grades

Field Major

Battle Captain

Lieutenant

Sergeant

Regular—aka 'Trooper'

INFERNUS MILITARY RANKS

Commandant Novus—Commander of all inferni

Novus—Three grades

Vulcanus

Pyrus—Two grades, Major and Minor

Infernus

MERCENARY LEGION RANKINGS

OFFICERS

Praetor—Supreme leader of the Legion

General—Rarely Seen—Used only once during the Fusion War when multiple legions joined together under one praetor

Colonel—There is usually an intrinsically understood hierarchy within the legion if multiple colonels are present

Major

Captain

Lieutenant

LEGIONNAIRES

Blood Poet—Highest ranking sergeant and spiritual leader of the legion

Sergeant—Usually assigned to squads, Sergeants act as natural extensions of the command structure

Adept – The regulars of a Legion, there are three classes: 1st, 2nd, and 3rd

Cadet—aka 'Blueback'

A Special Note on Mercenaries:

Many mercenary legions refer to themselves internally as Adepts (hence the rank, see above). It is believed this is a remnant of the mercenaries' attempt to distinguish themselves from the traditional definition of 'mercenary' from prior centuries (see appendix iii for a report on some of the mercenary legions and their root names). While internally we will refer to mercenaries as strictly thus, it is advised to all intendants that when dealing with mercenaries in any form of negotiation, use of the term 'adept' is highly recommended while referring to their operations. Despite the foolishness tied to such niceties, increased success rates and better returns have been achieved when using this 'polite' terminology.

Appendix II
CORPORATIONS OF THE WORLD
PHOENIX

'A Fading Fire'

Former Corporation Supreme.

Represented by the fiery bird of myth, Phoenix Corporation was a leader of medical research before rising to dominance. it was destroyed by the 'alliance of six' over two decades ago.

The corporate colors are red and orange.

Rubies and orange garnets feature prominently on many of its surviving works.

CERBERUS

'Emerging from the Dark'

Current Corporation Supreme

Represented by the three-headed guardian of the underworld, Cerberus is a leader in metallurgical advancements and created immutium. It is regarded without question as the most powerful corporation in the world today.

The corporate colors are dark purple and black

Amethyst and obsidian are frequently seen in Cerberus art and architecture

TITAN

'Gathering Strength'

Former Rival to Phoenix.

Represented by a massive elemental of earth and rock, Titan has lost a great deal of its power in recent decades. Master weaponsmiths, Titan created the fearsome zeus rifles.

The corporate colors are light green and brown.

Jade is overlaid on many of its sculptures and ceremonial weapons.

MINOTAUR

'An Empire on the Abyss'

Rumors of internal strife plague minotaur, despite its continued dominance in negotiating and managing trade between the corporations. Represented by the head of the bull-monster, Minotaur is known for its superior skill in construction, and is the developer of the behemoth transport so widely used by corporations today.

The corporate color is carmine

Rubies and ivory are often used in conjunction for minotaur busts and masks

MEDUSA

'The Lashing Snake'

Represented by the gazing face of the snake-haired creature known for turning men to stone, Medusa was once a powerful energy conglomerate. Despite its hand in creating fusion power, its loss in the resulting war changed its fortunes, and Medusa's influence continues to fade.

The corporate color is dark green.

Emeralds are often carved into snakes and worn as jewelry.

CHIMERA

'Poised to Strike'

Although one of the few remaining masters of daeduluses, ancient sophisticated computers that few know how to construct, Chimera has little influence upon the world stage. Some believe they are merely biding their time, while others believe they lack the population to make any large gains. Chimera is represented by a roaring lion with a scorpion's tail poised above it.

The corporate color is goldenrod.

Yellow topaz and gold thread are commonly found woven into articles of clothing worn by executors and overlords.

HYDRA

'Without Number'

Despite whispered reports of division and dissension among its underclass, Hydra remains the largest producer of food in the world, managing to export a large portion of its crop each year. Through black markets and legion trades this food keeps many of the most isolated communities in the world alive and well. This surplus has allowed Hydra to maintain one of the largest populations and armies of all the corporations. A lack of infrastructure and the ability to produce other goods, however, has weakened it.

The corporate color is blue.

Sapphire dust is often used in hydra paintings and dyes.

Appendix III
LEGIONS OF THE WORLD

A Brief Primer

O.D.I.N. Order for the Defense of Independent Nations

ODIN is currently one of the largest mercenary legions in operation today. Rising from obscurity over the past few decades, ODIN is rumored to have been started by outskirter colonies in an effort to defend themselves from Corporate raids. The origin of its mythology and rune system are unknown to the corporations. Although no legion can match corporate might, intendants are advised that ODIN should be approached cautiously, as the current Praetor, a man named Jennings, has developed a reputation for great cunning. ODIN is housed in a flying Avalon Class Fortress called Valhalla.

ODIN is represented by a red warrior astride a warhorse and carrying a spear. Some have suggested this is actually a representation of the God 'Odin', though such a god is unknown to corporate scholars.

S.H.A.D.E. Strategic Homeland Advance Defensive Enclave

A powerful legion, SHADE was destroyed in a great battle with Phoenix Corporation over two decades ago. Appearing in occasional reports from documents before the Fusion War, Some scholars have suggested that SHADE may have been founded before even the fall of the republics. Little evidence of this legion remains, however, though its impact upon recent history still lingers. Rumors of surviving members of this legion have all proven to be false. Its former home was the Avalon Class Fortress Elysium Fields.

SHADE was represented by a half-moon symbol, and is credited with developing several modern day mercenary techniques, including the infamous 'ghost dancing' that many legions claim to have mastered.

S.P.A.R.T.A.N. Society for the Protection of Allied Republics, Territories, And Nations

Perhaps the most powerful mercenary legion today, SPARTAN is recognized by all Corporations for a remarkably high success rate in its missions. Known for their ruthlessness in battle, SPARTAN mercenaries have developed a fearsome reputation and are considered one of the best values for corporate expenditures. Only ODIN is seen as a comparable alternative. It is rumored that SPARTAN and ODIN share a special rivalry, although the full details of this feud are unknown. SPARTAN operates from many bases across the world, and rumored to hold at least two Avalon Class Fortresses known as 'the Twins'.

SPARTAN is represented by a shield and helmet, and is said to control several smaller legions through territory and influence.

A Special Note on Legions:
Many Legions are present throughout the world. Only a few have been represented here, based on recent intelligence reports of their activity or impact.

Legions across the globe are considered loosely allied, although many appear to be little more than rabble living on the fringes of Corporate territory.

Despite appearances, however, all Legions should be treated with a measure of respect, as they possess enough weaponry and manpower to do significant damage to Corporate interests.

APPENDIX IV
BRIGG'S BALL

Brigg's Ball is an exciting game that has only recently come to the attention of the Corporations. Long played by mercenary legions, Brigg's Ball is a game the executors believe can easily be adapted for entertainment purposes throughout the Corporate hierarchy. As such, intendants are instructed to learn the rules of the game and determine any required modifications for implementation.

BASIC OVERVIEW

Brigg's Ball is a game played between 2 to 4 teams on a circular field approximately 60 meters in diameter. Each team attempts to score using colored balls called 'boomers'. the team with the highest score when the game ends wins.

RULES:

Teams:
The number of teams participating is determined before play begins, with each team requiring a minimum of 5 players. Teams may be adjusted based on group size, but generally each team will have 5 main players and 1 alternate. Generally, a Brigg's Ball match will feature two to four teams, though rumors of other variants exist.

Field of Play:

The Brigg's Ball Field is generally measured to a circular diameter of 60 meters, with 1 GOAL per team. the goals should be evenly spaced around the field, so each team has a clear portion of the field designated as their territory.

Each goal should be no more than 2 meters across, and preferably, 1 meter tall, at least 1 meter above the field of play.

Each goal should have a goal box that extends 6 meters in a circle in front of the goal. A small .75 meter squared region should be designated at the front of this box as a transition zone.

Equipment:

Boomer—The Boomer is a small ball 18 cm in diameter designed for throwing and passing. Usually consisting of a rubberized material, the Boomer should bounce to at least waist height when dropped from eye level. Although variations adapted for poorer regions use referees and static colors, a true Boomer should possess the ability to switch between red and blue at random intervals during a match. This switch time should be predetermined and last between 5 – 10 seconds.

Generally, for more informal matches, the number of Boomers in play should match the number of teams, but officially, the number of Boomers in play is calculated by taking the number of teams minus 1, with a minimum of two. No matter the ruleset adopted, 4 Boomers are generally not used, even in matches of 4 teams.

Armor—Highly recommended. Not Required.

Referee's outfit – the referee in a brigg's ball match should wear a full bodysuit (of preferred make and type) that features vertical stripes of alternating Orange and Yellow, at least 3 cm wide. Other colors are allowed, as long as they provide excellent visibility and contrast with the play field.

General Play:

A Brigg's Ball BATTLE takes place over a single, continuous 20 minute period.

Each team lines up in a staggered formation for the start of the game, with 2 STRIKERS at the front, and 3 DEFENDERS behind. The Strikers are lined up 10 meters in front of their goal, with the defenders 1 meter behind. Each player box should be spaced at least .5 meters from the others.

The 1st Boomer is launched by the ref or automatic system at the center of the field of play, equally spaced from all teams. When the Boomer reaches its apex, its color is determined, and play begins. Movement by teams before the Boomer reaches its apex is considered a false start, with the offending player or players moved onto the defender line, if possible.

Each team then battles for control of the boomer, using it to score points for their team, or against another. At least one Boomer will always remain in play at all times.

Scoring:

Scoring occurs when a boomer enters a goal, with the score of the team controlling the goal affected. Boomers that are blue in color give a team plus 1 point. Boomers that are red in color subtract 2 points. In this way, Blues should be scored in a team's own goal, and Reds should be scored against an opponent.

Multiple Boomers:

Every game of Brigg's Ball has at least one period of time where multiple Boomers are present on the field of play. In a general Battle, Boomers follow these rules for entering play:

At the start of play, only one Boomer is released. For the next 3 minutes, the teams will have only one Boomer on the field to battle over.

At the 3-minute mark, a second Boomer will enter play. Boomers will follow this pattern until all original Boomers have been released.

For example:

if there are 2 teams, a minimum of 2 Boomers are needed for play. As a result, Boomers will be released at start and the 3-minute mark.

for 3 teams, 2 Boomers are allowed, so Boomers will appear at start and 3 minutes.

for 4 teams, 3 Boomers are allowed, so Boomers will appear at start, 3 minutes, and 6 minutes.

After the max number of Boomers is released, Boomers enter the DORMANT CYCLE.

Dormant Cycle:

When a Boomer is scored, it disappears from play, remaining dormant and unusable until certain conditions are met:

If Half of the remaining time period goes by without meeting condition 2 (see below), release a Boomer. Continue this pattern until all Boomers have been returned to play.

If all Boomers are removed from play, immediately release all Boomers up to the max number allowed for the number of teams. This rule is in effect at all times, even at the start of battles.

Goalie:

Teams are allowed the option of a GOALIE – one player who transitions to the goalie position after the game has started. The goalie has several unique advantages and disadvantages.

To become a Goalie, a player must enter the goalbox's transition zone and wait for a period of 5 seconds. During this time, they may not interact with any Boomers or players, or the time resets. Once a player has transitioned to the goalie, they may not leave the goalbox without first transitioning back to play.

When a Goalie is active, opposing teams may not enter the goalbox without penalty. If another team's player enters the goalbox, they will receive a foul. If that player collides with the goalie – Willfully or Not – the team of that player will lose 1 point. Goalies may actively attack any player that enters the goalbox.

Goalies may hold onto any Boomer for up to 10 seconds, but may not score Boomers of any type. Goalies that hold onto Boomers for more than 10 seconds or attempt to score with a Boomer will acquire a foul, and no points will be gained or lost.

Fouls:

Each team is allowed 5 fouls without major penalty. Any foul acquired by a player is shared with the team. A team that acquires 5 fouls immediately loses one active player from their team, reducing the total number of players they can field at any time. This cycle will repeat until no more players can be lost and the team forfeits the Battle.

Brigg's Ball is a full contact sport, and a great deal of leeway is often given to teams as they engage in Battles. Any Player possessing a Boomer is considered fair game for engagement. Players that attack opponents not possessing a Boomer run the risk of acquiring fouls, generally at the discretion of the referee, and position related to the Boomer.

Although full contact is encouraged, certain behaviors are frowned upon and more likely to result in fouls. These include excessively violent attacks or attacks designed to inflict more grievous injury than simple bruising.

The most important rule to remember, however, is that "it isn't a foul if you don't get caught."

Victory:

The team with the highest score at the end of the 20 minute period wins the Battle.

Appendix V
IMPORTANT INDIVIDUALS

As Reported By Corporate Intelligence

The following is a list of Important Individuals our Intelligence Branch is currently monitoring. Intendants should refer to this report when needed.

ALASTOR
Alastor, Reginald
Rank: Overlord
Age: 59
Sex: Male
hair: Brown-Grey
Eyes: Grey
Notes: Technically the overlord for war for Cerberus, Alastor has developed a reputation for many of his own intelligence operations independent of Executor oversight. He appears to have a strong rivalry with <REDACTED>

CLARA
Clara – Last Name Unknown
Rank: None
Age: Unknown (Approximately Mid 30s)
Sex: Female
Hair: Black
Eyes: Dark - Unspecified

Notes: The name Clara has popped up several times in recent months in reports generated by <REDACTED>. She is a female slummer of unknown origin, with access to the upper levels through a special servant's position. She appears to be closely connected to 'janus', possibly as a mother figure.

CELES
Soltis, Celes
Rank: Adept
Age: 19
Sex: Female
Hair: Blond
Eyes: Blue
Notes: The origin of this young woman is unknown, but she has quickly become respected at Valhalla for level-headedness and wisdom, as well as for keen marksmanship.

DELACROIX
Delacroix – First Name Unknown
Rank: Executor
Age: Unknown
Sex: Male
Hair: White
Eyes: Unknown
Notes: Identified as a Titan Executor, little more is known about this mysterious individual other than he seems to be operating in the shadows as much as possible. <REDACTED>

HAWKES
Hawkes, Vladimir
Rank: Colonel

Age: 42
Sex: Male
Hair: Blond-Brown
Eyes: Blue
Notes: Known for his temper and fearsome fighting style, this is not the first time vladimir hawkes has appeared on Corporate Intelligence lists. He is believed to have originally had origins in medusa, and taken part in the "6th level rebellion" there.

JANUS

Janus – Last Name Unknown
Rank: Lieutenant
Age: 19
Sex: Male
Hair: Brown
Eyes: Brown
Notes: A newly promoted ODIN lieutenant, the name janus first appeared in a cerberus manifest report by <REDACTED>. For unknown reasons, he is considered a security threat by Cerberus. All individuals who come into contact with 'Janus' should be monitored.

JENNINGS

Jennings, Alexander
Rank: Praetor
Age: 62
Sex: Male
Hair: Grey
Eyes: Grey

Notes: Supreme leader of the ODIN Legion, Praetor Jennings is reported to be a cunning warrior and tradesman. An architect and designer in his spare time, he is said to have designed ODIN's current base of operations, Valhalla.

KEATS
Keats, Ananda
Rank: Colonel
Age: 37
Sex: Female
Hair: Black
Eyes: green
Notes: Perhaps the most respected officer in ODIN behind Praetor Jennings, Ananda (not Amanda) Keats is reported to be senior advisor to all of ODIN's operations. She is said to be soft-spoken and gentle – most of the time.

LYN
Cachin, Juliens
Rank: Adept
Age: 21
Sex: Female
Hair: Black
Eyes: Black
Notes: Identified as a go lucky, humorous individual, lyn is nonetheless developed a reputation for excellent scouting ability. along with ferros ramirez, she is said to come from the outskirts.

MARCUS
Auras, Marcus
Rank: Adept

Age: 20

Sex: Male

Hair: Black

Eyes: Brown

Notes: Originally from Medusa, Marcus is an extremely capable soldier with a reputation for getting the job done right. Although he is young and newly promoted from cadet, many of the officers in ODIN are watching him closely for future advancement.

MIDDLETON

Middleton, Victoria

Rank: Overlord

Age: Unspecified

Sex: Female

Hair: Unspecified

Eyes: Unspecified

Notes: <REDACTED>

NORM

Norm – Last Name Unknown

Rank: None

Age: Unknown – Appears to be in mid-70s, uncommon for a slummer

Sex: Male

Hair: Silver

Eyes: Blue

Notes: This individual recently met with Clara and seems to know her quite well. Further contact will be monitored although he seems unlikely to be anything more than a very old man.

NORTHCOTT

Northcott, Ishan

Rank: major
Age: 53
Sex: Male
Hair: White (originally Black)
Eyes: Brown
Notes: Master-at-arms at Valhalla, Northcott appears to be a well-respected member of the ODIN Legion's command staff. Reports of his personality suggest he is gruff, but measured.

RAMIREZ
Ramirez, Ferros
Rank: Adept
Age: 22
Sex: male
Hair: Brown
Eyes: Brown
Notes: Extremely tough individual, said to be as strong as a strength-enhanced Infernus. Known to be quiet and introspective. Believed to be from the outskirts and has a close bond with Juliens Cachin.

ROGERS
Rogers, Bario
Rank: Captain
Age: 30
Sex: Male
Hair: Brown
Eyes: Green
Notes: A captain in the ODIN Legion, Rogers is well respected for his Blade Mastery. He is rumored to have performed theatrically when he was a boy.

WOURIS

Wouris (Pronounced 'Worry') – First Name Unknown

Rank: Blood Poet

Age: 29

Sex: Female

hair: Red

Eyes: Green

Notes: Sergeant Wouris is ODIN Legion's Blood Poet and is highly respected. Her origin is unknown, though it is suggested that she has had contact with the upper echelons of multiple Corporations. Further investigation is required.

A Thank You To My Readers

To all whom have just read this book, Thank You.

Many of you have continued Janus's journey from The Phoenix Fallacy, Book I. Some of you may have started with Book II. In either case, thank you taking the time to read the next chapter in Janus' story.

These books have represented a tremendous personal journey, one that has been both instructional and life-changing. But no matter the highs or lows, the fact that you are holding this book in your hands right now makes it a journey that is truly, truly uplifting. The opportunity to shape a reader's world, if only for a brief time, is what drives the writer to share his or her story. Your support makes writing worthwhile.

I hope your voyage deeper into the world of The Phoenix Fallacy was exciting for you as it was for me, and that you will join me for the conclusion. But no matter how you felt, please review The Phoenix Fallacy online. Time is precious, and I thank you for spending some of yours with me. Help others decide whether they should do the same. And if you enjoyed it, please help other readers do the same!

For more on The Phoenix Fallacy, or to contact me, please visit www.phoenixfallacy.com. Thanks for sharing this wonderful adventure, and I hope we can travel together again soon.

Sincerely,

Jon